WAYPOINT
MAGELLAN

A Project Waypoint Novel

L. S. Roebuck

SHADOWLANDS PRESS
El Paso, Texas

Waypoint Magellan
© 2017-2021 L.S. Roebuck

ISBN 10: 0-9986090-0-5
ISBN 13: 978-0-9986090-0-3

1.5.1

Published by Shadowlands Press
5528 Last Waltz Dr.
El Paso, Texas 79932
www.shadowlandspress.com

For Cherissa

CONTENTS

7 | Prologue

13 | Waypoint Magellan (26 chapters)

329 | Epilogue

345 | Appendixes
A brief history of the birth of the waypoints
A listing of the waypoints between Earth and Arara
An account of the ships of Waypoint Magellan

PROLOGUE

waypoint (*n*) — *an endpoint of the leg of a long course; a stopping place on a journey.*

Waypoint Magellan, January 24, 2596

John Tyler rounded the corner at full speed, losing his balance, causing his feet to fly out from under him.

In his graceless fall, the young man hit his head sharply against the cold steel wall of the dimly lit capillary corridor. He instinctively placed his hand at the point of impact. He felt the sticky welcome of warm blood.

He scrambled to his feet, wiped his hand on his grey carbon polymer shirt, and peeked around the corner. The tall man, Järvinen, was nowhere to be seen.

Tyler strained to listen for footsteps, possibly the sounds of his pursuer, but heard nothing. This remote section of the waypoint, in the bowels of the environmental and life support storage tanks, was frequented by few, save the occasional engineer or technician. The only sound filling the hall was the continuous hum of air being pushed through scrubbing filters.

Tyler squinted, looking hard down the cramped capillary he'd just sprinted through. His chest heaved with heavy breathing, in part from running and in part from fear.

I should have never taken the Estrella job, Tyler thought. But the money was too good. The athletic man hoped he had given Järvinen, his boss, the slip. Even so, he wondered where he could hide from the grey-headed man on a waypoint? Tyler doubted the Marines would protect him. Would they even believe him?

What a bad idea to leave Arara in the first place, Tyler considered regretfully. But the siren song of earning a quick fortune trading on the waypoints was irresistible to a boy who grew up poor. So, when he was just 19, he started the long journey to *Magellan*.

Tyler leaned against the corner wall and was ciphering a plan to sneak back to his tiny room at the Hoover temporary housing center. Would Järvinen be waiting for him at his place? Tyler never thought taking a job as a glorified dockworker for a shady inter-waypoint logistic company would lead to him fearing for his life. *That son of a dirt licker is going to kill me.*

He listened again and then looked one more time down the metallic corridor. The hall's low clearance would cause anyone approaching two meters in height to frequently duck. *That would slow Järvinen down,* Tyler thought. Thirty meters down, a malfunctioning light flickered, but otherwise, he was alone.

Tyler exhaled a sigh of relief, quickly turned back around the corner and ran full body into Järvinen.

Shocked, Tyler fell backward to the floor, hitting his tailbone hard. Järvinen towered over the sitting Tyler. The tall man's silhouette blinked in the broken light.

"You're bleeding, Mr. Tyler," Järvinen said in a clear, eloquent voice. "We should take you to the clinic to have that looked at before it gets serious."

"I'm fine," Tyler blurted. "Just leave me alone."

"I don't mean to inconvenience you," Järvinen said evenly. "I just have a few questions I need to ask to find out … what you know." As he spoke, the older man produced a handheld weapon that Tyler immediately recognized as a common stun gun.

"Hey, look," Tyler said, eyeing the gun nervously, "really I don't know anything. Just, you know, the shipping schedules and manifests. You gave them to me."

"Don't toy with me, boy," Järvinen put some menace in his voice. "What did you overhear?"

Tyler started to stand up, but Järvinen closed the distance between them, kneeling and pointing his gun at the young man's head. "Don't get up on my account. Now tell me, do you know who Raven One is?"

"Who?"

Järvinen jabbed the stun gun into the bloody gash on Tyler's forehead. Tyler yelped in pain.

"I swear I don't know any Raven," Tyler said angrily. "I have no idea who he is."

"I believe you," Järvinen said slowly, letting the arm holding the stun gun drop to his side.

Tyler relaxed slightly. "It's the truth."

"But I can't have you going around and telling the Marines

about my threatening you with a stun gun. They'll ask why I was harassing you and more importantly, who is Raven One. And we wouldn't want that valuable piece of information floating around *Magellan*, would we," Järvinen reasoned.

Tyler's confusion reignited his fear. "What are you talking about?"

Järvinen lifted his stun gun and put two energy bolts into Tyler's body. The young man jolted a few times, as his muscles spasmed in an artificially-induced seizure. Then, Tyler grew still and slipped into blissful unconsciousness.

The older man moved quickly. He scooped up Tyler and carried him to the end of the capillary that opened into a small storage room of spare air filters. At the end of the room was a portal that allowed access into an airlock. This particular airlock was used mostly during construction of the *Waypoint Magellan* the and rarely in the decades since. Järvinen hoped that it was still operational.

He set Tyler down and tapped his comm unit.

"Raven One," he spoke into the radio microphone on his sleeve. "I've apprehended the worker who may have overheard my last communiqué."

"Did he compromise us?" came the reply from the comm unit. The voice was processed through a disguise algorithm.

"No, I don't think so," Järvinen said. "Still, we might be at risk."

"I am assuming you are going to clean up after this mess of yours, Järvinen," the voice said.

"Of course," the white-haired man replied into his comm unit. "I just need an override access code for airlock 18-c."

"I can open it for you from here," the voice said. Järvinen studied the interior airlock door.

It suddenly burst open.

Järvinen looked down at the unconscious Tyler, who was starting to stir and drug him into the airlock.

Järvinen had a horrifying thought. What if Raven One, displeased with his security lapse, would try to airlock them both? He rolled the body into the airlock and then quickly jumped out.

As soon as he cleared the interior door, the grey, windowless airlock slid shut.

"What the—" Järvinen half-shouted. "You almost trapped me in there! Are you trying to kill me?"

A guttural laugh sounded from Järvinen's comm.

Through the airlock door, Järvinen heard a familiar suction sound. He knew Tyler would be dead from space exposure in seconds, and hopefully it would be a long while before anyone realized the transient was missing.

"Don't be paranoid. I don't want to kill you, Järvinen. I have plans for you," the voice said. "Grand plans."

***

Thirteen-year-old Amberly sat cross-legged on her mother's bed, looking out the bedroom window into an immense star field. Her mother, Kimberly, stood behind her, running a brush through the girl's straight hair.

"It's that one, isn't it?" Amberly asked.

"Yes. The one twinkling yellow, next to that brighter cluster," her mother replied. "I'm pretty sure that's Viapos. And the fourth planet orbiting that yellow dwarf is Arara."

"Is the star named for a person, like *Magellan*?"

"No. It's short for the star's real name," Kimberly said. "It's Latin. *Vie Positis Finnis.*"

Amberly's mother set the brush on the bed and rested her hands on her daughter's shoulder.

"What does it mean?" the girl asked.

Kimberly appeared to ignore her daughter's question, and spoke absentmindedly. "No one has spoken Latin for a thousand years." She walked around the bed and placed a hand on the plexiglass, as if she could touch Viapos.

"It means 'waypoint's end.' Humanity's greatest journey terminates in that star's planetary system," Kimberly said, closing her eyes to accentuate a memory. "On Arara, you can feel the warmness of Viapos on your face as that glorious ball of fire pushes away the morning chill."

"Let's go there," Amberly said with a childlike sense of adventure.

"My dear girl, I want nothing more than to show you the deep green grasslands of the Lewis Islands where I grew up," Kimberly sat beside her daughter. "It's a long, lonely three-year journey from *Magellan* to *Arara*. By the time we'd get there, you'd be halfway through your adolescence. We'd have to find passage on a deep-space ship heading in the right direction."

"Dad says the *American Spirit* will be here, maybe in a year, and it's going to Arara," Amberly perked up, remembering the spaceship trivia her father, a pilot, liked to discuss with annoying frequency. "Could we go on that ship?"

"Maybe," Kimberly said, sadness lacing her voice. "But we can't go until my research is done here. Once I have finished, I *will* take you to Arara. I promise. But we must wait. My science, my research, is important. I can't stop working on it now."

"Why won't you tell me what experiments you are doing?" asked Amberly, who loved all things science.

"Amberly, you are the smartest 13-year-old I have ever known," Kimberly smiled. "Well, maybe not as smart as *me* when I was 13 —"

"Mom!"

"I said *maybe*. But the work I am doing is too complex for even you to understand. Someday I'll show you everything. Someday, you'll understand."

"Someday soon, I hope," Amberly said brightly. "Mom, I want to be a waypoint-famous scientist. I want to be just like you."

Kimberly smiled, pleased. "If you study hard and avoid distractions like boys—"

"Mom!"

"Amberly, they are not worth your attention."

"Okay, mom. I got it. Study hard, no boys. Waypoint's smartest scientist, here I come."

"The *galaxy's* smartest scientist." Kimberly reached behind her bed and picked up a blue duffle bag.

Amberly frowned. "Do you have to go right now? Let's identify some constellations together. Or maybe a game of chess?"

"I'm sorry sweetheart," Kimberly said. "Dad is already waiting for me in the hangar."

"How long will you be gone this time?" Amberly said softly, looking down and pulling absentmindedly on her red hair.

"A week, maybe two. It depends on how long it will take to complete the Spencer Minorem data collection," Kimberly said, referring to the weak star nearby. She slipped a finger under Amberly's chin and lifted her head until their gazes met.

"Listen to me. The time has come for you to learn how to be strong and independent. I won't always be here for you. You're still young, but you're old enough to decide your own future."

"So why do I have to listen to Kora when you and dad are gone?" Amberly asked.

"Good question. You're probably smarter than your sister, but she has almost three more years of life experience than you, and right now that experience means she's in charge. Don't worry. Soon you'll catch up and pass Kora."

Kimberly stepped into the living area and opened the apartment door that exited into an average *Magellan* corridor.

"Remember, never let anyone determine who you become. Use every resource you have to make what you know is right come true. Don't forget the best person always put the good of the community ahead of herself." Kimberly said, radiating intense conviction. "Good-bye, Amberly Macready. I'll see you in a few weeks."

Kimberly punched a control panel and the apartment's exterior door slid open.

"Mom!"

"Yes, my daughter?" Kimberly turned back.

"I love you."

"I love you, too."

Kimberly walked out the door, and it slid closed.

CHAPTER ONE

The gentle tapping on the hull sounded like rain dancing on street pavement during a light summer storm.

Amberly, 19, wouldn't have known that. Born and raised in space, she had never heard actual rain or even stood on a street. Still, something calmed her in the random soft pattering of sound and vibration that came as a cloud of dust and various gasses moved over and then past *Waypoint Magellan*.

The exterior view of the cloud colliding with *Magellan* was hypnotic. *Magellan*'s saucer-like cylinder hull rolled on its z-axis. The gently spinning station would twirl the cloud, already a cacophony of yellows and purples in color from the light of nearby stars, into a spectrum of odd colors – bright orange, deep red and even some blue-green.

Dust clouds were infrequent, but not unheard of, as the *Magellan* intersected with the galaxy in a way that kept the station in a raw sync — roughly 8.5 lightyears away — with the position of Earth. *Magellan* remained in a state of motion to maintain its relative position to the human home planet. Often *Magellan's* path of movement required the intersection with nebula-like interstellar bodies — great clouds in space.

From inside the waypoint, the dust cloud wasn't as aesthetically pleasing. Mostly it blocked stellar light. Still, "weather" was rare enough for Amberly to pause for a moment and look out the small viewport from her family quarters before stepping into the shower. She lived in the two-room apartment with her older sister, Kora. The quarters were not the most spacious on *Magellan*, but they were relative palaces compared to the visiting quarters, where spacefarers on their way to Arara or heading back towards Earth would stay during their layover.

Amberly stepped out of the shower, one of the most remarkable luxuries of *Magellan*, the most advanced waypoint ever built. The state-of-the-art waterworks system almost instantly recaptured, purified and reused wastewater. If one took a long shower on *Magellan*, the same water would run through three or four times, almost eliminating the need for water rationing that made life insufferable on older waypoints.

She toweled off her petite frame and short, reddish hair and quickly dressed. She looked in the mirror at her round face, and noted how much it looked like her sister's. Although they shared a facial structure, no one would have mistaken one for the other. Kora had long, dark hair and was nearly 15 centimeters taller than her younger sister. Amberly didn't know this, but on Earth, tall was stylish and desired. Not so much on a waypoint, where tall people often had to avoid bumping into a bulkhead in the more cramped areas near the station's extremities.

Today, Amberly wore her Science Corps dress uniform. She liked how she looked in the pressed, white pantsuit with green trim. The uniform reminded Amberly of her mother, who also served in the Science Corps. Amberly favored her mother in stature, though she inherited her red locks from her father. Six years had passed since her parents were lost in space, but she still thought often of her mother, the woman who inspired her to pursue a career of community service through scientific research.

Science Corps dress uniform was reserved for special occasions, and today most certainly was a special occasion.

Whenever a deep space transport came into dock, the whole waypoint bustled with excitement. In fact, since Amberly Macready was born on *Magellan* 19 years ago, only 12 deep space transports had docked — eight heading for Arara, and four in the direction for Earth. This one, *American Spirit*, had been to *Magellan* almost seven years ago. Then, the vessel was 16 years out from Earth, and only three years from Arara. Now *American Spirit* had delivered to Arara her payload of colonists, technology, supplies and military orders from the home world — and was on her way home to earth. Loaded with nearly 1,000 passengers, about half the ship's capacity, *American Spirit* would spend the next six weeks docked at the *Magellan* spaceport, before continuing the remaining eight and one-half light-year journey to Earth.

Amberly checked herself once more in the mirror, then activated the door into the residential corridor that lead to the Beltway transport. The lights on the door blinked red, yellow, green as the sensors in the door verified the safe air pressure on the other side before opening.

In the 102 years since the launch of *Magellan*, only one person had died from exposure to a vacuum — a careless engineer who miss-guessed the cause when the door to an exterior storage unit would not change from red to green. He assumed the problem was an instrument error, not an actual lack of atmosphere on the other side. The hapless engineer forced the door, and quickly all the air in the chamber he was in escaped out into space.

Amberly's infopad spoke: "Ms. Macready, you have a new message from North, and if I may say, you look so much like your mother when you are wearing your dress uniform."

Being like mom is good, thought Amberly. *Too bad just looking like someone doesn't give you what made her great.*

"Thanks Verne," Amberly replied to the infopad. Technically, Verne was a sophisticated virtual personality — a VP or sometimes called a VI for virtual intelligence — that could live on several different hardware platforms. To Amberly, Verne and its infopad hardware were one and the same, a gift from her father on her 13th birthday. She picked up Verne as she stepped into the hall. "Play the message from North."

Amberly wasn't looking at the infopad's screen, but she didn't need to look to know what North looked like. The tall, clean-cut Marine had a square jaw and a perfect smile. A slight scar decorated his chin. His dark brown hair was thick and matched his dark brown eyes. At nearly two meters, he was one of the taller Marines assigned to *Magellan*. He had a solid, fit build, compliments of the Marine exercise regimen. Amberly listened to the message as she strode away from her quarters into the common areas.

"Hey Red. Happy Ship Day. My unit drew the short straw, and we get to be honor guard for the debarkation. I just wanted you to know so you can check me out from your office," North teased in his message. Amberly blushed. She wasn't a shy person, even around the opposite sex, but North's bravado-infused flirting made her uncomfortable – mostly because she didn't know what it meant. True, North was attractive, and he had been a good friend to Amberly *and* Kora since he was assigned to *Magellan* nearly a decade ago.

Amberly didn't care much that he seemed to be friendly with

all the girls. Of all North's girlfriends, she and Kora were clearly his *best* girlfriends. But Kora had warned Amberly of his game years ago. "Steer clear of a guy who doesn't know how to focus his affections," Kora had told Amberly. Amberly remembered the day well. It was her 14th birthday, and she had just admitted to Kora that she had quite the crush on North, who was 24 at the time. Five years ago, Amberly pretended to dismiss her older sister's advice, but the seed was planted, and now the admonition was at the forefront of her thoughts.

Amberly listened to the rest of North's message. "Anyway, seeing as it's Friday, Skip and I are going to Rick's tonight to see if any of the *American Spirit* transients are young, single and looking for the hottest guys on *Magellan*. Why don't you and Kora come down to make the other women jealous?"

Typical, thought Amberly, as the flush in her otherwise pale face became even redder as her slight embarrassment turned to a slight anger. Still, Amberly knew that while his words were reckless, his actions had always been gentlemanly and marked by generosity and kindness.

Skip was a scrawny, annoying friend of North's who worked in *Magellan's* communication center as a news aggregator and general message operator.

Of the dozen or so clubs and cafés on *Magellan*, Amberly preferred Rick's. The name was a literary allusion to a popular early 20th century movie, *Casablanca*, which inspired the club's decor.

The hard heels of Amberly's dress boots clicked loudly on the hard, polished steel floor of the access hall. "You better pick up the pace or you are going to be late to work," Verne chirped. Amberly clicked the device into silent mode, annoyed, but nonetheless picked up her pace.

Every 10 meters or so, a portal was cut into the hall. The portals led into living quarters, supply manufacturing, station maintenance or central dining areas. Amberly passed a group of second grade students outside of the education quarters, just a few dozen meters from the waypoint's public transit system, which was known simply as the Tube.

Although the antimatter reactors provided more than

enough energy for *Magellan's* needs, the pneumatic tubes didn't tap the main power grid. Instead, a clever use of the waypoint's internal atmospheric pressure pushed the cars silently along the tube, which looped along the Beltway, the largest and main corridor that ran in a circle with a radius of about 1200 meters. The Beltway divided the waypoint into two rings. Everything inside the Beltway was known as the "core" and everything outside was known as the "rim."

The system housed about 25 four-person cars and had four "tubestops" that serviced the exterior ring of the *Magellan's* four quadrants: State, President, Science and Church. A queue of people had already lined up at this station. One had to be quick to board a tube car at the station. The doors would open, and a disembodied voice would chime out, "Next stop, Science Quadrant."

Although the line was lengthy, it flowed quickly. Amberly was surprised that she didn't see anyone she knew personally. Usually she ran into at least a few friends or acquaintances on the way to work. Because the waypoint's population only had infrequent immigration or emigration, one could, over the course of a lifetime — if not a few decades — get to know a large sample of the waypoint's 10,000 inhabitants.

The tubecar zipped around the Beltway. The car had no windows, leaving nothing to look at except a news feed monitor on the forward wall. News didn't interest Amberly much; Verne knew what she cared about and alerted her with items of interest.

Traveling to the next station took two minutes. The tubecar was sucked from Arkansas Station in the State Quarter to Lincoln Station in the President Quarter. The car was full for the quarter-circle ride — the three other passengers chatted about preparations for the arrival of the deep space ship, *American Spirit*, expected by 10:00 *Magellan* Standard Time that morning. They were part-time hospitality workers for *Magellan's* guest quarters, officially called the Herbert Hoover Temporary Housing Center, but known to the locals simply as the Hotel.

No one got into the tubecar at Lincoln Station, so the two-minute ride over to the Science quarter was quiet. Kepler Station in the Science Quarter opened into the manufacturing district, where scores of microfactories made hundreds of items — some luxuries, some necessities, either from recycled materials or mineral resources provided by the mining guild.

The main hallways through the manufacturing district twisted through rooms that were hidden from view. Amberly made her way towards the exterior of the waypoint rim, where her lab was located.

As a researcher, Amberly didn't have any official duties in conjunction with arrival of a deep space vessel, but the laboratory where she worked as a junior researcher overlooked *Magellan*'s spaceport and had a panoramic viewport in the lobby. The spaceport itself featured a gangway for the deep space ships and modest hangar for the smaller ships that made their berth in *Magellan*.

Amberly arrived at her office a few minutes late for her work, but none of the other researchers noticed, because they were all congregated in the staff lounge, looking out the broad viewport. Most, like Amberly, were dressed in the formal Science Corp garb. Amberly dropped Verne off at her desk and quietly joined her colleagues in the lounge.

"Wow," she said aloud, reflexively. "That ship is enormous."

American Spirit was docking.

"It's so beautiful," whispered Lydia, another junior researcher, breaking the silence. "I heard it runs faster than half-light."

Metallic silver streaks glistened on the warmly curved hull of *American Spirit*. Amberly could see the long vessel's tubular form silhouetted by the stellar light radiating from far away star clusters. From bow to stern, *American Spirit* was nearly a kilometer in length, with a diameter of 300 meters. The ship was slowing to a dead halt now (relative to *Magellan*), and Amberly could clearly make out the large windowed viewport of the ship's gardens. The window aligned with her laboratory's lounge viewport, with only five meters of space separating the portals.

She could see the faces of the *American Spirit*'s crew and passengers, peering back at the *Magellan*. Amberly thought she could feel the raw emotion in those faces, the excitement of arrival, the hope of leaving behind the loneliness of deep space travel, months and months confined to the narrow halls, isolated from humanity in inky-dark space.

The *American Spirit* was one of the fastest ships ever built, and could travel at a cruising velocity of nearly half light speed. Because of the effects of relativity, when the ship was traveling at maximum velocity, for every one year that transpired from the perspective of those on the ship, 1.1 years would pass on Earth. This extra tenth of a year meant that a child born on the *American Spirit* that traveled with the *American Spirit* for its full roundtrip voyage would be around 38, roughly 3.8 years younger than her counterpart born on Earth at the same time, not counting for layovers.

Although the *Magellan* was a finite structure, compared to existence on a deep space transport like *American Spirit*, the waypoint was a spacious oasis of life in light years of stellar desert.

Amberly spotted the ship's antimatter reactor in a fin-like superstructure that emanated near the stern. The reactor was designed outside of the main hull so it could be ejected in case of catastrophic failures. Such failures were rare, but could easily kill everyone on board a ship like *American Spirit* by radiation exposure or explosive force. If a deep space vessel was forced to eject its antimatter core when it was far away from a waypoint or planet, death may be the ultimate outcome, anyway. Massive amounts of energy were required for the ship's atmosphere conditioning, waterworks, food synthesis, and other life support functions. Suffocation, starvation, freezing or burning to death, were likely ends.

Floodlights from the *Magellan* suddenly snapped on, fully illuminating the hull of the visiting vessel. Painted near the bow was an enormous American flag, with the familiar pattern reflecting the powerful light beams casting a scattered red and blue hue back on *Magellan*. Beneath the flag in a lettering style that mimicked the calligraphy of the original Declaration of Independence, was the ship's name.

"*U.S.S. American Spirit*," Amberly read aloud to no one.

The red, white and blue flag was a symbol of nationalistic pride, something to which Amberly did not relate. The concept of nationalism was something she had studied at a young age as part of her civics education, but being born on and living her whole life on the waypoint, essentially an isolated city-state, belonging to a nation was more of an abstract thought than an emotional idea.

The people huddled in the *American Spirit* were now smiling and waving to the people peering through the various viewports that faced out from the docking side of *Magellan*. Those on *Magellan* did so in kind.

Amberly looked over and saw Lydia stifle a tear, laugh at herself and then say, "I always get emotional when these ships come in. I don't know how they can survive that long."

"You were born on *Waypoint Marquette*," Amberly said. "That's like more than a light year away. You survived deep space."

"Sure. But I don't remember *Marquette*, besides the vids and pics my parents gave me. I was three when we left, and five when we arrived here," Lydia said. She leaned her tall, broad frame against the window. She was fit, just "not exactly petite," as the not so subtle Skip once said. Lydia was minimalist and practical, well regarded characteristics for those who lived on waypoints. She kept her blonde hair cut short and often wore the sort of utility garb that was more popular among engineers than researchers. "I do remember arriving at the *Magellan*. I didn't know any place could be so big and open. It was the most incredible feeling."

"I bet that's what it would be like to go planetside," Amberly pondered.

Lydia squeezed Amberly's hand. "I bet somewhere on the *American Spirit* right now, a five-year-old-girl is about to have her first memories off a deep space ship."

Amberly turned from Lydia back toward the *American Spirit*, where the gangway was being extended and pressurized. The 40-meter gangway was attached further down the curvature of the *American Spirit*.

A young man on the *American Spirit* caught her eye.

Physically, he was unremarkable: not even close to two meters in height, a middling build, sandy brown hair, wearing nondescript khaki clothes. What *was* remarkable to Amberly was his solemn face. Everyone else on the *American Spirit* seemed to be celebrating joyfully, smiling, hugging, crying. But he was pensive, almost sad.

He looked across the vacuum through the viewpoint at her.

She realized she had been staring, blushed and turned away. Then something inside her forced her to look back, some burning curiosity to unravel the mystery of the stoic boy-man.

He must have been absentmindedly staring at her, because when she looked back, they locked eyes. She felt, or perhaps imagined, something intense boring into her head — unintentional, almost looking through her. In an instant, she was disappointed, as if some primal impulses made her want him to be staring at *her*. But clearly, he was just deep in thought.

Suddenly, the man realized he had been staring. His face changed, and he acknowledged Amberly with a charming, disarming smile, lifting his hand in a slight wave. She smiled back.

She started to return the wave as well, but the man's attention went to a beautiful woman who walked up beside him and took his hand. The woman was his opposite in many ways — remarkable in appearance, obviously dressed to catch the attention of wandering eyes, Amberly surmised. She roughly matched Amberly's stature, but was probably five to ten years older, and slightly more filled out. She had unusually long strawberry blonde hair, especially for someone who was on a deep space flight. Hair care was problematic on many deep space ships because of water rationing and sub-par bathing facilities, and the *American Spirit* was not an exception.

The young man turned with the woman, and hand-in-hand, walked back into the bowels of their ship.

Amberly opened her mouth to ask Lydia what she made of him, but then realized she was standing alone. The rest of the researchers had gone to their various offices that overlooked the main hangar. Most, of course, wanted to see the *Magellan's* civilian governor and Marine commander give the ceremonial permission to come ashore. Amberly scrambled to her office as well.

An honor guard of Marines lined the main hangar floor. Amberly could see North among the Marines, looking sharp in his dress uniform and standing at attention with the unit he commanded. Behind the honor guard, about 300 citizens of *Magellan* crowded into the hangar to greet the arrivals. Those on the hangar floor could hear a loud hiss as the gangway causeway opened. *Magellan's* governor, a short, round man, stepped forward and shook the hand of a gaunt, white-haired fellow who presumably was captain of the *American Spirit*.

The crowd erupted in a celebratory cheer. North broke from attention long enough to look in the direction of Amberly's office and wink.

CHAPTER TWO

Amberly and Kora ditched their work clothes to don something more appropriate for an evening at Rick's. The taller woman wore a single strap red dress that hung down to her knees, trimmed with glowing cords that gave off faint, ambient red light, shading Kora's figure. Amberly wore a more conservative black dress, sleeveless, that would have draped the floor if not for her heels. Amberly disliked dresses, and hated heels, but Kora convinced her to doll up.

For young single people who had not found love in the static mate market of a waypoint, the arrival of a vessel like *American Spirit* provided a rare opportunity to meet someone from outside the local dating pool. Focused on her work and following in her mother's footsteps, Amberly made little time for social activities. Kora, on the other hand, made plenty of time for getting out.

Amberly nearly tripped as they exited the Tube at Lincoln Station, just a few tenths of a kilometer from Rick's.

"Remind me why am I wearing these shoes?"

Kora looked at her sister. "They make you look gorgeous."

"And remind me why I care how I look?" grumbled Amberly as she stood upright and pulled her hiking dress down.

"Someday maybe even *you* will meet the right one and settle down. Even mom, the great progressive that she was, found her man," Kora said, saying the word "progressive" with a hint of derision. "Good thing too, or we wouldn't be here."

Amberly shook her head. "Mom regretted it. Also, she was a lot older than I am when she married."

"No rush," Kora said, turning down a broad promenade filled with a mixture of passengers of the *American Spirit* and *Magellan* residents. "Except … the *American Spirit* is only going to be here for six weeks, so, you'll have to move quick if you do meet a nice guy."

"I'm no good … at … this," Amberly grunted mostly at her wardrobe.

"No good at what did you say?"

"Nothing. Remember how dad always told us to look for men

at church."

"Yeah," Kora looked up as if recalling something. "I remember how mad that would make mom when he said that sort of stuff. She was always like, 'You sure as hell didn't meet me at a church, Alroy.'"

They came up to the double doors of Rick's. A middle-aged doorman leered at the sisters as he held open the door to the café.

Kora continued. "The problem is there are no lookers at church. I know; *I've* looked. And since you never go, well, that sort of makes dad's advice moot."

"Let's not hand-wring over relationships tonight. Let's just enjoy ourselves," Amberly said, smiling at her sister.

"I vote yes," Kora smiled back.

The pair linked arms and walked into the smoky salon. Raucous music and joyful conversation overlapped in waves of sound, crashing against the sisters.

Amberly had never seen the dimly lit café so crowded. Every chair was taken, and most people were standing around the score or so of high stainless-steel tables scattered through the center of the main hall. In-wall benches outlined the room, so the interior perimeter was clustered with standing and sitting patrons. The room was heavy with the scent of soaps and some faint perfumes and light sweat. Strong perfumes were considered highly inappropriate and uncouth on *Magellan* and other waypoints. One couldn't exactly open a window to air out the place.

Magellan's air temperature was highly controlled, almost always a constant 23 degrees Celsius. However, enough warm bodies were populating Rick's that the cooling system was falling behind.

A live band played an instrumental version of "Knock on Wood" as some of the club-goers attempted to use the crowded dance floor.

The sisters staked out a spot near a half-used tall table as Kato, one of Rick's bartenders walked up, collecting used beverage containers off the table and wiping it down.

"Well, it's my favorite Macready sisters," the thin waiter said. "So which one of you is going to be the lucky girl to be my date tonight? Or did you just want a drink?"

"Kato, you are too good for us humble waypoint natives."

"Just iced topis, please," Amberly said. Kora ordered something stronger, and Kato took the orders back to the bar. Topis was a bitter synthetic drink that was a poor imitation of black tea.

"Don't look now Amberly, but I think that guy is staring at you," Kora indicated with a flick of her head.

"Oh, it's him," Amberly said, a bit of surprise in her voice and her face growing flush.

"Wait … do you know him?"

"No, well, I saw him when the *American Spirit* docked."

"What do you mean, *saw him*?"

"I was in the lab, looking out the viewport, and I was staring at him … well, no … he was staring at me … well."

"Well, he is definitely the one staring now," teased Kora.

"Whatever."

Kato brought over the drinks and Kora reached for a cred chit to pay, but Kato waved her off. "Apparently the transient over in the khaki outfit with messy brown hair already paid for you. I did warn him that the Macready sisters were the most legendary ice queens on *Magellan*, but he still insisted."

"Ice queens? You are too kind, Kato. We're not ice queens. You just have to know how to get us to melt," Kora teased.

"Is there a class I can take –"

"Hey, Kato, how about a beer for Skip and I?" said a familiar baritone voice coming from behind Amberly. North and Skip pushed up to the table next to the sisters. "And I am paying for whatever these ladies are drinking."

"Too late, jarhead," Kato smirked, as he danced back to the bar. Kato generally disliked what any military stood for, and often shared his opinion that a military force on a peaceful waypoint like *Magellan* was a waste of precious resources.

North took no offense at Kato's slur. Although North wouldn't shy from a fight when it was upon him, he generally thought it best to avoid conflict. *In as much as you are able, live at peace with others*, North reminded himself of the ancient admonition.

North was content with the opportunities he believed God had placed before him. Growing up, he had loving, successful parents. He had known the best of both planetside and waypoint life. His friends brought him joy. He had a charmed career in the Marines, and with a little work ethic had enjoyed worthy promotions. For North, every day was a blessed gift.

"So, you got my message, Red?" North gave an infectious smile. "Have you scoped out any nice-looking, lonely ladies for us?"

"What's wrong with the ones sitting at here at the table?" Kora goaded.

"Well, you gals are sort of like my little sisters," North said. "Now Skip here should be making his move."

Skip was the sort of person who didn't enjoy crowds, and he certainly didn't enjoy being put on the spot. He and North were opposites in personality, skill sets and even appearance. Amberly wasn't even sure why they were friends.

"Um … please, North," Skip grabbed a beer from the just-returned Kato. "I mean, you are both pleasant to look at, but I'm not so backwards as to be looking for a permanent relationship. Seriously, I thought humankind had evolved past the need for any of these Neanderthal gender roles."

"Now that is a very narrow view, my friend," said the mysterious man who Amberly had seen on the *American Spirit*. He had made his way undetected from across Rick's to be standing right next to Amberly, and his presence startled her.

Amberly gulped her synthetic approximation of tea, and she had to fight a strong reflex to spew the faux-brew all over her tablemates.

"Excuse me, but the progressive view is *by definition*, the broad view," Skip said.

"Then let me, as a fellow progressive, suggest that by definition the progressive view is not so black and white. A true understanding of the waypoint era progressive movement would embrace traditionalism's view of gender roles when it is desired by the individuals involved."

"Well, I'm not super familiar with this philosophical stuff, but we do have manners here on *Magellan*," smiled North, who stuck out his hand. "I'm North, and this is my friend Skip. The redhead is Amberly and her sister is Kora. Welcome to Rick's, the best club within five light years. Join us?"

"I'm Dek, you know, from the *American Spirit*. Pleased to

meet you." Dek shook North's hand, but locked eye contact with Amberly. Amberly's face went flush again, and she hoped the café's dim lights had obscured her reaction.

"Hey, Dek, was it? Thanks for the drinks," Kora said.

"Oh, so you were *that* guy," North said. Amberly thought she caught a whiff of jealousy.

"What can I say? When you've been stuck on a deep spacer for a year, you're going to be a sucker for a pretty woman. Or two," Dek smiled.

Skip started again, "Now, you can call yourself broadminded, but if it acts like a traditional, and walks like a traditional and smells like —"

"Skip, can we please talk about something else besides politics," Kora said. "I'd for one, like to learn more about our new friend, Dek."

"Yes, Dek, what do you do on *American Spirit*? Passenger or crew?" asked North.

"Passenger. I am a researcher actually – attempting to catalog new forms of stellar radiation. The stuff that is emitted from stellar anomalies, black holes, stars in various states of nova. Nothing exposes you to weird forms of stellar radiation like a deep space trip."

"Boring," said Kora as she set her empty glass on the table. "But now that I think about it, Amberly don't you study stellar whatever as well?"

"Is that what they research at the dockside laboratory?" Dek looked intently at Amberly. "I'd love to see the labs on this waypoint."

"Well, a few of us research radiation, but I doubt our equipment is very impressive," Amberly said. "Our spectral analysis tools are at least 30 years old, but we are scheduled to get updated equipment next year when the *Magnus* arrives. But even when it gets here, I suppose whatever they are using on earth will be two decades newer."

"And that's if the *Magnus* arrives, and if it is carrying what people said they would put on it two decades ago when it left Earth," North said.

"That is the problem with Project Waypoint, isn't it? We serve a home planet few of us have ever seen or ever will see," Dek said. "We will always be, two or three decades behind Earth."

"*Magnus* should be on schedule," Skip said. "It has reported status green for as long as I have been working in Central Communications — my whole career. Well, there have been a few inconsistencies with the transmissions dates that I haven't been able to figure out. Probably just some bug in our triangulation software."

"Ugh ... why do we care about tia -ang- whatever- software," Kora yawned. "Anyone want to dance?"

As usual, Skip ignored Kora and kept talking. "We know *Magnus* arrived at *Waypoint Cartier* — that communiqué left *Cartier* just over two years ago and we just got it, so by now it should be at *Gilbert*. Of course, we usually only get about a six month heads up from ships when they leave *Gilbert*. Signals take just over half a year to reach us from there, while the ships take about a full year."

"We *know* that signals travel faster through space than deep space ships. We all learned that in grade school," Kora said with some exasperation. Skip looked perturbed. She continued, "So, Dek, since you are not so ideological about your progressive views, do you have a family tucked away on *American Spirit*? Wife? Kids? That sort of thing?"

"No, just a *sister*," Dek said, turning to Amberly. Amberly wanted to feel relieved or even hopeful that strawberry blonde she saw hanging on Dek's arm through the viewport on the *American Spirit* was not a significant other. Then she had a strange feeling that somehow the others in the group could somehow read that relief in her.

"I suppose today's Earth military tech is pretty awesome, too. We'll see in 30 years," North said, trying to change the subject.

"Or not," Dek said. "You think that Earth would ever send its best weaponry to the waypoints, or Arara? What makes you think that anything they are sending on *Magnus* was even top of the line when it left Earth?"

"I agree. Anyone who studies the news feeds can see the trends," Skip said. "Earth is dominated by traditionalists. Half of them are religious, anti-science freaks. We would do better to stop depending on Earth to send us their intellectual hand-me downs and start developing our own initiatives and evolving in our own ways."

A drunken Marine pilot named Croix stepped up to the table and pointed a figure at Skip.

"Excuse me, I but I think you need to show a little more respect for the homeworld. Our ancestors on Earth made this waypoint, and you progressives need to remember that we'd be nothing without Earth. Have some respect. Reeeespect," Croix blustered.

Skip stood up. "Who invited you to this conversation? The way I see it, as long as we keep following backwards Earth, we'll never reach our true potential."

"Who is 'we'?" Croix asked rhetorically. "'We' is all humanity, you cowardly little runt."

North stood up between Skip and the intoxicated Croix. "Listen friend," North said to his fellow Marine. "Skip doesn't mean anything by it. Why don't you let me buy you a drink?"

"Do I look like I need another drink? I'm already swim—swimming," the Marine said, with a slight slur, and turned to Kora and Amberly. "Your dad was a friend. He was a dirty hell of a pilot. Somewhere his ghost must be crying — cryyyiiing — because you stand by while these pra- pra- progs slander the great waypoint builders."

North, a strike commander in the *Magellan* Marines, held the rank of Lt. Commander. The corvette wing wasn't in his chain of command, but he was higher on the totem pole than the flyboy who was insulting his friends and making the women uncomfortable.

"That's enough," North said, his face becoming stony.

"I know you outrank me, North, but you're as bad as this scrawny civvy is, trash mouthing earth," Croix pointed at Skip, and then stood toe-to-toe with North. "How can you wear that uniform? You're defending this earth-hating, ungrateful, perverted scum —"

North handed the Marine his jaw. The flash of violence caused the conversation across the club to stop. The musicians joined the silence.

"Sorry," North said, as he shook his right hand. "Skip may be all those things, but he's my friend, and I can't let you get away with insulting him and —"

The Marine rubbed this mouth, blood running down his chin, and noticed he was missing a few teeth he had only a few moments earlier.

"Why you sonofa..."

The drunken Croix swung back, throwing his clenched fist into North's stomach, hitting North with enough force that the Marine knocked the air out of North's lungs. North doubled over and a glass of beer flew over his hunched body and right into the face of the intoxicated Marine, dislodging several more teeth. Croix reeled in pain, falling back into a table of transient women who were trying to mind their own business, alcoholic beverages flying off the table splashing on several bar patrons.

Amberly was shocked to see the outstretched hand of Skip, who had obviously thrown the glass.

"Who is the coward now? YEAH!" yelled an excited Skip.

"Skip, not sure that was such a good idea," Kora mumbled.

"No kidding, dirt licker," said one of the women at the table. "You better buy me a new drink!"

"Forget that," said another, who proceeded to break her glass over the head of Skip, rendering him unconscious.

Kora turned and slapped the woman. North righted himself, saw that Skip was on the floor, and assumed the two Marines flanking Croix had floored his friend. He picked up a chair and slammed it into the closest to him.

All hell broke loose.

Amberly dropped to the floor defensively as various projectiles and limbs were being swung throughout Rick's. She curled up and covered her head next to a booth and tried to spot Kora in the chaos. Her sister was nowhere to be seen.

Then, in a flash, she saw a metallic chair flying right at her, and she flinched, closing her eyes tight, preparing for the pain of impact.

And nothing.

She opened her eyes, and saw that Dek had intercepted the aluminum stool, catching it and tossing it aside.

The police had stormed the front door and were starting to zip cuff anyone who looked remotely guilty of throwing anything. The short-a-few-teeth Croix and Kora were both being apprehended.

Amberly started to panic. She didn't do anything wrong, but she was overcome with an irrational fear of the law all the same.

Dek slid beside her on the floor, behind an overturned table as the police were trying to subdue the still violent crowd.

"Let's get out of here," he said. "You don't want to get pinched. I promise."

"How do you know?"

"Trust me. We don't want to get in any trouble — at least not this sort of trouble. Come on, let's go," Dek stretched out his hand to Amberly. She hesitated for a moment, then considered his grey-blue eyes. She took his hand. His grip was firm, but gentle. She felt a jolt of … something.

Dek hoisted her up. He was much stronger than he appeared.

"This way," Dek half crouched toward an exit on the opposite side of the club from where police were pouring in.

Just as they were about to step out into the corridor, one of the police officers called after them.

"Hey, you two. Citizen. Girl with the red hair. Stop!"

"Run!" Dek prompted.

"But …"

Amberly didn't really have a choice. Amberly tugged off her heels as Dek pulled her out the door with a good amount of force. They were sprinting down the hall, away from the Beltway and toward the rim. Two teenage boys conducting some sort of mischief looked up from a wall panel they were removing as Amberly and Dek flew by. A man wearing a pilot's jumpsuit was across the corridor, several meters down, reading from a data pad, seeming to not notice the pair in flight.

A couple that Amberly knew, Nars Dino, a miner, and his new wife, Maria, were headed toward the Hoover Hotel to attend a welcome reception hosted by one of the mining companies. The hall at this point was barely wide enough for two people to pass each other comfortably.

Dek barreled through the couple, Amberly in tow. The Dinos were a bit stunned.

"Sorry Maria!" Amberly called out, as she and Dek rounded a corner out of the commerce district where Rick's was, and into an even tighter hallway that ran between a wall of apartments, not unlike the one Amberly lived in.

"What is going on?" Amberly heard Nars say from around the corner to the officer who was chasing them.

"Where did they go, citizen?" the officer said.

"Cut the citizen crap, Franco," Nars said. "You know good and well who I am. Just because you're a police officer now –"

"Fine, Nars," Franco said. "Just tell me where they went."

"I don't know," Nars fibbed. "I guess they must have slipped into one of the halls past here." Nars indicated down the corridor behind him, which had at least a dozen tighter halls branching behind him.

Franco growled and pushed Nars aside.

"Sorry I couldn't be of more help," Nars smiled, and took Maria's hand as they continued their walk.

Amberly heard Franco closing in. "Why don't we just turn ourselves in?"

"What's the fun in that?" Dek asked.

"Who are you, *really*?" Amberly said.

"I told you, I'm a researcher. Now where can we hide?"

Amberly pointed to a small Jeffries tube opening in the ceiling a few meters ahead with a ladder leading up. "Quick."

Amberly hopped up and grabbed the ladder, and pulled herself up, quickly ascending. Dek followed, pulling himself up as well. At the top of the tube was a door that locked with passcode access. The tube had barely enough depth to conceal the pair from the hallway below. Dek climbed up into the skinny tube so his body was pressed against Amberly. They were both out of breath from the sprinting. Her heart was beating hard. Dek was sweating, and Amberly could smell him. It wasn't an unpleasant smell, but it was definitely a man smell, mixed with a bit of alcohol, more than likely something that was spilled on them during the bar fight.

Below them, they heard footsteps. Amberly glanced down and saw Franco, although he was looking ahead and not up. Amberly and Dek held their breath.

Franco's police communicator crackled. "Unit three, where are you? We need you to help book some of these people."

"On my way back, sir." Franco looked around, but not up, and convinced he had lost the trail, he headed back towards Rick's.

Amberly and Dek both exhaled loudly, and their torsos brushed in the tight confines of the Jeffries tube.

"This is awkward," Amberly said.

"Not really," Dek said, with a more silly-than-charming grin on his face. "I sort of like it."

Amberly started to climb down.

"No, let's go up. Where does this go?"

"Into the topside gardens," Amberly said. "But I don't have the code for this door."

"Here. Allow me," Dek said, pulling a small metallic box from his pocket. He swiped it in proximity of the lock, and the small portal began to run the standard pressure check to assure there was atmosphere on the other side. It blinked green and slid open.

The pair climbed up. "Where did you get that little gizmo?"

"Let's just say I have some friends on the station."

"Friends? What sort of friends? Have you been on this waypoint before?"

The tube extended a half-meter above the floor of the next level. Amberly climbed over and out and stepped into a powdery substance that would best be described as dirt. The soft ground almost surprised her, compared to the metal surfaces she was used to walking on. She hadn't been to the topside gardens on *Magellan* in years.

Dek followed her out and resealed the door beneath them.

Standing up and taking in the scene, Dek gasped in reaction to the magnitude of the garden, and the encompassing beauty of the clear station exterior, which spanned for at least a half kilometer, like a never-ending window into the galaxy. This huge window allowed stellar light to help naturally grow the lush green plant life in the garden. Amberly paused to look up at the millions and millions of stars. This was the only "big sky" country on *Magellan*. Amberly had a vertigo-like sensation staring out into the vastness of space, like at any second, she would fall off *Magellan* into the eternity of loneliness that waited outside.

The topside gardens were not like the botanical garden in the station. The botanical garden was a park for recreation and relaxation for residents and guests of *Magellan*. The topside gardens were essentially an ultra-efficient farm for food production. Much of the food on *Magellan* was synthesized, using energy to matter conversion techniques, requiring enormous amounts of power. This was not a problem when the antimatter reactors were online. However, if they were ever offline, the station could survive for the short term off food that grew in the topside gardens. The gardens also created oxygen naturally, helping to support the air scrubbers and other systems tasked with the same job.

Amberly and Dek were the only humans on the farm that night, the work crew having long since gone home for the day. The air smelled sweet, of cantaloupe and strawberries. A slight breeze, created by the circulation of the air purifying systems, mixed the scents of the various flora. Being alone with Dek beneath the stars pulled some romantic strings Amberly didn't know she had. Her guard was down.

The pair made their way toward a horizontal irrigation pipe, and they sat down, taking in the peaceful, open view – the opposite of the chaos ensuing at Rick's. Dek took Amberly's hand like it was a natural thing to do. At first, Amberly felt as if she should withdraw, but didn't. *I like this*, she thought. She didn't know this man, but he had protected her, and showed interest in her, and had taken initiative. *Am I wrong to like his assertiveness? Mom wouldn't have approved.* She studied Dek's face for a few seconds then turned and considered the plant life in front of her.

After a few moments of lovely silence, she turned back to Dek.

"Who are you?"

"I told you. I'm Dek. Dek Tigona."

"No, I mean what are you doing here?"

"Running from the police."

"No, I mean on the *Magellan*."

"I came on the *American Spirit*," he said in a humorous tone.

"Tell me more, then," Amberly said as she did something totally unexpected and out of character: She rested her head on his shoulder.

CHAPTER THREE

In the warm breeze of the garden dome, Dek and Amberly conversed for hours. They talked about Dek being part of one of the first "cohort" generations from Arara. To increase the population rapidly, thousands of children were created by artificial insemination of donated eggs and grown in artificial wombs. These children were wards of the state, grew up in boarding school environments and encouraged on vocation paths in careers that desperately needed more manpower. Many of the traditionalists on Arara strongly objected to this parentless caste, but the social scientists believed this would help ensure the colony's survival. The progressives, who saw the traditional family as something of an anachronism anyway, welcomed the cohort technology that would let society abandon the inefficient traditional family altogether at some point.

Amberly wasn't fascinated with the cohort technology as much as wondering what it would be like to grow up with so many siblings.

"The woman I saw you with in the *American Spirit* portal, the one with strawberry blonde hair," Amberly asked, "she's your sister?"

"You mean Sparks? I call her a sister, but she technically ... I mean genetically, she's not exactly my sister," Dek replied. "We were *raised* as siblings, part of the same cohort. So, brother-sister is probably the best way to describe our relationship."

"Just friends?" Amberly half asked, half suggested.

"We were close when we were teenagers in preparatory school," Dek explained. "But she became a spaceship navigator and I went on to study physics and stellar radiation."

"So where did you study stellar radiation?"

"I did my undergraduate and graduate work at North Plate ... it's not the largest school on the Ingram continent —"

"North Plate!" Amberly echoed with a little excitement. "I took several virtual classes from North Plate. My favorites were ones with Professor Alpine. He really shaped my understanding of the nature of light and energy."

"Really? Dr. Alpine was a mentor of mine. Xander died a few years ago, just shortly after I left on the *American Spirit*."

"I can't get over that you took classes from Professor Alpine *in person*! That must have been something."

The pair talked late into the night, enjoying the sweet greenery of the topside garden. They talked about stellar radiation research, and what sorts of strange energies Amberly had found emanating from not-too-distant star clusters. They talked about Dek's cohort mentors, politicians on Arara who were now out of power, but still trying to influence the progressive movement behind the scenes. They talked about Amberly's parents, a scientist and a pilot, lost in space almost six years ago.

"Your mother sounds like she was a wonderful person," Dek said, as he played with a young cornstalk with one hand and slipped his other hand around Amberly. "Smart, attractive, proudly progressive, a great woman of science."

"I adored mom," Amberly said, staring through the plexiglass ceiling into the eternity of stars. "I miss her. I wish I were more like her."

The air circulators kicked on and a "wind" started to blow across the *Magellan's* topside farm, rustling and whistling through the various densely packed but tightly organized plant life on the farm.

"I love the sound of the airflow up here," Amberly said, briefly closing her eyes. "I imagine this is what it might feel like to sit in a field of grass on a planet."

She looked purposefully at Dek. "How does it feel to walk in a place with no end? To run through a grassy field? Like this?"

"Well, sort of, but not really," Dek said. "I've been on the *American Spirit* for almost three years now, so I've almost forgotten the feeling. On Arara, the grasses have taken over the planet — tall and wild and everywhere. The wind is always blowing, and the tall grass flows in waves, brilliant yellows and greens, as far as the eye can see. And then there are the oceans. They say the oceans back on Earth are not nearly as beautiful as the clear, blue waters on Arara. The water is warm. The waves are hypnotic."

"I can't even imagine what it would be like to stand next to an ocean, to bathe in an ocean," Amberly said. "I mean, I've seen videos and all. But it makes me sad thinking about the ocean."

"Sad? Why?"

"I always pictured mom playing in the ocean when she was growing up," Amberly said. "You know, she was born and grew up on Arara. And she told me stories of how she'd loved swimming in the ocean. But she also always dreamed of joining the stars. She would tell me how as a little girl the star-filled sky teased her – how the stars would call to her, that someday she would explore space."

Amberly absentmindedly pulled off a green blade from a corn stalk and then immediately winced. Destroying a growing thing planet side might be commonplace, but it was a bad idea on a waypoint.

She dropped the leaf to the ground and sheepishly looked around even though she knew no one else was on the farm.

"Ooops."

Dek and Amberly both burst out laughing. They both stopped laughing; stared at each other, snickered and then starting laughing again. Amberly had a case of the giggles. She could not remember the last time she had laughed so much and it felt good. Everything about Dek felt good to her. He was kind, and funny, a listener, adventurous, and mysterious, and even though his appearance was unconventional, he had a roguish handsomeness about him that was growing on her.

Dek, apparently taking advantage of the moment leaned in and pressed his forehead and nose against Amberly's. She hesitated, then turned her head away.

Now Amberly felt awkward. She was unprepared for Dek's advance, so she retreated into conversation. "I don't know why the people from Arara — and even the few people from Earth that I met – why they think space is a vast open place. I mean, here we are supposedly out in the wide open, but you can walk from one side of this waypoint to the other in an hour. Seems to me the real freedom is on Arara or Earth, planetside, where you can run in one direction for hours, or maybe even days, and you'll never reach the other side."

"Eventually, you'd come back around to where you started, silly."

"Mom really missed being planetside," Amberly said. "I think she always fought a deep depression because she missed Arara so much. The stars let her down. I suspect she only married my dad to escape."

"Escape what?" asked Dek.

"Escape the fact that she hated living in space, that she should have never left Arara, that the romanticized view of living on a waypoint was dashed when she realized how cold and empty and lonely living is space could be."

"She married your dad to try to shake things up?"

"I guess you could say that," Amberly said. "I mean, she loved my dad, but she was a progressive and didn't want marriage. Dad convinced her to marry him anyway — he was *very* persuasive. She always felt like she betrayed her principles by marrying him. Whenever she and dad fought, she would always try to hurt him by saying so."

"What did you think?" Dek asked again, in a way that seemed too innocent to Amberly.

"I didn't think about it. I stayed out of it. Now, if you pinned me down, I suppose you can call me a progressive. But back then, all I knew was I hated politics. Dad never pushed, but they were so different. I was only 13 when we lost them."

"Why didn't she leave him and go back to Arara?" Dek asked again.

The question hit a sensitive area, and for the first time since their evening adventure began, Amberly was beginning to feel the good feelings escape like air out of a punctured vacuum suit. "Why all the prying questions?"

"I'm sorry, Amberly," Dek stood up. "I didn't mean to offend. So much of who people become is because of who our parents are. I guess I am curious because I didn't have parents. Well, I guess I had a donor mother and father, but it's not the same."

Amberly took Dek's apology as sincere, grabbed Dek's hand and pulled him back down into a seated position.

"What did they see in each other?" Dek said.

"Hmm… Dad always called mom a 'dish.'"

"So that's where you get it from …"

"Stop it. Dad was handsome enough. They were both passionate adventurers, always exploring some gaseous cloud or asteroid in one of the *Magellan*'s corvettes dad piloted. They had their differences, but they both lived life to the fullest."

Dek smiled at the thought. Amberly continued.

"Dad wanted mom to go back to Arara. He wanted us all to go there together, because he thought mom would be happier there and maybe our family would be stronger. But when he suggested it, the idea just made mom angrier. She said her work in the labs was really important and she could not leave it and he should know that, and always scolded dad harshly whenever he brought it up."

"Seems like your dad didn't care about your mom's needs at all, just about family," Dek suggested.

"Oh, now Dek, I've gone and said too much, to a stranger, too." Amberly protested.

"Amberly, out here, no one can afford to be strangers."

"What I mean is that I want people to remember my parents' relationship for the good things it brought. You know, like Kora … and *me*. Mom had a conch shell that Dad have given her —"

"A what?"

"A conch shell. It's a seashell from Earth that they say if you listen to, you can hear the ocean. It sounds like waves, at least as far as I could tell. I don't know, something about the air pressure and acoustics. Anyway, mom loved it. She would always hold it up to her ear and close her eyes and pretend she was on some shore in Arara. It's a beautiful shell, pearl-colored with a nice round pattern. I have no idea how dad got it. Must have been from some of the traders he would hang out with in the pilot's lounge."

"Do you still have it?"

"I wish I did. Mom always took it with her when she and dad went on their expeditions. She would say that if for some reason they couldn't make it back, she wanted the sound of the ocean to be the last thing that she heard. When my parents were lost, the conch was gone, too."

"Do you ever want —?"

"Enough questions, transient," Amberly put up her hand in a stop gesture and gave Dek a warm smile. "I'm tired. Mr. Tigona, would it be too traditional for me to ask you to walk me home?"

"As I've always said, a progressive embraces traditional roles when it is desired by the individuals involved …" Dek smiled back.

"… but not forced on them by society," Amberly finished his sentence.

Dek popped open the Jeffries tube from the top, and the pair slipped back down on the quiet lower decks – it was the middle of the night, so most of the waypoint residents were sleeping. Although there were no real solar days on *Magellan*, the people living there still found it useful to structure their lives according to days that were approximately 28 hours. On Earth, a day was 24 hours; on Arara, the planet revolved on its axis every 32 hours. Originally, *Magellan* had been on a 24-hour cycle that matched Earth, but as more people of *Magellan's* population were Arara-born, the local government started making the days on *Magellan* longer. Eventually, settling on a 28-hour day was a sort of a compromise between those who liked the shorter earth days and those who liked the longer Araran days. Ultimately, even on Arara, time was always measured relative to Earth years, especially for legal purposes, like a person's age.

To match the Earth year, there were only 312 28-hour days in the *Magellan* year; on Arara, they counted a year completed when only 274 32-hour Araran days had passed.

Amberly and Dek walked quietly back to her apartment in the rim of the State Quadrant. They walked quietly, but the silence was not awkward.

At the tube station, Amberly noticed in her peripheral vision, a man reading an infopad wearing a black jumpsuit similar to those worn by the pilots who lived on *Magellan*.

When they got off the tube, Amberly noticed the same man got off the car behind them, apparently trying to seem like he was unaware of the couple, though at this time of night, they were the only other people in the vicinity of the tube station.

As they walked out towards the State Quadrant rim, Amberly whispered to Dek.

"That guy is following us. Did you see him?"

"What guy?" Dek asked, spinning around. The man was gone. "Are you sure there wasn't something recreational in your topis?"

"Very funny," Amberly said, because it wasn't. "Seriously, I've never seen that guy around here before."

"Seriously, what guy? I didn't see anyone."

"Really?"

"Really. Besides, Amberly, I'm here, and I wouldn't let anything bad happen to you."

"That's the sort of thing my dad would say to my mom. He meant it, but it still pissed her off."

"Does it bother you?"

Amberly thought about it. "No, maybe I kind of like it. I don't know," she admitted out loud, and was surprised she did.

"Hmm."

Amberly and Dek rounded the corner to face the main portal to the Macready home, and were surprised to find Kora giving a light kiss to a police officer in the partially open door. Amberly immediately knew it wasn't a *real* kiss. She had seen this act before. Dek on the other hand, was convinced, and it put all sorts of wrong ideas in his head.

Kora pushed the officer back and closed the door, the police officer turned to leave and was taken aback to find Amberly and Dek standing there. He was flush, perhaps wondering what they saw, but played it cool as he walked by the couple.

"Be safe, citizens and good night," he said as he rounded the corner.

When the officer was out of earshot, Dek and Amberly burst out laughing. Dek's grey-blue eyes were intense, and Amberly suspected that Dek wanted to play out the scene they just saw.

But she would have none of it; she knew better. She would sleep off this man-induced intoxication, and she would feel more sensible and in control in the morning, once the endorphins or hormones or whatever had worn off, and she would think nothing more of Dek. She stepped away before Dek could even make a second attempt at kissing her, so she wouldn't have to plainly reject him.

"Thanks for the … um … adventurous walk," Amberly said. "I can't think of another person I would rather avoid the law with."

"Meeting you was glorious, Amberly Macready. May we cross paths again soon."

"We'll see," Amberly said as she closed the door.

Amberly turned and faced her sister.

"Look at you, my little sister, bringing the man home," Kora teased.

Amberly scowled. "That's not true."

"What? You're not my sister?" Kora smiled.

"No. I didn't bring a man home."

"Looked like a man to me." Kora shrugged, then continued to poke sarcasm at Amberly. "I am so proud of you, running off with that transient to do God-knows-what. So, is he a good kisser?"

"I wouldn't know," said Amberly, not amused at Kora's teasing. "Unlike you, I don't kiss on the first date."

"So, it was a date. And that wasn't a kiss. More like a gentle peck."

Amberly let out a resigned sigh. "Change the subject. So, what happened at Rick's?"

"Well, the police took about a half dozen of us to the brig too cool off. Trot Wilder was the police officer who was booking us miscreants, and you know how he fancies me — he let me off the hook."

"Kora!" Amberly disapproved.

"Believe me, I wasn't trying to take advantage of him," Kora joked. "But would you really turn down a get-out-of-jail free token when offered?"

Amberly sat down on the bench seat opposite the front door in the living room in their apartment. The living room had an area of three-square meters and included an in-wall bench on two adjacent walls. The worn grey polyester cushions on the benches opened to reveal storage units, mostly filled with kitchen items and foodstuff. The walls without in-wall benches each had a portal – one that opened to the exterior corridor outside their apartment, the other that opened into the bedrooms and bathroom. In the middle of the living room was a square table, metallic and supported by one center leg that was welded to the floor.

Three similarly fashioned chairs, with slight curvatures in the backrest, were pushed in under the table. The table was covered with a blue cloth. The most common apartments on *Magellan* had only one bedroom and a combined living room and kitchen area – this one had two bedrooms. When the Macready's were younger, they shared one room and their parents, the other. Both rooms were connected to a shared small bathroom. After the

Macready parents were lost in space, Amberly moved into her parents' room. Both the bedrooms were located on the extreme rim of *Magellan,* making the apartment desirable because of the oversized viewports. From the bedrooms, occupants could quietly and privately look out into the maddening vastness of space.

"Still, it was only a kiss. I mean it was hardly a kiss," Kora debated, now feeling slightly guilty about leading Trot Wilder on. "That's all. Meant nothing."

"I knew that. But Trot didn't. But whatever. What happened to North? Is he still in the brig?"

"Why should you care?" Kora said as she walked into her bedroom and began to disrobe. "Looked like you were having plenty of fun all night with Dek."

"I'm not in the mood for your ...," Amberly said, not completing the sentence, grumpy with tiredness. She walked into her room and opened her wardrobe and pulled out a red nightgown and dressed for bed.

Kora put on worn black sweatpants and a loose-fitting white undershirt. "I don't know about North. I think they took all the Marines involved in the brawl down to the military brig."

"I hope he's not in any real trouble," Amberly said.

"Oh, North will be fine."

The dark-haired woman crawled into her bed. The head and port side of the bed butted up against the cold steel wall, taking up most of the floor space in the room. "Good night, Amberly."

"Good night, sister," Amberly, emotionally and physically exhausted from the day's unusual events, crawled into bed and looked out her window. She grew up looking out into the various star clusters that surrounded her waypoint. She knew one of the millions of points of light that glowed in the darkness was Viapos, orbited by Arara.

Mom looked out this same window, looking back for her home, Amberly thought, as she drifted to sleep.

In the place between awake and asleep, she thought perhaps she was floating out in space, flying in an epic streak like a meteor towards Arara. She was almost entirely unconscious when she saw a light blink on Verne. She reached over and saw there was a text-only message from North.

"Hey, Red. Heck of a ship day. I wanted to make sure you

were okay. Don't worry about me. I just got out of the brig. Commander Anderson is letting us all slide with a warning. Lucky break. Hey, I wanted to ask you something, but I didn't get the chance on account of all those flying fists at Rick's. Let's meet for breakfast tomorrow at the Church commons."

What in the waypoint does North want to ask me? Amberly thought as she drifted into the sweet oblivion of sleep. She had strange dreams that night of floating in space with Dek and North, but when she woke the next morning, she couldn't remember any of the details, just the feelings.

They unsettled her.

CHAPTER FOUR

Sitting across from North at the Church commons cafeteria, Amberly poked at the yellow blob of protein that was a poor facsimile of scrambled eggs.

Anybody who had actually eaten fresh scrambled eggs would have probably passed, but since chickens only existed back on Earth, most people had no idea what the real thing tasted like. Only a few people who lived on the *Magellan* came from Earth, and there was no one who had ever left *Magellan* for Earth and then lived to return to *Magellan*. The round trip certainly was possible, but it could be a 40-year proposition. Someone who left *Magellan* when they were 20 could make it to Earth and back by the time they were 60. Since the average lifespan of any human, whether they lived on waypoint, interstellar transport, or planet was 97 years, they might have about a third of their life left.

Thor Rillio, governor of *Magellan*, was Earth-born, and could remember what real scrambled eggs tasted like. His family, traders, left Earth when he was 18 years old, and he was nearly 40 when they arrived at *Magellan*. By the time his family had arrived on *Magellan*, they were relatively wealthy, having made a fortune bringing goods from Earth to the 16 waypoints (and then from waypoint to waypoint) before arriving at *Magellan*. Thor fell in love with the daughter of an asteroid miner, and settled on *Magellan*, while the rest of his family headed on to *Waypoint Cortes*. The Rillio family had planned on retiring on Arara, after over two decades of space travel and fortune making.

Unfortunately, the Rillio's transport, *S.S. Silverstreak*, had an antimatter failure six months out from *Magellan*, which blew out the ship's entire power system and primary batteries. Many died from the catastrophic explosion. The rest of Thor's family died from suffocation and extreme temperatures as the ship's life support system consumed the remaining power in the secondary batteries over the course of two months. No ship was close enough to reach the *Silverstreak*; and by the time the distress signal had reached the *Magellan*, the crew of the *Silverstreak* had been dead for months.

During the last two months of their lives, the crew of the *Silverstreak* – Thor's parents, paternal grandparents, aunt and uncle, brother and sister, three cousins, and a half-dozen "hired hands" – broadcast daily reports on their condition. Four months after each signal was sent, Thor would read the daily update, as the consecutive signals reached *Magellan* in turn. Day by day, Thor had no way of knowing if rescue had come, but he knew, as the days passed, that the daily messages were probably the voices of ghosts. If he had not stayed behind with his new bride, he would be dead, too.

Two years later, the mammoth cruiser *H.M.S. Victoria* arrived at *Magellan* with the remains of *S.S. Silverstreak* in tow. Thor inherited the wealth of his family, and he used those resources over the next 20 years to build a political empire on *Magellan*. He was currently in his second four-year term as the waypoint's civilian governor. Thor vowed never to travel in space again, and he never left *Magellan*, not even to go on one of the waypoint's short-range runabouts or corvettes.

As usual, North had a healthy appetite, owed to the intense physical regimen of waypoint Marines. He quickly ingested his "eggs" and washed them down with a vitamin-C rich glass of a synthetic orange breakfast drink.

"The brig, huh?" Amberly offered.

"Yeah, I want to try to avoid ending up there in the future. Not exactly the best place to pass the evening. Especially when you are sore from being bashed across the back with a chair," North said, absentmindedly rubbing his left shoulder with his right hand.

"I don't know why you stick up for Skip," Amberly smiled. "No, I do know why. Because, North, you are a good friend to many."

"Well, I ..."

Amberly lifted her glass and spoke with a faux-aristocratic accent. "Here's to North, protector of the weak, and good friend to Lydia, Skip, Kora and ...," Amberly dropped the accent, "... to me."

"Cheers," North chuckled at Amberly's display.

"So, thanks for breakfast and all, but what did you want to ask me that couldn't wait until you had some time to sleep off jail?" Amberly prodded.

"Oh, did I say it couldn't wait?" North asked. "Mostly I was just ... worried."

"Worried about what?"

"Well, I saw you running off with that transient, what was his name –"

"Dek."

"Right. Dek. The one who bought you the drink."

"The one who bought Kora and I the drinks."

"Yeah, that guy."

"Well, he actually ended up being pretty good at evading the police," Amberly said. "Dek's a neat guy. Brilliant scientist. Still, there's something about him ..."

"Something about him?"

"I can't quite put my finger on it. I really enjoyed our romp last night."

"Romp?"

"Yeah, we snuck up into the topside farms."

"Wait. *Romp*?"

"There was something thrilling and dangerous about him – yet calm and in control at the same time," Amberly said, looking away as if fixed on an imaginary image of Dek.

"Hey, I'm right here," North said, waving a hand in front of her face. "I don't think you should see this Dek character. I don't trust him."

North's unsolicited advice offended Amberly. She felt her strong, independent mother coming out. "Wait. Wait. Wait. Who are you to say whom I should be seeing or not? I am a good judge of character."

"I am just worried about you, Red, that's all."

"Do you think I can't take care of myself? You're not my father. What place do you think you — " Amberly's face was flush. She felt disrespected.

"No, no, kid ... it's just that you're – "

"It's just that *what*?" Amberly said, slightly annoyed. "If you have something to say, open up. What am I – "

But Amberly caught herself and didn't finish her sentence. She would never admit it to anyone, and she certainly didn't want to admit it to herself, but what she wanted to know was undeniable.

She didn't know how she felt about North – outside of being a friend. But she wanted to know how *he* felt about *her*.

Out here, on *Magellan*, light years of loneliness separated the pioneers of this waypoint from other human life. Amberly wasn't given to existential thought that often, but occasionally she thought about the millions of people on Arara and the billions of people on Earth and the life-sucking vacuum that separated her and her ten thousand waypoint keepers from where human life started. From home.

This desolate isolation burned places deep inside her. She wondered if this yearning for connection, this heavy, lonely feeling could be tamed if she bonded with someone solid, someone real, and close. Someone like North. She wished her mother were here, someone she could ask, is it better to suffer the void together – or is this just a precursor to later suffering an even more painful separation?

She suddenly felt vulnerable. What if North said he was nothing to her, nothing romantic anyway — and then she found out that she wanted to be with him?

She pushed *that* silly idea out of her head, and then decided for a tactical retreat.

"What am I going to do with you, old friend?" she asked rhetorically, transforming her annoyance into more of an exhausted smile.

North looked confused. Just was well, Amberly thought. "You wanted to ask me something?" Amberly pretended as if the awkward advice about Dek had never been given.

North went with it. "Well, Miss Macready, I have, in my possession, a private ship pass."

He pulled a blue authorization pass card from his breast pocket. The thin plastic rectangle bore the official *Magellan* civilian and military seals and had a highly encrypted micro-chit embedded in it, authorizing the use of one of *Magellan*'s public spacecraft. The cards were commonly used for keeping track of high value and transferable goods and services. This chip contained codes that were allegedly uncrackable, at least by any technology that had arrived at *Magellan* thus far.

"Wow. How did you get that?" Amberly marveled, genuinely surprised. "It's easier to space walk without a suit than get a private ship pass."

"Won it in a high stakes game of poker that I probably shouldn't have been playing."

"What are you going to do with it? Where are you going?" Amberly asked.

"The Shard Caves," he said and then smiled, showing his perfect white teeth, "And was sort of hoping you'd come with me."

"What? You mean, like a date?" Amberly asked with an uncharacteristic jocular coyness.

"Yes. Well, no, I mean we're friends … I mean, now … you can call it that if you want."

Amberly reached out and took the pass in her hand and considered it. "A poker game? Are you sure this pass is legit?" Amberly teased.

Going on a recreational trip, no matter how short, on one of the spacecraft assigned to *Magellan* was quite a luxury. Besides the privately-owned space vessels registered to the mining companies and traders, *Magellan* left Earth with a complement of four Valkyrie-class shuttles.

Magellan also employed a complement of about a dozen smaller, two-seater corvette-class shuttles. The Marines controlled eight corvettes, armed with repeating 50mm chain guns.

Mostly, the show of force was symbolic. There was no enemy. But even after thousands of years of not finding any extraterrestrial life, many people still religiously believed that man would have first contact with aliens, perhaps hostile. These alien-believers formed minority political parties on many waypoints – and on Earth and Arara, too. Centuries earlier, their political influence was essential to getting the intergovernmental support needed to make Project Waypoint a reality. Many of them believed ET would be making an interstellar call. But the aliens had not yet rung, and many lost faith. The political power of the alien hopefuls ended up splitting evenly between the progressive and the traditionalist parties.

The possibility of rogue humans needing to be engaged in space battle existed, however remote. History, up to his point, had never recorded any space battle of any kind – but with so many unknowns facing Project Waypoint, the hawks outvoted the doves, arguing it was better to be prepared than caught defenseless. Arming the corvettes was a compromise to avoid arming the Waypoints themselves. Unlike the Valkyries, the corvettes were severely limited in range. Running on battery power only, a fully charged corvette would have a reliable range of 100,000 kilometers. After that, passengers on a corvette risked life-support failure, or insufficient power for deceleration when the corvette reached its destination.

Several corvettes were publicly owned. These were not armed and available for public use by lottery. North had won his pass card from an unlucky schoolteacher who had won them in the 2602 lottery. The teacher, Jonus Ramon, a greying man in his 60s who had never been off the waypoint, put them up for collateral in a regular poker game held in a side room at Rick's. Ramon thought he would be walking home with North's monthly salary when he drew an inside straight. The blood drained from his face when he saw North lay down a full house, deuces over jacks, and then scoop up the authorization chit from among the credit coins in the pot.

North was going on a vacation to the Shard Caves, and he knew just who he wanted to go with him. Ramon, on the other hand, was going to be unpopular with his wife.

"When I won the corvette pass, I thought long and hard for about three seconds about who I wanted to take," North said. He smiled and teased, "Of course, I thought about Lydia and Kora, but those corvettes are a tight squeeze, so I though some one more petite might be a better co-pilot."

"You know how to fly one of those things?" asked Amberly, incredulously.

"Well, I am not as good as –" North caught himself, but Amberly finished.

"As my father?"

"You have to admit, he was a great pilot," North said. "But yes, I can fly a corvette. It's been a year since I've been out in an actual one, but I am required to log 10 hours a month in a simulator just in case."

Amberly poked at a bowl of mostly uneaten cereal, then took

a drink of vita-water. "You know, I haven't been out on a ship since my father died. In fact, now that I think about it, I've only ever been out on ships that my father piloted." Amberly spoke aloud, but absentmindedly.

"Does that mean you'll go with me?"

"Sure, I'll go with you," Amberly looked at North. Why wouldn't she go with him? North was the closest thing she had to a big brother or any male family member, and he had always been there for her, especially after her parents disappeared. She enjoyed North's company, and the thought of being in close quarters for what amounted to a daytrip seemed … pleasant.

Being with North was comfortable, she decided, and right now, comfortable was good. Besides she had never seen the Shard Caves.

Just then, Verne announced: "Amberly, if you don't start heading for the lab, you are going to be late for work."

"Sorry North, gotta run."

"No problem." North pushed back his seat and stood as she did. North smiled as he watched Amberly leave the Church commons eating area *en route* to the Tube.

Amberly sat alone in the tubecar as it quietly sped to the next quadrant station. For so long, she was the object of no one's affection. Now suddenly and out of nowhere, she had two men courting her attention: North, the good friend who maybe wanted something more, and Dek, the mysterious adventure, waiting to happen.

Caution was the only imperative she was sure of. She didn't want to lead anyone on, especially North, because of their friendship. But as the car decelerated, she knew that she didn't know what she wanted, and she didn't know how to figure out what she wanted, and she didn't like the feeling of not knowing how to know what she wanted. She thought about asking Kora for advice, but then imagined her mother telling her she needed to figure this out by herself.

As she stepped out of the tube car, Verne inquired, "Would you like me to set up an appointment for a corvette outing with North on your calendar?"

"I don't know, Verne," Amberly told her infopad. "I don't know."

The Shard Caves, known for their colorful, crystalline formations, were found deep within the Spencer Belt, a group of asteroids that, depending on its orbital cycle, came an amazingly close 40,000 kilometers to *Magellan*. When astronomers, physicists, engineers and others determined the best spot to "anchor" *Magellan*, they did not know about the existence of the Spencer Belt. However, within a few years of the waypoint reaching its anchorage, the residents searching for raw resources needed for continued sustainment and economic development found the asteroid cluster.

Spencer Belt was composed of several thousand chartable asteroids, with diameters ranging from a few hundred meters to the largest, Sonnet, which was more than 70 kilometers in diameter. The Spencer Belt was in deep orbit around the closest star to *Magellan*, HD 238921, a dim, relatively cool, low mass stellar object, know to the inhabitants of *Magellan* as Spencer Minorem, or Spencer the Lessor. The Spencer Belt was just over 14 billion kilometers from HD 238921, around twice the distance of Pluto to the Sun.

Magellan itself never fell into the orbit of Spencer Minorem, not only because the gravitational pull of the starlet was so weak, but also because *Magellan* deployed powerful antimatter-fueled thrusters to maintain a rough synchronous travel pattern with Earth and its solar system, 76 *trillion* kilometers away.

The Spencer Belt was in range of a runabout or corvette with the *Magellan* for about one Earth year of its six-year orbit around HD 238921. The proximity to the Spencer Belt ended up being a huge economic boon for the waypoint. The asteroids were rich with raw metallic ores, silicon, magnesium, sulfur, sodium chloride and hydric acid. Although most water is recycled on a waypoint, slow loss occurs over decades through atmospheric venting, and by resupplying deep space vehicles. With the frozen hydric acid found in pockets of the Spencer Belt, *Magellan's* miners could collect water not only for themselves, but also for nearby waypoints. This made the waypoints less reliant for their water on the supply convoys that came from earth every two score years, and provided a profitable export that employed many on *Magellan*.

In 2554, 29 years before Amberly was born, a team from the *Magellan* attempted to establish a permanent settlement on Sonnet. The construction of the 10,000-square meter facility began about one earth month into the yearlong window when the asteroids were accessible to *Magellan*. Construction fell behind schedule, and by the eleventh month of the orbital window, there was some question if the settlement, which contained the facilities needed to survive for the five years the Spencer Belt was out of contact with *Magellan*, could be completed successfully. *Magellan's* then-Governor Ingo Fuentes had pushed the construction of the Sonnet colony against the advice of several of *Magellan's* leading engineers. Convinced the colony was not folly, but what would help *Magellan* economically, culturally and politically dominate its waypoint neighbors, Fuentes resigned from his governorship to be the team commander of the Sonnet Colony itself. Corners were cut, sacrifices were made, tradeoffs considered, and with two days to spare, the final runabout, *M.S.S. Normandy* left the Sonnet Colony for the last time, carrying back to the *Magellan* the last of the construction crew. Left behind for the five-year dark cycle were three Marines, four miners, two medical specialists, two domestic logistics specialists, a greenhouse technician, an environmental engineer, a structural engineer, a researcher, and Fuentes, the mission commander.

The success of the first two years of the colony — three years before the shuttle travel window would open again and people and supplies could be ferried between the Sonnet Colony and *Magellan* – was beyond the dreams of Fuentes. They did not have to rely entirely on the food synthesizers because the greenhouse technician had successfully coaxed an incredible farm yield that, square meter for square meter matched the *Magellan's* topside gardens. The miners had found several new veins of rare ores, and the stellar researcher had been able to develop some new theories on small mass star origins based on data they gathered from the Spencer Belt's orbit.

Then little things started to go wrong. Doors between the colony building segments would jam. Both the air refreshers would clog and the environmental engineer did not have experience repairing this smaller model based on the *Magellan* refresher design. She would get one of the units fixed, but only for a short time before they would fail again. The mechanical battles were constant. Too many errors had been made adapting the life support systems for the ultra-low gravity of Sonnet, as opposed to the artificial gravity of *Magellan*.

The thermal units were hard pressed to be able to keep up with the extreme colds, which were harsher than expected when the colony was blocked from direct rays of HD 238921 by other asteroids in the belt. To preserve heat and energy, Fuentes was forced to order the greenhouses shut down and sealed, meaning the colonists had to rely on the food synth machines alone. Then the food synth machine broke for two days straight, giving the colonists their first real taste of hunger.

In May of 2557, the mining team was out of the colony in spacesuits on an expedition where they were attempting to access pockets of hydric acid. They were using small explosive charges to remove the surface rubble and access the invaluable substance below. One of the explosives went off unexpectedly and threw a miner off the almost zero-G asteroid into the inky void of space.

Reacting quickly according to training, a second miner, Illius Burke, put down a tether and anchor line and then leaped after the first miner in a vain attempt to save him from a frozen death in the vacuum of space. Unfortunately, in his haste to save his friend, he didn't test the rock he tethered himself to. It was unsecured and floated up after him. The third miner, Rachel Risa, grabbed for the tether but missed it by centimeters.

The blood drained from Rachel's face as she saw Illius, a secret lover, float out of her would-be saving reach into the cold embrace of certain space death. Horror flashed briefly over Illius' otherwise warm face. Rachel could still see the glint of the small, cold star in his eyes.

Illius had often thought of what would ever happen if he were spaced, and knew his anchoring error would be fatal as he floated off into oblivion. In four or five hours, his spacesuit's life support would give out. He quickly accepted his fate, and a sweet, sad smile washed over him – a smile for Rachel, who would only be able make out his face for another minute at most. He wanted his last contact with another person to be one of peace, one of love. And it was.

Illius floated away slowly, like a balloon with barely enough helium to float, after being released by a child on the surface of the earth. Illius wore a bright white suit, which reflected stellar light for kilometers. Rachel sobbed openly as she saw him float away, salty tears running down her smooth mocha-colored cheeks. Inside her helmet, the tears could not be wiped away. Instead, they started to levitate and bounce into each other, floating drops of pain and loss and grief. She fell to her knees, resisting the temptation to jump after him, to join him in his endless grave of space. She would stay with him, and she could make out his suit as a speck of light for a few hours. And then he was gone. And Rachel, who had departed the Sonnet Colony that morning with a friend and lover, slowly walked back to base alone.

Because of the time constraints during construction, Fuentes ordered that the corvette bay and docking station not be built, so they decided to not take a corvette with them. There was no ship to go after the men as they floated out of the Spencer Belt and into open space. Rachel knew a corvette could have easily recovered her colleagues before they perished.

Once safely inside the base, Rachel forcefully, verbally attacked Fuentes for rushing the project and letting them leave *Magellan* before they were ready. She said they were fools for thinking they could get the colony ready in a year, and they should have waited for the next cycle. Fuentes, unsympathetic to Rachel's protests, reminded her she knew the risks. A week later, Rachel seduced one of the Marines and stole his sidearm. She coldly and quietly went around the colony and put a bullet into the head of the remaining colonists. She left a message detailing what she had done and why, and then donned a spacesuit and left the safety of the colony for the surface of Sonnet.

She jumped as hard as she could, pushing off the asteroid, and plunging into the darkness. Rachel wrote in her message that she would find Illius, even if she had to chase him to the edge of the universe. As she floated away, she turned and looked at Sonnet, the large rock that floated near the center of the Spencer Belt. The asteroid had a unique symmetry that made it stand out from its brothers. She was nearly a kilometer away, and she could see the opening to the Shard Caves now, on the opposite side of Sonnet from the colony base. She closed her eyes, thought of when she once explored those beautiful caves with Illius, and froze to death.

When they discovered the massacre, the powers-that-be on *Magellan* found little appetite to revisit creating a permanent colony on Sonnet. The colony's structures were converted into an unmanned emergency survival station. In the future, should anyone find themselves stranded in the Spencer Belt, if they could make it to Sonnet, they would find a cache of supplies that would last 200 people about 10 years, or two people 1,000 years. Otherwise, the site was a memorial to the misjudgment of Governor Fuentes, and a tragic reminder of the quiet rage of Rachel Risa.

"Wait. North asked *you* to go with him to the Shard Caves?" Lydia seemed incredulous.

"What's that supposed to mean?" Amberly asked, as she punched up logs from the *Magellan*'s radiation sensors at her research station.

"I'm surprised he didn't ask Hannah or Ilia. I heard last week he went to the Wyoming Theater and to that new expensive restaurant in the Science commons with Flora," Lydia reminded her.

Flora Dillington. Just thinking of her put Amberly in a sour mood. The two were alike in many ways. They had both been born on *Magellan*. Both were the same age. They attended the same schools and had many of the same classes, had strong math and language aptitude, and were encouraged to seek careers in science. Amberly was fortunate to get an appointment as a junior researcher in the Science Corps; Flora secured lucrative work in the private sector for the Waypoint Research Group, the largest for-profit research company off planet. The women were even similar in size and appearance, except Flora was a dirty blonde. Amberly and Flora had been friends until they were 12, when Amberly told Flora about the crush she had on Theotinine Metopolin, a scrawny teenager who liked to recite romantic poets at length from memory. Flora then decided she wanted to be Theo's girl, and proceeded to flaunt herself to that end. Amberly was too shy to act on her crush, and she never forgave Flora. Theo moved with his parents to *Waypoint Estevancio* soon after. Amberly and Flora rarely spoke after that. She admitted to herself that it was a silly grudge, but the thought of her middle school nemesis getting her hooks into North was somewhat unnerving.

"Flora? With North? Please Lydia," Amberly said. "What would North see in her?" Amberly examined the logs on her screen and saw that there were no anomalies. She cleared the screen, and punched up new logs that needed processing.

Lydia pushed back an errant lock of her short golden hair that had slipped out from under her headband. "Please don't tell me you are interested in that Neanderthal. He's nice to look at, but nothing between the ears. You are so above him."

"North's not *that* bad."

"You *are* interested in him!"

"I hadn't really thought about it," Amberly lied.

"Well, there's no reason to be jealous of Flora if you are not interested in North."

"I'm not jealous of Flora. How did this become about Flora? North asked me to go to the Shards with him, anyway."

"Well are you going with him or not?" Lydia looked up from the terminal where she was tracking thermal spikes to offer an inquisitive look.

"I think I am."

"Of course you are," Lydia giggled.

North had arranged for the use of the corvette exactly one week after the incident at Rick's. The week went by fast for Amberly, who was kept busy working late hours at the lab analyzing the data collected by the *American Spirit*. When deep space vessels docked with waypoints, it was customary for the ship and waypoint to exchange sensor logs. A lot of data – locations of high-radiation zones in space, new micro-nebula, uncharted space junk, and more – was transferred via tight beam transmissions between the waypoints, but even with the best data compression, bandwidth for inter-waypoint transmissions was in high demand, and allocated as a scare resource. Secondary data collected by various sensors, data such as the intensity of infrared rays, or gamma radiation emission variances, were not shared over tight-beam communications. Instead, passing ships would capture and share this secondary data when they made a physical network connection.

Amberly was trained to search this data for anomalies that

were suspicious. In doing so, she could detect potential hazards, like lethal radiation from distant solar flares. This information, once analyzed, was fed into the powerful navigational computers, so waypoints and ships could avoid being burnt to a crisp from some unwanted stellar outburst by simply moving out of the way.

The technology application project Amberly was just starting to work on was to create predictive models based on the anomalous data – so not only could they locate and chart interstellar hazards, but perhaps they would also be better at predicting when solar bodies would misbehave. Amberly's research was ambitious, and the only reason her superiors in the Science Corps let her work on her pie-in-the-sky theory was because her mathematics aptitude was off-the-charts high. In the standardized theoretical mathematical test administered to those applying to be in the Science Corps, she was in the 99.9th percentile of everyone who had ever taken the test, on any waypoint or planet.

"You're working late tonight, ma'am," a deep voice came from behind her workstation. Amberly, startled, whirled her chair around to see a burly, blond man of average height, who had moved past middle age.

"Delivery," he said. "Just have a new box of data cards. I'm Midas."

Amberly was not in a mood to chat it up with some ancient deliveryman. "Um, thanks, do I need to sign for those?" Amberly offered her thumb for biometric verification and, when Midas put his info pad forward, she placed it on the scanner.

"You're a Macready girl, aren't you?" Midas offered. "The red hair. Alroy must have been your dad. Dirty shame, what happened to Alroy and Kimberly."

Many on *Magellan* knew either one or both of Amberly's parents, so it wasn't uncommon for her to run into people who had a story or a fond memory of the Macreadys. Usually, Amberly smiled and politely listened, but today she just wanted to get her work done. "You really look like your mum."

"Thanks, um, Midas," Amberly said, grabbing the box. "I'll take those now. See ya!"

Midas took the hint, tipped his head and headed out.

When he was gone, Amberly woke Verne up.

"Verne," she said to her info pad AI, "Do I know that guy?"

The AI responded flatly, "According to my visual records, Midas has delivered about 20 packages when you have been here in the past two years."

"I've never noticed him before," she said, as she absentmindedly returned to the stellar data she was processing. "Kind of creepy."

Over the course of the week, Amberly had half-expected to see Dek pop up again unexpectedly, after his rejoinder that they might cross paths again. She was sort of disappointed he didn't. She didn't see Dek's "sister" around either and wondered if Dek lied about that being his *cohort* sister. Perhaps they were cavorting back aboard the *American Spirit*. She knew Dek was brilliant — maybe not her level brilliant, but still sharper than most. If North was the epitome of brawn, Dek was a beacon of intellect. North was a man of rough honor; Dek seemed more to favor roguish charm.

Amberly was taking a day off work for the trip to the Shard Caves. The Spencer Belt was nearly at its closest point to *Magellan*, so the timing for an expedition to the Shard Caves was excellent. They should be able to reach the Spencer Belt in five or six hours, spend a few hours in the caves – Amberly didn't know exactly what North had in mind – and then about six hours on the return.

Amberly was walking home from the lab to her apartment the night before her trip when she noticed him again. It was the same man who she had thought to be following her the night she escaped the police with Dek – the one Dek denied seeing. He wasn't wearing a pilot jumpsuit anymore, but a large and heavy overcoat. If the man was trying to be inconspicuous, he wasn't doing a very good job. The temperature in most of the public areas of the waypoint was well regulated, around 25 degrees Celsius, eliminating the need for heavy clothing, like the man's heavy coat.

Amberly decided to confront the man. He was tall and middle aged, maybe 50 years old. As she approached him from across the tube station lobby, he pretended to ignore her.

She walked right up to him.

"Hey, I'm sorry to be rude, but I've noticed that you have been … well … spying on me lately. Who are you? Did you come on the *American Spirit?*"

The man was startled for a second, and scanned the lobby to see if anyone else was listening.

"I was wondering if you were with us," the man said, a smile of friendliness melting across his face. "You look so much like your mother, though I see you've inherited your father's mane. I am so glad that Dek could recruit you to the Chasm. Your mother would be proud."

"Chasm? You know Dek?" Amberly was confused and it showed as her eyes narrowed. "And how did you know my parents?"

"Wait … you mean Dek hasn't … I mean, I must be going now." The man turned from Amberly and in a near sprint made for the Tube. Amberly didn't know if she should chase the man or not. While she was considering, the man vanished into an empty Tubecar.

Was he dangerous? Or just crazy? Or both? Amberly had some questions that needed answering, and she knew that she would, indeed, be crossing paths with Dek Tigona again.

CHAPTER FIVE

"Wow, I think we should tell the police. Do you want me to call Trot?" Kora said, sitting backwards in one of her living room chairs, leaning over the clear table.

Amberly was lying on an in-wall bench. One arm was draped over the side, with her hand skimming the floor. The other was covering her eyes, as if the lights that illuminated the living room were bothering her. She was still wearing her science lab work uniform, though she had removed the form fitting white jacket and had tossed it on the floor. Kora, who worked as a nurse in the Church medical wards, was still wearing her classic white nurse uniform. Many of the nurses wore practical uniforms — scrub-like garments that were easy to clean and otherwise bland. Kora's uniform was a bit more feminine than most — she took pride in being stylish, but also enjoyed the extra attention.

Amberly told Kora everything she knew about this mysterious man who seemed to know their deceased parents.

"What would we tell them? Some crazy guy from the *American Spirit* claims to know our parents? It's not like any law has been broken," Amberly said, sitting up and straightening her undershirt. "Do you know anything about a 'chasm'?" Amberly asked her sister.

Kora pulled at her dark hair. "No clue. If you don't want to tell the authorities, maybe we should let North know, you know. Maybe this Chasm is a military thing?"

"Ha! Dek is anything but military," Amberly snorted. "Besides, all we need is North going on some protective man rant."

"I don't know, having a man protecting you doesn't sound like a bad idea to me."

"If mom could hear you —"

"Mom can't hear me, Amberly," Kora said. "And even if she was here, I mean, I loved mom more than anything, but I think she was wrong about so many things."

"Because you know so much better than our silly, unintelligent mother," Amberly projected sarcasm.

Kora sat down. "I know you were a little bit younger. But I

saw how much dad loved mom. And how lucky she was to have him. Either of us would be lucky to marry someone like dad. And don't say it — you are not going to get married."

"You never appreciated mom, Kora. You just lived in dad's fantasy worlds. And I am *not* going to get married. I am not having this conversation with you again," Amberly exhaled in exasperation. "I need to sleep. I'll figure out what to do about our crazy guy in the morning. North and I have an early start time tomorrow."

Kora stood up and stepped toward her room, then turned around and sat down next to her sister, placing a hand on Amberly's shoulder. "Sorry for going there again. It's just that – "

"You don't need to be." Amberly interrupted her sister gently. "I'm just tired and cranky."

Amberly stood and picked up her jacket from the floor and started undressing for bed while calling back to her sister. "I'm sort of looking forward to tomorrow."

"And why shouldn't you. North's a good guy. You'll have fun tomorrow. I may actually be jealous of you."

"Come on Kora, if you wanted to, you know you could have North eating out of your hand," Amberly suggested.

"I think you underestimate him," Kora said in seriousness. "He knows what he wants. Maybe he's ready to stop playing around. I mean, North didn't ask *me* to go with him to the Shard Caves after all."

"So you are saying he is interested in the younger, better looking Macready model?" Amberly teased.

"Let's not have delusions of grandeur. You are *not* better looking than me," Kora quipped back. "North's a good man."

"You said that already. Good night, sister."

"Good night."

Most of the residents of *Magellan*, and the guests from the *American Spirit*, were still asleep when Amberly met North at the hangar. North had already been there for an hour, going over the preflight checklist with the early shift dock master. North was wearing civilian clothes: cleanly pressed brown trousers and a bright white collared shirt with buttons, half-way buttoned up, taught against his broad shoulders. Underneath, he wore an undershirt, also white as a clear night star. Buttons were not unheard of in the fashion of *Magellan*, but most common clothes used plastic lock strands, adhesive strips, or even metallic zippers. Buttons were still seen in traditional military dress uniforms, but were usually only worn for formal or important occasions.

His hair was neatly cut and framed face perfectly. The scar on his chin, about three centimeters long, was the only blemish on his otherwise clean-shaven face. His brown eyes were dark, but still managed to reflect a twinkle of friendly, comfortable light.

North had won the right for a personal use of the corvette *M.S.S. Claire De Lune*, a new ship built from scratch on *Magellan*. The ship was a testament to how independent the waypoint had become. The *Claire De Lune* was brilliant metallic silver, the exterior a shiny polished alloy that one might mistake for chrome. Not only was *Claire De Lune* entirely built on *Magellan*, but most of the materials used to forge the ship were also harvested from Spencer Belt asteroids.

The corvette was seven times as long as it was wide, which was just wide enough to hold two humans sitting side by side. The *Clair De Lune* was mostly cylindrical in shape, though it had three rear fins, which were cosmetic in purpose, giving the vessel a sleek, cosmopolitan design.

Powered entirely by batteries, the corvette had no antimatter generator, severely limiting its range. The forward viewport (the only viewport on most corvette-class ships) was generously large, offering the pilot and the co-pilot a spectacular view of whatever the bow was facing. Behind the tight two-person cockpit was a small zero-gravity restroom and galley. The galley was little more than a place to store pre-made meals, beverages and emergency rations in case, for some unforeseen reason, a corvette was temporarily stranded. The galley also had space-certified suits that the pilot and passenger or co-pilot could don in the event the cockpit was compromised. When she was a schoolchild on *Magellan*, Amberly had been trained to put on a spacesuit. However, that was 10 years ago. She was out of practice.

North saw Amberly enter the dock, and he smiled his captivating grin. He half expected Amberly to stand him up, even though the cost of their trip was enormous. He was slightly nervous, though he tried to hide it. Amberly wore an emerald green dress made from synthetic cotton. The dress was modestly cut, though it accentuated Amberly's natural curves. Her short hair was pulled up into a single tight bun with Oriental sticks holding the bun in place.

"Wow. You look beautiful," North said to Amberly, as she appeared from behind a private runabout. North again shot her his trademark smile, with just a little bit of dimple. "Are you ready?"

"Thanks," Amberly said with simple, sincere gratitude. "Kora said she was *very* jealous."

"I'm sure she'll get over it."

Magellan's dock was still full of parked vessels at this hour of the morning with more than 20 private, public and military vessels still in port.

The deck officer, Jimbo Tunabi, a friend of North's, walked up to the pair.

"You're approved for departure, North. No other traffic from *Magellan* scheduled for a Sonnet run today – looks like you have the run of the place. A Marine corvette is going to be out today for testing and maintenance, but it should be nowhere near your flight path."

"Thanks for the update," North saluted Jimbo and he returned the gesture.

"Shall we dance?" North said, pointing toward the exterior access port to the corvette. Amberly climbed up a small ladder, slipped into the port and slid into the co-pilot's seat. North followed her, deftly slipping his larger frame through the portal. Once inside, North had comfortable maneuvering room. Jimbo sealed the port, turned off the artificial gravity, and gave a visual signal to North that he was clear to test fire the *Claire De Lune's* engines.

"You sure you know how to fly this thing?" Amberly asked.

"You already asked me that. This is just like the Marine corvettes, only no guns. I got this, no problem."

And with that, North released the magnetic locks, and the ship began to float freely.

"*Magellan* dockmaster, this is *Claire De Lune*, requesting depressurization and opening of the hangar doors," North said into the radio communication headpiece he had put in during preflight preparation.

"*Claire De Lune*, this is dock master. Please have all crew and passengers do thumbprint verification at this time." Both North and Amberly complied, in turn pressing a thumb against the ship's biometric reader until a positive ID indicator chimed.

To let a ship out of dock, first all the air had to be evacuated from the bay into storage tanks. Specialized pressure inlets sucked the air from dock into the tanks – so valuable atmosphere would not be lost into space during the airlocking process for the small ships inside the dock.

Once the atmosphere from the docks was captured, creating a vacuum, the dock master would open the doors. Ships not magnetically attached to *Magellan* could float out.

Of course, they did not want to evacuate the air in the hangar when people were inside, so everyone who entered the hangar was required to authenticate entry and exit with a thumbprint. When it was time to launch a ship, people cleared the hangar behind an environmental curtain that fell before the space doors opened. *Magellan's* computers then did a headcount to make sure no one was accidentally exposed to a vacuum.

The hangar doors were large, copper-colored and opened slowly. Normally, the view out of the hangar door was just a star field, but today, the gleam of the docked *American Spirit* radiated just outside.

Amberly belted into her seat to keep from floating as the *Claire De Lune* slipped out of the *Magellan's* artificial gravity well into open space. Amberly noted North's familiar command of *Claire De Lune's* navigational thrusters.

"How about a spin around *Magellan*, before we head out?" suggested Amberly, as she peered out the viewport.

North nodded. Apart from the Tube, people who lived on *Magellan* almost never enjoyed any kind of mechanized travel. The float out into space was more than a joyride to Amberly, however.

Amberly took in the view of the *American Spirit*, as they skirted the gangway. She looked at the American flag painted on the *Sprit's* hull. Technically, having been born on an American waypoint, she was an American citizen, though one's Earth nationality did not have much relevance on a waypoint as it did planet side. Earth's nationalistic governments persevered, though on Arara there was one planetary government, divided into federal districts.

"You, know, the ship I was born on was about the same size as that one," North said, nodding to the *American Spirit*.

"Which ship was that?"

"*Il Lungo Viaggio*. That's old Italian for 'the long voyage'," North explained. "We landed on Arara when I was five."

"How could you ever come back into space after living on a planet?"

"I dunno," North said. "Duty called. Someone must be ever vigilant to defend the waypoints from foes external and internal. Someone must be always ready. Heaven forbid something happen to one of the waypoints, and we lose our connection with Earth."

"Except we don't have any foes," Amberly said.

"Hopefully the Marines will never be needed for any real battle," North agreed. "But you must admit, you feel a little bit safer knowing we are around just in case."

"Well, maybe safer knowing *you* are around," Amberly joked, and she patted her hand on North's.

The *Claire De Lune* cleared several kilometers of distance from *Magellan* and the docked *American Spirit*. "I'm bringing the engines to full power," North announced by habit.

North and Amberly talked continuously about nothing important for the next few hours as they sped along at thousands of kilometers per hour toward the Spencer Belt. It wasn't an awkward nothing – it was a familiar nothing: details about the minutia of daily life on a waypoint, the sort of banal information discussed by close siblings, old friends or lovers. Amberly was comfortable alone with North; she didn't know what they were romantically, but she knew they were friends. Somehow, she knew they would always be friends. Why wouldn't they be? They had been friends for eight years, nearly half of Amberly's life and a third of North's.

"And then Skip says, what did you mean, 'wider than a tubecar'?" North said.

"He did not. You're making that up," Amberly responded.

The pair of joyriders giggled through sandwiches North had

packed when they made visual contact with the Spencer Belt. Sonnet stood out because it was significantly larger than its sibling asteroids. Amberly pressed a hand to the viewport.

"The Shard Caves are on the far side," North announced, quickly slipping into his military pilot training. "I am going to bring us down to a few hundred meters, and then we'll circle relative north to the caves."

"That is a big rock," Amberly smiled. She spotted an artificial structure on the horizon. "Is that the abandoned settlement over there?"

"Yeah, good ol' Fuentes Memorial," North said. "I thought we'd do a fly-by since we were out here."

"I remember reading about that in middle school history," Amberly said. "Everyone died. I am surprised we've never tried again."

The chrome and white shell of the old colony building was coming clearly into view.

"Hey, is that a light? I thought the thing was abandoned?" Amberly said.

"Where?"

"There."

"Where?"

"Oh, it's gone now. Maybe I was just seeing things."

"Well, I thought it was abandoned. Mining runs aren't expected to start for another three weeks. Maybe we should radio, just in case, North said, as he activated the radio that was standard for all spacefaring craft – a universal local communication system. "This is the *M.S.S. Claire De Lune,* broadcasting a general hello to anyone in earshot."

The pair listened for a response. There was a long period of silence followed by a quick series of clicks. Then more silence.

"Was that something? Sounded like someone opening and closing a comm channel?"

"Probably just some magnetic radiation interfering with the radio," North shrugged.

Amberly reached over and activated the radio. "Hello? Hello?" she said. "Anyone out there?"

The response was more silence.

"On to the main event," North said.

Even at reduced speeds, the corvette zoomed quickly around the asteroid, and within a few minutes, the *Claire De Lune* was at the opening of the Shard Caves. Amberly couldn't see directly into the cave mouth from her angle, but could see a soft glow emanating from inside.

"I didn't think we should put down and hike in," North said. "Too dangerous unless you are experienced in space suit walking."

"I hate the things. You feel claustrophobic and vertigo at the same time," Amberly said. "But how are we going to see the shards?"

"We're floating in."

"Whoa. Are you sure about that? It's a pretty tight squeeze," Amberly said, trying to hide the sudden nervousness in her voice.

"Absolutely. Hold on."

North accelerated the *Claire De Lune* and pitched the craft skyward for a few hundred meters. A bright field of stars filled the viewport, raining beams of light on the couple. Then he slowly rounded the vertical ascent back into a descent – a controlled nose-dive, and the rocky Sonnet filled the viewport again. North was threading a needle, heading straight towards the cave mouth.

That mouth is twice as wide as the ship, thought Amberly, as she tried to reassure herself. *Any good pilot could manage that. I think.* She glanced over at North who was looking over at her, clearly amused at her anxiety.

"Pay attention to the rock in front of us!" Amberly shouted. North chuckled, smiled and looked forward again, guiding the corvette expertly into the crevasse. The ship glided in as if it were made to fit, like a well-engineered cog or a finely tailored glove.

And then they were inside the cave. Amberly gasped as her anxiety was replaced by breathtaking awe.

The intensity of the glow emanating from the crystalline structures seemed to grow on all sides. The cave was brighter than Amberly expected – not waypoint day bright, but surprisingly bright for a naturally occurring phosphorescence phenomenon. Each crystal had a unique glowing color: turquoise, amber, violet, rose and a spectrum of others. The largest crystals growing out of the rocks were several meters tall and had smaller crystals of varying colors growing out of them. Most of the shards were semi-translucent, and colors from the other shards could be seen though them.

The scientist in Amberly was trying to figure out how enough outside light could even penetrate the cave to create this much afterglow. The smaller, poetic voice in her whispered to her heart, just enjoy the show.

So she did.

The caves went on for several kilometers, and the deeper *Claire De Lune* made its way into the caves and away from the mouth, the dimmer the shards were. About two kilometers in, the corvette floated into a large cavern, about half the size of the *Magellan's* hangar bay. North brought the ship to a full stop, and powered the main engines down. The glowing rocks were dim here, and seemed to flicker like candles, although Amberly did not associate flickering with candles, as open flames were uncommon on *Magellan*. Scientifically, she couldn't figure out what was causing the flickering, and it bothered her a little bit. Then she looked over at North, and she thought he was looking at her funny.

"Why are you looking at me like that?

"I'm not looking at you in any way."

"Yes, you look a little goofy."

"I guess it's you."

"Me?"

"You're amazing. Look at you, Amberly. You have it all: the most beautiful girl on *Magellan*, and you're probably more intelligent than anyone else on the station. You're only 19 and people respect you like you're 40. Your friends adore you. You're considerate, kind to everyone you meet. You are practically perfect."

"*You* said it," Amberly said, putting her hands up palms forward.

"Amberly, I've been doing a lot of thinking lately, about the people God puts in our lives. I've been thinking about where we are heading and –"

"What we? We 'humanity'? We *Magellan*? We us?"

"All of the above, I suppose, but mostly 'us'," he smiled his winning smile. "What if we were to become more than friends?"

"You mean, like dating?" Amberly said, with an almost sarcastic tone and a look in her eyes like North had just asked her to airlock herself.

"Sure dating, courtship, you know, boyfriend, girlfriend," North said.

"Leading to what?" Amberly said, getting testy.

"I am not trying to get ahead of anything here," North said, confused by Amberly's tone. "You're pretty good. And, well, I'm not so bad. What if together, we can be great?"

"North, you know me … better than this," Amberly said, starting to feel confusing emotions erupt inside.

This is wrong … all wrong, Amberly's brain flashed. Not the location. The view of the soft glowing cavern of the shard caves was romantic as any place within light years of *Magellan* to be sure. And North was good looking. And just plain good. But she was not going to be defined by an outdated institution born of ancient religion. If her mother taught her anything, instilled any value in her core, it was how the deceptive comforts of tradition would hold her back.

North *knew* she felt this way. He knew her mother felt this way. If he cared for her, wouldn't he know better?

Perhaps, after all these years, North still didn't understand her, Amberly wondered. He was too simplistic, too naïve. He was 10 years her senior, and in many ways, a man of the worlds. But Amberly also thought of North as being a bit backwards, a smidgen old-fashioned, and perhaps on the macro-level, dully unimaginative. He was always playing checkers, and she was playing chess.

"Amberly, I've known you for a long time," North said. "If you give us a chance, you would see how much we could do together."

"You sound like my dad, North."

"Is that a bad thing? Alroy Macready was a good man."

"Yes. Because I am like mom – I choose to be like her. I want to be like her, more than anything. And she regretted her relationship with my dad. Even if she never said it. I could see it, even when I was a girl. She was never happy. It was unfair to dad, because he could never make her happy. I saw him suffer, too."

North looked at the young woman, not sure how to respond to her. After a few moments, she filled the silence. "You are gentle and kind. But we would just end up like mom and dad: I would be disenchanted and disappointed and you would be eternally frustrated that you couldn't make me happy."

"You don't know that Amberly."

North's wrong, Amberly thought. *I will not disrespect my mother's memory by not learning from the mistakes she made. That's what she'd want.*

"North, don't be an idiot. I would never be with you," Amberly said, and immediately regretted using such an ugly tone with her friend. Her cheeks burned crimson with embarrassment and she quickly covered her mouth with a hand and looked away.

"Oh, I'm sorry," Amberly stammered, "I didn't mean —"

"You must be right," North flatly said, looking out the window and away from Amberly.

North was not a spoiled man, or someone who felt entitled to the best life had to offer. But for 29 years, life had seemed to always go his way. Amberly meant so much to him, and he was sure that she had the same feelings. But to be so wrong, and to be denied something he thought was right and good broke something in North. *How naïve am I?* thought North. He wasn't sure what had changed inside him, and North wasn't prone to excessive focus on his own feelings, but this would be something he'd need to process, to pray about.

Amberly reached across her seat and took North's sizable hand in hers. Her cold fingers felt tingly holding his strong, warm hand.

"I'm sorry, North," Amberly said. "It's not you. I'm never going to be any man's anything. I've got too much of my mother in me."

CHAPTER SIX

Amberly was wearing a spacesuit. *How did I get this on?* she thought. *Where am I?*

She looked down, and saw her feet planted on a dusty, rocky ground. She looked up and saw hundreds of asteroid rocks floating in the heavens around her. A quick look a few dozen meters behind her, the white-silver gleam of the Fuentes Memorial glowed. Something suddenly blocked the light from HD 238921. Standing in shadow, she looked up, and saw it was the *Claire De Lune*, floating viewport down, just a few meters above her. She could see North in the pilot's seat. His eyes were red, as if he had been crying.

Oh no, what have I done? Wait, why am I out here? Amberly thought.

The *Claire De Lune* rotated slowly and now she could see the co-pilot's seat – her seat. But … someone else was sitting in her seat! Flora Dillington! How? Flora was laughing, though Amberly was not sure how she could hear Flora through the vacuum of space.

North waved at Amberly — not a hello wave, but a goodbye one, and she started to panic. *Wait, don't leave me here!* The *Claire De Lune*'s engines fired up and the ship started to pull away, out into open space away from Sonnet.

No! Don't leave me, North! North!

Then suddenly, the *Claire De Lune* exploded in a ball of fire, and smoking fragments of metal and flesh streaked along the disintegrated corvette's trajectory.

North! Amberly reached to her mouth and could feel a trickle of drool out of the side of her mouth. *How could she feel her mouth with her space suit on,* she wondered?

Dreaming. Amberly had leaned her head against the portside bulkhead juxtaposed to her chair and had fallen asleep. Well, the drool was real. Amberly was relieved, and went back into a soft sleep, albeit a more peaceful one.

North didn't process emotions quickly. He was patient, letting his feelings simmer before internalizing them. He looked over at Amberly, who was breathing heavily as she slept. The

Claire De Lune was *en route* to *Magellan*. Watching the authentically beautiful Amberly sleep unexpectedly made him feel raw and exposed.

When Amberly woke an hour later, the mood was awkward. North broke the silence.

"Of course, I'm not for you Amberly," North said, matter-of-factly. "Totally unfair to you. I don't know what I was thinking. We live on the same waypoint, but really, we've always been on two separate worlds. You are a brilliant researcher with a future brighter than any of the dim stars out here. I'm just a guy who can point a gun."

"It's not like that, North, not really."

"Isn't it, though?" North insisted with calmness. "In your world of stellar anomalies and quantum whatevers, I really have nothing to offer. Why would you desire someone who brings nothing to the table? The best I can do is be cannon fodder for an enemy that doesn't exist. We don't match. The waypoint needs you. It doesn't need me."

Amberly wanted to say, "I still need your friendship," but she remained silent.

A question struck North. "Why *did* Kimberly marry your dad?"

"I don't know North; if she were alive today, I'd ask her," Amberly said, a little annoyed at where this was going. "Why are you so hung up on getting married anyway? It's a meaningless tradition."

"Meaningless? Can't you see how relationships affect society, and even human history? I'm not the greatest thinker, but it's sort of obvious that strong families build strong societies, and strong societies are what enable us to do great things, like build the waypoints. Some people — maybe even you — think this is silly, but a man and woman committed to each other forever is an awfully powerful thing for good."

"Please, North," Amberly rolled her eyes. "Applied science allowed us to create Project Waypoint."

"No, you don't understand what I mean," North said, trying hard not to be condescending or disagreeable. "Strong societies need *order* to function. Marriage and the traditional family are the building blocks of social order. Patterns of relationships that create a foundation for everything else we do. We would not have the space to pursue science and art in a world of chaos. Chaos destroys societies."

"Yes, I've heard this before. What you call chaos, I call freedom and self-determination. What, are you running for office now or something?"

"What? ... No," North sighed. "You know I don't give a dirt licker's spittle about politics. I just respect our forebears from Earth and the traditions they gave us, like marriage."

"But what is Earth keeping from us?"

"Keeping from us? Now you sound like that progressive crazy at Rick's ... Dek. What nonsense did he put into your head?"

Now Amberly was offended. Her cheeks burned and almost matched the color of her hair. "*How dare you?* I am not a puppet of whatever idea I heard most recently from the last man I spoke with – you or Dek. I'm done talking to you."

"What? I didn't say that. Have I ever —"

Then Amberly did something North thought childish: She got up from her chair, took two steps into the small galley, and pulled the sliding door closed, ending the conversation. Maybe he gave her too much credit; she was, after all, only 19.

There was standing room only in the galley, though Amberly was able to sit cross-legged on the floor, where she floated slightly. She stubbornly waited in the galley for the next three hours until they arrived safely in the *Magellan* docks.

Amberly was never happier to see her apartment door. She burst through the door and straight toward the bathroom. All Amberly wanted was a shower and her bed. But Kora lay in ambush in the common area.

"Will there be a second date?" Kora asked, barely able to contain her excitement.

"No!"

"What? Are you crazy? You turned North down."

"Wait. You knew North was going to propose something?"

"Of course, I knew," Kora said.

"And you didn't tell me?"

"I didn't know *know*. North never said anything to me. But anyone with eyes knows. For someone who is supposed to be so smart, Amberly —"

"Don't start with me," Amberly said as she stepped into the shower.

"Oh. Did you guys have a lovers' quarrel?" Kora teased.

"WE ARE NOT LOVERS. We will never be lovers. North and I are just friends. And I don't know if I want to even be friends anymore after what he pulled today."

Kora dropped her teasing attitude and grew concerned for her sister. "I'm sorry Amberly. I didn't expect — this is about Dek, isn't it?"

"No, Kora, it's not like that," Amberly called out from the shower.

"You don't even know that transient. And I would be careful about accepting expensive gifts from people you don't even know."

Kora listened for a reply from Amberly, but all she heard was the running water.

"Did you ever report your mysterious stalker?" Kora asked.

"No," Amberly said. "Not yet."

Amberly wasn't finished with her shower, but she turned off the water, partially opened the door, and stuck her head out and looked at her sister.

"What expensive gift?"

"While you were gone, your new boyfriend brought you a present. I thought it was kind of morbid actually, but I have no idea how he got one. I left it on your bed."

"Ugh... he's not my boyfriend," Amberly said grabbed a towel and wrapped it around herself and stepped into her bedroom. There, lying on top of her neatly made bed, was a beautiful pearly-pink conch shell, exactly like the one her mother used to have.

As Amberly examined the shell, Kora continued. "I mean, why is this guy so interested in our dead mother? What kind of freak is that? And this shell must have cost him thousands of credits. He kept asking me questions about where you were and who you were with. I didn't trust him, so I lied to him and told him you were making out with Skip at the movies, like you did every Tuesday. I don't think he believed me. He wanted to leave you a message. I told him to send a voicemail to Verne, but he wanted to leave a written message! On paper! I guess the guy has money to airlock. Is that why you like him more than North? No, of course not, but — are you listening to me?" Kora asked as she stepped into Amberly's bedroom.

Amberly was shaking. "Kora, this isn't a conch shell just like mother's. I think it's the same shell. Let me see that note."

"Mom's shell? How is that possible? She took it with her. You *must* be mistaken," Kora said, as she handed the note over. The folded paper bore a wax seal.

"You're probably right." Amberly had seen old vids where paper notes were sealed with melted wax to ensure privacy, but she had never seen a wax seal in person before. Finding wax products at a waypoint marketplace was unheard of. This far out in space, even a birthday candle was hard to come by. With a little hesitation, Amberly broke the seal and then read the note to herself:

Dear Amberly: I am returning this shell to you because I wanted you to think about your mother. She loved you very much, and she always wanted you to be a part of Chasm. She was loyal to Chasm, and she gave her life to Chasm. More than anything, we know she wanted you join Chasm, and continue her important work. Join me tomorrow morning for breakfast in the Hotel Commons at 06:30, and you will learn the truth about your mother, and I believe, about your own destiny. – With respect and admiration, Dek.

Postscript: Please don't share this with anyone.

"What did the note say?" Kora asked as she stepped into the living area. "Did he say where he got the shell?"

"Just an invitation to a date, that's all," Amberly said, trying to quickly process how much she should keep from her sister. She didn't trust Dek, but she thought she should honor Dek's request to not tell anyone. Kora might tell the police or North if she knew, and then maybe she would be prevented from finding out this secret about her mother.

Mom, what were you up to? Amberly thought. She never thought she would have an opportunity to have some real closure, but now, that possibility seemed imminent.

"You're not going to actually go, are you?" Kora asked. "North would be crushed."

"Oh, you too. First off, North is nothing to me. Not like that anyway."

"Nothing? He's been a friend for more tha —"

Amberly interrupted her sister. "You know what I mean. There is no reason to get our good friend North worked up over this … date. He doesn't have to know."

"I don't know … that sounds awfully deceptive. But if you have a thing for this Dek —"

"I don't have a thing for Dek! Argh! You can be so frustrating sometimes," Amberly felt like pulling her hair out. "I'm going to bed."

She crawled into bed, but she could not sleep. What in the world was Chasm? Did Dek really know Kimberly Macready? How could he even have known her mother? But he did have her shell. All questions, no answers.

Amberly would find out in the morning.

The Herbert Hoover Temporary Housing Center Commons in the President's Quarter was one of the larger open spaces on the waypoint. The room was a quarter circle arc filled with stainless steel cafeteria-style tables and benches. When deep-space ships were not in port, the Hoover Commons served as a multipurpose room and was used for a wide variety of functions, from political party caucuses, to large private parties, to training sessions and even for academic testing. The Commons uncomfortably seated 500. Because of the extra transients from the *American Spirit,* most of the seats were taken.

The room was warm with crowds as many were taking advantage of eating someplace else besides the limited galley of the *American Spirit.* At both ends of the commons were kitchens, which offered buffet service. Lines of those waiting to eat snaked about the room.

The chatter was loud and frenetic. Amberly normally disliked chaotic noise, but the tone of the conversation sprung with overtones of excitement, relief and joy, so she didn't mind it so much. Besides those from *American Spirit,* many of *Magellan's* permanent residents showed up for breakfast as well — mostly for the free meal. Because the charter purpose of *Magellan* and all waypoints was to service those ships making the long trip to and from Arara, all hospitality and basic survival supplies were provided to the travelers with no charge.

Because it was so crowded, a few *Magellan* natives stayed clear of the Hotel Commons, preferring to visit their usual eating places, even if they had to pay. For some of the less affluent *Magellan* residents, and some cheapskates as well, free food was worth the wait. Others came because the Hotel Commons represented a great (and sometimes, the only) opportunity to meet new people and perhaps start a new life adventure.

Often during layovers, deep space ships would pick up new passengers and crew from waypoint natives. Some were people who dreamed of going planet side and were willing to sacrifice years of their life in confinement on a deep space ship to find it. Others were just down-on-their-luck locals who needed to try something different. Signing up for service or even as a passenger aboard a deep space ship presented plenty of risks and rewards. Some found deep space life satisfying and adventurous compared to life on the waypoint. Others grew disenchanted and depressed before they even reached the next waypoint.

Amberly scanned the room looking for Dek. She couldn't see over the heads of the hundreds of people milling about looking for a place to sit. Amberly thought about standing on a chair to get a better vantage point, but before she could execute her plan, a firm hand landed on her shoulder and spun her around.

She let out a surprised "Whoa!" and then let her mouth melt into a smart smile when her eyes fell on Dek's messy brown hair and grey-blue eyes. Something about his face was growing on her. He looked young, but not immature. The quiet dignity in how his brows framed those eyes seemed to muffle noise around them.

"I am elated to see you. This way…" Dek gently pulled at Amberly's elbow and led her out of the Hotel commons and into a crowded corridor that flowed into banks of guest rooms. "Let's go someplace we can talk in private."

"*Elated*? Did you think I wouldn't come?" Amberly asked.

"I didn't know. I was worried that the shell may have freaked you out once you realized what it was."

"Who says I am not freaked out?"

"You do not have the countenance of a woman under pressure or stress," Dek said. "In fact, if I didn't know any better, I'd say you're happy to see me. I'm certainly happy to once again lay eyes on your … crimson locks."

They entered an elevator. The doors slid shut, and they were alone. Dek entered his room's floor and number on the door pad.

"Don't be too presumptuous," Amberly said in a flirtatious manner. "Maybe I just wanted to get the free food."

"Oh, breakfast," Dek shrugged. "We'll have to get that later."

After traveling several floors, the door to the elevator opened again.

"What is this Chasm, anyway?"

"Not here, Amberly." Dek led Amberly a few paces down the hallway into the interior of the Hotel, which was lined with doors on either side, about two meters apart. Between some of the doors, prints of impressionistic paintings had been affixed to otherwise unmarred steel walls, giving the hall a bit of warmth. Dek stopped at one of the doors, next to a replica of Monet's *Japanese Footbridge*, and punched in his key code giving the pair access to his temporary home on *Magellan*.

"Inside here."

The two escaped into the room, and Dek closed the door behind them. The Hotel room was commonplace in appearance and configuration, about two-by-three meters in size. The bed rolled up into a seating unit next to the wall. The opposite wall had a pull-down table. Across from the hallway door they just entered from were basic restroom facilities: sink, shower and vacuum toilet. A curtain could be pulled for privacy, and it was drawn when they entered the room.

"I had really hoped your mom had left you some sort of coded message about Operation Chasm. That would have made this all a lot easier. I hope you'll still help us."

"Help you with *what*?" said Amberly.

"Help us complete your mom's mission."

"Whoa. Slow down. Start from the beginning. What is this Operation Chasm? What does my mom have to do with it?"

Dek took Amberly's hand and gently pulled her down onto the bed-roll couch, so they were sitting beside each other.

"It's a long story," Dek said, "Let me explain. About 60 years ago, a group of influential patriots suspected what we now know to be true: The colony planets are meant to be, in a sense, slaves to mother Earth. This group of separatists believed that Earth's leadership would always hold back on key technology and human advances to ensure that Earth would be the dominant planet in the relationship between Earth and Arara."

Why does it always have to be politics with men, Amberly thought. "Yes, I've heard this theory before, and all the windbag politicians on both sides go on and on about it," Amberly sighed, almost disappointed with the direction the conversation was going. This was not the mystery she had hoped for.

"Yes, yes, but the difference here, my dear Amberly, was that this group of Arara loyalists decided to do something about it. They had seen the decades of talk and theories just like you, and were no longer interested in a political solution. They wanted to take action. That is why I am here today. Your mother, another true patriot of Arara, wanted to do something and be part of the solution, too, and that is why she joined Operation Chasm."

"Mom? I don't understand," Amberly rubbed her head. "Why wouldn't mom have mentioned this to us? And what exactly did she decide to ... um ... do about it?"

"I suspect your mother was just trying to protect you," Dek shrugged as he offered the suggestion. "While the group had many plans to boost Arara, the only plan that gained any traction was code-named Chasm. Eventually, Chasm was the whole effort. We've spent 30 years planning Chasm, and another three decades putting the pieces together."

Amberly was trying to get her head around what Dek was saying.

"So, mom was a part of this how? Did you know her?"

"I don't know — didn't know — Kimberly personally, of course," Dek said, picking up his data pad and absentmindedly flipping through some random photos that were on display. "I was just a little older than you are now when I joined Chasm. I was still working on my stellar physics major at the North Plate when I was recruited. It was Xander who recruited me — I mean Professor Alpine. He was also part of Chasm, of course. He was a great mentor and a friend."

"The professor is part of Chasm, too? Popular bunch."

"Not really. As you have seen, Chasm is a … clandestine operation. With his role in the university, he could recruit the best minds easily without drawing attention to himself. I believe Xander recruited your mother as well."

"Really? Professor Alpine knew my mom?" The whole story was on the verge of unbelievable, and if it weren't for the fact that Dek had produced his mother's conch shell, she certainly wouldn't have given any credence to his tale.

"Yes. It was he who got me my first Chasm assignment. I was lucky to be the support agent for your mother. I exchanged correspondence with your mom before she disappeared. I logged her reports. Chasm provided me with my first real gainful employment, besides when I worked as a harvester on the farm."

"What? You worked on a farm? In the dirt? Get out." Amberly was truly impressed. Manual labor jobs in an open world were highly romanticized by waypoint natives.

"All males on Arara are required to work on the farm at some point. It's not as glamorous as some say. But you wanted to know about your mother."

"Yes … to the point."

"I worked in the secret communications office for Chasm. I was responsible for decoding messages from our … agents … and then working with the senior … officers … to compose and send back appropriate messages with instructions, updates and sometimes to just offer encouragement. You see, for those who loved Arara so much, like your mother, it was hard to leave for the stars."

"This all makes sense," Amberly thought aloud. "This is why she was so stubborn about staying on *Magellan* even when she hated it so much and even when dad offered to take us all back to Arara. She had a mission to complete."

"Yes. There was a lot of correspondence from your mother to HQ about your father. The Chairman was furious when she married your dad. But I suppose that's the advantage of being several light years away from your boss. Not much she could do about it."

"And a good thing, too!" Amberly half-joked, but also allowing a bit of impatience to surface in her voice. "Otherwise I wouldn't be here. What was mom doing?"

"That, indeed, would be tragic if you did not come into being. Sometimes the randomness of the universe produces a rare gem," Dek said, with enough sincerity that Amberly did not feel the comment to be as cheesy as it sounded.

Every detail Dek teased left Amberly hungry with new questions. "Who or what is the Chairman? What was mom's mission? What were you guys trying to accomplish here on *Magellan*? Quit stalling." Amberly wasn't interested in Dek's slow, expositional story telling. She wanted a concise version of the truth. Of what happened to her mother, whom she loved dearly, and lost suddenly.

She wanted so much what she believed was in Dek's head. She had a growing desire — an unfamiliar one — to kiss Dek, caught up in his mysterious game and infatuated with his adventurous tale, and then alternately to beat the answers out of him, so frustrated with his slow play. Her heart started racing, and she became quite flush.

"So many questions, young one," Dek said, reaching over and slowly intertwining his olive-toned fingers into Amberly's hair just above her left ear, then resting his palm on her cheek. Amberly didn't know how to react to Dek's touch. "You must be patient."

"You said…" Amberly struggled to say, somehow losing her voice as Dek stared intently into her eyes, "you said that you would tell me about mom."

"Amberly, I want to tell you everything," Dek spoke softly as he slowly ran his fingers back though her hair. "But we have to know if we can trust you. Sixty years of preparations are riding on what happens on *Magellan* before the *American Spirit* leaves for the next waypoint. And there are people who would do anything to stop the good thing we are trying to do."

"You can trust me," Amberly asserted, reaching her hand to grasp Dek's and hold it still. "I don't care about the politics of Earth and Arara. I just must know about my mother. Who was she, really?"

"I believe you Amberly. Moreover, I believe that you are on our side, and when the time comes you will be an ally to the cause. But some of the others aren't so sure. They are great patriots, but they are dangerous. They would airlock someone before they would let them jeopardize Operation Chasm."

Airlock. Just the uttering of the word made the warmth between Amberly and Dek's clasped hands cool. When capital punishment was required, or when someone wanted to cleanly murder someone (both cases rare in the history of waypoints) forcing a person out an airlock into the endlessly cold oblivion of space was the prime method. Every child that grew up on a waypoint was made to fear the method of disposing of the unwanted.

"Don't you see, Amberly, that if I tell you too much and I am wrong, and you do not take our side in this… epic … conflict, this historic struggle, then they will make sure you cannot stand against us. And I have come to care about you, too much to risk your invisible death. Ever since I first learned about you, the daughter of Kimberly Macready, I've always known somehow we'd have a connection."

Amberly gently pulled Dek's hand off her face. "I am really flattered that you care about me, and I genuinely don't even know what to think about that," Amberly spoke resolutely, "but what you need to know is that I would do almost anything to learn about what happened to my mother. What do I need to do to prove to your … friends that I am not a threat to their operation?"

"As a matter of fact, they have given me a task for you."

Amberly sighed audibly. *Why was Dek making this so hard?*

"Okay, okay, who are they? What would you want *me* to do?"

Just then, from behind the restroom curtain, stepped out a man who Amberly immediately recognized as the one who had been tailing her for days. He was holding some sort of weapon, which was trained on Amberly's chest.

Amberly was not a weapons expert. In fact, she knew very little about firearms. But she knew that the gun trained on her shot actual bullets. Most guns on waypoints were some sort of advanced electronic weapons – stun guns and burn rays. Those could bring harm to a flesh-and-blood human, but stray shots were unlikely to damage the waypoint. On the other hand, a stray bullet that hit a window or other weaker part of the waypoint exterior hull, could theoretically create a breach, which could be lethal to both the shooter and his target.

Amberly was shocked, and only her momentary confusion

kept her fight or flight instincts from kicking in. She looked to Dek, expecting him to physically engage this restroom spy, but Dek looked calm and even a bit amused.

"Joti, put the gun down," Dek said.

"Wait, you're with this guy?" Amberly frowned. Thoughts quickly ran through her head about the life-ending instrument pointed at her, and the obvious threat of imminent death, and she was surprised to find herself more annoyed at Dek than concerned for her life.

"I am 'they'," the man said. "I am the Chasm operation director here on *Magellan*, and I need you to know how serious our need for secrecy is, hence the weapon."

"I said, put the gun down," Dek repeated, with a little emotion rising in the voice.

Joti looked at Dek, and smiled. "Please Dek, I am the one who gives orders arou– oh, you actually like her don't you? And here I thought it was just an act for your mission." Joti turned and addressed Amberly, hiding the weapon away back in the folds of his coat.

"I actually *do* trust you," Joti said. "How can I not? You have your father's hair for sure, but the rest of you is *all* your mother. I knew her well — we came together on the same deep space ship to *Magellan*, those decades ago. I was the only person on the station who knew who she truly was —"

"You! You somehow got her shell and gave it to Dek. Who was she? What was her secret?" Amberly nearly shouted. "Why have you been following me? Tell me what you know."

"Impatient, just like Dek," Joti smirked. "If I told you now, how do I know you would still complete an important mission for us?"

"Joti, it doesn't have to be like this. Amberly will help us. She has no love for Earth. She'll do it. Now cut the games, and let's get started."

"I'm sorry Amberly, you will learn everything in time. For now, we need you to recover something for us that we need. Your friend, the Marine… what's his name?"

"North," Dek interjected, and Amberly detected just a hint of jealousy.

"Yes, North," Joti continued. "What a silly name, to be named after a cardinal and live on a waypoint. Back on Arara, north means something. It's cold in the north, where strong women and men go to test their mettle. Back on Earth, centuries ago, people used to cross vast oceans — you do know what an *ocean* is don't you Amberly?"

Amberly nodded her head, growing more annoyed and frustrated with Joti.

"Right… well true explorers, like Ferdinand Magellan, no doubt, used the North Star to guide their way. But I don't suppose this North of yours is any special guide to you?"

"North doesn't mean anything to me, if that is what you are getting at," Amberly lied to herself more than to Joti. "I mean, were friends and all, but nothing more."

"Well, I've noticed that he is keen on engaging your affections," Joti countered. "We need you to take advantage of that little fact to get something of his, something relatively worthless, and then I swear on Arara herself, I will tell you everything I know about your beloved mother." He spoke of Kimberly not sarcastically, and Amberly realized that he was almost reverent toward Mrs. Macready.

"What do you need me to get? And why do you need it?"

Dek jumped in. "His corvette access pass, the one he won in a game of poker."

"But he's already used it. The codes are authenticated and only work one time. It's worthless, what do you want it for?" Amberly pressed.

"Does it matter?" Joti asked.

"Obviously, it does. I mean why would you go through all this trouble, all this cloak and dagger, to get a worthless code chip? It has to have some use," Amberly said.

"You are quite insightful, just like your mother. But don't trouble yourself with that detail," Joti said. "Bring us the chip by this afternoon, and before you go to sleep tonight I promise you will know things about your mother that will be joyous to your young heart."

"I am not really planning to see North anytime soon. Are we in a hurry?"

"You ask too many questions, young Miss Macready. The *American Sprit* will not be here forever, so we are on a timeline.

Do you have a problem with that?" Joti was getting annoyed and started fingering the weapon concealed under his coat absentmindedly.

Dek jumped in again, standing up and squaring off shoulder to shoulder. "Quit patronizing Amberly. Do you think you can win her over with the stick or the carrot? She's not just beautiful, she's brilliant. To anyone with half a brain, what we are fighting for is obviously right and the best path for humanity. She'll see that if you'll just quit trying to manipulate her."

Joti grew red. "Dek, you impotent little snot. Why I ought to —"

"Don't threaten me, Joti," Dek said, suddenly filling the room with a powerful, charismatic presence Amberly hadn't seen before, as if he had been holding back. "I know we have rank and file in Chasm, but that is a necessary evil to get the job done. And right now, it's you and your heavy-handed ways that is threatening our mission. You go ahead and report my impudence to the Chairman. I'll report your incompetence."

Amberly was somewhat surprised that the two Chasm operatives were so openly combative in front of her. She believed Dek did trust her and had faith that because of her intellect, she would reason things the way he did. *Dek is probably right*, Amberly thought, *once I have a chance to process all this, I probably will side with him.*

Everything he did up to this point seemed planned, rational, methodical. Dek's new stand up performance also attracted Amberly. Something primal about Dek challenging the alpha male made her heart beat a little faster.

"Three years from now, when you are back on Arara, do you want to be standing in glory for a mission accomplished? Or do you want me to massage your ego now, and you can go home a failure," Dek said with a calm power in his voice.

"You are just saying these things because you think you love her, don't you?" Joti said, slightly diminished and sounding defensive. "You think you are the only person here who ... I loved K–"

Dek reached up quickly and put his hand over his mouth, encouraging Joti to be silent. Amberly expected Joti would respond with some sort of violent or emotional display to being physically silenced, but instead the older man just relaxed, gave Dek a knowing look, and a wry smile curled on Joti's lips as Dek slowly removed his hand.

"She'll get it done," Dek said slowly and deliberately to Joti, then turned to Amberly. "Right?"

Amberly, tiring of the conversation and being in tight quarters with a cryptic guy welding a lethal weapon, followed Dek's cue. "I'll get it done. Back here by 16:00."

"Excellent! Amberly the things I will show you, it's going to disintegrate your paradigms of everything," Joti promised, his smile almost expanding into a happy laugh.

Amberly smiled tightly in return and said nothing else as she exited the stuffed apartment with Dek in tow. She remained silent as they passed out of the hotel and by the commons. Amberly was headed straight for the tube, walking at an impressive pace. Dek had trouble keeping up without breaking into a mild sprint.

There was a line at the tube. Amberly grunted something barely audible in disappointment. She tugged on Dek's shirt and pulled him toward a hallway that ran in a concentric circle next to the tube.

This hallway connected to a private storage area where a little extra space could be purchased for a significant price. Dek and Amberly passed by several banks of these storage units toward the back of the facility. Amberly saw a few people accessing units toward the front door, but the back area was presently deserted.

The pair was alone in a back corridor. Amberly pushed Dek up against a storage unit door. She reached up and kissed Dek. He was a little surprised, but he quickly transformed from a passive receiver into a full participant. He started to drape his arms around Amberly's back, but she broke the kiss and took a step back.

"What was that about?" Dek said.

"Research," Amberly said, already turning from Dek and walking back toward the tube.

"And?" Dek asked, already two paces behind her and trying to catch up.

"Inconclusive," she called over her shoulder.

"That's it? Nothing else to sa—"

"So many questions, old one," Amberly said. "You must be

patient. Besides, I've got a mission to do."

She turned her back to Dek and walked away. The secrets of her late mother, which Amberly had sought desperately but had escaped her, were at hand. She felt alive and excited.

Dek stood bewildered.

CHAPTER SEVEN

Sitting at her lab station, Amberly's excitement from hours earlier had decomposed into confusion. Deep in thought, she absentmindedly clicked through stellar reports from the *American Spirit*. Normally, Amberly would be judgmental of colleagues who went through the motions without engaging with their work. What if they missed a key detail? Some bit of information that would foretell a coming radiation storm or the discovery of extraterrestrial life? But the redhead was so gripped by recent events that even her own work ethic could not keep her from getting lost in thought.

She was hoping that somehow a spontaneous kiss with Dek would create some sort of chemical-biological imperative, that she would know she could trust that Dek did care for her and had her best interest in mind, and that whatever this Chasm business was about was in everyone's best interest.

Amberly knew the hope was irrational, and she was starting to regret she had given that irrational kiss. She was a woman of science, and her worldview was based on the tangible and knowable and rational.

Kora would not approve of kissing Dek, Amberly thought. In many ways, though Kora had taken care of Amberly after their parents disappeared, Amberly was, she thought, the more mature of the two. Amberly valued Kora's love as a sister, but didn't really value her approval or her wisdom.

What she desperately wanted, but could never have, was her mother's approval. It was another irrational desire; one she didn't realize was so important to her until this opportunity to understand her mother in a new way appeared. *If only I knew more about this Operation Chasm, and what mom was doing*, Amberly thought. *Am I going to steal from North? Steal?*

The clandestine nature of Operation Chasm didn't bother Amberly. She was old enough to realize that sometimes you need to keep secrets from others to protect the people you love. The gun waving was a new experience for her, and she didn't like it. She had seen plenty of gunplay in the various movies and other vids, and the real thing didn't seem much different than she would have imagined. Dek's step-up move in the shadow of Joti's gun was still strangely attractive.

"AMBERLY!"

Amberly was so lost in her own thought, Lydia had to shout at Amberly to get her attention.

"I'm sorry," Amberly smiled sheepishly at the tall blonde. "Did you need something? I was just focused on finishing these stellar —"

"Sure. You've gone from zero to too many men in your life, and now you can't think straight. It's unlike you."

"I'm sorry, it's just…"

"Oh don't be sorry," Lydia smiled. "I'm just jealous. I wish I had guys chasing me that I could daydream about."

"Whatever. Need something?"

"Skip is here to see you," Lydia said. "I was pretty sure that you didn't like *him*, but you seem to be taking in all kinds of new territory these days."

"Skip? Give me a break," Amberly said. "I don't want to see him. Did he say what he wanted?"

"Well I figured you didn't want to see him, so I told him that you were busy adjusting some very sensitive radiation receptors and couldn't be bothered," Lydia seemed to be taking a perverse joy in deceiving on Amberly's behalf. "But he was insistent. He's waiting in the observation lobby."

"Why didn't he just send a message?"

Amberly's info pad beeped to life.

"He did send eight messages," Verne said. "You just weren't paying any attention to me." If Amberly didn't know better, she would have thought her infopad had a hint of exasperation in its synthesized voice.

Lydia shrugged, Amberly sighed, and Verne spoke, "Do you want me to read them to you now?"

"No, I'll just go see Skip myself," Amberly scowled severely, clearly annoyed to have to deal with the imp.

"Hey, Amberly, what is the big deal?" Lydia put her hand on Amberly's shoulder. "Don't you think you are being a bit snobbish? Skip is annoying, but he is a person. Where is this animosity coming from?"

"You're right," Amberly said. "I'm just tired of boys right

now, and Skip has the great misfortune of being the wrong gender."

"Oh, don't say that," Lydia joked. "Skip would make a horrible girl."

Amberly walked down into the reception area of the Science Corps laboratories, and found Skip pacing, impatiently. Lydia was in tow.

"Amberly! Didn't you get my messages?" Skip said. "This is important."

"What's so important?" Amberly said ungraciously.

"Hi Lydia," Skip acknowledged the woman who towered over them both.

"Hi Skip. How's life down in Communications?"

"Fine. Fine. Listen, Amberly, I think this Dek guy is trouble and …"

"That's the hot tip that had you interrupt my —"

"Just listen. I was monitoring inter-waypoint traffic, and, well, the message sent to Dek didn't sit right—"

Lydia interrupted Skip. "You were spying on Dek?"

"Yes. Yes. So anyways I was decoding the message and —"

"Wait," now Amberly was interrupting Skip. "You were spying on Dek? Why? Isn't that illegal?"

"Wait. What? No. Well, maybe a little. That's not the point. The point is—"

"Why were you spying on Dek?" Amberly projected a demanding tone.

"Um… well… mother of dirt, you are probably going to find out anyway. North asked me to keep an eye on Dek's transmissions."

Amberly burned. "When I find North, I am going to rip him a —"

Now Lydia was interrupting Amberly. "Wait. Don't get ahead of yourself. Maybe North didn't have Skip spying on Dek because he was jealous that you liked Dek's brain better than his brawn… But now that I think about it, probably that's exactly why."

Lydia turned to Skip. "Why *did* North have you spying on Dek?"

"Would you two stop it?! I think this could be … you know…

maybe a matter of life and death." Skip had grown flush.

"Come on Skip, don't be so dramatic," Lydia started to chastise the scrawny man. But Amberly held up her hand to silence Lydia. She didn't know what Dek was up to, but she did know that Dek's associate, Joti, threatened to use lethal force, even if it was just masculine bravado posturing. The thought that Operation Chasm might be more of an existential threat to her and *Magellan* entered her mind for the first time.

"What did the message say?"

"Well, if you would quit interrupting me," Skip said indignantly. He pulled out his infopad. "I actually couldn't read the message, which is what I thought was weird. It was encrypted with a manual key that probably only Dek has."

"So what?" Lydia said. "Maybe it's an intimate message from a secret lover?"

Amberly grew flush at that thought. Partially because she had a natural jealous reaction, partially because she was embarrassed that she had a jealous reaction.

"I doubt it. This was top-secret type encoding that we only get from Earth brass," Skip said. "Why would a run-of-the-mill glorified star librarian like Dek be using military grade encodings?"

"I'm sure it's nothing," Lydia said, thinking Amberly must be explosively furious with both Skip and North over this snooping.

Amberly looked out the *Magellan* window at the Stars and Stripes painted on the exterior of the docked *American Spirit*. She spoke plainly, "We have to find out what is in that message."

"We do?" Lydia said, surprised. Amberly realized that her sudden interest probably seemed to be driven by some hormonally-influenced reasoning. It would seem that way to Amberly as well, had she not had the strange interaction with Dek and Joti earlier.

"Trust me, we do," Amberly said. "I think Skip might be right. This might be serious. How can we break this encryption?"

Skip was ready to answer this question. "It depends on how fast you want it. My computers down in Communications are decades old and it would take years to break this security level. You guys have much better stuff here in the Science Corps. You could probably hack it in a week or so. Maybe a few months."

"We might not have a few months," said Amberly quietly.

"What? Why?" Skip asked.

"The *American Spirit* will be long gone by then," Amberly replied. "Is there a quicker way?"

"Not without getting the hard key from Dek," Skip replied.

Lydia whistled. "Transfer me the message. We have a few processor banks that were taken down for routine maintenance, and I haven't brought them back online yet. I am sure no one will miss them if they stay off the main process grid while I use them to see if we can crack this message. Who knows, we may be lucky and successfully guess the key without having to go through too many of the permutations."

"I think I can get the hard key from Dek," Amberly said, glancing knowingly at Lydia.

"How?" Skip asked.

"She has her womanly wiles," Lydia responded, using her two hands to draw the silhouette of a woman's body for Skip.

"North won't like that," Skip said, matter-of-factly.

"North doesn't need to find out," Amberly replied, "In fact, it's probably best that we keep all this to ourselves until we figure out what is going on."

"Fine," said Skip.

"It's a race, Lydia. You see how fast you can crack this message, and I'll see how fast I can 'borrow' the key from Dek," Amberly said.

"Why do I get the feeling you know more than you are letting on?" Lydia smiled weakly at Amberly.

"Because you are right."

"Are you sure North's shift ended a half hour ago?" Amberly asked Verne.

"Based on your correspondence with North over the past year, I have been able to construct a crude approximation of what North's schedule is. However, I am not sure. Why don't I just call him?"

"No, no. I want to surprise him."

Amberly was hanging out in a junction lobby just outside of the main entrance to the *Magellan* Marine headquarters. An on-duty Marine did a manual check of identification even after the biometrics of those entering were computer-verified. Amberly tried to casually wait outside the door and not draw attention. The Marine on guard didn't seem to pay her heed. A regular stream of Marines and support staff came in and out of the main door. Amberly played with Verne as if reading the latest news, etc., so as not to look awkward. She would periodically glance up when the sliding door opened, but had not seen North exit the HQ yet.

From Marine Headquarters, one could get direct access to the military's half of the main hangar bay, to station-wide environmental controls, and to the civilian central command, where bureaucratic engineers could monitor and control much of the waypoint's functions.

In the center of civilian central command, or Cencomm, was a three-dimensional map that showed locations of tube cars, temperature readings, and live status conditions of all the runabout Valkyries and corvettes assigned to *Magellan*. Authorities could, with the right code and a flip of a switch, broadcast emergency commands that would be heard everywhere in the station.

Across the lobby from the sliding door was a portal that opened into a barracks unit. The barracks housed about half of the *Magellan* Marine contingent. The rest of the Marines, like North, lived in civilian housing around the waypoint.

Besides access to the headquarters and the barracks, the lobby connected to a broad corridor that led directly to a tube station a few tenths of a kilometer away. Contractors' offices and other non-military Marine support operations could be accessed from the hall, and on the far side, where it opened into the tube station, were several restaurants and a food market.

It was well past 14:00, and Amberly told Joti and Dek she'd be back with North's expired ship access card by 16:00. That gave her two hours to make up enough with North to get access to his apartment, and then hopefully find his used access card.

The sliding door to HQ opened, and Amberly heard a young, energetic baritone voice she immediately recognized as North. Amberly smiled, messed with her hair and pinched her cheeks. She had her plan in place to fish an invite back to North's place, and plan or not, she did want to patch things up after the disastrous Shard Cave date.

She was about ready to pounce on North when she realized he was not alone. There was a shapely dirty blond hanging on his every word — and hanging on his biceps: Flora Dillington! Flora was wearing a tight black dress and her hair was up in a beehive, exposing her ivory neck. Amberly decided to retreat and quickly ducked through the Marine barrack door and out of sight. Amberly heard Flora giggle.

"Was that Amberly Macready? I swear I just saw her duck into the barracks," North said to Flora. Flora ignored the questions, and pulled North by the elbow.

"Come on, I'm hungry! Let's have Asian!"

"Sure, Flora," North replied, and the two headed for Chinatown, a popular Chinese-themed restaurant with an open dining area on the Beltway that faced the tube stop nearest the Marine HQ. North wasn't positive he saw Amberly, though her red hair made her hard to mistake for someone else.

"May I help you?" the Marine manning the barracks reception, surprised at the sudden entrance, inquired of Amberly. She wasn't positive, but she thought she recognized the Marine as Eli Wong, one of the low-IQ grunts in the strike force under North's command.

"Um, actually, no I was just hiding from someone," Amberly opted for the truth.

"Is everything okay? Do I need to contact civilian police?"

"No, no. Everything is fine, Eli. It is Eli Wong, isn't it?"

"Yes ma'am," Wong replied, and then after about 30 seconds of silence spoke again. "Oh, a lover's quarrel is it then?" the guard teased.

"What?! No," Amberly thought the question was awkward and rude. "We're not lovers."

"Oh good! Then North won't mind if I ask you out?" Eli said in a half-serious way as he examined Amberly. *North was right*, he thought. *She was one of the most beautiful women on* Magellan.

"Wait… how do you know about North and me. I mean, there's nothing to know, but how do you know?"

"Oh, I just assumed you were North's girl," the guard smiled, seemingly amused to put Amberly on the spot. "The red hair and all. Also, North just got off work, and you said you were hiding from someone, and, well I did the math."

"What?! Is North calling me his girl?"

"No ma'am. I just assumed because he took you out to the Shard Caves. I mean, wouldn't you think that if a man takes a woman on a posh trip like that, there must be something between them. But far be it from me to judge the Lt. Commander."

"Does everyone know about that?"

"Yes, ma'am."

"Well, Private Wong, you can tell everyone it's not true. I am not North's girl, woman, lover, anything."

"Very well, ma'am. Means there is hope for the rest of us," Private Wong joked.

Amberly shot a pointed glance at Wong, and quickly slipped out the door. Once she was back into the lobby she glanced down the hall past a half dozen or so pedestrians to see North and Flora as barely recognizable dots on the far side of the hall. She started to pace toward them, keeping her distance because she did not want to be seen by them — yet.

"Verne," Amberly activated her infopad. "Would you send a message to Kora? Ask her if she's interested in having dinner with me in 15 minutes. Maybe at Chinatown?"

"Request acknowledged. Do you want me to reserve a table for you and go ahead and order your most popular menu choice?" the helpful infopad replied.

"Wait for Kora's reply," Amberly said. "I'm not really interested in a table for one tonight."

"If Kora says no, shall I invite someone else?" Verne asked, as Amberly noted that North and Flora did indeed slip into Chinatown, so she slowed her pace. "May I suggest Lydia, Skip, North, Kato, Maria Dino or Dek Tigona? I took the liberty of adding Dek to your contact list."

"No Verne, that won't be necessary. Just let me know when Kora responds."

The corridor that ran from the tube stop to the Marine HQ was about five meters wide, spacious for a waypoint. In the way of decor, the hall was sparse. The military contractors had simple doors and some of them had windows that exposed reception or lobby areas or just office space. One of the larger offices on this corridor, however, had invested in a bench with two planters on either side of the seat. Amberly sat there and waited. The short shrubs grew with artificial light as well as some natural stellar light that was "piped" into the interior of the waypoint with fiber optic cabling. Connecting fiber optics to an exterior viewport of the ship that had regular stellar light was expensive, but this office belonged to Waypoint Research Group, the largest off-planet science corporation, and they had credits to burn.

Amberly couldn't help but bring to mind that Flora worked here, making quite a mint, and potentially having access to North nearly every day. She couldn't rationalize these feelings of jealousy concerning North, and she wished they would escape like atmosphere from a hull breach. She did care if North and Flora were – she cut off the thought before she could complete it.

Amberly found herself studying the thin leaves of the plants while she was waiting. She did not know enough botany to identify the species, and she was disappointed in herself, making a mental note to study up on *Magellan's* plant life when she had a chance. The hallway had a steady stream of traffic, with people walking in pairs and trios, mostly leaving work and heading for the tube to catch a car to one of the residential districts, or perhaps out to eat at a restaurant or the commons.

Verne chimed. "Kora confirms she will meet you at Chinatown in five minutes. I've made reservations."

Amberly stood, smoothed her blue blouson jumpsuit. Kora had the outfit custom made for Amberly for her 18th birthday. Kora repeatedly told Amberly the jumpsuit was very flattering, exposing Amberly's pale shoulders, and hanging delicately off her petite frame. Amberly thought the outfit inappropriate for professional use, so she rarely wore it to the lab. *Perhaps she wore the blouson to impress Dek this morning*, she thought. North, aware it was a birthday gift from Kora, always complemented Amberly when she wore it.

Chinatown was a marvel of waypoint environmental design. The front of the restaurant opened into the tube station lobby, making the eatery appear larger than it really was. The tables offered significant privacy for a waypoint because each was surrounded by an elevated indoor rice patty. The restaurant was laid out like a checkerboard, with table squares surrounded by rice patty squares, where green rice shoots grew several feet above the three-foot-high planters. Rice took a lot of water and space to grow, so the restaurant grew some of its own, at the expense of seating capacity. Still, the restaurant was one of the lushest places on *Magellan*, and the scarcity of seating made the restaurant all the more in demand.

The maître d' of Chinatown was one of Kora's myriad of admirers, and after Amberly had filled in Kora that she was spying on North (though she said nothing about Chasm or Skip's intercepted message), Kora convinced the host to discreetly seat them at the closest table to North and Flora.

"Okay, I'm starting to worry a little bit about you," Kora said, as she poked at her soy tofu on rice. Natural rice was an expensive meal on *Magellan*, but not out of the reach for an occasional outing. Some people liked to top their rice with tofu or artificial protein cubes, but Amberly preferred to eat the delicacy plain.

"I'm not being as stupid as you think I am," Amberly told her older sister. "There is a lot going on that you don't know about that I can't tell you right now, and you'll just have to trust me. But I think I'll be okay."

"You know I trust you. Just remember you can trust me, too," Kora said, taking sip of hot topis. "I'm here if you need me. … Don't look now, I think North spotted us."

Amberly was trying to decide how she was going to play this. She needed to figure out a way to get into North's apartment and hopefully find that access card. Her back was to North and Flora, but she could tell by Kora's expression that North was coming over to see them. Amberly turned in her chair to see the Marine a few paces away, smiling that infectious smile, and tracing his hands through the rice grass.

"My two favorite Macready sisters," North stood at the end of their table and took each of their hands. His grip was strong, firm and gentle. Amberly gave his hand a squeeze back and then withdrew hers from his.

"Hi North," Kora said in a saccharine tone. "Didn't I just see you with that one girl, um, Flora, right? Flora Dillington?" Kora knew perfectly well who Flora was, but she was playing Amberly's game now.

"Oh, her," North said, suddenly embarrassed as if he hadn't

thought the Macready sisters had noticed Flora was his dinner companion. "That was just business, I mean... Waypoint Research is going to be providing new cartography for our unit, and we were just having a business dinner to discuss the details... and... really it was just business. She's already gone back to her lab." North was answering Kora, but he was looking at Amberly's face at this point. Amberly face was stone, not giving any emotional hints for North.

"Not really our business who you do business with, right Amberly?" Kora looked at her sister and smiled slyly. "Thanks for coming by and saying hello, North."

"Well, good to see you both," said North, who was disappointed Amberly had said nothing. He figured she was still steamed about the Shard Caves. He shrugged, turned and started walking away.

After he had taken a few paces, Amberly called out, "Wait."

She rose and walked over to him as he stood between the growing green grasses. Kora wanted to follow, but she knew better and just looked down at her plate and played with her food.

Amberly walked up to North, and, facing him, took both his hands in hers. "Listen, I feel like I have been unfair, and I ... wanted to say thank you for taking me to Shard Caves. I mean, I should have been flattered. I was flattered. I *am* flattered. And I want you to know even though we disagree sometimes, I am thinking about what you said. You are a true friend."

North didn't expect this apology. Amberly was getting more and more confusing to North every time he talked to her. "That's kind of you to say," North said.

"What I am trying to say, if I can spit it out, is that I have something that I wanted to give you to say thank you. May I bring it by your place, in say 30 minutes?"

"Sure. That would be great. Maybe we could finish the conversation we started?"

"If you think it's a good idea," Amberly said.

"It's always a good idea ... and a bad idea, I suppose, to talk with you."

North turned and walked away. Amberly thought she would be able to pull this off. She felt bad because she realized deep down, she was going to be using North's attraction for her own purposes. But Amberly wanted few things more than to connect with her late mother. North's emotions seemed a small price to pay: she needed that access card.

Amberly returned to her table and sat down to eat again.

"Well, how did it go?" Kora asked.

"I need to hurry up and finish this," Amberly answered as she attempted to maneuver a clump of grain into her mouth with her chopsticks. "I have a date with North in 30 minutes."

Kora smiled. "That's good, right?"

North had commonplace quarters on *Magellan*. In some ways, he was fortunate because he did not share barracks with the other Marines. His parents, farmers on Arara, were wealthy enough to help North buy his own place when he arrived for service on *Magellan* in 2594. His parents grew corn, soybeans and ligrains in the fertile plains on Arara's small continent, Ingram. Ligrains were a bland grain that was a genetically modified cross between lupins and lentils.

They also bred cattle. It wasn't until 2580 that the first breeding bovines had successfully made the journey from Earth alive. That it didn't happen sooner wasn't for lack of trying. Bovine just didn't survive well in space, and with an average lifespan of 15 years, they had to get the cattle to give birth to at least one generation of offspring in space.

On some of the first attempts, it was unclear if the cows died of space trauma, or if some of the homesick passengers on the deep space ships went stir crazy and really started craving beef. Eventually, an enterprising soul named Jabari Mandela managed to get two sets of breeding cattle to Arara. Upon arrival, North's family traded half of their farmland, several million credits, and a farmstead home to Jabari in exchange for a pair of his cattle. The investment ended up being a good one, because Jabari's cattle did not adjust well to planet side life, and his bull would not mate. North's family's cattle did breed, and soon they purchased Jabari's cow and had built enough of a herd to start selling cattle for beef to wealthy Ararans.

By the time North had enlisted in military service, his family was one of a few growers who owned their own deep space freighter, which exclusively delivered foodstuffs to the three waypoints closest to Arara: *Waypoint Marquette, Waypoint Cortes* and *Waypoint Magellan.* In the first six years of service, the freighter had made two roundtrips to *Cortes,* with stops coming and going at *Marquette.* On its third trip, the ship took in one more waypoint. It brought tons and tons of foodstuffs when it arrived at *Magellan* two years ago. North's father, Ogdin, captained the vessel himself, leaving Jabari in charge of his farm on Arara, because he wanted to visit his son. North's mother had died two years earlier from the Araran Sweats, a flu-like illness caused by a superbug that evolved from a virus that was probably brought to Arara on one of the first colony ships.

Ogdin had sold his stock of vacuum-sealed beef on *Cortes* and *Marquette,* but he did have about 20 pounds of beef jerky for his son as a gift. North, who had not had animal protein since he left Arara, vowed to make his jerky last until his father returned again, which would be in seven years. North had not been as disciplined as he had hoped, and had eaten through half his stock in two years.

Today, he wanted to be generous and impressive, and with Amberly on her way over, he set some jerky out along with some crackers on the table in the center of his living area. The table was just over a meter wide and took up more than three quarters of the floor space in the living area. The table could be folded up into the wall, but usually North would just leave it out.

North was military neat, and his apartment was straight and clean. He had only three adornments hanging on his wall: A photograph of his parents set in a rare ornate oak frame, a photo of the earth city Vancouver, Canada circa 2000, and an abstract painting of three crosses meant to depict the Christ's crucifixion scene as described in the New Testament.

The doorbell rang, and North, seeing it was Amberly on the security monitor, voice commanded the door open. North was still wearing his well-fitting uniform.

"Come in, Amberly," North stood and motioned her to sit at the table. She did, and did not speak, instead, looked around the room, slowly taking it all in. She'd been in North's apartment a hundred times, but to North, it seemed like she was acting like the whole place was new to her.

Amberly was, of course, thinking about where the access card could be. She was counting on the fact that North hadn't already sent it to the recycle center.

"Hey, Red. I'm glad you came over. I've been thinking about our trip and I wanted you to know I can see how you think what I suggested would be offensive and I wanted to–"

Amberly reached over and put a finger over North's mouth.

"Shhh. Let me talk first," she said, dropping her right hand first to the surface of table, then, moving it across the table to take North's left hand.

"You know, I've been ungrateful, and a bad friend," Amberly said. "You opened up to me, and as your friend, I was really rotten to you." Amberly again felt guilt in her manipulations. Still, she rationalized, everything she said *was true*, and finding out about her mother surely justified these means.

North smiled warmly and squeezed Amberly's hand, then released it.

"That's kind of you to say, but you're not the first filly to turn me down," North said, with a comfortable confidence that made Amberly feel childish and keenly aware of the 10 years that separated them. North smiled. "But you were *the best*. Don't worry on my account. I'm made of stern stuff."

Amberly was about to respond, but she didn't know if she was offended that he'd apparently moved on so quickly. On the other hand, she felt strangely attracted to him because, suddenly, with a phrase and a hand gesture, North had gone from desperate to unattainable. Another feeling flashed in her chest: Had she let a good thing get away? She didn't know what to say, and after a few seconds of silence, North filled the air.

"You know, before I left Arara, I'd look up into the night sky, and see the billions and billions of stars staring down on me. I knew the stars would be brighter if I was closer, but I never dreamed I'd find a star as bright as you. You are too good for me; you know it; I know it. I've made peace with that."

Amberly was about to protest, but realized she was forgetting why she was here. She had to know about her mother.

"Any woman who was looking for a husband would be a fool not to take an offer from you," Amberly said. "You're a fine specimen. You have a great pedigree, a farm back on Arara when you retire. I'm sure your children will be gorgeous. You're a Marine, so you have that whole protection thing down for any woman who is into that sort of thing."

"You said you had something for me," North said, trying to change the subject. Amberly wondered if maybe he was more broken over her rejection than he was letting on. The moment of truth had come.

"Taking me out on a corvette, choosing me to go to the Spencer Belt over all the others, that means a lot, and I didn't really show my gratitude." While Amberly was speaking, she had slid from the chair that was across the table from North onto the wall bench he was sitting on.

North seemed unsure about where this exchange was going, and he started to talk again, but this time Amberly was quicker to place her pointing finger over his lips. North sighed, and Amberly reached deep inside to find motivation to put her plan into play. The guilt was growing, but she hoped everything would come out all right in the end.

"I lied a little, I don't have something to give you," Amberly said to the shushed North. "I have something to trade for something you have that I'd like. I wanted to have a memento from our outing. My dad always had those ship passes every time he went on an adventure, and I never managed to snag one for my keepsake box. I suppose I could have just tried to get any old one, but you know, they are actually really hard to come by, even the used ones, and besides, I want one that has meaning, something that I shared with a man I care about."

North gently pushed her finger from his mouth.

"You want the ship pass card? It's just a hunk of circuits and code." North was amused at what seemed to him an odd request. "I'm supposed to turn this in to recycling. It's possible that someone might miss it."

"Oh, you know no one will miss it," Amberly said and she causally slipped an arm over North's shoulder. "Besides, don't you want to know what I am willing to trade for it?"

"Okay, I'll bite, what are you willing to tra—" Amberly put her hand to North's mouth for a third time, this time, index, middle and ring finger. She looked deeply into his brown eyes, her green ones blinking in slow motion.

Amberly leaned in and kissed North. The kiss was full mouthed and active, moist, hot and sweet. She liked this kiss too much, and after a time that seemed too long and, yet at the same time, too short, North pulled away from Amberly.

"I'm sorry, Amberly, I don't understand what you are trying to do here," North said. He enjoyed the kiss, but he knew Amberly was playing some sort of game, and he didn't want to play. This wasn't an affirming affection between partners. This was childish.

"Amberly, I care for you deeply, but this isn't right."

Amberly resisted the urge to panic. Did North see through her? Was she in over her head? She started to wonder what unintended consequences might transpire because of her manipulation of North — and Dek.

"I'm sorry, but I need to go," Amberly said, nervously. "May I have the pass?"

North shrugged, went a little stone faced, and stepped into his bedroom. Amberly could hear him ruffling though his belongings.

North emerged with the card. "Here you go," North handed Amberly the card, and she slipped it into her handbag along with Verne.

"I really have to go," Amberly repeated, moving for the portal. And she slipped out the door.

The feeling of naïveté North had when Amberly rejected him on the Shard Cave trip returned. No, this was the taste of ignorance, North reasoned. He scratched his head and started wondering if he really knew Amberly at all. North picked up a stick of beef jerky, ripping it with his teeth.

Amberly was nearly sprinting down the hall to make her next rendezvous. She was not a liar, at least, she hadn't been one until now. *Manipulation isn't a lie, not necessarily*, she reasoned.

A small part of Amberly realized that she had not only successfully deceived North, but she had deceived herself, too.

CHAPTER EIGHT

"I have it," Amberly said through the intercom at Dek's temporary apartment. "Let's finish our deal."

Amberly wasn't surprised when she didn't hear Dek's voice, but Joti's in reply. The door slid open and Joti reached out and yanked the petite woman inside, the door sliding closed as quickly as it had opened.

Amberly surveyed the room. Joti was standing next to her, and seated on the folded down bed was Dek, and next to him was a woman with long strawberry blonde hair. She was the one who spoke, "Let me see it."

Amberly reached into a pocket and fingered the access card.

"Are you really Dek's cohort sister?"

The woman just snorted with some disdain.

Amberly looked at Dek, who looked down at the textured metallic floor. "Tell me, what do you need with a ship pass that has been already used?"

"Silly girl," the woman said to Amberly, and then looked at Dek. "You didn't tell her, did you? She's in for a shock."

The woman turned back to Amberly. After a moment, she spoke.

"Dek isn't anything romantic to me if that's what you're worried about. We're cohort mates. We did grow up together, and we both joined Chasm about the same time. That's all we are – now. The stories of your mother Kimberly, before she left for *Magellan*, inspired me to join Chasm. She's a legend to us, you know."

"No, I don't know," Amberly blustered. "Why don't you tell me?"

"The card please?" the woman said. Joti's eyes widened as Amberly pulled the pass from her pocket and handed it to the woman. The woman in turn handed it to Joti, who put it in his pocket, and in a flash, exited the apartment.

"Joti has a lot of work to do in a short time," the woman said. "As do I. Let me tell you what is going to happen tonight, Amberly. The first thing you should know is I am not going to tell you my name. You can call me Sparks, because I am the spark that will light this revolution."

Amberly was growing weary of the theatrics. "Whatever, Sparks," she said sarcastically. Sparks laughed in reply.

"You see, we are going to take *M.S.S. Firebird* tonight. We have to recover some personnel from the Spencer Belt," Dek said, speaking for the first time. "You have to come with us. We can tell you all about your mom on the trip over there."

Amberly was confused. "You guys know this pass will not let you launch with the *Firebird*, or any ship right? The launch code is used already. You need a new launch code."

"Of course, you are correct Amberly," Dek said. Sparks rolled her eyes. "We have the ability to write a new code on the card. We just needed a used card to put a new code on. As you know, those cards are hard to come by. *Magellan* security never figured someone could do what Joti is doing right now — forging a new launch code to overwrite an old one."

Amberly remembered the evening with Dek and the strange device he had to access the topside gardens. "Your hacking box. It's how we got into the topside gardens. But that's different than a launch card—"

Dek reached into a parachute pocket of his khaki pants, and pulled out a few assorted items and set them on the table. Amberly recognized Dek's device from the evening at Rick's, which Dek presented to her. But Amberly was keenly interested in another item Dek had emptied out of his pocket: a hard decoder key, probably for accessing encrypted messages like the one Skip had intercepted. She had to figure out how to grab the hard key without arousing suspicion.

"And there is the hacking box now," Amberly said.

"It's a thing of beauty, really," Dek replied. "Time to start giving you what you asked for. Your mother … was one of the most gifted people to ever work on cryptology. Writing unbreakable encryption algorithms… breaking everyone else's. She was amazing. A prodigy. She had spent every free moment on *Magellan* working to crack every encryption and security code on the waypoint. A long, boring and arduous task reserved for only the most disciplined geniuses. And Kimberly was the best."

"Nearly 30 years ago, we started sending code crackers to the five closest waypoints," Sparks explained.

"But why?"

"All in due time," Sparks smiled. "Trust me, you are going to be pleased."

Dek jumped in. "Your mother cracked the code first among her colleagues at the other waypoints, but she feared she was compromised. Some conversation intercepted or something. She figured she didn't have years for the rest of the Chasm code crackers to do their work. Then she disappeared with your father. Your mother was dedicated to Chasm like no other. And as you now know, she paid dearly for it."

Amberly's head was spinning. She knew her mother was sharp, but a super genius? Learning about her mother's secret life was enough to stir her emotions. But this secret plot, which apparently cost her mother her life, could have unknown consequences. It was a lot for Amberly to process. "Why do you guys want all the codes? What are you planning to do?" Amberly was becoming worried about what would happen next.

Sparks laughed. "Sorry sister. Telling you the details about Chasm wasn't part of the deal. But I guarantee you'll want to be on the *Firebird* when we borrow it tonight. After we show you our… secret, you can decide then if you want to join us, and if you join us, then you get to know everything."

Sparks reached out and put a hand on Dek and smiled. "It's time. We have our orders. Let's change history."

Dek smiled excitedly, reached out his hand and clasped it on Sparks' shoulder.

"Go and help Joti prepare for the trip. I'll make sure that Amberly gets to the hangar bay in time for departure," Dek replied. "It's so surreal, after all this time, after lifetimes of work, we're finally ready. I thought I wouldn't be sure about going through with the plan, but I have never been more sure about anything."

Sparks leaned in and kissed Dek on the cheek. Amberly unintentionally sighed aloud.

"Jealous?" Sparks said. "Well you should be. You may be the daughter of the iconic Kimberly Macready, but I've earned my place, earned the admiration of my peers. Don't worry. Stick with me, sister, and someday you might be great, too."

Sparks turned back to Dek, who wasn't giving anything away

with his expressions. Amberly fumed.

"There's no reason to get her worked up," Dek said to Sparks.

"Can't a girl have some fun?" Sparks tossed out as she exited Dek's temporary apartment. Amberly and Dek were alone.

"What was that about?" Amberly said. "You and she…"

"It was nothing and it was a long time ago," Dek said, taking Amberly's hands into his. "Don't listen to Sparks. You are twice the woman she is."

Amberly leaned into Dek and embraced him.

"Dek, I want to trust you, but I'm sort of getting worried," Amberly admitted, looking up into Dek's bright grey-blue eyes.

"There's nothing to fear," Dek said. "We are on the edge of history, and you have a front row seat."

"That's what I mean, Dek," Amberly said, standing back. "You and your weird crew are acting like Armageddon is knocking on the outer hull, and somehow my super-genius mom was the harbinger of the apocalypse."

"Look, we could be in the Spencer Belt for a few days. Why don't we go by your place and you can get some stuff?" Dek asked.

Amberly didn't want to get on the ship with the Chasm team. Not without knowing what was going on. Stealing a runabout, even borrowing one, was not an insignificant crime, and not one that you could easily get away with if you ever wanted to set foot back on *Magellan* again. On a closed environment like *Magellan*, there weren't a lot of places you could lay low for a while. And Amberly didn't want to accidentally exile herself from her home. Of course, Dek knew this, and it seemed unlikely he would put himself in so much trouble without an escape plan.

She thought he might try to get away on the *American Spirit*, but it wasn't scheduled to leave for another four weeks. Were they planning on being out in the Spencer Belt for that long? Amberly's absence from her normal routines and the missing runabout would point to her culpability. Was she just going along to be framed?

On the other hand, Amberly was intensely curious about what Joti, Sparks and Dek weren't telling her. She knew they were holding out, and they were holding out something big about her mother. Every morsel of information they fed her only made her want more. Amberly, who had spent the last six years obsessing over her dead mother, was vulnerable to making irrational decisions when tempted with the idea of becoming closer to Kimberly Macready, posthumously.

They also might try to compel her to come. Joti certainly liked to wave around his weapon. While she did trust Dek, she certainly didn't trust Sparks and definitely kept a wary eye on Joti. Dek was different, she thought. Or maybe she was just hoping he was different, because she was attracted to him — a strong intellect, who believed in a cause and was willing to take significant measures, someone who took command in a situation and took care of the people around him.

Just a week ago, Amberly was just a bright, young scientist on an obscure waypoint in the far-off reaches of space. Now she was involved in a… in a what? She didn't know what she was involved in: plot, conspiracy, protest? She thought the best course of action would be to play both sides, at least until she had all the information.

"Yeah, let's go to my place. Do you mind if I use your restroom first? I know this is awkward, but I really need to go. And would you be a gentleman and, well…" Amberly motioned toward the door of the small apartment. Even though there was a privacy curtain, Dek knew the polite thing would be for him to step outside, and he did.

"Wait for me outside," Amberly called out, "I'll be right out."

Once Dek was outside, she moved quickly. She turned on the water in the restroom sink and let it run. She sat down and pulled off her boot, and then grabbed the hard key Skip needed and slipped it inside the shoe. She quickly pulled the boot back on, careful not to crush the hard key with her foot. The key was uncomfortable when she stepped on it, but she ignored the odd sensation in her shoe and tried to walk normally.

She washed and dried her hands, pulled the curtain closed, and then grabbed the hacking box and stepped outside the door.

Dek was waiting for her, and she immediately handed the hacking box to Dek.

"I figured we might need this, so I grabbed it," Amberly said as Dek took the device and slid it into his pocket. Amberly started for the tube car at a rapid pace.

"Let's go," she said. Dek turned away from Amberly and took

a step back toward the door. Was Dek was thinking about the hard key he left in the apartment? Amberly's heart started to beat a little faster, and she was worried her face would become flush.

"Come on, let's go. Kora is going to call the police or something to find me if I don't get back to my place to check in," Amberly called back to Dek.

Dek looked at the apartment door, and then looked at Amberly. He reached for the door, but instead of opening it, he just tested it, to make sure it was locked, and then he jogged the few paces between the door and where Amberly was waiting.

"Yeah, let's go," Dek said. "It's going to be a long night still. Once we get underway, I am going to try to catch a nap. I'm tired."

Amberly took Dek's hand as he looked behind him again at the door. Amberly took a risk.

"Did you forget something?" she asked. "We can go back for it."

"No, nothing," he said, and Amberly exerted a significant amount of self-control to keep from breathing a sigh of relief.

Within a few minutes, the pair had reached the tube, and there was a significant queue.

"Maybe it will be quicker if we walked," Dek said, obviously frustrated at the line.

"No, this will go quickly. Besides, it's more than a kilometer to my place from here. Maybe two," Amberly said.

"It's your home, you know best," Dek said.

As they waited, Amberly took Dek's hand and leaned her head on Dek's shoulder, and spoke softly, so only he could make out her words. "Dek, I need you to tell me something," she spoke.

Dek nuzzled her soft red hair with his chin. "Yes?"

"I need to know if anything really bad is going to happen."

"If we do our job right, nothing really bad will happen."

"What's our job?"

"You know I can't tell you that right now," Dek said, lifting his head. "But once we get to the Spencer Belt, you'll know everything that I do."

Amberly and Dek reached the front of the queue and stepped into the tubecar. A portly man in his 30s, who looked like someone who worked in a microfactory by his uniform, also tried to get into the car with them.

Dek gently put his hand up.

"Friend, do you mind if we take this car alone," he asked the worker.

"What? Come on, I want to get home. You transients need to learn to share," the man objected and started to step in the car. Dek reached into his pocket and pulled out a credit chip and tossed it on the ground outside the car. The man reached down to pick it up, and Dek pushed him clear.

"Hey!"

The door sealed closed and the tube car started to move, and Dek and Amberly were alone again. Dek sat next to Amberly and turned her head to him. His gaze pieced her green eyes, and he had gently placed each of his hands on Amberly's cheeks.

"I need you to trust me, Amberly Macready. Your mother trusted us. And even if you don't trust us, trust me. I only want what is best for you."

"I want to trust you; I really do," Amberly said. "But how do I know you are not just playing me, using me for who knows what? How do I know my mom trusted you?"

"It's because your mom trusted us that we have the shell. She knew it would be a message to you, and now it's critical that we get you to the Spencer Belt so your mom's work can be complete."

"That makes no sense," Amberly said, protesting with her mouth.

But her eyes seemed ready to give in to Dek. She couldn't deny she was attracted to Dek, and quickly started to think about where that path would lead. Would he leave on the *American Spirit* once his mission was done? Would she be okay with a quick-burning relationship? It was very unattached and progressive, and that appealed to her. North would never do that. North was a now-and-forever kind of guy, and the kiss she stole from him made her second guess herself.

Amberly was lost in the middle of that thought when Dek leaned in to kiss her. Amberly retreated, and with a flirting wink said, "Slow down, Romeo. There will be time for that later."

Amberly wanted to kiss Dek. She loved his powerful eyes and his progressive idealism. But she had to keep her head clear. And she had to keep him hungry. Too much was at stake. She felt so close to learning everything about her dead mother.

Dek was disappointed, but he could be patient. Amberly leaned her head on Dek's shoulder. As she relaxed, her foot slipped slightly and the hard corner of the hidden key pressed into her heel. She winced and reflexively withdrew.

"Are you all right?" Dek asked, confused.

Amberly thought for a moment that maybe she should come clean with Dek about the encoded messages Skip had intercepted, and about swiping his hard key. She opened her mouth to confess.

Then she closed it.

No, she wouldn't tell him. She would stick to the plan. Maybe her heart trusted Dek, but her head didn't, and Amberly was hell-bent to let her head keep running the show for now.

"I'm fine. Sorry," she said.

The tubecar started slowing at the next stop.

"Dek, I trust you," she half-lied with a confident tone, as the door slid open and the pair stepped out. "Let's do this."

Within a few minutes, they were standing in front of the door to the Macready residence.

"I need to go in alone and talk with Kora," Amberly said. "Don't worry I won't be long."

"You know I can't let you go in there alone," Dek protested. "You might tell Kora about our plans to commandeer the *Firebird*."

"Look, there is nothing I want more than to find out everything about my mother and what she was doing, and that means staying with you. I am not going to mess that up now," Amberly said. "And honestly, you are the person I want to be with right now, Chasm or not."

Amberly was so mixed up right now, that she didn't know if she was lying or not, but she was sticking to the plan. She hoped she could get the hard key to Lydia and Skip.

"Don't say things you don't mean," Dek fished. "What if a kiss is just a kiss?"

"I want to find out what we are, Dek. I trust you are going to make history, and I trust it is going to be a good history. I am putting myself in your hands by going with you tonight. Now it's your turn to trust me. I need to talk to my sister, alone. Please, trust me like I trust you."

Dek briefly considered her test. "Okay, Amberly, please hurry. I'll be right here."

Amberly punched in her unlock code and slipped into her apartment.

Kora was watching a vid in her room. She called out.

"Amberly, there you are. Lydia has been trying to reach you all day, she seems worried —"

"Kora, listen. I don't have much time. This is important and my life could be in danger. Dek is right outside…"

"Dek? I thought you were on a date with North?"

"Well, I was over at North's place, and, it doesn't matter."

"Dek is threatening you? How is he putting you in danger?"

"Would you just listen!?" Amberly sat down on the bed next to Kora and pulled off her boot. "After I leave, I need you to take this hard key to Lydia or Skip right away. Don't tell anyone. Just give it to them. Don't lose it."

"I don't understand," Kora protested. Amberly had moved from Kora's room to hers, and she had pulled out a small bag and was stuffing a jumpsuit and some extra undergarments and toiletries inside.

"An overnight bag? Listen Amberly, I know I have encouraged you to develop relationships with men, but what you are doing here looks like a bad idea."

"No, it's not like that. Not even close."

"Uh-huh. Really. Who is it? North? Surely not. Wait. *Dek*?"

Amberly stopped packing for a moment to consider the question. Her flash reaction was that the question was juvenile, but then she just made the connection she had kissed both men within the space of a few hours.

"Both," she answered truthfully. "And yes I am going crazy, and no, I don't know if it meant anything yet. But none of that is important tonight."

"What? Amberly, you are not making any sense," Kora said, concern tightening her brow.

"No time to explain. After you give the key to Lydia or Skip, find North and tell him about the key and that he should find Skip. Don't talk about this with anyone else. This is important. Don't tell anyone, and find North."

"Okay, deliver key. Tell North."

Amberly grabbed her infopad and her mother's conch shell and added them to her bag's contents before zipping it and slipping it on her shoulder. She stopped and faced her sister, and pulled her into an embrace.

"No matter what happens, I love you, Kora," Amberly said, and turned to the door. The door slid open, with Dek waiting in the access corridor. Amberly walked out of the door, and Kora ran after her.

She eyed Dek unhappily. "Amberly, be safe."

Dek and Amberly stopped and turned to face Kora.

"Amberly... I," Kora started to speak, but Amberly gave her a hard stare that Kora correctly interpreted as an indication that she shouldn't say anything in front of Dek. Kora looked straight at Dek.

"I have no idea what the hell is going on between the two of you, but you better make sure my little sister doesn't get hurt, runt." Kora put a finger into Dek's chest. "If she does, I will personally airlock you."

Kora swung on her heels and retired to her apartment. When the door had closed and Amberly and Dek were alone once again, Dek turned to Amberly.

"Is she going to be a problem?" he asked, not threateningly, but out of genuine concern.

"No, she thinks I am going with you for a sleepover," Amberly said.

"That's a nice idea," Dek quipped.

Amberly's hand struck out like lightning, as she slapped Dek's face with a sudden fury that surprised them both.

"Don't assume too much, Dek Tigona," Amberly seethed. And as quickly as her temper flared, it subsided. "You should put that thought away before you get into real trouble."

They walked silently toward the hangars. Dek's face had a welt where Amberly's petite fingers had struck him. She thought he might even bruise. She was upset about his arrogant, presumptuous suggestion, but she was also starting to feel sorry for her flash of violence.

"Maybe we should stop by the commons and get some ice for that," Amberly suggested.

"No time," Dek said flatly, and the two quickly walked toward the main hangar, which was right next to her workplace.

About ten minutes later, they were closing in on the lower lobby that gave access to the hangar and the Science Corps main labs. It was 27:30 — nearly midnight — and the access corridors were mostly deserted, so both Amberly and Dek jumped a bit when the Science Corps main door slid open and a tall blonde walked out.

"Lydia!" Amberly shouted. "What are you doing out so late?"

"Amberly, you know I am working on the —"

Amberly cut her off. "I'm sorry, how rude of me. Lydia this is Dek, you know, the fellow from the *American Spirit* I've been telling you about."

Dek reached out his hand.

"So nice to meet you, Lydia," he said. "I don't know if Amberly told you, but I do stellar cataloguing, too. She's promised me a tour of your labs. But not tonight."

Amberly wanted to telegraph the precarious nature of her stroll with Dek, but couldn't figure out a way how without tipping her hand to Dek.

"So what are you two out here for? An evening stroll?"

"Dek wanted to give me a tour of the *American Spirit*. So here we are, headed to the hangar docking port. By the way Lydia, Kora has been looking for you all day. I just came from over there and I know she'd appreciate it if you dropped by."

Amberly glanced over at Dek, and if he thought her comments to Lydia were anything but innocent, he didn't show it.

"Good night, Lydia."

"Good night, Amberly. Mr. Tigona."

"Lydia, it was a great pleasure to make your acquaintance," Dek said.

Lydia had rounded the corner and was gone. A few paces later, Amberly was at the main door for the hangar. During working hours, a Marine handled admittance, but at night, you had to enter the authorized passcode. Since Dek was a passenger on the *American Spirit*, he had been given a passcode to open the door so he could have access to his ship. Likewise, because of her position in the Science Corps, Amberly also had an access code.

"After you," Dek said to Amberly, motioning to her to enter her code.

"Oh no, you put your code in. They log those you know, and it doesn't make sense for me to be here at night, so when this whole thing comes apart, they will come looking for you, not me," Amberly replied.

Dek sighed and reached a control pad on the door and entered a 10-digit code. "In the end, I promise you no one will care who entered the hangar when."

"That's easy for you to say, Dek. You know the plan. I'm flying blind here."

"Right."

"So even if you do have a working pass code to take the ship, how do you know the flight deck isn't going to be suspicious and try to confirm the launch codes?"

"Our guy is running the flight deck," Dek said as he looked around the hangar for the runabouts and started walking in that direction.

"How many of you are there on *Magellan*?"

"I don't know the exact number. Let's just say hundreds," Dek said. "Joti knows an exact count, I believe. Sparks will tell you she does, but she doesn't. Your mother — would have had access to that information."

All three of the runabouts were in dock, and Amberly didn't know the *Firebird* by sight from the others, but when she saw Joti and Sparks standing in front of the furthest ship from the safety vacuum curtain, she figured that was their ride.

Sparks looked curiously at the finger welts on Dek's face. "What happened to you? Wait, don't tell me you got frisky with Amberly? Shame, shame."

"Hurry," Joti said. "The sooner we get underway, the better." From the bottom of the runabout protruded a ladder, and Joti started climbing it. Sparks followed.

"Ladies first," Dek indicated the ladder to Amberly. Amberly climbed into the belly of the ship, and finally Dek ascended the ladder. Once he was in the ship, the ladder retracted and the hatch sealed.

At the top of the ladder, Joti was waiting for Amberly. She could see he had a firearm holstered near his hip.

"Did you happen to bring an infopad? If so, hand it over."

Amberly opened her bag and produced Verne.

"Can't have you making any calls while we are in range of *Magellan*," he said.

"Don't trust me huh?" Amberly entered a lock command on Verne and handed him to Joti. "I don't trust you either."

"I'm glad that's clear," he said. "You have too much of your father in you."

Dek climbed out of the stairwell. Joti addressed him.

"Sparks and I are going to get this ship underway. Would you make sure our guest is comfortable? And by that, I mean lock her up in one of the sleeping quarters." Joti headed toward the cockpit.

When Sparks and Joti had disappeared onto the bridge, Dek turned to Amberly.

"I'm sorry, Amberly, but I'm going to need to lock you in—"

"Don't worry. I understand," Amberly said. Dek pointed her aft. They walked to the back of *Firebird* along the main corridor.

"Your friend Joti is a real ball of starshine," Amberly mused.

"His bedside manner is horrible, but he's loyal to the cause and willing to do what needs to be done."

"He's a horrible spy," Amberly said. "You can lock this from the outside, right?"

"Sure, but I can stay here with you if—"

Amberly gently pushed Dek back into the hallway, and winked at him.

"Thanks, but I need some alone time anyway. Maybe you should go to the bridge and keep an eye on crazy. Both of them. See you soon," Amberly pressed a button, the door slid closed and Dek heard Amberly locking the door from the inside. He thought about entering a lock code on the exterior door, but in defiance of Joti he did not and just headed for the bridge.

This bizarre conspiracy wrapped in this ultimate tease about the fate of her late mother had pushed Amberly to the emotional limit. She reclined on the lower bunk and tried to push back the emotions so she could think clearly. Amberly suspected she'd need to stay sharp as possible just in case this whole unauthorized trip backfired and she needed to act quickly.

She needed to rest, but Amberly was too wound up to sleep,

so she just listened to the hum of the engines and started speculating about the outcome of her second trip to the Spencer Belt in as many weeks.

CHAPTER NINE

After hours of silent waiting, Amberly was still queasy from the *Firebird*'s artificial gravity, which felt different from the gravity on *Magellan*. She was disoriented and tired, but kept running through the details of what was becoming the longest day of her life.

Amberly was desperate for any information. *Did Lydia get the hard key?* She tried to clear her mind, to think clearly.

She instinctively reached for Verne to check her messages, but then remembered Joti had confiscated the infopad. Across from her bunk, almost within arm's reach, was a communications terminal. Amberly flicked it on, but it asked her for the ship's master passcode for access.

"Let's see if we can guess this," Amberly said aloud to no one. She typed in C-H-A-S-M and got nothing. She thought for a while, and then typed K-I-M-B-E-R-L-Y, knowing how much these people allegedly respected her dead mother. No access. Not wanting to get locked out for bad guesses, she let the terminal be.

At the end of the short, tube-like room was a round portal that Amberly suspected opened into a restroom. She was right. She grabbed her night bag, slipped into the tight shower unit, bathed, and put on a cream-colored fitted tunic with black leggings.

She laid back down, but still couldn't sleep, so Amberly decided to explore the ship and see what Dek, Joti and Sparks were up to, and maybe get a better picture of exactly what they were going to do in the Spencer Belt. Sparks had said they were going to recover "personnel," implying they were picking up people. But how did such people get to the Spencer Belt, and what would they have been doing? Amberly thought it was highly unlikely Chasm would have some sort of permanent base. *Only one way to find out*, Amberly thought as she reached to open the sleeper room door.

She half expected the door to be locked from the outside, but the door came open, and Amberly peered down the central corridor, which ran the length of *Firebird*. She could see the door to the bridge open at the far end, so she started to make her way along the ship.

Nowhere near as cramped as a corvette, the runabout boasted a luxurious 300 square meters of cabin space over two decks. The top deck had sleeping quarters, galley, navigation and communications centers, and the bridge. The lower deck had engineering, life support resources, a cargo hold, two escape pods, a small lounge, and the airlock for docking with ships that had no hangars. The airlock also could be depressurized to allow direct access to space.

Because Marines could theoretically commandeer this ship, the airlock room had a small armory. It was more of a locked hard case, but when stocked, it could carry enough stun weapons for everyone on board to arm themselves.

Amberly peered through the open hatch onto the bridge. Three windows opened to the bow of the ship, offering a natural view of straight ahead, slightly port, and slightly starboard. Visual confirmation was rarely used however, as the *Firebird* was mostly piloted by sensors and navigational computers. Three chairs were tightly arranged in a U-shape that put each station roughly in sync with one of the windows. On a minimalist pillar in front of each chair was an interface pad, enabling authorized personnel to pull up the appropriate controls.

When the controls were activated, any number of floating pixels (small, reflective metallic bits) would arrange, directed by a complex magnetic system, into various screens on various planes perpendicular to the physical interface pad. Tiny lasers would be shot from the pad, and then reflected or refracted into visible light by the floating pixels, creating a three-dimensional screen. Motion sensors would then track the user's hands relative to the floating pixels to register input. A hand inserted through a floating pixel screen would feel little resistance, as if pushing through dust in the air. When the hand was removed, the magnetic screen controllers would rearrange any pixels in the wrong place in a few milliseconds.

Amberly was not a pilot, but she had been around ships enough with her father to know what the three stations typically were. The navigator was responsible for programming the destination into the ship's computers and performing traditional, manual piloting when necessary. From the engineering station, all the ships vitals could be maintained, including running the anti-matter reactor, life support and artificial gravity. The captain's chair on a Valkyrie-class ship would be able to access all the commands of engineering and navigation, in addition to communication (shipwide and ship to ship) and basic weapons systems (if the ship was carrying weapons). The *Firebird* had no real offensive weapons to speak of. It did have a repulsor beam, which could tap the artificial gravity field generator to push any asteroids or attacking ships off course.

Only Sparks was on the bridge, sitting in the command chair. She turned to look at Amberly. "Hey. Joti let you out of your cell? Pick a seat."

Amberly sat down in the vacant engineering chair. "So, you're like Dek. You really believe in the Chasm cause?"

"Sure. Chasm is where the action is. Dek wants to change history. That's great, I am just jazzed to be here. And believe me, things are about to get exciting."

"So Dek is in this because he believes he is making better worlds, and you are in this for ... an adrenaline rush?"

"People aren't that simple. We have complex motivations. Joti has his ... secrets. And Dek's mind I can't figure out. For example, Dek *really* likes you," Sparks smiled. "Why is that? He hardly knows you, and he's never expressed any interest in long-term relationships. What do you think?"

"I wouldn't know," Amberly said, looking out a window with the Spencer Belt appearing larger as they sped closer.

"Hmm... you're not bad to look at," Sparks thought aloud. "Maybe it's your hair. Not many redheads on Arara — at least not natural ones. Of course, it could be that he likes you because he's obsessed with your mother. We *all* are, to some degree. She ... was an incredible woman."

"She was. Mom was the most important person in my life when she left," Amberly said in Sparks direction, but not really to Sparks. Amberly peered down at some readouts on the engineering monitor. "We are going to Sonnet?"

"Yep, to Fuentes Station," Sparks said.

"Why am I here? You are not going to kill me, are you?" Amberly said, nonchalantly considering the topic.

"Kill you?" Sparks seemed tickled at the idea. "She'd be real pissed if we killed you."

"Who? The … chairman?"

"The Chairman? Don't have any delusions of grandeur. I wonder if she even knows you exist. Besides, I don't think Dek would let us kill you."

"But you *are* going to kill people?" Amberly asked, trying to sound nonchalant about the morbid question.

"Well, I hope not," Sparks smiled. "But it may be unavoidable. You must understand that freedom from tyranny is worth dying for. And I suppose *anything* worth dying for is worth killing for. That *anything* is often a lot of fun, too."

"Taking life and giving up your own life are not morally equivalent," Amberly said, sort of taken aback by Sparks' ethical calculus. "Tell me what you guys are doing — tell me what mom's mission was — and maybe I'll understand and maybe I can help."

"The *Magellan* mission leader will want to tell you personally. That's who we are picking up," Sparks said.

"But Joti said he was the leader of Chasm on *Magellan*," Amberly said.

"Joti was the ranking operative on *Magellan*, but he is not our leader. Speak of the devil —"

Joti and Dek marched onto the bridge. Amberly stood.

Dek was wearing another khaki jumpsuit, slightly darker in color than the one he wore when he and Amberly first met. Joti, on the other hand, had completely transformed himself. He was clean-shaven, with pressed black pants and a white, traditional Zhongshan jacket. His hair was smartly parted; his teeth were freshly whitened.

"Dressed to impress, Joti?" Sparks asked. Joti ignored Sparks, who turned to Dek. "What brings you boys to the bridge?"

"My proximity alarm indicated we were getting close to Sonnet," Dek said.

"Look outside," Sparks indicated to Dek. "See for yourself."

Sonnet loomed larger as the *Firebird* sped toward the large asteroid.

"You sure you know how to land this thing?" Dek asked.

"Please, I've logged, like, 300 hours on the simulator," Sparks said back to Dek. "I could do it with my eyes closed."

"I thought Fuentes Station was abandoned," Amberly said aloud to no one specifically.

"Oh, officially it is," Sparks said to Amberly, and then turned to Dek, who was sitting in the navigator's chair now. "Have you seen the all clear land code?"

Dek was peering through the closest portal to his station, and Amberly moved behind him and looked as well. They were making a pass at Fuentes Station, but moving way too fast to land.

A quick flash of light came from the station.

"I got her," Dek responded.

"*Magellan* chief, this is Dek Tigona," Dek spoke into his open channel comm. "Please confirm visual signal, over."

"Wait, when I was here with North, I saw a flash," Amberly said. "That was a signal."

"Yes, and because you didn't know what it was, the commander wasn't compromised, and could go silent," Joti offered. "Now that she knows we are friendly, she'll give the all-clear signal."

Just then from what appeared to be a main window on the station, came a series of three flashes, followed by a single flash.

Dek spoke into his comm unit again. "Confirmed chief. We need to dust off quickly, so no time for a social visit. Also, we don't know if our automatic docking clamps are working properly, so we are going to recommend a spacewalk out to us once we touch down. Please double flash for confirmation."

Two flashes of light quickly followed from the surface.

"Confirmed, chief. Pack your things, it's time to make history," Dek replied, and then switched off the comm. "Let's set her down nice and gentle, okay Sparks?"

"Three hundred hours, moron."

The final descent was quick, and soon the *Firebird* was resting on skids and anchored to the surface of Sonnet. Gravity on the asteroid was barely perceptible.

Amberly peered through the center portal and could make out a lone figure in a space suit, low-gravity bouncing towards the *Firebird*. Dek and Sparks seemed very excited, but Joti was visibly nervous. Sparks noticed his nervousness and sighed aloud.

Amberly moved to be close to Dek.

"What is up with Joti?" she said under her breath. "And why

did he… clean up?"

"Wow. You asking me that particular question at this particular time has to create some ironic rip in the space/time continuum somewhere," Dek frowned.

Amberly was genuinely confused, "What?"

"I don't know how to explain this in a fashion that won't become profoundly awkward. Let's just say that Joti was an old boyfriend of the *Magellan* chief. Well, at least in his mind. I am reasonably sure she just used him. It was a long time ago; long before I knew the *Magellan* chief."

Amberly glanced at the suited figure on the surface. She would be at the ship's airlock in a minute or less.

"Does the chief answer to the Chairman on Arara?" she continued to question Dek.

"Well, yes. All the Chasm waypoint chiefs report directly to the Chairman," Dek said. "But, of course, they have some autonomy because of the message lag."

"Every waypoint has Chasm agents?"

"No, no. Just *Gilbert*, *Magellan*, *Cortes*, and *Marquette*."

"Why only those four?"

"We didn't want to let our eyes get bigger than our stomachs."

A computer spoke at the engineering station, where Joti was now seated. "Agent Raven One is requesting Airlock access."

Sparks spoke into her comm unit. "Sparks to Raven One. Confirmation code is: Alpha-Two-Tango-Zeta-Zero-Zero-Beta. Please reply with the response code."

A female replied, but the signal was practically inaudible because of tremendous amount of static.

"She's a few meters away," Dek said. "How come we can't hear her? What if this is a trap or something?"

"Who the dirty hell else would be out here?" Joti said, the edginess in his voice hanging in the air. "Let her in!"

"Be quiet!" Sparks commanded. She took out a set of headphones and placed them over her ears so she could hear the woman more clearly. "Sparks to Raven One. Can you repeat? There was a lot of static on your last transmission. Please repeat the response code."

Dek, Joti and Amberly watched Sparks nod her head, but they couldn't hear what she was hearing. "Yes, I can hear you now.

Good. Thanks. Code checks. Welcome back Chief. We have a surprise for you. Opening the airlock now."

Sparks turned to the engineering station. "Go ahead Joti. Let her in."

Joti stuck his hands into the engineering holoscreen and inputted the codes to allow ship access. He then stood up and made for the aft ladder to descend to the lower level. Sparks quickly followed Joti. To depressurize the airlock only took a few minutes, and they both wanted to be there to welcome back their chief.

Dek looked like he was going to bolt after his comrades, but instead turned and faced Amberly. She reached out and took his hand.

"Dek, noting seems right. What are you guys doing? Are people going to die? Am I in danger?"

As she finished the last question, Dek's face of concern turned to one of amusement.

"Amberly, I promise I will not let any harm come to you," Dek said. "And I suspect that the chief will work twice as hard as I would to keep you safe."

"I don't understand."

"Come down and meet her. She'll answer all your questions."

"I've heard that before, but so far you have been just leading me on," Amberly said, frustrated. "I don't know who taught you progressive values, but my mother clearly indicated that honesty was near the top of the list."

"Funny you should mention that. No, Amberly, by bringing you down here I am fulfilling a promise to you, and to her."

"A promise to my mother?" Amberly asked, the pronoun reference unclear.

"To the *Magellan* chief," Dek corrected.

She followed Dek back down the upper level access hall to the aft access port to the lower level. The port in the deck floor was round and had a hinged door attached. The door was entirely mechanical and could only be opened manually. It could be sealed from the top with a latch lock, but otherwise could be opened from both sides.

This was Amberly's first time on the lower deck. A hall parallel to the one on the top floor ran the length of the ship. In the bow, situated immediately below the bridge was the airlock. Amberly and Dek walked that way, and Amberly could see the chief — Raven One – was talking with Joti. Her back was facing Amberly, as was Sparks. Joti's face she could see, and he was crying.

Raven One was still in her space suit, though she had already removed her helmet and gloves. Amberly noticed she had in her hand one of the little code breaker key boxes like the one Dek had used the night Amberly met him.

Amberly stopped two meters short of the group, not wanting to interrupt what was clearly a private and awkward conversation. Dek also stopped, a pace behind Amberly.

"If *she* is onboard, *he* definitely cannot stay with us," Raven One said, pointing a finger at Joti. "And she is here?"

That voice, that voice, Amberly thought, and shook her head, as if to clear it.

"She's here," Sparks said.

"Joti, fetch me a gun," Raven One said, pointing at the armory locker in the airlock room.

"Are you going to shoot me?" Joti said, his voice trembling.

"Joti, Joti," Raven One said, sweetly and condescendingly at the same time. "I am not going shoot you. Why would I do that? And if I was going shoot you, why would you even hand me a gun?"

It's her voice. Amberly's heart started beating rapidly, and she stood watching the scene unfold, paralyzed.

The muscles in Sparks arms and legs tensed, like a predator about to pounce on her prey.

"You know why. I'd give you the gun because I love you. I'd do anything for you," Joti said, through blubbering tears.

"Then get me the gun," Raven One said, calmly and coolly.

"The armory is locked," Joti said, looking though the open interior airlock door at the metallic box inside.

"I'll unlock it for you," Raven One sighed, then punched some code in her key box, transmitting a signal to unlock the armory.

"Just do it, Joti," Sparks said. "There are probably no guns in there anyway. I don't think the Marines keep it stocked."

"Go to hell, dirt licker!" a highly agitated Joti spat at Sparks.

He stepped into the airlock and reached for the unlocked armory door.

Dek quietly stepped behind the speechless Amberly and embraced her, putting his arms around her and locking his hands together at mid-torso. She was so entranced by what was going on, she didn't notice Dek securing her.

Joti's back was to Raven One and Sparks now, and Raven One lifted her hacking device again and punched in another code.

At the same time, Joti opened the armory door to reveal that Sparks was indeed right; no weapons were to be had in the locker. Just as he turned around to show the empty container to the women standing just outside the airlock, the interior airlock door slid shut.

Joti's eyes became wide and he immediately started pounding on the window of the closed door. Raven One just shook her head as the airlock computer started the normal airlock safety count down.

"Confirm initiate ten seconds until chamber decompression," the computer spoke.

"No! Don't start it!" Joti screamed.

Raven One typed some commands into her box again, and the computer ignored Joti.

"Ten…"

"But I love you…"

"Eight"

"And you said you loved me…"

"Six"

"I don't love you, you moron," Raven One said, spittle from her mouth spraying on the airlock window. "I never loved you. You are now and always were a tool. Now die miserably. You failed me, so you failed Chasm."

"Two"

"No. No. No." Joti banged the window desperately. "I love you Kimberly! I love you! I —"

A klaxon sounded. The atmosphere, far too valuable to be vented, was sucked into vacuum canisters, a process which took about 10 seconds.

Amberly screamed. "No! Why would you kill someone?!" She started to thrash, but Dek restrained her.

Raven One swung around. "Amberly!" she shouted. "Oh my…"

Amberly looked at Raven One and the asphyxiating Joti, floating in clear view in the window behind her.

Raven One *was* Kimberly Macready.

"Mom? Mom. But… I thought you were… you were … dead."

Kimberly Macready grew flush with anger and glared at Sparks, then at Dek.

"Mom… he's dying!" Amberly pointed to the airlock.

Dek whispered in Amberly's ear, "He's been a dead man walking for years."

"Dek, go lock her in a sleeping room or an escape pod. Do it now! I can't deal with this," Kimberly barked at the man restraining her younger daughter.

Dek responded by pulling Amberly, who was now crying and thrashing, away from Kimberly. Amberly was strong, but Dek managed to drag her away with some exertion.

As Dek gently but firmly pushed the struggling Amberly up the access tube, she saw Joti's lifeless body float out the door and into space.

Dek and Amberly emerged through the access tube onto *Firebird*'s upper deck. Amberly slumped down to her knees, sobbing hysterically. She was starting to hyperventilate when Dek lifted her back to her feet.

"I'm sorry about all of this Amberly," Dek said as he gently nudged her toward the sleeping compartment she had occupied earlier. "You must be in shock. But it will all make sense soon. You'll see that your mother knows best."

"Was *that* my mother? *My* mother wouldn't kill someone in cold blood," Amberly croaked softly between sobs. She then looked up at Dek with a hot bolt of anger in her eyes.

"How is my mother alive?! Why didn't you tell me my mother was still alive, you ass!?" She pulled back her hand to strike Dek for a second time. Dek resolved to take the slap in a manly fashion, but he still flinched. A swing later, Amberly had imprinted a hand-shaped welt on Dek's face.

Amberly's fury burned deep as red blood boiled to the surface. Now she pulled back her fist to as if to punch Dek, but before she could strike her blow, Dek moved to restrain her with a gentle but firm grasp. She collapsed in his arms, spent emotionally and physically. She sobbed, quietly, into the shoulder of his khaki jumpsuit.

"Dek, what is happening?"

Dek slid open the door open to Amberly's sleeping quarters, and motioned her to her bed.

"Why don't you just rest here? Let me get you a protein bar or something for you to eat. You must be in shock," Dek said as he opened the mini-pantry high on the wall opposite the bunk beds.

Amberly sat down on the lower bunk. She was too overwhelmed to process that not only was her mother alive, but she was the leader of this Chasm movement, and she was capable of killing someone in a horrific fashion.

"I need to go and see what is going on," Dek said, giving Amberly's hand a quick squeeze. "Please stay here until your mother or I come for you."

Amberly used the back of her hand to wipe tears and mucus from her face. She looked up at Dek. "Am I a prisoner here?"

"No, of course not," Dek said. "Listen. Eighty percent of who you know your mom to be is true to who she is. We shouldn't cross the other 20 percent. I told you she is dedicated to Chasm like no one else. You just saw that." Dek handed Amberly the protein bar, but she brushed it away.

"I don't know what to think. Is that really my mother?"

"Please, Amberly, just stay here until I figure out what is going on," Dek said so firmly that Amberly felt it was not a request. She spread out on the bed, and lying down on her back, closed her eyes.

Dek figured that he was lucky to have her calmed down this much and decided that he didn't want to be away from whatever schemes Kimberly and Sparks were planning for too long, so he left Amberly, sliding and latching the door tight behind him.

Amberly lay quietly, still tearing up, and then she was struck with a thought she was surprised hadn't hit her sooner.

Where's dad?

CHAPTER TEN

"Are you sure the message was correct?" Kimberly slammed her hand hard on the dining table in the middle of the mess of the *Firebird*. She looked sternly at Dek.

"It was encoded, it followed the protocol, it was passcode authenticated. How could it not be?" Dek said. "Why would anyone send that message besides the Chairman? She is the only person who would want that. Our enemies certainly would not. They don't even know we have the capacity to do such a thing."

Sparks was sitting across the table from Dek and Kimberly, leaning back against the wall and rubbing her temples. "Did you have to airlock Joti? I mean, I didn't really like him and all, but did he deserve that?"

Kimberly put a finger up. "Shush. There were secrets that only Joti and I knew that I never wanted Amberly to find out. Ever. Now I'm the only one who knows them. I don't want to talk about it anymore, understand? I need to focus on the problem at hand. I need to visualize every detail."

Kimberly bowed her head slightly, closed her eyes halfway, and her lips started moving rapidly, as if she was having a silent conversation with herself. Dek thought that this was no doubt the amazing mind of Kimberly Macready at work. This same mind cracked the operational codes of *Magellan* without detection, and plotted the genius plan of her own "death" and her multi-year exile in preparation for this very day, the day when Arara would separate from its past, thought Dek, to fully embrace its future.

This was supposed to be the day *Magellan* would be under Chasm command, except for Dek's message.

Kimberly, with her head still bowed, spoke. "Dek, read me the message again. Be very precise. I want to hear every word."

Dek pulled up an infopad and tapped it a few times.

He read: "Dek. Meeting resistance on *Marquette*. We'll make the stand here. Initiate contingency code Scorched Earth. You have discretion on Friend or Foe protocol. Eliminate foes. Retrieve Raven One at all costs. For the future, Chairman: signature code X-120-Tiger-Alpha-321-Pi."

"Are you sure Scorched Earth means we have to destroy the

entire waypoint?" Sparks said.

"Of course, I am sure," Kimberly snapped, her head popping up. "Remember who I am!"

"This isn't fair," Sparks said in a particularly whiney voice. "We did our job. We can take *Magellan* by force. Why should we not claim the Spencer Belt and all its resources for Arara?"

"Sparks, Sparks, Sparks. Don't be a simpleton," Kimberly sighed. "Out here, in this great expanse of nothingness, the resources of the Spencer Belt may be invaluable. But back there, back home, on the golden fields of Arara, it's commonplace and worthless as dirt."

"Dirt's not worthless," Sparks said.

"That's my point," Kimberly said. "Here in deep, cold, lifeless space, you give hundreds and thousands of credits for the amount of dirt needed to grow a bean plant. But on Arara, we have a different economy."

Dek continued where Kimberly left off. "Don't you see, Sparks, humanity was not meant to live in space. Not like this. The waypoints were a necessary evil at best, to help us get to Arara. Besides, I've been given friend-or-foe authorization. We will save those who are sympathetic to the cause."

"How?" Sparks demanded. "How do you save people while blowing up the only life-sustaining port within a half lightyear?"

Kimberly raised both of her hands, palms-forward, to calm her companion. "Do not worry. I'm making a plan. Just give me an hour or so to work out the details. Then we can head back to *Magellan*. And then," she smiled, "And then... we can finally go home and breathe the fresh fragrances of the grasses of Arara again."

Kimberly was suddenly lost in thought, staring through Dek and Sparks.

"Kimberly?" Dek asked in response to the glossy look in her eyes.

"It's been decades, and the memory is so real. I can hear the oceans calling me home." Kimberly closed her eyes and smiled, "But first I better tend to my daughter."

Kimberly suddenly snapped her attention on Dek.

"Dek, what is the nature of your relationship with Amberly? Speak, *boy*." Kimberly put a particularly condescending twist in the word "boy," and it irked Dek. He was 24 after all, five years superior to Kimberly's daughter, and certainly had proven himself a man in his own right.

"Amberly and I aren't intimate, if that's what you mean," Dek said, barely hiding his indignant feelings. "She fancies me no doubt, and I actually think highly of her. She's sharp, probably inherited your genius wizardry, but she certainly has an attractive spirit, and a zeal for life that shines brighter than most."

"She's not the marrying kind, so don't make any long-term plans," Kimberly baited Dek, measuring his response.

"And maybe you don't know Amberly anymore," Dek said, pushing Kimberly just a little to measure her, as well. He wanted to know if she would keep her composure under pressure, if all those years in practical isolation affected her sanity, and he was testing her resolve, especially where it impacted her loved ones. What was to come would stretch the moral fabric of them all, and Dek wanted to make sure their leader's heart was as committed as her head.

When Kimberly remained silent, Dek continued, "Not that it matters. Marriage is just another old tradition that will vanish when we create this chasm between us and Earth. Apparently, you were the marrying kind, Raven One, and that was a bit surprising to Chasm – especially the Chairman."

Kimberly smiled slightly. Dek gave the right answer before the snide follow up, she thought, but his profession of belief in the common good rang true. Still, she had seen far too many intelligent men Dek's age fall to romantic notions when an attractive woman was in their sights. She used it to her advantage when she could, but otherwise, such notions just made men weak.

"If what you say is true, that Amberly would consider marriage, that's the influence of my firstborn, her disappointment of a sister, no doubt."

"The Marine, North, also seems to have somewhat of an influence on her," Dek said. "Although she was quick to betray him to get us access to this ship so we could recover you before we began our final *Magellan* operation."

Sparks was visibly frustrated, and playing with her strawberry blonde hair. She was not interested in the topic of marriage. "Can't you guys talk about Dek's social life later? I'm still not sure how we are going to be able to take *Magellan* offline and not get ourselves killed in the process. I still think it's a horrible idea, to destroy a waypoint, especially one close to Arara."

"It is a shame," Kimberly admitted. "But if we take *Magellan*, and our comrades cannot take the other waypoints between here and Arara, it will be for nothing. If it came to war, and we didn't capture *Cortes*, we would be behind enemy lines. They would starve us out. But if we destroy *Magellan*, it makes the gap too big for Earth to stage an attack. And it would take Earth three or four decades to build and replace the waypoint. By that time, we'd be ready. We would finally be free of the shackles of dear Mother Earth."

A thought dawned on Sparks, and she grew pale. "But we have teams on *Cortes*, *Marquette* and *Gilbert*. Of course, they fight for *Marquette* because it is the closest to Arara, and possibly defensible. But then would the Chairman really have ordered the destruction of *Cortes*, *Magellan* and *Gilbert*? There are like 25,000, maybe 30,000 people on those waypoints."

"There is an old Earth saying," Kimberly said, deadpan. "You have to break a few eggs to make an omelet."

"I've never even tasted eggs, well, not real ones," Dek said to no one in particular.

"I have friends on *Cortes*. Good friends. Not part of Chasm. From our cohort, Dek," Sparks said. "Are we really going to allow them to die?"

"We don't have any choice," Dek said. "There is nothing we could do about it now. But if we follow Scorched Earth Protocol, we may arrive in time with the *American Spirit* to save the Chasm loyalists, at least."

"And if Scorched Earth Protocol really is in effect, wouldn't we have heard from Chasm operators on *Gilbert*?" Sparks asked.

"In an ideal situation, yes," Kimberly said. "But Scorched Earth was never meant for an ideal situation. If the Chairman has invoked the protocol, it means she must believe that saving the waypoints is not an option or too risky to the whole operation."

"But what about —"

"Enough, Sparks!" Kimberly raised her voice, and then calmly continued. "Enough. I need to go see Amberly right now."

She rose and headed for the corridor that led to the sleeping quarters.

"Besides, I have my plan now. Go to the bridge and get us headed back toward *Magellan*. But take it slow."

Amberly was starting to recover from her state of shock. *I need to be calm, so I can be ready to do the right thing when the time comes*, Amberly thought. *I just wish I knew what the right thing was.* A rap came from the door.

"Amberly, I am coming in," Kimberly said, in the sort of tone a mother would use when she was about to spray painful disinfectant on her child's open wound.

The door slid open, Kimberly stepped in, and then the door slid closed. The two of them were alone.

Amberly looked up, tears streaming down her face. She wore one of the most pained expressions Kimberly thought she had ever seen. She sat down next to her daughter and gently took Amberly into her arms.

The last time Amberly felt the comfort of her mother's arms was six years ago, when she was a very young 13.

"Oh, Amberly," Kimberly was crying now, "I've missed you so. My dear, sweet Amberly. Oh, I know you have a million questions, and you may be very angry at me. I understand. But for now, let me just look at you."

Kimberly stood up and stepped back, holding both of Amberly's hands up. The family resemblance would be obvious to anyone with sight. Amberly's round face was clearly a younger copy of her mother's. They were the same height, and though Kimberly was nearly 30 years older, she had almost the same figure as her daughter. Although Kimberly's bust and hips were slightly larger than Amberly's, Kimberly still had more of a wiry, scrappy look to her. This was probably due to her long-term isolation where she had tight rations and plenty of time to do strength-building exercises. Amberly had felt her mother's strength through the embrace, and it was new and something she didn't remember. Her grip was powerful.

"Look at you," Kimberly said, as she took one hand and ran her fingers through Amberly's hair. "So beautiful. No wonder that Dek boy likes you. I gave you some great genes, even if you did get your father's ginger hair."

Amberly took her hands and placed them on her mother's cheeks. "Mom," she spoke slowly and deliberately, "Where is dad?"

"Your father is dead."

"What happened to him? What happened to you?"

Kimberly stepped back from Amberly and sat down on the far side of the bed.

"What happened?" Kimberly asked herself slowly, with monotone evenness. "What happened? I can't really say. It was horrible. I can't talk about it. It's too hard. Maybe later."

Kimberly stared vacantly for about 10 seconds and then shook her head as if clearing cobwebs.

"Let's talk about you! Dek tells me you are in the Science Corps now. I'm so proud."

"No mom, we need to talk about you first. I mean, you run away for six years, you were secretly part of this Chasm group, and you can't tell me how dad died. All you need to know about me right now is that I grew up while you were gone." Amberly fought to control her emotions. She had already grieved the loss of her father, but seeing her mom alive had reopened old wounds.

Kimberly stared warmly into Amberly's eyes, trying to measure the emotional fortitude of her favorite daughter. *Can she handle what is to come*, Kimberly thought, *and more importantly, will she be friend or enemy?*

Kimberly had never thought about what she would have to do if Amberly did not side with Chasm. But once she did think about it, she knew she would do the same to Amberly that she did to Joti if it came to it. If she was willing to sacrifice an entire waypoint for the cause, then surely, she knew she must be willing to sacrifice what was closest to her as well. *In a way*, Kimberly thought, *I have already proven I am willing to make the sacrifice because I was willing to walk away from a daughter I loved dearly for the most formative years of Amberly's life.*

"Fine, Amberly, fine. We'll do this your way," Kimberly said, breaking the stare and semi-reclining on the bed. "By now, you know what I think of Earth: they want to control and oppress Arara by holding us back from our true potential, teaching our young to worship their fantasy god, and denying us the technological advances that belong to all humanity. As long as we have an umbilical cord to earth — the waypoints — we will never mature and come into our own. Reliance is slavery. Arara cannot grow in the shadow of Earth. It's time for us to leave the nest, and the only way to do that is to create a chasm."

"You mean a literal chasm? You mean to … destroy the waypoints?"

"Originally, we had hoped to spare *Magellan*, only destroying *Waypoint Gilbert* to create the interstellar gap needed for Earth to leave us alone. But now it seems we have orders to destroy *Magellan*, too. And I wonder if the Chairman means to destroy all the waypoints in her reach, minimizing the chance of Earth closing the gap."

Amberly was immediately horrified at the thought. The case her mother made about how the connection to Earth retarded Arara from reaching its full potential made sense, but at what price? North, Lydia, Skip and even Kora, dead? She was about to challenge her mother's apparent inhumanity, but two thoughts flowed nearly instantaneously through her head that held her tongue.

First, Kimberly could be right. Maybe sacrificing *Magellan* was the most utilitarian action. It was hard to fathom, but Amberly was mature enough to know sometimes hard choices had to be made for the good of … the most? Second, she knew that while the woman in front of her was her mom – the woman who pushed her to excel in school, taught her to dress sharply, have manners, and be independent – she was also someone else who Amberly never saw.

Kimberly was someone who was willing to toss Joti out of an airlock for some reason unknown to Amberly. Clearly, nothing was more important to Kimberly than the cause, than Chasm. If Kimberly was willing to leave her daughters behind for Chasm for six years, there was a good chance she was willing to airlock them as well, reasoned Amberly. Either way, she knew the best thing to do now was to allow her mom to believe she leaned toward Chasm.

"Sometimes you must sacrifice the things you love most to do what is right," Kimberly said. "Perhaps even *Magellan*. She's been a true friend, and I know that she is all you know."

"Mom, it's home, my home," Amberly said. "There has be

something else that can be done."

"No, Amberly, you have never seen a *real* home," Kimberly said. "Soon, the time of sacrifice will be at an end, and we will reap the rewards of a free Arara. Do you remember what I promised you? I will take you to your true home. Mother Arara is beautiful and unspoiled – unlike Earth."

Amberly reached into her duffle bag and produced her mother's conch shell.

"I believe this is yours," Amberly said, and handed the artifact over to her mother.

Now it was Kimberly's turn to be emotional. The older Macready looked as if she would burst into tears. "Yes, your father gave me this." She traced the pearled exposed interior surface with her pale finger. She held the shell to her ear, and then slowly smiled. "I've heard the real great waters of Arara. I'll hear them again soon. I won't need this anymore."

Amberly thought for a moment. "What about the people on Arara who don't want to lose the connection to Earth? Surely there must be —"

"Yes, we may have to subdue an enemy on Arara who don't see our vision for a real future, for owning our own future. For a chance to make a perfect world. No worries. The Chairman has it in hand, if she hasn't already put her plans in motion. Don't you see, Amberly, we are finally going to be able to build the perfect society," Kimberly said as she stood up. "But enough of this. I'm tired. I need a shower, and I need to prepare for the task ahead. Please stay here until Dek or I come for you. Will you do that for me, sweetheart?"

"Mom, wait," Amberly called out. "People are going to die, right? How did you become okay with innocents dying?"

"Sweet Amberly," Kimberly said as she stepped for the door. "Death is the way of things. Plants and animals die so that we can live, eventually our forefathers die to make space for us to grow. The old way must die to make way for the new."

"What about Kora?"

"Well, hopefully she'll make the smart choice and join us," Kimberly frowned.

"And if she doesn't?"

Kimberly took the conch shell, which traveled for decades

and eight lightyears from earth, and threw it to the floor, shattering the priceless object into a thousand fragments. "Some of the old things must die."

Kimberly slid out the door.

CHAPTER ELEVEN

Skip handed North his data pad. The two were sitting in the mission prep room at Marine headquarters. The room had no viewports, but was brightly lit – too brightly lit for Skip, who preferred to work only in the soft glow of a magnetic interface screen. In the middle of the room was a cold steel table, bolted to the floor. Two rows of matching aluminum chairs surrounded the table.

Skip shook his head. "We are in deep s—"

The door slid open, interrupting Skip's expletive, and Lt. Smythe Johnson, in standard Marine uniform, came in followed by an-out-of-breath, disheveled Lydia and an amazingly well made up, composed Kora. Lydia wore a basic brown jumpsuit common for normal lab work. Kora wore a snug red dress with black stockings and a black beret.

Lt. Johnson, who commanded one of the two Marine strike units on *Magellan* (the other commanded by North), was originally from Arara, and had been stationed on *Magellan* for the last four years.

North noticed the energy-discharging stun sidearm normally carried by uniformed officers was missing on Johnson. Instead, he had an automatic rifle that used bullets. North was about to ask Johnson why he was packing solid ammunition when Lydia spoke.

"I came as soon as I could," she apologized. "I wasn't able to crack the code, but Am... er ... Kora was able to get the decoder key. Is that true?"

Skip pulled the key out of his pocket. "Bingo. And I've only decoded the newest message so far, and it's kind of cryptic, but sounds bad to me."

"What did it say?" Johnson demanded, in a commanding voice as if Skip were a Marine under his command. "Can I see that keycard?"

Skip handed the keycard to Johnson. Johnson inspected it carefully.

North pulled up the coded message on his data pad and began to read: "Dek. Meeting resistance on *Marquette*. We'll make the stand here. Initiate contingency code Scorched Earth. You have discretion on Friend or Foe protocol. Eliminate foes. Retrieve Raven One at all costs. For the future, Chairman: signature code X-120-Tiger-Alpha-321-Pi."

The blood drained from Johnson's face, and he muttered under his breath, "Scorched Earth. No."

North couldn't make out what he uttered and looked at the pale Johnson, "Come again?" But before Johnson could repeat himself, Kora jumped into the conversation.

"Well, I'm no military gal, but I don't like the 'Scorched Earth' and 'Eliminate Foes' part," Kora said.

"I am military, and I don't like it either," North fumed. "And you said Amberly left with Dek, who is no longer on *Magellan*. I knew Dek was trouble. I am going to give that guy a piece of —"

"Wait, what do you mean, 'No longer on *Magellan*,'?" Kora pressed. "Where's Amberly?"

"Apparently, someone stole the *Firebird*," North said. "My guess is Amberly and her precious Dek are on it." North could barely contain his combination of hurt and jealous anger. His fists were clenched, and his gaze was hard as his biceps.

"What? It's impossible to get a ship off this station without a pass card," Lydia said. "Even if they subdued or bribed the dock watch, the electronic safeguards wouldn't release a ship out of *Magellan* dock without it."

"Apparently," North said again, slowly for emphasis, "Amberly swiped my expired pass card and someone — maybe Dek — created a forged card."

"No way, I mean, no one is that smart. That would require someone to crack the master *Magellan* security codes," Skip said. "I mean, with those codes cracked or bypassed, someone could steal the ships, control the Tube, access the police and Marine armories, shut off power to anywhere in the *Magellan*, even turn off life support and if they were real creative, vent our atmosphere."

"Well, someone is that smart," said Lydia. "But I don't think that Amberly is in league with Dek. It seems pretty clear from the message that Dek is involved in some sort of ... conspiracy."

"Why would Amberly steal from you, North?" Johnson asked.

"Well, she didn't exactly steal the pass, she sort of swindled it from me," North's anger had turned to dejection, and slight embarrassment. "I sort of ... traded it for a kiss. I know it sounds quite idiotic when you say it out loud."

"A kiss?" Kora said knowingly. "That's interesting."

"This isn't the time," Lydia said to Kora with a half scowl.

"I saw Amberly leave with Dek, and she did seem secretive, but also under duress," Kora said. "I don't think she's involved intentionally in some sort of trouble."

"Seems like she can't make up her mind," Skip said to the table.

"Dek better have some answers," North said. "I better inform Commander Anderson."

"Are you sure this Dek is some sort of a danger to Amberly?" said Johnson. "What makes you think that?"

"Well, when I decrypt the rest of his messages, I'll know for sure," said Skip. "Let me get back over to Central Communication and I'll pull some more —"

"I'll go with you, Skip, wait till I get back from Anderson's office," North said, and he looked over at Johnson. "You coming?"

Johnson eyed Skip, Lydia and Kora skeptically. "You guys should all wait here until we get back."

North and Johnson took off down the hall towards the commanding officer's quarters and office.

"Shoot," Skip said. "Johnson didn't give me the encryption keycard back."

Anderson sat at his desk. He was a quiet man, and at 83, was the oldest serving officer in the Marines on any waypoint. A bit of grey stubble grew on his face and his shaved head. His eyes were small and dark and calm.

"So, you helped this Amberly girl steal a Valkyrie?" Anderson said evenly, but with an intensity that revealed his anger.

"I'm sorry sir," North said. "But I didn't help her. And I think she may be operating under duress." He stood at attention, looking straightforward.

"Wasn't it her mother that was responsible for our last Valkyrie disappearing? Do you know if this one is coming back?" Anderson said, disappointment filling the air.

"Commander, perhaps we should summon the Wing Commander here," Johnson suggested. "We should get some corvettes out looking in the Spencer Belt for our missing bird. And shouldn't we inform the XO as well —"

"Good idea. Get Jindal down here. But no need to bother Rita," Anderson said, pleased with Johnson. Anderson was a man of action, who respected other men of action, who worked quickly to solve issues before they evolved into problems.

Johnson produced his infopad and started sending a message to *Magellan's* Wing Commander, Devansh Jindal, who led a unit of 10 combat-rated pilots, though none had ever seen action outside of a simulator.

"Jindal indicates he'll be here in a moment, sir," Johnson said.

"Sir, with all due respect, I think we have a bigger problem," North said. "This message that my friend Skip intercepted and decoded indicates there may be some larger conspiracy threatening the *Magellan*."

"I need hard evidence, North. What do you have?" Anderson sounded skeptical.

"Besides the message and the theft of *Firebird*, nothing," North sighed. "But we have a military-grade decryption key that belongs to a transient from the *American Spirit*, a Dek Tigona. I was just about to head down with Skip to Central Communication to see if we can decode some more of his messages."

"North, do you have no sense of what you are asking?" Anderson stood up now, and some of the calm was leaving his voice. "Do you know what the governor will do if he finds I authorized snooping though civilian communiqués without an appropriate warrant? The guy already wants to do away with the Marines altogether and absorb us into the civilian police force. I better talk to the governor first. I am already on notice with those guys after the bar fight you started last week."

"Sir, Croix had it coming —" North was interrupted with a finger from Anderson indicating he wasn't interested.

Jindal entered the room. "Reporting for duty, sir."

"Devansh, please sit down," Anderson said, motioning for a chair. "We have a missing Valkyrie I need your flyboys to hunt down."

"Missing?" said Jindal as he took the chair indicated. "Which one?"

"The *Firebird*."

"Awww, that's my favorite."

"I want you to sweep the Spencer Belt, I can't imagine where else they could be hiding. It's not like they'd make a run for deep space," Anderson stated the obvious.

"Now, show me this message key you have," Anderson said and turned and looked to North and Johnson.

Johnson pulled the device from his pocket and slowly set the device on the edge of Anderson's desk.

Then in a snap, Johnson brought the butt of his automatic rifle down hard on the key, shattering it into worthless pieces.

"What the hell!?!" said North. Anderson looked taken aback, trying to figure out what Johnson was doing. Jindal had a disinterested look on his face. In a split second, North surmised Johnson's motive, and North's hand went for his sidearm. But North wasn't fast enough.

Johnson had already flipped his gun around and disabled the safety. He loosed a spray of bullets at the heads of the seated officers. Several punctured into the brains of both Anderson and Jindal.

North's right arm suddenly erupted in pain, causing him to drop his energy gun to the floor. He had taken a bullet to the elbow, had suddenly lost the use of his lower arm, and his blood spurted out over the now dead bodies of Anderson and Jindal. Jindal's body had fallen out of his aluminum chair and now laid face first on the floor.

"You bastard! You're one of them."

Johnson leveled his gun at North and smiled. "Correct."

At the same moment, North let his body drop to the floor and Johnson's second spray of bullets only ended up grazing North's ear. Ignoring the pain in his arm, North swung his legs so they caught the chair just occupied by Jindal not even a minute ago. His shin pushed the chair solidly and it flew into the legs of Johnson causing him to stumble forward onto the ground and lose control of his gun. A few shots went off as Johnson hit the ground, but none of them hit targets. Johnson's face slammed into the cold steel floor and his mouth began to bleed.

North struggled to get to his feet, almost passing out from the intense pain in his elbow, where blood still flowed freely. Johnson rubbed his mouth as he started to rise, noticing that he too was bleeding, though not profusely. Johnson thought that North might go for the automatic rifle, so he started to scoot towards it, knowing that he could beat North to it.

North however, wasn't going for the gun. He threw himself at Johnson, and landed on the back of the crawling man. Johnson tried to free himself, but couldn't quickly escape with the 190 pounds of North straddling his back.

"Get off me, you lug!"

"Why? So you can kill me too?"

"We are all going to die, moron."

Using his left hand, North began to wail on Johnson, hitting the pinned man on the temple with powerful left hooks, until the fourth shot knocked Johnson unconscious. "Dirt licker."

North found some binders in Anderson's drawers and cuffed Johnson. Then he ripped off the sleeve of Jindal's shirt and wrapped it around his upper right arm in an attempt to make a tourniquet. He was already feeling woozy and lightheaded from blood loss.

North attempted to assess the situation. Clearly Johnson and whoever he worked for was attempting to eliminate as much of the senior leadership of the Marines as possible in advance of who knows what, North thought. With Anderson and Jindal gone, it was just him, the murderer Johnson and XO Rita Moreno, the chief of base operations.

He was about to comm Moreno, when the thought struck him that maybe the reason she wasn't here already was because she was in on whatever Johnson had planned. If they took North out, they would control the resources of the Marines.

But if she wasn't compromised, then he could use her help. He couldn't take the chance. Instead he decided to comm one of his own grunts, someone he could trust completely, like Eli Wong.

"Eli," he spoke into his infopad. "I need you in the commander's office immediately. Come armed and come silent. I'll fill you in when you get here. And bring a first aid kit, too. Hurry."

"Yes sir," came the deep, drawled voice of Wong. "Is everything okay, sir?"

"No. Hurry."

North righted the chair that he used to take out Johnson, and lifted Johnson's limp body into it. Johnson was starting to regain consciousness. North grabbed a second and third set of binders, and used one to link the binders around Johnson's hands to the chair. The other he used to bind the chair to the late Anderson's desk.

North recovered the automatic rifle, sat down in Anderson's chair, and punched up the communication terminal, entering his own password into the magnetic screen. He called up Skip's communicator.

"Skip, are you there?" he said, as he looked around for something to clean some of the blood from his hands and face. The red splatter was everywhere and was starting to thicken and congeal.

"What's up?"

"Grab Lydia and Kora and get to Commander Anderson's office. It's just down the hall and to the right from the conference room. Hurry. I've been shot and Anderson and the Wing Commander are dead."

"What?!" Skip said, shocked and confused, "Dead?"

"Hurry. We're in dan–"

North didn't finish his sentence, but instead fell to the floor, stunned by an electronic side arm. Every nerve in his body felt like it was exposed to the vacuum of space, and he writhed on the floor, conscious, but unable to control his body. He saw three Marines, one with his weapon drawn, clearly the one who had shot North.

These three were part of Johnson's unit – Mooney, Phan and Boro. Mooney was of Irish descent, but was third generation *Magellan*. He was an average build and otherwise unremarkable. Phan, who had shot North, was short and muscular, Asian – probably of Vietnamese descent. He joined the Marines after being recruited on Arara. Boro was dark skinned, tall and muscular. His ancestors left earth on *Waypoint Cortes* centuries ago, and all they had ever known since was life on the waypoints.

North was trying to piece together what was going on and force himself to recover from the stun gun's effects. But he couldn't control any of his muscles and still involuntarily twitched on the floor, as if having a seizure. The pain had subsided slightly, but North could tell he would soon lose consciousness as his body went into shock.

Johnson was fully awake now, and North, lying on the floor, could see Johnson's men freeing their supervising officer from the binders.

North heard the now free Johnson give some orders to the trio of Marines.

"Just bash his head in or something," Johnson said to Boro.

"Kill him? Are you sure? I don't know," Boro said. "It isn't right. North was a Marine like us and at least he should have the dignity of dying on his feet."

"You dirty idiot," Johnson said and uttered a string of expletives at the dark-skinned man. "Scorched Earth means that they are going to destroy *Magellan*. We don't have time for traditional obsolete notions of honor. Kill or be killed, survival of the fittest time. Get it done. Phan, we need to go kill his friends waiting in the briefing room. And then both of you meet me in the hangar bay so we can find out what the plan is when *Firebird* gets back. Mooney, Boro is going soft. Please off that knuckle-dragger North."

Johnson seemed unsteady, but put his arm around Phan. "We must move quickly, or this will all be for nothing." The two of them left the room.

Boro looked at Mooney, who had picked up the automatic rifle and pointed it squarely at North's head. North still did not have enough control of his body to speak, but his eyes were wide and defiant.

Boro spoke, "Don't do it, Mooney. He deserves better. Let's get out of here before we run into someone from North's unit."

Mooney just laughed. "North has always been a self-righteous traditional prick. It's going to be great to bury him in the past he loves so much."

Boro grabbed Mooney's arm, pointing the gun away from North.

"What the hell, Boro?"

"It doesn't have to be like this," Boro said. "We can liberate ourselves from Earth without violence. It isn't right."

Mooney jerked the gun out of Boro's grasp. "You see, Boro,

you never really were one of us, were you? There is no right and wrong. There is just might. The mighty will define morality, not some misguided sense of tradition, based on some magical dead god."

Boro started to talk, "I'm not saying that—"

"Just shut up," Mooney fumed, condescension dripping in saliva droplets from the corner of his mouth. "You have so much to learn. Raven One will teach you."

Mooney turned and looked at North. Madness sparkled in Mooney's glassy green eyes. He slammed the butt of the rifle into North's face, making a loud cracking sound that triggered a reflexive smirk on Mooney's face. "I'd say 'See you in hell' but there is no hell, North. There is only oblivion. You are over." Mooney was glib, almost intoxicated at the thought of wielding the ultimate irreversible power over someone else. He was taking his time, enjoying the sick rush of depriving someone of life – a tactical mistake.

Mooney's index finer caressed the gun's trigger, and his eyes were fixed on North. "Who is going to stop me?"

North closed his eyes.

"Wha…" Mooney started to utter, when his torso caught the full force of strong-armed shove. Boro's powerful two-armed underhanded swing lifted Mooney off the ground and tossed him over the administrator's desk into a corner. Mooney clutched at the gun, but lost his grip. The weapon skidded to a rest near the dead bodies of Jindal and Anderson.

"No!" Boro shouted. "You will not kill today."

North noticed he was reflexively clenching his hand into a tight fist, and then he realized the effects of the stun blast were starting to wear off. With great concentration, he lifted his left hand to his chin, and rubbed it. He felt hot blood, his own, oozing from a gash on the left side of his face. The movement came with intense pain, and North almost passed out. *Focus on what's important*, North thought. He thought about having drinks with his friends, Skip, Lydia and Kora, at Rick's. He started to force himself to stand, only to have screaming pain explode through his whole body. *Focus on what you love.*

And he thought about Amberly – her beautiful form, her round face, her intense green eyes, each curl of her radiant red hair. He thought about how he would never understand the complexity of her thoughts and feelings, how he could never match the power of her brilliant spirit, and how he would never be good enough for her.

And then he thought about Dek, and how he tricked Amberly or kidnapped her or was taking advantage of her somehow, and his feelings of love turned to anger, then rage. The pain meant nothing to him now — North would find Amberly, save her if he could, and Dek, the pretender, would pay dearly for his transgressions.

North stood fully erect now, large and imposing, like a wounded animal, ready to strike for the kill.

Boro turned from a shell-shocked Mooney, who was painfully moaning in the corner, and saw the rising North, anger burning bright in his bloodied face. In a flash of self-defense, Boro grabbed the rifle and pointed it at North's heaving chest.

When he saw that North was not going to pounce, Boro slowly pointed the rifle down and then at himself as he offered the weapon, butt end, to North.

"I'm sorry, sir," Boro said, as North took the weapon. Boro clasped his hands behind his head, interlocking his fingers, and kneeling on the ground, in an obvious position of surrender.

"No, you fool! Why didn't you kill him?" Mooney had come around, and in a quick motion had drawn his stun pistol and taken cover behind the desk. Mooney took aim at North.

Exposed and with no real place for cover in the tight quarters, North had no choice. If he hesitated, Mooney would stun him, and this time Mooney would not delay in recovering the gun and putting some hot lead in North's skull.

North did not hesitate.

He let loose a spray of bullets that tore up the commander's desk. He unloaded the clip and the gun fell silent. Mooney's stun gun fell from his loosened grip and toppled to an exposed patch of floor. Mooney's body followed, with a half dozen holes oozing life, as the man slumped to the floor. North dropped the automatic rifle, and kneeled at Mooney's side. Boro did the same, propping up Mooney's head.

Mooney weakly coughed up some blood.

"I hope … I'm right…," he gasped at the two men huddling

over him, "… that there … is … no … he… he… hell." His body grew limp, but his eyes were wild and afraid. "Hope … I'm… right." His eyes grew distant. Mooney was gone.

North closed his eyes, and mouthed what looked like a silent prayer. He stood again, looked at Boro, and then collapsed from the pain and blood loss.

"Boro…" North said, "If you could get me to the briefing room, that would be good."

Boro was a strong man, but North was a big man. Boro gently leaned his shoulder into North's abdomen and then with a heave and a grunt tossed him over his shoulder and carried him out into the hall and down toward the briefing room.

As they were walking out, Tricia Moreville, a short woman of medium build with nearly white hair, came running up. Moreville was on Anderson's executive staff.

She gasped loudly when she saw the bloody North hoisted over Boro's shoulder like a sack of potatoes.

"You better call the XO and get her down her," Boro said. "Anderson is dead. Jindal is dead. Johnson did it, and he got away."

"Did I hear North right? Did he just say Commander Anderson is dead?" Skip said, putting his hand on his chest in a vain attempt to slow his rapidly increased breathing. He tapped his comm unit, but the connection to North had been cut.

Lydia was shocked. Murder was rare on a waypoint, and for someone who represented the safety and security of the *Magellan* to be murdered in his own stronghold was particularly jarring.

The cool head of the trio was Kora, who quickly closed all the doors to the mission prep room. She turned to Skip. "Is there any way to lock these down?" she asked, indicated the sliding doors.

"Why would you want to lock them down?" Skip asked.

"Because whoever killed Anderson may want to kill us too," Kora said.

"I'll try," Skip said and pulled out his infopad and tried to interface with the doors' locking mechanisms. "I don't think I can do it."

"Keep trying. Lydia, call the police and tell them what is going on."

Lydia clutched Kora's arm. "Is North dead? Is this all about that message? Do you think they killed Amberly?"

Kora pushed away those thoughts. "On second thought," she said, looking at the tall and gracefully formidable Lydia, "I'll send the message to security. You see if you can find something heavy to swing in case we have to fight."

"Hey, I actually got the locking mechanisms on," Skip said with some surprise in his voice. "But anyone with an access card will be able to unlock it."

Lydia looked around the room. There was nothing in the room but the table and chairs. The table had a built-in magnetic resonance display and, Lydia noted, was bolted to the ground. The chairs, on the other hand, were not bolted to the ground. She lifted one up — it was made of lightweight aluminum, but she imagined she could do some damage on someone if she flung it.

Kora noticed Lydia considering the chair's heft. "That's my girl," Kora said, then she used her info pad to start a voice chat on the emergency channel. "Huh? It is giving me this weird error message." She handed her infopad to Skip.

"Yeah, someone locked down communications in the Marine base as some sort of security precaution," Skip said as his fingers fluttered over the info pad's flatscreen. "Yep, see here. Lt. Johnson ordered the lockdown, and we'll have to get his permission to bypass this. We really ought to try to find out what happened to North."

Lydia wasn't so sure. "Maybe he's okay. Maybe he'll call back."

Just then, the door unlocked. Someone had used a code to open Skip's door hack. Lydia picked up a chair. Skip crouched behind the table on the opposite side of the room's door. Kora spun around a chair, sat down facing the door.

The door flew open, and standing in the door was a bloody Lt. Johnson with an unfamiliar Marine.

Skip looked visibly relieved to see a Marine officer instead of the rogue attacker who had apparently killed Anderson and Jindal. "Thank goodness it's you," he sighed.

"Are you okay?" Kora said, looking at the blood-soaked Johnson. "What happened?"

"I can't talk about it now," Johnson said. "I need to go get some help. This is private Phan. He'll make sure you are all safe. Please stay in this room with him until help arrives." Johnson turned back toward the door, and moved in double-time.

"Wait!" Skip called out. "Can you unlock the communications block so we can call for help?"

"Sorry," Johnson called back as the door slid closed, "Security protocol."

Johnson was gone.

CHAPTER TWELVE

Phan nervously smiled at Skip, Lydia and Kora. "Why doesn't everyone take a seat? I'd like to ask you some questions to see if we can figure out what is going on here."

Phan indicated the chairs that faced the door, and the trio sat down as instructed, Skip between the two women.

Phan paced behind the three of them. Skip craned his neck to keep eye contact, clearly uncomfortable with Phan's pacing out of his sight. Kora was a little unnerved by Phan slipping behind her and her seated companions. Lydia, on the other hand, sat straight up and looked ahead, not seeming to be bothered at all.

"I need to know what you know about … Chasm," Phan said, with an edge of menace hanging in his voice. "And who you've told."

"I don't like your tone, Private," Kora said, standing up. "What happened to North? Do you know? Did you see him?"

"Are you with North? Did you know he killed Commander Anderson and Wing Commander Jindal?" Phan lied.

"Bull dirt," Kora said. "North would never …"

"I saw it with my own eyes," Phan said, and drew his stun gun and aimed it at Kora. "Now sit down before I am forced to use this."

Phan waved the gun at the chair.

"Are you kidding me?" Skip said. "I want to see my legal counselor. You can't keep us here at gunpoint."

Phan just grunted. "Sit down," he threatened. Kora complied.

"We don't know anything about Chasm. Is that what you want to hear?" Kora said. "Do you know if that is what Dek Tigona is involved in? He kidnapped my sister."

"I believe you don't know anything about Chasm," Phan said. "But Dek didn't kidnap your sister. She went of her own accord."

"What?" Kora stood up again. "How do you know that?"

"Because Dek is Chasm. And so am I," Phan said, pointing his gun again directly at Kora. "And now, I am sorry to say I am going to have to kill you. It's for the greater good."

At this, Skip stood up, and Phan waved the stun gun in Skip's direction.

"Don't make this harder than it is. Accept your fate. I am not an evil murderer," Phan said, almost as if he was trying to convince himself of something that he didn't really believe. "Please, I will stun you first, so you will be unconscious, so your death will be painless. If you are one of those crazy religious people, you have about 30 seconds to pray to your god."

Skip was defiant. He stood and pointed a finger at Phan's chest. "You better hope someone gets North before he gets you. He will rearrange your anatomy before he airlocks you into oblivion. North will —"

Skip was interrupted by a bolt of energy from the stun gun. He cried out from the burning sensation coursing through his nervous system, then his eyes rolled back into his head and he fell awkwardly to the floor, convulsing.

Lydia was still sitting straight up in her chair, with her back to Phan. She was like a mannequin, fixed and unmoving and saying nothing. Kora was kneeling next to the table now, taking Phan up on his offer. Her head was bowed and her hands were folded. She was praying softly, but not inaudibly. "Dear Father in heaven, I pray for my dear sister Amberly. I pray that she would come to believe in you. May your angels protect her."

Although he was an atheist, Phan wasn't anti-religious like many of the Chasm operatives were. In the old regime, he always had advocated a live-and-let-live compromise position between people of "faith" and people like him. That compromise position had ended a bloody civil war hundreds of years ago on Earth, and the sacred and the secular were both given space under the then newly formed North American alliance. But Phan firmly believed that a pure world, one without religion, which Chasm was building on Arara, would be a better world — a much better world.

Phan didn't have many religious friends, so hearing a prayer was a novelty to him, and he decided to wait for Kora to finish before stunning her next.

"Lord, please forgive this man. His eyes are closed, and he doesn't know what he does. Give me courage now. Amen."

Phan was genuinely surprised to see Kora pray specifically for him, even as she faced death.

Lydia slowly slipped off her chair, as if to join Kora in prayer, but instead of falling on her knees, she simply squatted and clutched the chair back. Phan admired Lydia's body, tall and muscular, and for a brief moment entertained a a romantic fantasy in his mind.

In that moment, Lydia took her chance.

The blonde flung the chair right at Phan's head. He threw his arms up, and the chair smashed into his forearm, causing a brief sharp pain and knocking him back a meter. Much to Lydia's dismay, he held the gun tight.

Lydia jumped at Phan as he was trying to regain his footing, but she was too far away to catch him before he could aim and fire his stun gun, and in less than a second Lydia was convulsing on the floor next to Skip.

Phan wasn't going to take any more chances. He pointed the gun at Kora and pulled the trigger. Kora shrieked in pain, and then collapsed with her companions. The three were incapacitated on the floor, and Phan felt a sense of urgency. He had toyed around with them too much, and he had forgotten that Scorched Earth protocol was in place. He would have to move quickly or he was in danger of joining these three in their impending deaths.

Phan had a sheathed four-inch knife attached to his belt, and knelt next to Skip's head. He exposed the knife's shiny, serrated blade and moved to pull it across Skip's neck.

He heard the meeting room door slide open and a voice boom behind him.

"Don't do it Phan," said the voice, which Phan immediately recognized as fellow Marine and North suck-up Eli Wong. Phan decided to try to surprise Wong by quickly spinning around and throwing the knife at Wong's head. Phan thought he could take out or at least distract Wong enough to give himself the time he needed to draw his stun gun. Quickly triangulating Wong's location, based on his voice and knowing that Wong was likely standing in the door, Phan put his plan in action.

He whirled around in a blur and his arm was in motion when he suddenly felt one of his knees give out. The knife, misdirected as Phan lost the ability to remain erect, careened harmlessly off the wall and came to a rest near Wong's feet.

As Phan went down, he realized his mistake. Wong was not

alone. Executive Officer Rita Moreno, chief of base operations, stood next to Wong holding a bullet-based assault rifle trained on Phan. She fired it again, this time the bullet capped Phan's other knee. Phan screamed in pain as he lay on the floor, clutching his left leg. That bullet ripped clear through his thigh, the entry and exit point bleeding. His right knee took the second bullet, and now all that was left was a sausage factory of sinew, cartilage and ligaments.

Moreno was a sharp-featured olive-skinned woman in her late-30s. She had not had time to don her military uniform when Anderson's assistant, Tricia, had burst into her quarters on the far side of the base. Instead, Moreno wore a jade green kimono robe that seemed out of place with the all-purpose work boots she slipped on after recovering her assault rifle. She had ordered Tricia to gather the remaining Marines in North's strike team and then go report to North.

Moreno ran into Wong on the way to Commander Anderson's office, and as they passed near the briefing room, they heard the chair Lydia had flung hit the interior wall, and went to investigate.

Moreno flipped the safety on her gun.

"Secure Phan," she ordered Wong. "Get him stable. I want to interrogate him. Now." Wong nodded at Moreno and proceeded to handcuff Phan, and then tend to his wound using a first aid kit attached to the bottom of the conference table.

"Wong, I need you to get a medic here on the double," Moreno said. "We need to lock this base down. Now get going Marine."

"Yes, ma'am," Wong replied and immediately exited.

Moreno checked the pulse of Lydia, Kora and Skip, relieved to find them all alive and as well as could be expected for three people who had taken a stun bolt at point blank range.

Moreno accessed the emergency control through the magnetic screen on the conference table and offered a palm to be scanned and then keyed in a password. A menu came up offering several options, and she noticed briefly that the communication security lock had been engaged. She pressed the "BASE GENERAL QUARTERS" and immediately a klaxon sounded, followed by a recorded voice announcing, "General Quarters, this is not a drill. Please report to your stations immediately."

Moreno hoped that whoever had killed Anderson and Jindal could be captured before escaping out of Marine Headquarters. The general quarters locked down the entire base, including the adjacent *Magellan* Central Command, from where most of the station's functions — such as life support, port control, and communications — could be overridden from the decentralized control centers scattered around the waypoint.

The door began to buzz with someone entering the access code on the outside wall. Moreno drew her weapon, flipped off the safety and leveled it at the door as it slid open.

Standing in the door was Private Boro, holding a poorly patched up North.

"Boro," Moreno gave orders reflexively, "Lay North down on the table."

Moreno, who was incredibly strong for a woman of her stature, jerked Phan off the table and into a chair. Phan screamed in pain.

"Sorry about that," Moreno said dryly to Phan.

Boro, as gently as possible, set North on the table, relief flowing through his stressed muscles as they lowered the heavy Marine.

Moreno re-cuffed Phan's arms behind the chair back. He started to laugh uncomfortably. "Boro is one of us... auuggghhmfp." The pain of his torn flesh interrupted his sentence.

Boro frowned, and immediately clasped his hands behind his head, and knelt as before. "I surrender myself per military code title four, section 2A. I am sorry. I should be charged with treason."

Moreno looked around. She had three stunned civilians lying on the floor, one murderous traitor handcuffed to a chair, another who had just taken a surrender position, and one of the waypoint's strike commanders bleeding out on the table. She didn't have another set of handcuffs and she knew that it could be five minutes before Wong came back with a medic. Moreno couldn't take a chance. She took the stun sidearm from North's belt and pointed it at Boro.

"Sorry. You ready for a nap until we sort this out?"

North raised a weak arm and pushed on Moreno.

"He's alright," he said, smiling at Boro. "He saved me from that dirt licker's partner…" North waved a few fingers in Phan's direction. He moaned slightly and closed his eyes.

"Boro, I'm watching you closely," Moreno said, "only because North vouched for you."

"I understand," Boro said calmly. "How can I help?"

"Get those civilians upright and revived from the stun bolts Phan no doubt hit them with."

Boro silently got to work.

Moreno grabbed the first aid kit Wong had procured and started pulling out medical supplies. As she did, she started shouting intensely at Phan. "Tell me everything about this Chasm group now."

"I'm not talking," Phan said, and spit in the general direction of Moreno.

"I'll tell you everything, XO," Boro offered.

"Go ahead and tell them. It doesn't matter. Soon we'll all be dead, I suspect. If she makes it back, she'll make sure we go through with Scorched Earth protocol," Phan blabbered.

Moreno taped healing gauze to North's elbow and moved next to Phan, drawing the stun gun she had taken from North. Phan eyed the stun gun. "If you stun me," he said, "I will never wake up before we are all dead."

"What is the Scorched Earth protocol? How many Chasm agents are on *Magellan*?" Moreno barked questions.

Phan silently bowed his head and said nothing. Moreno turned to Boro.

"I don't know what Scorched Earth protocol is. Sounds like bad news," Boro said as he propped Lydia against the wall. "But Chasm I do know. Our ultimate goal is to divide and separate from Earth, making it impossible for Earth to influence the future development of Arara. We are going to make a real Utopia. A beautiful place where there is no money, no war, where everyone has a place, and the smartest people have the power they need to build systems that help us all. No more popularity contest elections, where the rich influence with secret power. We've been planning this moment for generations."

Boro hung his head shamefully. "But I didn't know it would

come to this … cold blooded murder."

"Not murder. We take life only because it serves the common good, not randomly or out of some sort of righteous fury," Phan seethed. "Don't impose Earth's binary morality on us."

"I know what you believe, Phan," Boro said calmly and evenly. "And it sounded like wisdom. But look around you now. How much death has happened already? How much more to come? My brain understands what you say, but my soul … my soul… convicts me."

"How dirty stupid can you be! There is no soul. That religious myth made people slaves to for centuries, for millennia," Phan said, struggling in his restraints. "So what if more people die. Individuals do not matter. Only the great Arara rising matters. Only the common good, which Chasm will define when this day is done. Raven One is returning soon and when she does, you will all be —"

Phan started to twitch and then slumped in his chair.

Moreno holstered the discharged stun gun. "I've heard enough from this traitor," she said.

North forced his eyes open again, and exchanged a glance with Moreno, letting her know he was okay. North spoke to Boro in a commanding tone. It was clear he was weak from his recent injuries, but there was a steel resolve in his voice. "How many Chasm operatives are there? Speak now, private."

"I don't know for sure, but I suspect maybe 100 or 200 well-trained sleepers on *Magellan*. Some have been here for decades," Boro said. "We brought another 500 from Arara on the *American Spirit*. The plan was to take control of this waypoint. And *Cortez*, and *Marquette*. We were going to force evacuate *Gilbert* and then destroy it in space. But something has gone wrong… I think Scorched Earth may be a contingency plan."

North painfully sat up from the table. "I need some water," he said, focusing back on Moreno. She pulled a silver pouch filled with an electrolyte-infused drink from the first aid kit and handed it to North. He took a swig, and then turned to Boro.

"Seven hundred against a few dozen civilian police and less than 100 Marines." he thought out loud. "I don't like those odds. And who knows how many traitors we have in our Corps."

"Where are your weapons?" Moreno jumped in. "Is the plan

still on?"

"As far as I know ma'am. I was on the lowest level of need-to-know. There is a secret armory on the *American Spirit* with probably enough firearms for a thousand."

"Who are your leaders? Who is running the show?" Moreno demanded.

"We have several cell leaders, I don't know who they are. My cell leader was Johnson. Half of his unit are Chasm," Boro said.

"Good, that's means we should still have 30 strike Marines who are loyal," North said, sitting up. The painkillers and stimulants Moreno had administered were starting to kick in.

"That's assuming none of your unit is sleeper Chasm," Moreno said.

"My guys are solid. None of them are capable of being traitors," North said defensively.

"I hope you are right," Moreno said, nervously running her fingers through her short dark brown hair. "The leaders, Boro?"

"The cells reported to the *Magellan* Triumvirate – sort of a three-headed command group. Raven One, that's a code name and I don't know who she is, except that she went deep undercover several years ago. She is the *Magellan* leader. Also, a merchant named Joti, he was in charge of intelligence. In addition to leading his own cell, Johnson was in charge of coordinating the muscle. I know that on the *American Spirit*, they had a Triumvirate as well. Dek Tigona was the *Spirit's* leader, and their military operations director was some woman by the name of Sparks, I think that was a code name, too. And the third member was the *American Spirit's* captain. Järvinen."

"Captain Järvinen? And that dirthead, Dek Tigona," North growled his rival's name with guttural disdain. "Now I have a real excuse to put a bullet into that traitor's head."

"North, we'll bring this Dek character to justice," Moreno warned the injured Marine in a calming manner. "But remember your rules of engagement."

Lydia started to stir, supremely groggy and suffering from disorienting pain, typical side effects from a blast from a stun gun. "North? You're not dead…" she croaked. She tried to stand, but almost immediately collapsed. Boro lunged and caught her. She smiled at him as he moved her into a chair.

Skip had also come around. "This is the worst hangover I've ever had." He successfully tried to stand, and leaned over the table North was sitting on. He laid his hand on North's uninjured arm, partially to steady himself, partially as a quasi-embrace with his best friend.

"I'm glad to see you are alive," Skip weakly smiled at North. "What is going on?" North nodded his head toward Boro and Moreno.

Moreno continued her interrogation of Boro. "What else?"

"Also, you should know that Raven One, the leader of Chasm on *Magellan*, personally cracked the master waypoint controls five or six years ago," Boro explained. "So, if Chasm can secure the Central Command, they will be able to control the station electronically, blocking communications —"

"— or turning off life support," North completed.

"Impossible," Moreno said. "The command protocols are uncrackable. I mean, it would take centuries."

"Raven One?" Skip asked, "Why the code name?"

Lydia, who was tending to the still unconscious Kora, ventured her opinion. "I suppose it's so if someone intercepted a message, like we did, that operative wouldn't be compromised."

"Well, I've sounded general quarters, so Central Command is locked down right now. I better get down there and take command of this situation as soon as possible. North, can you gather your strike team and bring them to secure Cencomm until we figure out what is going on?"

"Yes, ma'am. But we need to make sure you have armed escort. Johnson is still on the loose, and he's already killed two officers. If you are lost, God forbid, I'll have to take command of all the Marines on *Magellan*. I do not want that responsibility."

"You are right of course," Moreno said. "Wong should be back soon. And I have Tricia rounding up the rest of your strike team."

North put pressure on his wound, causing him to wince. He asked Boro, "How in the world did they crack the code? And why didn't they take over the station then?"

"You don't understand. Raven One is beyond genius," Boro said, his words painted with awe and reverence. "Everything is about timing. They needed a way to get enough troops out to secure a waypoint by force if need be. Also, we wanted to make sure there wasn't time for the waypoints to ready a resistance. Finally, we needed a ship to get people off *Gilbert*, which was to be destroyed, scorched earth or not."

"The *Magnus*," Skip said. "I've noticed that the transmission date stamps and the computer's telemetry on the ship's likely position have never matched up. I always assumed it was some sort of relativity effect. And it's on the way. Is it possible that *Gilbert* is already gone?" Moreno and Boro spun around, and North turned his head quickly towards Skip.

Kora was coming around as well. Moreno pulled some pills from the first aid kit, and distributed them to the trio.

"Chew this," Moreno said. "It should reduce the side effects of the stun gun." Kora pulled herself into a chair with an assist from Lydia. The brunette reached over and gave North's hand a reassuring squeeze.

The door chime went off, and the room's intercom sounded. Tricia's voice came over the speaker. "North, are you in there?"

Moreno unlocked the door and opened it, revealing a frazzled Tricia flanked by five members of North's strike force, decked in full assault armor and each armed with an automatic assault rifle.

"Thank God," North said.

"Commander, are you all right?" asked one of North's troops, Mac Dillington, Flora's older brother. The other troops expressed similar sentiments until North raised his hand.

"I'm all right, guys," he said. For an officer, North was friendly with his subordinates to a fault – at least that is what Anderson had told him on several occasions. He acted more like a friend than a commanding officer. Still North engendered great loyalty among his troops, several of which were a decade older than their young team leader.

"What is going on?" Mac asked. "Anderson and Jindal are dead?"

"Johnson killed them," North said. "I saw it. He tried to kill me, too, but Boro saved me."

"I don't understand," Kora said. "What does this Chasm group want?"

"They want to cut off ties with Earth by destroying a few waypoints," North replied, "so they can reorder Arara society into some socially engineered super utopia and –"

Moreno cut him off. "North, I have a plan, and we are going to have to move quickly. Most of the passengers are off the *American Spirit*, and I can only hope that those loyal to Chasm are among those who have disembarked. If they are going to take *Magellan* by force, they'll need to get to their weapons, which Boro has said are still on the *American Spirit*."

"But what if they are just going to destroy *Magellan*, not take it over?" Skip asked nervously.

"I'm betting that the Chasm operatives want to live to see their grand Arara rise, if possible, so they'll want to be well on their way on the *American Spirit* before they destroy *Magellan*. And unless they have a nuclear weapon tucked away on the ship, the only way they can destroy *Magellan* is to trigger some catastrophic event from Central Command, like forcing a reactor explosion or venting the atmosphere."

"No, they need *Magellan* gone, not just incapacitated," North said. "They must want to blow the whole station to kingdom come, and the only way to do that is to overload the reactor. And if Boro is right, they have the codes to do it."

"It would be a lot easier to use a nuke," Mac said.

"No way they have a nuke on *American Spirit*," Skip spoke up. "Radiation alarms would have picked it up as soon as they were within a few hundred kilometers from *Magellan*."

"Unless Raven One had somehow tampered with the monitors," Boro suggested. "My colleagues will stop at nothing, take any risk, sacrifice their very lives if needed to build the perfect Earth on Arara. Do not underestimate their resolve."

"Either way," Moreno said, wanting to end the conversation and get into action, "we will have strategic victory as long as we secure the Command Center and keep anyone from boarding or leaving the *American Spirit*. I am going to take these five with me to secure central command." Moreno indicated the five Marines that had come with Moreville.

"Once I have Cencomm, I'll start coordinating with the civilian government. This is going to get messy." Moreno took North's hand. "North, you round up the rest of your troops, and position yourself in the docks and make sure no one gets on *American Spirit*. Hold the landing bay. Nothing lands and nothing takes off without my authorization."

"Understood," North replied.

"When Wong gets back, send him to coordinate with the MPs and Boro to attempt to apprehend any Marines Boro says are turncoats. Boro will you be willing to give us the names of your conspirators?"

"I don't know them all, but those I know, yes," Boro said with a bit of shame, head hanging.

"North, wait for Wong to get back, get whatever medical help you need, and then secure the landing bay," Moreno said, as she exited the briefing room with the Marines and Tricia in tow. "Now let's see if we can stop this revolution before it begins."

CHAPTER THIRTEEN

Amberly awoke alone in the room that had become somewhat of a holding cell for her on the *Firebird*. Her mother, the so-called Raven One, had ordered Sparks and Dek to keep Amberly locked in the plain sleeping quarters, under threat of airlock.

Amberly shivered. The room was cold. She slid off the thin bed and walked over to the computer console and tried to log in again. She had to get some message to Kora or, better yet, North, that *Magellan* was in danger. Her biometric password was rejected again. Still locked out. She wondered if she could find out where Joti hid her infopad, Verne.

She moved toward the lavatory door, opposite the room's access door to the hallway. She activated the sink, an upward-facing semi-sphere, with its flat side covered. She waved a hand, and the cover retracted. Another wave and a small jet of pressurized water shot up. Amberly cupped some water in her hand and then splashed her face. She tapped the sink, and the cover returned. The runoff water in the sink was vacuumed out.

Amberly was still trying to reason out her mother's plan. When she thought about it, of course, what Chasm was trying to achieve was clearly rational. The history of Earth was one of disorder and chaos, replete with preventable wars and famine driven by individual pride, differences of creed, greed, identity politics and often some combination of the four. If Chasm could, relying on the brightest and most clever people as guides, build a planet where everyone was truly equal, and peace wasn't optional, wouldn't that be the desired state of society?

Amberly also understood that in order for Chasm's utopia to be built, that the individual had to submit to the greater good. *Millions of people had died on earth because of the chaos of individualism*, Amberly reasoned. *Why is it so hard to accept that a few thousand might need to die for a perfect world?*

She didn't understand how her mother and this so-called Chairman would build the perfect world. But she wasn't so arrogant to think that she was anywhere near the brightest humanity had to offer. Her mother was obviously gifted beyond what Amberly had been aware growing up.

But as much as Amberly held onto the reason, she couldn't blot out their faces: Kora's pale face crowned with her mother's raven-black hair; the imposingly beautiful Lydia, even that runt Skip. They had all been her friends in good and bad times. *Would friendship have any meaning in this new Araran order? Would love?*

And she thought of North. She pictured his strong form and the solitary scar on his face. He was physically attractive and would make a good mating partner should she ever decide she wanted to have natural children. But was he more than a friend?

North loved Amberly; she knew it now. Part of her longed to reciprocate that love — as if someone loving you is reason enough to love them back. *That was too simple*, she decided. She wanted more. She wanted someone who challenged her, who thrilled her, who puzzled her, slowly teasing her with piecemeal revelations of the depths of his soul in a mysterious dance of ideas and passions, someone who believed in something greater than himself. She thought about the revolutionary Dek Tigona, his messy brown hair, his deep eyes, his calm confidence, and his mind, open and full of ideas.

Could she love Dek? Did she even believe in love? A chemical response to a mate designed by eons of evolution? Or an irrational emotion that poets had tried to mystify and even deify?

No, love is real, Amberly thought. It wasn't an empirical reality, but something transcendent. There must be more to life than simply what could be observed. The proof was the ability of people to be selfless. Selflessness had no place in evolutionary theory, where survival alone was the great guiding hand. She had seen selfless love. She remembered how her father was willing to sacrifice so much for her mother, to try to make her happy. *What happened to dad? What is mom hiding?*

Amberly fought tears. *Dek? North? What does it matter? Will we all be dead?* She thought about her friends.

A white-knuckle resolve began to grow in Amberly. She needed to plan, to think strategically and tactically like her mother. What were her goals, and how was she going to get there? She thought again about her friends. *I have to save them. I must.*

Amberly reasoned that she may agree with Chasm, but she

knew her strategic priority was to save her friends. She didn't have enough knowledge about what was going on to develop tactics so, for now, she would prioritize information acquisition. And probably the only way she was going to get any real information was to convince her mother that she was in the Chasm camp and ready to follow orders.

Amberly wasn't sure of the exact time, but she knew they had to be getting close to *Magellan*. Which meant she needed to work quickly. The first step of the plan that was developing in her brain: drive a wedge between Dek and her mother.

Amberly knew just how to do that. She pulled out her fresh clothes and makeup and went to work.

On the bridge, Dek knew that Raven One's threat to airlock anyone who didn't follow her orders about Amberly was not idle. She would airlock any Chasm member for the slightest insubordination at this point, Dek thought, as he sat at *Firebird's* navigation station. "We are in instant communication range with *Magellan* and the *American Spirit* now. Looks like our ETA is unchanged, so we'll be at *Magellan* in about one hour and 30 minutes," he said to Kimberly, who was sitting in the command seat.

Of course, Dek agreed with Kimberly's hard line. Too much was at stake now. Everything they had been working toward for their entire lives, and generations before them, could come down to what would transpire in the next few hours. The Chasm team's resolve had to be hardened, now more than ever. And if the promise of glory in a perfect world did not steel a Chasm believer, then fear of death might keep the weak on course.

Kimberly's dark black hair was wound into a bun, efficient and tight. She had changed into a white European-cut karategi, which did less to hide her petiteness than the bulky protective garments she had worn under her space suit. Dek had heard the rumors that Kimberly was not only a genius of Einsteinian proportions, but she was also a master of many hand-to-hand combat forms. Dek had never witnessed Raven One in combat, so her fabled melee skills may only be a myth, perhaps of Kimberly's intentional creation. Or she really could be a fighting master. Either possibility wouldn't surprise Dek.

"Dek, go check on Amberly," Kimberly said. "I need to fill Capt. Järvinen in on the plan. Our agents on the *American Spirit* are going to need to be ready to do their part."

Moreno stood in the center of Central Command, a gleaming white round room consisting of a multi-story atrium circled by three floors of workstations. Each workstation opened into and faced the center of the atrium. Those working at the stations – 12 stations on each balcony, 36 in total — could view whoever was on the platform that Moreno was standing on now. She was barking orders at a half-dozen civilian workers. The command platform was designed for a crisis workflow to facilitate quick and accurate communication between the person in charge and the various technocrats and military officers supporting operations. Every major function of the *Magellan* from life support to harbor control was represented with a primary and backup station. The person in the middle could orchestrate the operations of the station like a maestro directing.

Moreno was conducting.

Twenty minutes earlier, she had arrived with the detachment of five of North's Marines to a chaotic Cencom. Seven people were in the center when Moreno's general quarters was ordered, five civilian operators and two Marines — from Johnson's unit. Both Marines were undercover Chasm operatives, who had realized that the final plans for *Magellan* had been or were about to be set in motion by a signal from Johnson.

Worried that a non-Chasm force might prevent Raven One from taking control of Central Command once she returned, the two drew their weapons and attempted to take the civilians hostage to force them to initiate whatever commands, however destructive, into *Magellan's* control computer.

Unfortunately for the Chasm operators, just as they were drawing weapons on the technocrats, Moreno and her Marine detachment entered. One of the mutinous Marines lost his cool right away, figuring that Moreno already knew everything and they were going to be doomed as traitors. He pointed his stun gun at Moreno, but before he could pull the trigger, Marcos DeLeon, one of North's privates, had already gifted his traitorous colleague with a half dozen pieces of hot lead.

With Cencom secured, Moreno started reestablishing control over the chaotic waypoint headquarters. She told the computer to undo Johnson's communication lockdown. Moreno looked at DeLeon, now at the communication station on the second terrace, and gave him orders. "Call the governor on his emergency channel. Get North on speaker as well."

Moreno started waving her hands at the magnetic imaging screen, causing the three-dimensional display to jump to life.

"I have North," DeLeon looked up from the communication station.

"North, Moreno here," the acting commander said, "Report."

"We've secured the docks," North's voice was tinny and slightly garbled as it sounded though micro speakers on Moreno's console. "Just outside the civilian access one of my troops noticed that Johnson and some of his men were congregating with the civilian police… hold on…"

"Johnson? What is he … oh dirt," Moreno cussed. She could hear the public intercom in the background of her connection with North.

"Lt. North, you are under arrest for the assassination of Commander Anderson and Wing Commander Jindal. You and your men have two minutes to surrender before we will use deadly force to apprehend you," a voice called out. Moreno assumed it was just outside the main civilian access to the *Magellan's* space dock, two plexiglass retractable double doors about three meters wide and that many high.

"Did you hear that?" North called over the channel to Moreno. "The bastard Johnson told them I did it."

"I got it. Your orders are to hold that position, copy?"

North had strapped his field infopad to his forearm and was using it to speak with Moreno.

"Wilco." North looked through the plexiglass at the gathering force in the corridor. He could see down the corridor to Chinatown, the restaurant where he met Amberly the night before this violent conspiracy started to unravel. He was desperate to talk with Amberly. Was she a part of this Chasm cult or just an innocent bystander?

The five Marines with North were preparing for a firefight. Two of them had assault rifles, the other half just their stun sidearm.

"North, we're now tracking the stolen runabout," Moreno's voice came over North's radio. "Looks like she is headed back to port. Just more than an hour out. I am not going to allow *Firebird* to dock until we have full control of the station and we have defused the situation down there."

North thought about Amberly, hopefully safe aboard the *Firebird*, being abducted by Dek, and he ground his teeth in frustrated anger. At least he hoped she was abducted. *Is it possible she was one of these Chasm butchers?* The thought overwhelmed North, but then he quickly cleared his head. *Got to stay in the game.*

North could feel a hardening deep inside. His joyful life was imploding. Amberly's rejection in the Shard Caves threw him off center. He hadn't time to process the trauma of seeing Anderson and Jindal murdered in front of him — and narrowly escaping with his own life. He knew he would never be the same, and he knew that if he didn't hold fast, he could be overwhelmed by what was yet to come. "We'll take care of everything down here, XO."

"I am going to send you whatever reinforcements I can," Moreno said over North's communication unit. "I'm am trying to raise the governor now. He can call off his police. And I've locked down the hangar access door from here — no one is going to override it, so if they want in, they'll have to break it down."

The main floor of the *Magellan* docks was one of the largest open spaces in the waypoint, nearly 200 meters from the hangar doors to the inside wall. The civilian access point, with its large translucent doors, was situated on one inside wall corner; the other inside wall corner led into the Marine base. On the far exterior wall were the main space doors and gangway access.

A few meters from the civilian access point were a processing center, cargo scanners, decontamination materials and a collection of desks and other office furniture. Behind those was the air pressure curtain, currently up. Before a ship left the hangar, a failsafe required all personnel move to the area between the pressure curtain and the interior wall. When the curtain was engaged, its atmospheric seal protected dockworkers and others from the deadly vacuum of space, which could then be opened.

North and his men had taken up positions behind the processing desks but in front of the pressure curtain drop line. This way, Johnson or the others could not simply try to perform a normal hangar traffic depressurization to eliminate North's forces.

North's men were all crouched below the counter now, so Johnson's forces and the civilian police did not have a direct line of sight on them.

"Snyder, can you get a bogey count for me?" North, still crouching behind the counter, called out to the Marine the furthest away.

Snyder was above average height, with a conservative haircut and average build. He was old for an enlisted Marine at age 42. Born on *Waypoint Cortez*, he tried to make a living as an artist. His digital paintings of Earth scenes (based on both photos and his own imagination) were somewhat popular on two or three waypoints, but those brought him little income. So, he enlisted in the Marines and eventually was transferred from *Cortez*, which had a surplus of recruits, to *Magellan*, which at the time had a shortage.

Marines did drills, maintenance work and other tasks, but because there was little to no threat of real battle, Snyder thought signing up would bring him many days of peace where he could use his free time to pursue his art.

North looked over at Snyder, both men crouched behind cover. Snyder's face was pale, and North thought he may vomit.

"Snyder!" North grunted. "Are you okay?"

"Yes sir, I've just never been in a real firefight before. I mean, we could get killed," Snyder said, with a slight shake in his voice. *None of us have*, thought North, but knew he must instill confidence in his men in this hour they never thought would come. *The Magellan Marines will defend our waypoint, from enemies without, and enemies within*, North recalled the oath from his commissioning.

"No more people are going to die, Snyder," North insisted. "Do you hear me? No more. We will defend this waypoint from enemies within."

On the other side of North, another member of the unit, Leo

Kendrick, chuckled as he checked the ammunition clip on his assault rifle.

"You know, Snyder, if you do get killed, maybe your paintings will become worth something," the blond, baby-faced Leo snarked. "You know, like Van Gogh. The guy was a beggar while he was alive, but now his paintings are worth *billions*."

North shot Kendrick a glare. "Not helpful." He turned back to Snyder. "Get me a bogey count, now."

Snyder peeked over the desk. He counted five police officers, flanked by at least that many Marines. He slipped back under the cover of the desk.

"Ten, at least," Snyder said. "Half of them are police. It looked like they were rigging some sort of explosive to take out the door. They were in a two-line formation, police in front, Marines in back. I saw Johnson for sure. He looked pretty beat up"

"Idiots," North shook his head. "If they damage the fail-safe, no one is going to be able to use the docks."

"Or worse, they could disable the fail-safe with an explosion, and someone pops the hatch. We'd all be frozen space debris," Snyder said.

The third Marine, Jana Smith, was shaking. Smith was perhaps the smallest Marine, no more than one and one-half meters tall. A mess of her shoulder-length brown hair stuck out of her hastily donned combat helmet over part of her eyes. She was small, but kilogram-for-kilogram was perhaps the strongest Marine in North's strike force. When she wasn't taking care of her official Marine duties, Jana frequented the Marine's private workout gym, doing calisthenics routines, while watching documentary vids about animal wildlife back on Earth.

Snyder fancied Jana, who was a decade younger, though he would have never acted on the feeling. Snyder had found loneliness a better muse than any women. Still, occasionally he would daydream that he and Jana married and moved to a homestead on Arara, raising corn and children.

However, now seeing Jana was frightened for her life, a wisp of bravado entered his lungs. He would be strong now, no matter what end came.

North's radio buzzed. Moreno's voice came through.

"North, do you copy?" Moreno asked. "I have Governor

Rillio on the line."

The governor's dark face appeared on North's infopad.

"Lieutenant North," Rillo spoke directly to North. "Lieutenant Johnson says you killed your commander and Jindal, as well. XO Moreno, however, says you are innocent. Can you help me out here? I am not sure who to believe."

"Sir, I witnessed Johnson do it, but that doesn't matter now," North spoke quickly, but evenly. "Johnson is part of a conspiracy to take over or destroy *Magellan*. They have hundreds of trained militia —"

North could see the governor frowned. "That's a bit of a stretch. Why don't you turn yourself in, and we'll sort all this out at the civilian justice center?"

Moreno jumped in the radio conversation. "Sir, I have a confession from one of Johnson's co-conspirators. This is no joke. We must take it seriously. Anderson and Jindal are dead, and we know Johnson was hoping to kill North and me, too, so he could completely control the military."

"This doesn't make any sense, Rita," the governor said.

"I know, Thor," Moreno said. "You are going to have to trust me on this one. We have some intercepted transmissions that also corroborate North's story."

"I don't know," the governor said. "I need to confer with my police chief on the ground there. Hold the line."

North peered around the side of the desk. He saw Chief Allison Kim take a call on her radio. He also saw officers Franco and Ioder, both nervously fingering their stun guns.

She looked over at Johnson, and then spoke excitedly back into her radio. North imagined she was incredulous that what she was hearing from the governor was true. Kim, an average looking 30-something, was close with Johnson. North had always suspected they were romantically involved.

North's radio crackled to life.

"Lieutenant? This is the governor again. Listen, if Johnson and his men put down their arms, will you do the same and let the police bring the lot of you in?"

North immediately bristled at the idea of going down to the brig with Johnson, but realized that the governor didn't have a lot of options. If a mutual surrender could prove the real threat from

Chasm to the governor in the shortest amount of time, North would have to do it.

"XO?" North asked Moreno, who was still on the line.

"Do it. I promise I'll make sure this gets worked out, hopefully with no more deaths," she said to North. Although the words seemed like an order, Moreno did not put the finality of command in her voice. North knew the decision was up to him.

"Fine. We'll put our guns down as soon as we see Johnson's men disarm. Then Moreno can open the front door here, and we'll all take a stroll to the brig. It hasn't been that long since I visited anyway," North agreed.

"You are making the right choice, son," Thor said. "I'll signal Chief Kim to collect Johnson's team's weapons now and you put yours out on the floor in plain view. Hold the line."

North could see Johnson and Kim arguing, and then North realized their mistake. There was no way Johnson would agree to disarm. He reached for the radio to have Thor call Kim off, but he was too late.

Kim was clearly frustrated with the uncooperative Johnson, but didn't view him as a threat, North saw. He strained his ears, but he couldn't hear the conversation through the plexiglass doors. Still, even though he couldn't hear, it was clear Johnson wasn't giving up his weapons.

Kim reached to grab at Johnson's rifle, but he stepped back and pulled the trigger, and shouted an inaudible command to his unit. They all opened fire.

"Holy smokes," Snyder yelled. Smith let out a brief scream of shock as she saw a splattering of blood on the other side of the plexiglass doors. Johnson himself efficiently put several rounds into Franco, Ioder and Johnson's former lover, Kim. They collapsed.

Within seconds, all five of the civilian police officers were lying on the floor, bleeding out with multiple bullet wounds, likely all dead.

"No! No!" North shouted.

"What is going on?" Thor's excited voice came over the radio.

"That traitor Johnson just killed all your officers on the ground here," North yelled, barely able to contain his raw rage.

North stood up, discharged his rifle, and sent a string of

bullets shooting at Johnson, but they did not penetrate the bullet-proof plexiglass doors. It did, however get Johnson's attention.

North made eye contact with Johnson. North saw a gleam that looked like a mixture of evil and madness. North knew one of them would not survive this.

"I'm going get you, you son-of-a-bitch," North shouted. Though Johnson could not hear him, he guessed at what his hotheaded colleague was saying. He smiled coolly.

Johnson barked some orders at one of his men who North saw was that suck-up Dallas, an explosives engineer, who moved up to the bomb-like device on the other side of the plexiglass.

"They are going to blow the door!" North shouted into his infopad, and then to his Marines, "Everyone duck!" The Marines dropped behind the desk.

The explosion ripped open the plexiglass door.

The sharp knock at the door startled Amberly, who was deep in thought. She had changed into an emerald green jumpsuit, both practical and comfortable for space travel, and was using the mirror over the sink to straighten her hair. Seeing her mom again reminded her how much she had her mother's face, round with a button nose, slightly oversized eyes and a perfectly proportioned forehead.

But as she tied up her naturally red hair into an out-of-the-way bun, she couldn't help but think about her dad. His face was oval and tall, and his dark eyes were piercing. However, the mop on his head and his well-trimmed beard were the same color as Amberly's hair. She missed riding around on his back as a young girl, the way he would throw her up in the air and catch her, the tickle fights and falling asleep on his shoulder while they watched old Earth movies like *Casablanca*.

The knock came again, along with a voice.

"Amberly, may I come in?" Dek was here, and Amberly was ready to start driving her wedge. *Showtime*, Amberly thought. She briefly wished she had Kora's confidence with the opposite sex. Still, she knew that Dek was attracted to her, and she would use that to help save her friends now.

She briefly did some ethical gymnastics in her head, trying to justify that it was okay to use Dek's male weaknesses against him. She did in fact like him, and she did in fact long to know him more. *In another time and another place …*

"Amberly? I'm coming in," Dek said, now more as a statement than a query.

The door slid open, and Dek filled its frame. He seemed taller than normal in this sleeping room with lower than normal ceilings. His dark khaki slacks were pressed, and he had put on a brown faux-leather jacket. The bright light flooding in from the corridor made him appear as a silhouette from where Amberly sat on her bed in the dark room.

"Dek," Amberly smiled. "I'm glad it's you."

"Kimberly… er… your mother wanted me to come and check on you," Dek said, stepping all the way into the sleeping quarters. The door slid closed, and now Amberly could more clearly see the features of Dek's face — his messy brown bangs, curling over his deep blue-grey eyes.

"Do you really think, Dek," Amberly said gently, taking his hands firmly in hers as she stood up to face him, "that Chasm is the right thing? Do you really think we can make a perfect world?"

"Am I sure of our success? No," Dek said. "Still, we have to try."

"But so many people have tried to create a utopian order. So many faiths, so many governments. They have all failed. What if people are, deep down, essentially, bad?"

"I can't believe that," Dek said. "Societies are bad. Ideologies are evil. People, if we are trained properly, with enough time and education, can be good. People are merely the product of the environment they live in. If we create the perfect environment, we create perfect people."

Amberly reached one hand up and touched Dek's face. "You, you are good, Dek. I can feel it. But other people, can they be good? I don't know. Are we really smart enough to build that perfect world?"

"I'm not. And you, well the jury's out. But people like your mom, like the Chairman — you have no idea how brilliant they are. They are the brightest lights in the darkest voids of space. If we uplift them, Amberly, they will show us the way."

"Don't sell yourself short, Dek Tigona," Amberly said, as she leaned into Dek. Dek was only a few inches taller than Amberly, so their foreheads gently touched as she tipped her head toward him. She closed her eyes. Dek spoke softly, yet with passion.

"You have to see that the only way we can build a world where everyone is equal — and we have eternal peace and order — is by leaving all the past behind. By leaving Earth behind. Too much history. We must let go of all that is holding us back. We can't be afraid to say goodbye."

Amberly opened her eyes, pulled her head back a few centimeters, and her green eyes gazed intently into Dek's clear eyes. "Yes, I see."

Time to put the plan in action, Amberly thought.

She gave Dek the best "I want you" eyes she could muster. He responded, leaning in to kiss her, but Amberly played the full tease, stepped away, smiling and tracing a finger across his face.

She turned her back to him, looked down to the ground, and spoke.

"Oh, Dek, we shouldn't. We can't. What would my mother think?"

She turned around with a sudden spring in her step, face beaming and took Dek's hand. "I have an idea. Let's go see mom."

CHAPTER FOURTEEN

Leo's hands were covered with blood as he attempted to stop Snyder from bleeding out. A plexiglass fragment had lodged into Snyder's neck, shrapnel from the bombed door. Snyder's jugular had been severed, and no amount of pressure applied by Leo could stop the inevitable.

North wanted to help Leo, but he assumed that Johnson and his traitorous Chasm-loyal Marines would be taking advantage of the chaos caused by the bomb to finish them off, and North was not about to give up yet. Smoke filled the air, and emergency alarms were blaring.

North, Leo and Snyder were all still hiding behind a reception desk. North strained to hear above the sirens for footfalls and he was rewarded with the unmistakable sound of boots crunching debris — Johnson's men were advancing, cautiously, to ascertain if North and his men had survived the blast.

Five to five, even odds, North quickly processed. Well, five to four, because Snyder wasn't going to be able to fight. In his left peripheral vision, he saw Leo trying to make a makeshift bandage from a sleeve he tore from Snyder's shirt. The forth Marine who was holding the line in the hangar was Romero Topez. North glanced to his right, and saw Topez lying in an unnatural position, clearly snapped to death, likely caught in the force of the blast. Smith was crouched next to Topez's body, and appeared to be in shock, trembling. Five to three. The odds were looking worse.

North decided to chance surprising his enemy. He popped up from behind the counter, simultaneously pulling the trigger on his assault rifle, releasing a spray of bullets.

In the second he was up, North saw at least a dozen in the enemy ranks. The Chasm operatives were massing now. His bullets caught one Chasm trooper in the shoulder, but otherwise found no targets. Johnson's troops hit the deck and scattered for cover.

"There!" shouted Johnson, and indicated with a finger the area where North had left cover.

Bullets and stun rays flew in North's direction, but he had already dropped out of sight. North knew it was only a matter of time before they just tried shooting up the whole counter to get whoever was still alive behind the massive metal reception desk.

North caught Leo's eyes and indicated Snyder with a flick of his head. Leo shook his head slowly. A few bullets sprayed overhead and North hugged the floor tightly. He shimmied a half-meter to where he could see Snyder.

"Leo, it's so cold," Snyder said. Leo leaned over the prone Snyder, one hand uselessly covering Snyder's wound. Snyder's eyes wondered over to North. "Don't lie to me, Commander. I'm not going to make it, am I?"

North shook his head.

Snyder slightly trembled, tears running down the side of his face, mixing with his blood. A Chasm troop shot a warning volley over the desk causing North to jolt involuntarily — North knew they were closing in now. "Looks like none of us are going to make it, Snyder."

"It's okay, Commander," Snyder said. "We're going to a better place. I'm ready."

"I'll see you on the other side, buddy," North said, tearing up.

"Just make sure Leo survives," Snyder whispered, his eyes rolling back into his head. "He has several of my paintings. He's going to be rich."

Snyder went limp.

"If we survive, I am going to put a bullet right between Johnson's eyes," Leo said, wiping tears from his eyes.

North cursed. Anderson, Jindal, Snyder and Topez, all good men, now gone. North looked over to an overturned processing table a few meters away from where Jana was hiding, clutching her stun gun. She made eye contact with him, and North put a finger over his mouth, indicating silence. He didn't want Johnson's men to realize she had retreated to that tactically superior position.

If he could coax Johnson's men closer to his position, she might be able to flank them and stun the lot of them, or at least get them caught in cross fire.

An alarm sounded that North recognized as the waypoint-wide emergency alert system. The governor's voice was heard speaking. Surprised, Johnson's men appeared to stop their advance.

"This is governor Rillio speaking. This is not a test. This is a real emergency. We are all in grave danger. A terrorist group of radicals known as Chasm is attempting to take over *Magellan*, with the goal of destroying our home. They have sleeper agents on *Magellan* and on the *American Spirit*. They have already killed senior Marine officers Anderson and Jindal. Please return to your quarters immediately, lock yourselves in, and await further instructions from Marine XO Rita Moreno. Under the authority of Waypoint Charter regulation article four, section five, I am declaring martial law and placing XO Moreno in charge of this waypoint until the situation is managed and Moreno and I agree to return the station to civilian control."

Chasm was now revealed to all. Johnson was clearly not pleased that Chasm had lost the element of surprise. Still, if they could get to the armory on the *American Spirit*, they could muster an armed fighting force of as many as 500, which he imagined would be more than enough to subdue a hostile populace of nearly 10,000 — and the population *would* be hostile now that Thor announced Chasm intentions. Only North and few Marines stood between him and control of the armory. He already had nearly 30 trained fighters who had assembled at the hangar door.

Not all of them were armed, however. Johnson knew he could use unarmed men as cannon fodder, but in order to save as many of his Chasm comrades as possible from the coming annihilation, he would have to access the armory on the *American Spirit*, and then successfully distribute those arms. Raven One was about ready to initiate Scorched Earth, and Johnson felt, as one of the Chasm triumvirate on *Magellan*, he was honor-bound as a leader to save as many of his Chasm loyalists as possible.

Kimberly would most certainly burn *Magellan*, of that Johnson had no doubt. Johnson knew her loyalty to the Chairman was absolute. Macready would airlock her own children to please the Chairman, so she certainly wouldn't have second thoughts about destroying *Magellan* while he was still ashore.

I am not like that, Johnson attempted to reassure himself. *I would only abandon our comrades if absolutely necessary. What good is building a utopia if those who sacrificed the most aren't around to enjoy it?*

Johnson knew that to flush out North and the Marines who remained alive, he would have to risk some of his pawns. He signaled with a series of hand motions to two Chasm operatives, Dallas and Amir, who had come to *Magellan* on the *American Spirit*, to walk around either side of the table. Both looked tense, and Amir glared at Johnson as if he was crazy. The pair was unarmed, though Dallas carried an explosive ordinance.

Johnson nodded toward his assault rifle and lifted the scope to his eye level in a gesture meant to show Dallas and Amir that he would be ready to shoot anything that popped up. Johnson didn't know what kind of training the troops on the *American Spirit* had received under the tutelage of Sparks on their three-year voyage from Arara, but he hoped Amir understood to walk slowly around the counter that hid the *Magellan* Marines, making no sudden moves. Johnson and another in his Marine unit, Kyung-ah, held their guns, eye at the scope and finger on the trigger, waiting to peg North or one of his Marines the minute they left cover.

Dallas had his hands up in a mock surrender, knowing the *Magellan* Marines would be less likely to shoot an obviously unarmed man. Amir, just about to round the corner in sight of anyone behind the desk, was sweating.

"Steady," Johnson whispered to Kyung-ah.

North could see the shadow of Amir, and from his crawl position, his assault rifle was aimed right at where he thought Amir's head would first come into view.

"Don't come any closer," North warned. In response, some shots rang out from one of Johnson's troop's rifles sailing in the direction of North's voice, but they passed harmlessly overhead.

"Give up, North," Johnson called out.

"I'll never surrender to you, crazy murderer," North shouted back. He didn't have an angle on Amir, but let a few bullets loose in his general direction. Amir shrieked, covered his head and dropped to the floor.

"There is no way you survive this, North!" Johnson yelled. "*Magellan's* service is coming to a quick end. It's for the greater good. The only question is, how many people will go with this station into oblivion, and how many will get safely off."

"The greater good can go to hell, Johnson," North shouted back, clutching his rifle. He had been ignoring the pain from his wound. He wanted to lie down, to rest for a few minutes so he could clear his head and relax his torn muscle. Instead, he was forced to crouch behind the makeshift cover, and the pain flared like a flame with a fresh supply of oxygen.

"You know, North, there is no way to stop the inevitable," Johnson said. "As for me and my comrades, we are prepared to die for this great moment in the history of humanity. You keeping us from that ship will not stop Raven One from destroying *Magellan*. We'll all go to oblivion together."

"I don't believe you all have a death wish," North shouted back. To North's left, Leo saw Dallas trying to sneak by the side of the desk with an explosive of some type. Leo made some hand signals to make sure North was aware Johnson's forces were going to try to blow them up with some low-grade explosives.

North whispered to Leo, "Make the shot if you have it."

Leo had never shot anyone before. He'd killed tens of thousands of virtual people in the video game-style simulator where all Marines trained, but now he was having doubts he could pull the trigger and take another man's life. This was real now and he was awash in emotion, still in semi-shock over his friend Snyder bleeding out.

Leo thought about the landscape of the hangar reception area, and knew Dallas would cross his line of fire briefly while positioning to toss an explosive. Dallas would try to move behind a cabinet to Leo's left.

I can't do it, Leo thought. *I can't take the life of another man.* But Leo knew if Dallas did get behind that cabinet, he'd be able to launch an explosive assault, and they'd be forced to retreat into the open and then be mowed down by Johnson and his men.

"It doesn't matter if we have a death wish or not," Johnson explained, shouting to the surviving Marines. "As I said, there is nothing we can do now that will stop Raven One. If we do not get off, we will die. North, I don't believe you are so selfish as to stop my comrades from getting off *Magellan* before it's too late, condemning them to death, just to prove you are right about something irrelevant."

Johnson then changed his tone and addressed North's troops. "Listen to me, fellow Marines," he said. "I do want to live. And you have a chance to survive too. Join us and come with us to Arara. Help our collective build a new world, a perfect world. You don't need to die today. Just come out of cover slowly with your hands up."

North looked quickly at Leo, and smiled cynically because they both knew Johnson was a dirt-licking liar. He would put a bullet through them the minute they showed themselves.

North turned to Smith and saw a hopeless look in her eyes.

"Smith! No!" he shouted.

But North was too late. She desperately wanted to live and believed Johnson's lie.

She set her stun gun down, put her hands up, and stood slowly.

North could see her from his position, but couldn't see Johnson or his men.

Shots rang out, as a scattering of bullets from multiple rifles held by Johnson's unseen men filled the air where Smith stood. Her eyes opened wide in shock, and Smith fell hard to the floor.

North took advantage of Johnson's attention on Smith and popped out of cover long enough to let loose a volley from his own rifle. This time, his discharge was more effective, as three of Johnson's troops took critical hits and went down. Kyung-ah was the only one who had kept a calm demeanor during North's brief offensive, and took aim at North's head. North was harmlessly grazed by Kyung-ah's bullet as he dove back behind cover.

In the chaos, the weaponless Amir, who was still crouched on the floor just a few meters from where Smith lay, saw her stun gun open for the taking. He quickly crawled over and stretched for the gun, hoping that he could recover a weapon and return to cover and survive.

Leo had seen Smith fall, and figuring his days, rather, his minutes, were numbered anyhow, decided now was as good a time as any to be heroic. Johnson's troops were still in a chaotic state from North's assault. Less than two meters of open space separated the main desk from the overturned table, and Leo sprung into a sprint to cover the distance.

Leo almost collided with Amir, who quickly grabbed the stun gun and discharged in Leo's direction. At the same time, the leaping Leo pulled the trigger on his assault rifle. Leo took a direct hit from the stun gun, and almost instantaneously lost consciousness. His momentum carried him behind the table, and he slumped next to the fallen Smith, drool running from the corner of his mouth as he twitched from the aftereffects of the stun shot.

Amir rested peacefully on the floor, his arms spread out in front of him, his left hand clutching the stun gun, his head and torso perforated with several bullet holes.

North looked over at the motionless body of Smith, and the twitching body of Leo, and swore again. He looked over his shoulder to his left where Leo had been keeping watch on Dallas, and realized they were now exposed. He saw Dallas standing up, and pulling a pin out of what appeared to be some sort of grenade. North knew he had no time as Dallas pulled back his arm to toss the explosive. North curled up into a ball and covered his head with his arms.

A shot zipped in between Dallas' eyes. On the far side of the hangar, Marcos DeLeon, the best shot of the *Magellan* Marines, had emerged from the control center side portal with Tricia Moreville laying down covering fire. Boro and Wong were close behind, armed and armored.

Dallas collapsed, and instead of following through with the throw, his limp, dead body dropped the grenade where he had been standing.

Both Johnson and Kyung-ah, not too far from where Dallas had repositioned, saw Dallas and the armed grenade go down, and they leapt for cover.

The explosion blew twisted pieces of aluminum files and chairs several meters in all directions. While Johnson and his troops scattered to avoid shrapnel, the Marine reinforcements moved to press the advantage. Marcos, Boro, Tricia and Wong all began firing simultaneously and continuously toward the destroyed plexiglass door.

"Fall back, fools, fall back," Johnson said, realizing that he was going to lose at least half of his recently assembled force. Johnson himself rounded the corner away from the hangar reception door and made for a full sprint towards the Chinatown restaurant at the end of the passage.

"Kyung!" he called, looking back. He saw his friend sprinting behind him, escaping the Marine reinforcements.

In total, Johnson counted ten running with him down the

deserted hall. North was going to pay for this, Johnson thought angrily, letting his emotions fuel his hasty retreat.

Boro and Wong immediately starting shifting any large piece of debris or furniture to make a makeshift barrier where there had once been a door to the hangar. Tricia was checking the life signs of the fallen enemies. At least three had only been taken down with stun bolts, and she cuffed their hands and feet where they lay. Most of the Chasm agents who had taken bullets were dead.

North stood up and ran over to Smith and Leo, shouting at Marco, who was chasing Johnson's men down the hall with warning fire. "We need some medics, Marco!"

"Already on their way," Marco said as he dropped back to support Tricia.

As if on cue, two military nurses, guarded by a pair of MPs, emerged through the control center side portal. Behind them came Skip and Kora, who hoped to put her civilian nursing skills to work.

"Kora, get over here," North indicated Leo. "He's been stunned."

Skip ran up as well, and looked at North. Skip, not used to seeing so much blood, became nauseous.

"North," Skip said, "your ear!"

"I'm fine. I'm fine," North said, waving off his friend. "Help Kora with the others. He was hit by a stun." North pointed at Leo.

"Yeah, I'm still hungover from the same thing," Skip rubbed his head, and pulled Leo into a sitting position, revealing the blood-soaked Smith.

Kora kneeled over Smith, placing two fingers on her neck.

"You! You!" Kora pointed at the MPs. "This woman is alive. Help me get her back to the medical center. She's bleeding everywhere."

Kora produced a can of foam bandage from the first aid kit she was carrying, and she sprayed it where she thought the bullet holes were — it was hard to tell because of the ubiquitous blood. The foam contained antiseptics and a coagulant and would keep Smith from losing any more blood while being transported.

"North," Moreville shouted from the makeshift barrier at the front of the hangar. "Moreno wants you back in Cencom ASAP. The *Firebird* is back."

North looked at the damaged hangar doors. Thanks to the assault by Johnson, the hangar could not be used without creating a major hull breach.

Kora looked up at North from where she was treating a fallen Chasm agent. The concern in her eyes spoke for her.

"Amberly is trapped out there," North confirmed.

CHAPTER FIFTEEN

Capt. Järvinen was attractive for a man with no spine, Kimberly thought, as she ran her fingers through her dark black hair. Järvinen tall and walked with a slight hunch, no doubt from years of walking through portals on the *American Spirit* with not enough clearance to accommodate his above-average height. He had a muscular build, but not too bulky, and his head was crowned with brilliant white hair.

Kimberly was surprised Järvinen had grown so squeamish, so weak. He hadn't always been unwilling to get his hands dirty when the greater good demanded it. Six years ago, he'd even airlocked an unfortunate soul who accidentally came across Kimberly's real identity.

This was the second time Järvinen had visited *Magellan*. The first time was nearly eight years ago when he was first mate on the supply ship *Sucellus* from Arara. Even then, Järvinen was already high in the Chasm ranks. Järvinen's mission was to take command of the *American Spirit,* at the time *en route* to Arara from Earth, more than two decades in transit. He would intercept his quarry at *Magellan.*

Järvinen had more than a year to prepare for his ascension to the master of the *American Spirit*, while waiting for the deep space vessel to arrive. He worked as the dock master for the privately held Estrella Logistics, a Chasm front firm that did long term waypoint supply planning and fulfillment.

When the *American Spirit* first arrived at *Magellan*, Järvinen had made friends with the captain, Lars Olaf, who had a weakness for gambling and alcohol. The first officer on the *American Spirit*, Montgomery Rice, was, unlike his captain, completely by-the-book and incorruptible. Järvinen's secret Chasm commanding officer, Raven One, gave the order for Järvinen to dispatch Rice in a manner that seemed fit.

While ashore supervising freight transfers, First Officer Rice was crushed to death in a freak "accident" at the Estrella Logistics transfer station. Meanwhile, Kimberly Macready hacked Olaf's communiqués and found that he had been taking bribes from waypoint residents for transport on the *American Spirit* — a highly illegal act, as space transport, by law, had to be sold in lottery at a controlled price.

Macready, using anonymous communication, threatened to expose Capt. Olaf. Olaf knew he would be ruined, and probably marooned, tossed off the *American Spirit* and jailed on *Magellan*, never to set foot planet side again.

He quickly asked Kimberly through the anonymous communiqué what her terms were, expecting to have to pay a significant portion of the millions of credits he'd extorted out of desperate travelers. She replied with a simple message, "Hire Järvinen as your new first officer and the condemning evidence will disappear."

Olaf took the deal, not wanting to look the gift horse in the mouth and counted himself fortunate to not have to part with the ill-gotten lucre he'd collected to set himself up as a king on Arara.

Raven One didn't know how Järvinen was planning to handle the rest, and she didn't care. She was pleased to hear the news that before the *American Spirit* had reached *Waypoint Cortez*, Capt. Olaf had developed Deep Space Dissociative Disorder, an all-too-common occurrence for space travelers who just couldn't psychologically adjust to years of space travel. Olaf had gone stark raving mad, and as first officer, for the good of the *American Spirit*, Järvinen had to have the captain committed mid-voyage. Järvinen temporarily assumed command while Olaf recovered.

Of course, Olaf wouldn't recover as long as Järvinen kept slipping hallucinogenic drugs into the captain's nightcap. Once Olaf was committed, covertly slipping him the crazy pills was easier; just a simple swap with the captain's regular medication.

Because of space limitations, psychologically unstable and potentially dangerous individuals had to be incarcerated in the brig unless they were being chaperoned by one of the two mental health professionals that served full time on the *American Spirit*.

Although the captain was supposed to be on suicide watch, Olaf was somehow still able to commit "suicide" within a few weeks of being committed.

Järvinen had already gained the confidence of the senior crew, and the full crew gave a positive vote of confidence, making Järvinen the new permanent captain of the *American Spirit*. Järvinen held a quick funeral for Olaf, and they buried his body in space without doing an autopsy, sending it on a collision course with a nearby star. Järvinen had confidentially shared the incriminating bribery data with the ship's chief judicial officer, suggesting Olaf's guilt got the better of him. Järvinen convinced the JO that nothing would come of publicly disgracing Olaf now, but he'd arrange to return the bribe money to the passengers quietly.

By returning the bribe money quietly, Järvinen made the nearly 100 *American Spirit* passengers who paid the bribe both love him and fear him. They loved him because they were suddenly tens of thousands of credits richer. They feared him because they knew that Järvinen had something on them, that offering a bribe in the first place was a criminal offense. The offense of making the bribe wasn't as grave as taking the bribe, but it was enough to potentially get thrown off the *American Spirit* at the next waypoint. He was able to convert about 90 of those passengers into Chasm agents by the time they reached Arara. The 10 who rejected Järvinen's recruitment efforts all ended up meeting unfortunate ends within a few months of reaching Arara.

Clearly, the Järvinen who was willing to set aside irrelevant personal morality for the cause of creating a perfect society was not the man who was talking with Kimberly Macready now. She sat on the bridge of the *M.S.S. Firebird*, stolen days ago from *Magellan's* hangar bay, with the help of her daughter and that witless Marine, North.

"Järvinen, I am trapped out here and I can't land," Raven One said, "You have to take everyone who is still onboard the *American Spirit*, find out who is loyal and who will join us. Charge the hangar, then the command center. You have plenty of weapons in the armory. Once you have control of the command center, I'll figure out a way to get off the *Firebird* and onto *Magellan*, perhaps via escape pod, and I'll meet you in the control center."

Järvinen's image flickered on the magnetic screen.

"That's not the plan," Järvinen said. "The plan was for us to wait here on the ship until Johnson and his troops came to us and we were to turn the contents of the armory over to him."

Sparks was sitting in the navigator's chair. She was frustrated with Järvinen's new hesitance as well.

"Listen, Jarve," Sparks said over Kimberly's shoulder. "Plans change. Turns out Johnson is the loser we all thought he was, and he isn't going to get to you anytime soon. So, either you prove you are worthy to wear the captain's bars and assault the command center — or we're about to flush decades of planning out into space like refuse."

"Kimberly, tell that whelp to shut up," Järvinen said through the secure communication line. Sparks seemed unfazed by the insult.

"She's right, Järvinen, and I'm Raven One to you. Don't think we are familiar. If I had the chance to put Dek or Sparks in your place right now and put you out in cold space, I'd do it like that," Kimberly snapped her fingers. "Your time for great things has come, Järvinen. Are you on the side of victory, or are you going to be a frozen body, floating forever in space, waiting for the warm embrace of a star to finally erase your existence?" Kimberly knew she needed his absolute commitment to the task. The value of the carrot with Järvinen had long since expired. The time had come for the stick — the deadly one.

Järvinen obviously was attracted to Raven One, and for a long time, he thought that maybe with her husband out of the way, they could be something more than fellow passengers pushing forward the most significant revolution in human history. But now he realized, too late, that he was nothing to her, just another stupid man caught up in Raven's magnetic beauty and feminine charisma.

He had laughed when he saw Joti twist in her web, but now realized he was caught even deeper.

He knew he was powerless to resist her, even now when he had nothing to lose, when he knew he would never be anything more than another peon in the pile of suckers who sacrificed themselves on the fires of her ambition. All his life, the Captain of the *American Spirit*, the grand man, was master of his destiny. It was all an illusion. Her illusion. He had been her pawn since the day he met her eight years ago. Worse, his power was always hers. Self-hatred oozed from his pores.

"Look, maybe I could muster 100 or so people to hold a gun," Järvinen said. "We'd lose about half of those at least in the assault. Maybe more. And what am I going to tell the people who might reject us?"

"The time for half measures has expired," Kimberly said. "Just show a few the airlock. The rest will fall in line. Make sure they understand, either they will join us or die. Report back to me when you have taken the command center."

Kimberly could taste the victory now, and it tasted like blood. She never thought of herself as one to succumb to bloodlust. But Raven One began to understand now why Alexander cried when there was no more world to conquer. She felt she was becoming a kindred spirit to Joseph Stalin, Che Guevara, Mao Zedong and Sarah Wilmington. They were fellow travelers whose shoulders she was standing on now. They all had visions of a greater good, a perfect society of order. They were willing to extinguish millions of souls because they understood it was the only way for true progress.

Kimberly realized she was no different. She would kill *ten million* people if needed, because she knew this was the one opportunity humanity had to shed its corrupt past, full of selfish individualism and greed. The waypoints created the opportunity to start over on a new Earth, but not to carry the sins of the fathers further into space. They had served their purpose, and now they could only be conduits for bringing the horrible legacy of humanity from Earth to Arara. Kimberly would not allow it. Humanity's new future started today, this day.

If only these fool men could hold themselves together. *Men are so rarely balanced*, she thought. She thought that men, as a group, had almost perfectly bifurcated themselves. On one side, spineless suck-ups like Joti and Järvinen, who held onto the illusion of power as if that gave them significance, but inside full of self-doubt, mixed with pure weakness. On the other side, boorish bravados like her late husband and that brainless Marine, North. They feign caring and compassion, but Kimberly knew that really, these alpha males used micro-aggressions and misogynistic cultural constructs to dominate mostly women, and perhaps weak men as well. Even though it didn't have the trappings of power, these men wielded real power, influencing the weaker people in their lives, creating tribes and making themselves *de facto* chiefs. They had inner strength, and they were real threats to the success of Chasm.

Three and a half centuries ago, society came so close to eliminating religiously imagined gender walls completely, Kimberly thought. But the great Islamo-Occidental War kept faith in the supernatural alive, along with the rest of Western Civilization, and the price of peace was the survival of religion. Kimberly did admit that humanity was probably better off after the alliance of Christians, pluralists, Indian Hindi and Chinese Buddhists defeated the odd axis of totalitarian leftism and Islamic jihad. But the great compromise between the factions ensured religion endured, and Kimberly believed that even the milder forms of Christianity were just vehicles for males to dominate females.

She was disgusted at the memory of being married to a religious man for so long. Christianity was just another reason to burn the bridge from Earth to Arara. *Let the Terrans pray to their imaginary gods. We'll be building a real heaven on Arara.*

Kimberly's thoughts were interrupted when the door to the bridge slid open, and both Kimberly and Sparks looked up to see Dek and Amberly.

"What is the status?" Dek asked. "Did Johnson take control of the harbor?"

Sparks looked uncomfortably at Amberly, and pointed an open hand at the redhead, and spoke to Kimberly. "Well?"

"We can trust Amberly," Dek said. "She understands the stakes."

Amberly nodded. "I understand if you don't trust me, Sparks … mom." She looked intently at both in turn. "But I am ready to go home now, I mean, ready to find a new home."

Kimberly looked intently into Amberly's green eyes. She saw Amberly's father in her crimson hair, and she doubted Amberly's resolve. Amberly took her mom's hands.

"Mom, I love you. I am never going to leave your side again."

"What is love, Amberly?" Kimberly said. She felt a familiar emotion crawl up her throat.

"It's my choice to feel what I want to feel," Amberly said. "So, I choose to love you."

"And your friends? North? Lydia?" Kimberly asked. "Kora?"

"I am not going to lie to you, mom," Amberly lied. "I hope we can save them, but saving them is not what is important. We are such little pieces in the big picture now."

Kimberly smiled, pulled her daughter close, and held her in a solid embrace. "I love you too, Amberly. I am never going to leave you again."

Sparks frowned.

"It's settled then," Kimberly said. "We have a spot on the *Magellan* leadership team that Joti ... vacated. Welcome to the triumvirate. Let's get control of the station."

"Nepotism at its finest," Spark snarked, absentmindedly working a knot out of her long strawberry hair.

"Amberly's qualities are apparent even if she didn't have my genes," Kimberly said. "I am certain the Chairman would agree. Amberly will be one of the great leaders of the new order of Arara. Maybe as the head of the ministry of science, or... who knows. Once Chasm is complete, we have only to ascend from glory to glory."

Amberly took a deep breath, and calmed herself as if she was about to recite a speech in school. She slipped out of the embrace of her mom, bounced twice like a giddy schoolgirl, and turned to hug Dek.

"You were right about mom, Dek; she does still love me," Amberly said with an ear-to-ear grin on her face. Then she pushed up on her toes and smashed her lips into Dek. Dek was caught off guard, and for a split second thought he should withdraw at the risk of offending Raven One. But the kiss was too sweet, and he accepted it. She gripped his lower lip between her lips and slowly pulled away. Dek's face reddened.

"There will be plenty of time for that when we get to Arara," Amberly said, looking to see what sort of reaction she was getting from her mother. "We have so many plans to make together."

If Dek's face had gone red, Raven One's face was ashen. She was not pleased at what appeared to be the seeds of a traditional subjugation of Amberly to Dek in a non-platonic relationship, but chose to hold her tongue while she tactically analyzed the situation. There was never any need to panic. She would see to Amberly's well-being and her daughter's ascension in the new world order that would rise in a post-Chasm Arara. If Dek became a distraction to Amberly, well, Raven One knew there were plenty of ways to deal with Dek, permanently.

Dek cleared his throat awkwardly; Kimberly stared uncomfortably at him, wondering what his motivations were, and Amberly just smiled, as if ignorant of the tension she had cultivated with her sultry kiss.

Sparks broke the silence.

"Been there. Done that. Whatever," she said, trying to indicate she was above the little family drama that was unfolding. "You wanted a status report, Dek?"

"Yes, how long has Johnson had control of the harbor?"

"Lt. Johnson?" Amberly asked. "He's one of … us?"

"Yes, try to keep up," Sparks said condescendingly. "Johnson, your mother and Joti — the *Magellan* Triumvirate — in charge of the Chasm operations here. Looks like you were fast tracked in to replace poor Joti. Don't worry, I am sure that everyone will think you deserve this on your own, not because your mother is the famous Raven —"

"That's enough of that," Kimberly cut in.

"Your boy toy over there," Sparks indicated Dek, "Capt. Järvinen and moi are the *American Spirit* Triumvirate. Each major Chasm operation has three leaders, for redundancy and to help make sure we make rational judgments. We keep each other in check."

"But I thought mom was in charge," Amberly said, and eyed her mother.

"She is the first among equals, if that's what you mean," Sparks said. "But honestly, your mother seems to have everyone wrapped around her finger, even the Chairman."

"Enough!" Kimberly shouted, and even the precocious Sparks backed down. "We don't have time for this. Johnson failed at his mission. We do not have control of the control center or even the hangar for that matter. In fact, that idiot Johnson damaged the hangar so it cannot even be opened without compromising the *Magellan*."

"I thought that's what we wanted," Dek said.

"We don't want a crippled *Magellan* that may survive after we are gone. Scorched Earth requires a clean kill," Raven said. "And I have to get to the control center and complete the command code sequencing."

"So even if we regained control of the hangar, we can't land,"

Sparks said.

"Why can't you just take control remotely?" Amberly asked.

"Two reasons," Sparks interjected. "First is that the *American Spirit* is flooding the area with all sorts of radio noise. One of my projects was to create a jamming mechanism that interferes with radio transmissions. I've spent the better part of three years building it, and I must say it works like a charm."

"Because…" Amberly was reasoning in her head, "we don't want *Magellan* tipping our hand. But wouldn't the Marines and the central communications know right away if the comms were jammed, and they would clue into Chasm?"

"The corvette is already out of that hangar, sister," Sparks said, with a silent "duh" rolling of her eyes. "More importantly, we don't want *Magellan* warning the other waypoints, until it is too late. Second, is that the central command features we need to access — life support and power systems — do not have any connection to outside networks to protect them from being hijacked remotely. We have to be there in person to … do whatever Raven One has planned."

Dek was confused. "Johnson was unable to decapitate the Marines?"

"Yes, and apparently the governor has declared martial law. They are onto us. Rillio made some sort of waypoint-wide announcement."

Amberly worked to hide the flash of alarm in her eyes. On the one hand, she was glad people knew what was going on and were taking the Chasm threat seriously. On the other, the "decapitate the Marines" part seemed drastic.

"What do you mean, 'decapitate the Marines'?" Amberly asked as nonchalantly as possible.

"Johnson was supposed to get the other top Marine officers together and incapacitate them," Sparks said, standing up from her seat and taking a step toward Dek. "Apparently he had to make his move early because someone else screwed up."

Sparks pointed her index finger into Dek's chest hard. Dek winced, and then Sparks seductively trailed her fingers down Dek's chest to near his belly button as she looked at Amberly. "Someone stole your communication key, and they were using it to decode your messages. Johnson said they only got the 'Scorched

Earth' command decoded before he could destroy the key. Of course, this exposed him. He was able to kill Anderson and Jindal, and he apparently wounded North. Moreno survived, too, and she's running the show."

A shock of adrenaline hit Amberly as she thought about North being injured and possibly her other friends too. How badly? She did not dare ask, not now. Apparently, the deaths her mother promised had started.

"In other words," Raven One said to Dek while stealing a glance over at her daughter, "You ended up being just as weak a link as Joti and Johnson. Maybe more. Not only is the whole station on alert looking for us, but the command center is also under extra guard."

Amberly was fighting the urge to panic. Did North tell anyone where he got the communication key? If she came clean now, what would they do to her? Airlock, for certain. All she could now was hope they didn't discover her theft — and play along waiting for an opportunity to escape back to *Magellan*.

"Dek, how did you lose your communication encryption key?" Raven One asked coolly.

Dek was dumfounded. He was running through his mind the last time he saw the keycard. His heart rate also was elevated. "I didn't lose it — I left it locked in my transient quarters."

Sparks smelled blood, and she was in the mood for fresh meat.

"Are you sure, Dek?" Sparks said. "Maybe you let in someone who swiped it."

"Amberly!" Dek said, as if jolted by a defibrillator.

"What… no… I…" Amberly looked for a door to escape through, as if she could run away on a runabout. She knew Dek was about figure out her deception.

"Amberly… was a witness," Dek said. "She was there when I double-checked to make sure my room was locked before we came to secure the *Firebird* to come and get you."

"Yes, I was," Amberly said, relieved suddenly. "We had left the hotel room heading for my apartment, and we had walked a few meters and Dek said he wanted to go back. I saw him go and check to make sure his door was secure."

"You should have kept your communication key on you,"

Sparks said.

"We have more important things to worry about," Kimberly said, clearly satisfied with Dek's explanation and wanting to move on. "Like coming up with a plan just in case the good Capt. Järvinen doesn't capture the hangar and control center."

"You know *I* don't think highly of Järvinen," Sparks said, sliding back in her chair at the navigation point. "But he should be able to pull off an assault with the element of surprise. He might have a five to one advantage. We should have him coordinate with Johnson, who could lead a distraction assault from the access door."

"They'll be waiting for Johnson to regroup and assault again," Kimberly said. "They must know he wants to get on the *American Spirit* and it seems like Moreno is hell bound to keep him from reaching it."

"Yes, that should work nicely," Sparks mused. "Järvinen sneaks in the back with his men in a surprise attack just after Johnson leads his cannon fodder assault. It will be a suicide mission."

"I love a self-cleaning mess," Kimberly smiled. "Johnson is no longer useful to us anyway. He's a liability. Sparks, contact Johnson and Järvinen and coordinate the attacks. Amberly, Dek and I will figure out a way to get back on the *Magellan* without docking."

Even with the setbacks they had seen, Kimberly could still see many paths to victory. The thought of victory, of accomplishing the mission after years and years of sacrifice, thrilled her like nothing before.

Her excitement was contagious, and Sparks sported an uncharacteristic grin.

"Let's start the fire."

CHAPTER SIXTEEN

North paced the executive conference room, which was connected by a secure hallway directly to the command center. In the center of the room was a rare mahogany table three meters in length with matching wood chairs, ten in all. The room was well lit and spacious. Three of the walls surrounding the room featured in-wall seating. The fourth wall was a floor to ceiling window into space. The reactor fin of the *American Spirit* could be seen through the window, glistening in the starlight.

Lydia loved this room. Being a glorified lab tech, she'd didn't even know the Marine base and command center had a meeting room like this. But the view of open space called to her curious spirit, and made the universe seem large, but somehow accessible. She felt as if should could reach out and grab a stellar object, examine it, classify it, and then set it back.

The window wall unsettled Kora. Looking out into the infinity of space with just a strip of some transparent polymer to keep a person from getting sucked out didn't inspire Kora. When she looked into space, she felt a faint sense of vertigo mixed with fear, so instead she focused on the attractive figure of North.

Skip, Lydia and Kora sat on one of the in-wall benches, welcome to be present but not necessarily welcome to comment. In the room at the head of the table sat Acting Marine Commander Rita Moreno. As the ranking pilot under the late Jindal, Lt. Wing Commander Twig occupied a seat as well. Next to him sat Gov. Thor Rillio and his chief of staff, Micha Gonzalez, a young, round woman with unremarkable features. *Magellan's* chief judicial officer, Counselor Jayden Adams, stood behind a chair. Slightly overweight and middle aged, Adams was sweating, either because he had been running or because he was extremely nervous; North wasn't sure which. Finally, the four police sub-captains, one from each quadrant, were in attendance.

"How do we know any of us are not Chasm agents, like Johnson and half his men," North said, his voice full of anxiety and adrenaline.

"Relax, North," Moreno said calmly, but with the power of command in her voice. "Here is how we are going to do this. This is the leadership team here at the table. Everyone does everything, and I mean everything, from here on out until we restore civilian rule, together. We make decisions together; we go to the bathroom together."

"That sounds unpleasant," Gonzalez said.

"Next, everyone caries one of these emergency transponders," Moreno passed out small round devices that clipped to clothing. "I know the Marines are familiar with these, but let me explain them to the rest of you. These are all hard coded with your ID. Once clipped on, they are activated. If you are in trouble because you think one of us is really Chasm, you press the transponder button. It shares that with everyone else wearing the transponder that something is amiss."

"What about the radio interference being broadcast by the *American Spirit?*" Twig asked. "Won't that interfere with the transmission?"

Skip, an expert in radio communication, spoke up. "Naw. The interior of *Magellan* is shielded. Our internal ship transmissions are working fine, through our internal repeating wireless hubs. Well, working fine if we can keep central communication under control. Whatever that ship out there is filling up the space around us with so we can't get communication in or out, is not radiating inside. Eventually, if they jam us long enough, someone will notice that we are not making our regular check-ins. Of course, that will take a year or so, and then a year or more to investigate, and — "

"Thanks Skip," North said. "So basically, if one of us is going to be assassinated by another one of us, press the button before you die?"

"Well, it's not foolproof," Moreno said. "That is why I have a second action item for us to consider. If you all agree with me now, I will use my power under martial law as acting Marine commander to bring swift justice to our enemy."

Thor shifted in his chair, looking uncomfortable. "What do you mean, Rita?"

"Again, if we all agree, I will issue a general proclamation under my martial law powers," Moreno said, evenly and slowly, "to suspend habeas corpus for known Chasm conspirators, and the right to trial by jury. Henceforth the punishment for conspiring with Chasm will be death by airlock, with guilt determined by military tribunal, to be convened immediately."

The room was silent. Moreno scanned the room, looking to see reactions in the faces. Thor nodded slightly.

Twig spoke first, "I agree. The measure is extreme, but the situation warrants it."

"I don't understand," said Adams, wiping perspiration from his brow. "How will this help us identify traitors in our midst?"

"Upon issuing the execution order, I will also issue an amnesty rider. Chasm conspirators who surrender to us within two hours will be considered for executive commutation — the death sentence will be reduced to imprisonment in exile," Moreno clarified. "My assumption is that if any of you are Chasm, you don't want to see the outside of the airlock."

"So, if you are Chasm, and we capture you, it's a quick march into space," Gonzalez mused. "But if you surrender to us, the alternative is a free ticket on a penal ship headed to…?"

"Earth," Thor said, leaning back in his chair. "It's like a 20-year sentence. Prison labor on a ship."

"But what happens when they get to Earth?" North asked.

"Well, if they live that long, who knows? We'll leave that up to the politicians back on the mother planet," Moreno said.

"But what adverse impact could issuing this edict have if Chasm ends up taking control of this station," Twig said, placing his hands palm down on the table. "I'm all for it, but we have to know that if we can't regain full control and somehow Chasm gets the upper hand, we are all destined for the airlock ourselves."

"If Chasm gets control of this station, we are all dead anyway," Adams said, "Isn't that what this Scorched Earth is all about?"

"Yes, Jayden," Moreno confirmed. "At least that's what we were able to gather from the Marines who were turned Chasm by Johnson: private Boro and Phan. Boro surrendered to us and has since been cooperative."

"And he saved us from Johnson's assault," North added.

"Whoever is pulling the strings of this um… terrorist group seems to have ordered *Magellan* destroyed," Thor said. "Let's act. I move we endorse Rita's proposal, giving her the support she needs to enforce her martial order."

Heads nodded around the table.

"Very well," Rita said. "I want everyone here to understand the actions I take I do with the greatest sobriety, and I deem them necessary only because all of our lives are in peril. I will appoint Thor and Twig to serve with me on the military tribunal."

She reached onto the table and activated the intercom and signaled a Marine who was sitting at the communications station in central command.

"Moreno here. Please patch me through to the ship wide broadcast system so I can make an announcement."

"One moment, XO," the Marine said, businesslike. "Okay, biometrics verified, XO, confirmed you have all internal channels hot."

"Attention. This is acting station commander XO Rita Moreno. Please stand by for a critical message about the survival of this station."

Rita pressed the mute button, and then looked around the room.

"Are you all sure we should do this? We can't bluff on this. If I announce the Chasm tribunal, we'll have to go through with it. We are going to be putting live people out of the airlock."

Thor looked around at his colleagues and friends. "We have to do it. And if anyone goes out an airlock, it will be for good cause. These Chasm people have stuck it to the good people of *Magellan*. What, did they think we would go down without a fight?"

North nodded in agreement.

Rita looked at him. "Before you are too quick to support the plan, North, ask yourself if you'd push the button to open the airlock."

"I would," he said and then doubled-down. "I will."

Kimberly, Amberly and Dek were sitting in the *Firebird's* small galley. Amberly was using a microwave wand to heat up a package of noodles. Dek and Kimberly were both pouring over infopads, looking at schematics of *Magellan*. Kimberly had suggested they don spacesuits and make a jump for an exterior portal. The problem with the plan was that all exterior "manhole" hatches only opened from the inside.

The hatches were of course locked and required a high-clearance passcode to open. Hacking this was a trifle for Kimberly — if she were on the inside. There were no interface consoles on the outside of the door, and the *Magellan* was radiation shielded, meaning wireless access of the hatch locking mechanisms from the outside of the ship was impossible.

"Can I make you a bowl of something, Dek?" Amberly said, trying hard to sound subservient.

Kimberly bristled with disgust, and she had to work hard to stay focused on the mission. She was pained to see how easily Amberly slipped into a female domestic servant role. Clearly, the six-year absence of her guidance during Amberly's adolescence left her daughter susceptible to negative influences. No doubt Kora kept the ideas of their father alive even though the man himself was dead.

"Sure, that would be nice," Dek replied, sweetly. "I'll have some—"

Sparks burst through the portal. "Just heard from the tight beam optical spynet ... Moreno is creating tribunals. You need to hear this."

Sparks turned and sped back toward the bridge, and Raven One and Dek quickly fell in behind her, sensing the urgency in her voice. Amberly, left alone, sat down and ate her noodles.

After a few quick paces, they were in the bridge, standing around the communication terminal listing to the audio only transmission.

"This has repeated a few times across *Magellan* now," Sparks said. "I'm not sure if they are able to broadcast this on the *American Spirit*."

A female voice was heard speaking evenly with just a little bit of static distortion. "This is Acting Commander Rita Moreno. Under the authority granted to me by article four, section fourteen of the Waypoint Charter, I am suspending habeas corpus and convening a tribunal to prosecute and punish any known persons who are affiliated with, members of, co-conspirators to, or providing comfort or aid to the treasonous organization known as Chasm. I have compelling evidence that Chasm is presently involved in an attempt to disable or destroy this station, and in light of this existential threat, I am ordering the death by expulsion into space for anyone implicated and convicted by the tribunal of treasonous actions against the state."

Sparks rubbed a hand over her throat, which suddenly felt a little tight to her.

Dek sat down in the navigator's chair. He knew death was a risk, but he had always though he could be more clever than death. He self-assessed as a man of significant talents, someone who could flirt with an unnatural end, but through force of will would find a way to endure, at least until he reached a mature age and nature got the better of him.

Dek pulled out a serrated knife from a sheath that was neatly hidden on the calf of his khaki pants and played absentmindedly with the point. He often fiddled with the easy-to-conceal four-inch weapon when deep in thought.

As he considered the sharpness of the blade, he was forced to concede the possibility that death coming soon was already inevitable. If Johnson and Järvinen could not take the control center, and North and his Marines took control of the *American Spirit*, there would be no place for him to hide, no place to run. The *Firebird* could escape, to be sure, but to where? The vessel was not capable of interstellar travel. It had neither the speed nor the supplies to make it to another harbor. And likely the elder Macready would rather die in a blaze of glory than turn tail and run. Could they live in exile in the Spencer Belt? Dek knew Sparks was a survivor.

Maybe together they could mutiny against Raven One — no, Dek stopped himself from that thought. This line of thinking is premature, Dek reasoned. *Kimberly Macready is a tactical genius.* She was capable of stratagems that would completely confound Moreno. Chasm would not fail today.

Amberly walked onto the bridge, and Dek saw what would keep him strong today: the hope of a future with Amberly. He felt it wrong to hope for this, but in this desperate hour, Dek needed to draw strength from wherever he could get it. Right now, that source had a soft round face and deep green eyes framed by attention-grabbing red hair.

Amberly started to talk, but her mother quieted her. Over the audio channel, Moreno continued.

"Also, by executive order, I will commute the death sentence, with a reduction to exile and imprisonment on the next earth-bound ship, for any Chasm conspirator who surrenders to us unconditionally by 14:00 hours. Those wishing to surrender should come unarmed to the *Magellan* brig facility in the Science Quarter."

"Clever girl," Kimberly smiled, clearly pleased her new opponent might offer her some challenge. "We should not underestimate Moreno. She'll try to thin our numbers with the stick of death and the carrot of amnesty."

"What does that mean for us?" Sparks asked.

"It means Järvinen and Johnson need to make their assaults now, before weak-willed people on our side decide to take the offer. We need to show strength, so everyone knows that they need to side with us to survive. Right now, survival is a seat on the *American Spirit*, so we must establish a supply line to move people and supplies easily on and off that ship."

Sparks, anticipating Kimberly's next command, sat down in the communication seat. She waved her hands and brought up the magnetic screens, and entered in commands to create a tight beam optical signal. "I have Järvinen and Johnson on the line," Sparks said pulling an earpiece over her strawberry hair. "I suppose you want to do the battle briefing yourself."

"Raven One to Johnson," Kimberly spoke on the bridge, and the sophisticated microphones located throughout the room picked up her voice and beamed it to Johnson's portable receiver. "What is your troop strength and status?"

Johnson's voice crackled through the bridge speakers. "I have a headcount of about 30 troops now, and we have secured the tube station and are positioned about two tenths of a kilometer from the hangar. Only about half of our force is armed with guns, the rest have makeshift melee weapons."

Sparks spoke up. "Any defections after hearing Moreno's ultimatum?"

"Only two," Johnson said. "Once they had left, I sent Kyung-ah to make sure the cowards didn't make it to the Science Quadrant. I'll have to admit, Kyung-ah has style. He cut an ear off both and brought it back to show the others."

"He killed them?" Dek said, sounding a little surprised. Dek knew he shouldn't be. For Chasm to succeed now, sacrifices must be made. Compassion for those who would abandon the cause now would only undermine their endgame. It was a cruel calculus, but it was a hard truth.

"Yes," Johnson said. "And now that everyone else knows the consequences, I don't think Moreno is going to have many more takers, at least from my group."

"Good work, Johnson. You may end up not being a total loss to Chasm," Raven One said matter-of-factly. Sparks rolled her eyes, but only because she knew Kimberly was looking the other way. "But I think Moreno is forcing our hand, and we have to push her off her throne now. I need to get to *Magellan's* control center so I can finish this. I'm patching in Järvinen — Järvinen can you hear this?"

The captain's voice came over the speakers, calm and confident, a marked change from the last time Kimberly had spoken with him. She wondered what had changed. "Yes. I've been listening. Let's make our assault. My troops are prepped."

"Did you hear Moreno's proclamation on the *American Spirit's* shipwides?" Sparks asked.

"No, I disabled the communication link once I found out Johnson had launched the Marine coup. Some people with individual comms linked in at the time might have heard it, and we picked it up here on the bridge, but I've dismissed all the non-Chasm officers up here, and for the most part the ship is in the dark."

"Her little death tribunals won't matter once we have taken the control center," Kimberly scowled, tired of the irrelevant discussion. "Listen, here is the plan. In five minutes from my mark, Johnson leads a frontal assault through the main passenger door."

"That's a suicide mission," Johnson protested. "They've dug in now; we'll be slaughtered."

Kimberly spoke without emotion. "It is necessary for the success of Chasm. Don't go weak now. Besides, you only need to distract them, not take the hill. However, if you should perish, your sacrifice will be remembered in the coming utopia."

"Yeah, like Joti," Sparks snickered under her breath.

"Five minutes after Johnson has launched his assault, ten minutes from my mark, Järvinen will launch his attack through the gangway. Järvinen, split your troops into two groups. The first should join Johnson's in making a distraction, drawing attention and *Magellan* troop power away from the command center. Your second group should charge the access corridor from the hangar to Central Command."

"If they think all we care about is getting access to the *American Spirit*, the *Magellan* Marines might not be expecting us to take Central Command," Dek offered. "It's very likely they have gathered all their strength in the hangar itself."

"Järvinen, listen to me," Kimberly warned, pressing her petite, strong hand against her round face and then tugging slightly on her black hair. "You must get through the gangway quickly. And be careful if you are discharging bullets not to put a hole in the wall. We don't want to depressurize *Magellan* until our people are safely off."

"Yes, Raven One," Järvinen said stoically. "I'm sure all of us would like to make sure we keep air flowing in our lungs."

"Once you have control of the command center, I want you to release the locks on all external portals. Dek, Amberly and I will space walk to the nearest portal and enter the station that way. I must get in the command center to enter the command code response sequence."

Sparks called up a schematic of *Magellan*. "Looks like the closest portal to the command center is off the science lab observatory.

"I know that portal," Amberly spoke up. "It's near my work lab. But I've never done a spacewalk."

"Don't worry, Amberly," Dek said protectively with reassuring tones. "I'll make sure you make it safely inside." Dek's words made Kimberly bristle.

"Prepare for my mark," Raven said, activating a timer on the captain's station control panel. "Three, two, one, Mark. Go, for the glory of Arara and an everlasting uplifted humanity. If you should perish, die with honor and know your sacrifices are necessary for the greater good. In the new order, for millennia in the future, our descendants will build the perfect life if we succeed today. For the common good, do not fail Chasm now."

Amberly had listened carefully to the Chasm strike plan. She was trying so hard to stay emotionally in one piece, to figure out how she could help her friends while feigning Chasm allegiance. Warning them directly about the coming attack would be next to impossible, and even if she could get a radio signal off, there was no way she could do it discreetly. Would her mom airlock her if she revealed her intentions now?

And then Amberly had a more horrific thought. What if Chasm failed like she hoped it would, but then everyone believed she helped Chasm of her own volition? Would Moreno's tribunal take her word she was only playing along to save her own life, and perhaps those of her friends? North would vouch for her, wouldn't he? But she had stolen the used ship pass from North. Was she already a condemned Chasm conspirator?

It didn't matter now. Amberly had to get back onto *Magellan*, and then as soon as she could, she had to escape from her mother and find her sister and their friends. She might not be able to change her fate now, she reasoned, but at least she could stand by the people who meant the most to her.

She looked over at Dek, who was busy monitoring comm chatter between Johnson and Järvinen's unit. His eyes glowed with excitement. If she could convince Dek that the ends did not justify the means, that the individual mattered as much as the collective, maybe he could be turned. But what argument could she make to dissuade Dek, ever reasonable and intellectually sure, to see Chasm for what it was?

Just then Dek looked up at Amberly and caught her staring at him. Her soft cheeks turned crimson and she quickly turned away, irrationally afraid he could read her thoughts. Realizing how silly that was, she forced herself to look back at him, and he smiled at her warmly.

And she knew how she could turn him. She smiled back and opened her eyes wide and welcoming. If she could convince Dek that she loved him, no matter what she truly felt, Dek could become a critical help to make sure that Chasm was dismantled. He must know things, she believed, that would give the Marines the edge in fighting this generations-old conspiracy.

The egalitarian philosophies instilled in Amberly by her mother from a young age made her hate relying on her femininity to manipulate Dek. But even at the young age of 19, Amberly clearly saw the differences between women and men were more than just biology. There was something more complementary, something more symbiotic that defined natural relations between the genders.

Though her mother taught Amberly that men and women were equals in every way, in the short time she had been reunited with Kimberly, she saw that the so-called Raven One looked down on men, and saw them as inferior. She had harbored vile antipathy towards men. Moreover, she saw that Kimberly was more than willing to use a man's attraction to manipulate him. Amberly did not like that she had resorted to using her mother's tactic, but she believed she had to use every resource at her command to save *Magellan.*

Sparks had been slowly navigating the *Firebird* around *Magellan*, to get the roundabout in position for the spacewalk.

Magellan's metallic hull gleamed in the stellar light, with hundreds of viewports from private apartments, micro-factories, restaurants and public recreation areas dotting the exterior. Many of the windows were illuminated with internal activity, and others were quiet with darkness. Anyone who had seen an old city skyline back on earth would have seen a likeness: *Magellan* resembling a dark skyscraper rising against a starlit, moonless night sky, with a checkerboard of lit windows creating an ambient glow as half of the tower was alive with activity, and the other half rested in obscurity.

Amberly peered out of *Firebird*'s bridge viewport. *Magellan's* topside gardens filled the view. The gardens were the pinnacle of agrarian engineering, providing the luxury of fresh, natural foods to complement the artificial consumables generated by Magellan's replication tech. Underneath the clear polycarbonate dome, Amberly could clearly see the rows and rows of green leafy plants, arranged in a large circle, centered evenly on *Magellan's* top. The lush farm had a diameter of nearly three kilometers. They were close enough that she could make out the various crops growing — corn, soybeans, potatoes, green beans, sugar beets and tomatoes. The yield on the core crops had even been good enough this year that the waypoint's agrarian directors had allocated some of the land to create a vineyard.

In the center of the circle, under the domes highest elevation, stood an orchard of trees, brought to *Magellan* on the deep space ship, *The Caddo Warrior,* nearly two decades ago. Bright yellow lemons, sweet smelling oranges, fatty avocados and tart Granny Smith apples grew on the 30 or so trees in the orchard. The company that imported the trees, Waypoint Produce Company, had an agreement with the *Magellan* government that in exchange for acreage in the topside garden to grow the trees, half of the orchard's output would be given away via a lottery system to the people of *Magellan.* The other half could be sold on the open market or exported as luxury cuisine.

Amberly had never had the chance to visit the orchard — few people were allowed access because of the delicate environmental balance of the garden — and now she wished she had that fateful evening when she last visited the topside garden with Dek. She knew now she may never have that opportunity again.

Though just over a week ago, that exciting night with Dek seemed like ages past. Dek was the enlightened man, just a romantic, mysterious visitor to interrupt the monotony of Amberly's charmed life. How did she go from her life of intellectually engaging lab work by day and joyful evenings with friends taking in jazzy music at Rick's to this crisis threatening everyone she cared about?

In the middle of the orchard stood a flagpole, the only one on the waypoint. The topside garden was the only place that had both the vertical clearance and something of an air current where it made sense to fly a flag. The background of the flag was a deep blue, and in the center of the blue field was a silver, monotone image of the earth. The globe-like icon was focused on the western hemisphere, centered on the Americas, in honor of the pan-American space alliance that had been responsible for the construction of *Magellan* more than a century ago. Surrounding the blue field were 14 white stars, one representing each of the waypoints that had been built before *Magellan.*

Sparks was also taking in the view of the gardens as the *Firebird* smoothly cut a circular path parallel to the *Magellan's* exterior hull. "Where are all the workers?"

"Martial law curfew?" Dek guessed.

Amberly ignored the banter, deep in thought. Amberly wasn't a person enslaved to personal wants. Her mom had instructed her on the importance of community above self, and at the time the community that Kimberly was talking about was the immediate Macready family. Now Amberly could see that the "community" her mother cared about was much larger.

Seeing *Magellan* in its full glory, Amberly realized she didn't give a damn about the greater good or the perfect utopia. Though at some level it felt wrong, she wanted her old life back. She knew she was willing to do anything to see that end.

In this resolve, she thought she was more like Kimberly than not, and the thought scared her. Both were willing to do whatever it took to get what they wanted. For Kimberly, it was a grand revolution that would reshape the human experience. For Amberly, she just wanted to go to her home — *Magellan*.

CHAPTER SEVENTEEN

Twig was an excellent pilot and had little trouble maneuvering the *Clair De Lune* in the tight confines of the hangar. The thrusters were firing at minimum strength to give the corvette just a little lift off the deck. Twig's delicate touch on the yoke caused the ship to gracefully rotate 180 degrees, from pointing toward the space doors to pointing toward an interior opening in the hangar, wreathed with twisted metal, carbon scoring and jagged, cracked plexiglass.

North had the idea to use a corvette's 50-mm chain guns as a defensive turret should Johnson muster up a force and try to make a run at getting access to the *American Spirit* again. The corvette could not get a clear shot down the corridor, but anyone attempting to charge the hangar from within the Waypoint would be mowed down with a spray of bullets.

Twig peered out of the cockpit window as he slowly lowered the *Clair De Lune* into position. When he was a few centimeters off the floor, he killed the thruster power, and the artificial gravity pulled the corvette to the floor with a clanking thud.

The Marines had the *Magellan* hangar set up as a forward operating base. North's vital orders from Acting Commander Moreno: Keep the Chasm forces from gaining access to the *American Spirit*.

Near the portal that led to the command center, Kora and some of the Marine support staff carefully placed the deceased Captain Kim, Private Snyder, Topez and the traitor Amir into body bags.

Kora's dress was stained with the blood of the dead. She was tired and wanted to sleep, but knew that her nursing skills were needed now more than ever. She finished sealing Snyder's body bag, stood up and walked over to the center of the hangar, where North, Leo and Marco were looking at a large infopad that displayed a two-dimensional floorplan of the *Magellan* hangar and surrounding compartments.

"Leo takes up position here, and he should be able to keep a clean sight nearly down to the tube station. He should be able to give us some advance warning if the Chasm troops decide to make another run at the hangar," North said.

Kora pushed into the circle of Marines. "North," she said, looking up at her friend, "Do you have any news on Amberly?"

North dismissed Leo and Marco to their positions. "Resupply your ammo and get to your points and report in every five minutes." The pair headed toward the main entrance, stopping to pillage a supply crate about halfway to the portal.

North turned back to Kora. Her eyes were dark, sleepless circles. Her bare forearms were caked with dried blood. Her cheeks were dirty, and her hair was pulled back into a messy ponytail that was becoming formless.

North realized he must not look any better than Kora. He was bloodied twice: his ear, grazed by a bullet, and his elbow, which had an entry and exit wound. The medi-foam Moreno had applied back in the Marine conference room had done its work, killing bacteria, stopping the bleeding, and deadening his blazing nerves. In the observation room off of the central command, Kora had put a brace on it to limit North's left arm movement. He had already been ignoring the pain, and Kora feared that he would permanently damage his arm. North protested, but ultimately gave in. The brace kept his elbow bent at about a 15-degree angle, though North still had full mobility of his arm at the socket.

North was a strong man, and he was still able to wield his assault rifle with only his right arm. His accuracy was diminished, but once the brace was on, he practiced using the left arm to help him stabilize the weapon by extending the arm and laying the gun on top of it.

Physically spent, Kora leaned into the sturdy North, pushing her raven-haired head against his chest. North wrapped his good arm around her and hugged her. The strong arm around her called out a mix of feelings in her, probably, she thought amplified by the traumatic events taking place. But although she always loved North, she knew she could never be with him. For one, he was too much of a brother. And two, she knew that his heart was for Amberly. And Kora hoped that someday Amberly would come to see the great man North was.

Amberly is too much like mom, Kora thought. *That's why she'll never be with North, either. Too bad for the Macready sisters. If Amberly is still alive, that is.*

The last thought caused her to shudder, and she took a half-step back from North and looked up into his dark eyes.

"Is there any hope for Amberly?" she asked.

North took Kora's hand with his good arm.

"Of course there is," North said. "We know the *Firebird* has returned to *Magellan*, so as soon as we get this situation under control and this Chasm uprising snuffed out, we'll get this hangar repaired or send out a rescue ship or something."

"What if Dek killed her?"

"Do you really think Dek is the killing type?" North said.

"You're right," Kora said, her face brightening with hope. "He doesn't seem like a killer. I think that he really likes Amberly a lot."

As soon as the words escaped her mouth, Kora wished she hadn't said that last sentence. North winced at the thought that not only was Amberly trapped on the *Firebird* with this traitor, Dek, but that Dek may like her and Amberly may like him as well. A slow, jealous anger burned in North's stomach. He was slightly ashamed at the well of emotions over Amberly. He had no claim on her; she wasn't his property. North knew deep down that Amberly would never be anybody's property. But if the desire to own, and be owned, by a mate was encoded in the fabric of both the male and the female of the human species, North knew he was not immune.

"I need to report to Moreno. We're planning some sorties to see if we can flush out the Chasm troops." North gave Kora a reassuring side-hug with his good arm. "The minute I know anything about Amberly, I'll comm you."

A bullet whizzed by North's good ear.

"Incoming bogies," Leo shouted.

"Get back to the command center, now!" North ordered Kora. "Take Skip and the civilians with you."

North hoisted his rifle and sprinted the 10 meters to the makeshift barricade where Leo and Marco had taken up positions.

"There are at least 30," Marco said, looking with binoculars down the corridor through a gap in the barrier. "Make that 50. Many of them are unarmed."

North signaled to Twig. "Time to saddle up." North indicated the *Claire De Lune* with a wave of his bad arm. Twig just nodded in reply, keyed open the corvette's portal and then slipped into the cockpit. He spun up the machine guns, but held his fire.

Wong had joined North as part of the squad defending the hangar, along with Tricia Moreville. "If they keep coming, they'll be slaughtered. They'll be fish in barrel advancing up that hallway."

"Tricia, if we let them get to the *American Spirit*, we may all be dead," North said. "Leo, fetch me the bullhorn."

More fire came from down the hallway. Leo's survival instinct kicked in, and he hit the floor. There was no way for the advancing Chasm troops to get a clear shot, but bullets were ricocheting everywhere. Leo crouched and made his way to the emergency supply closet at the far end of the hangar.

"Marcos, fire some warning shots," North ordered.

Marcos swung his assault rifles over the top of the barrier and let out a few rounds of bullets. Tricia peeked through peephole.

"Still coming," she announced, as Marcos withdrew his rifles and reloaded. A flurry of pings and bangs bounced off the barriers, causing several of the Marines to jump. "And they are returning fire," Tricia stated the obvious.

Leo handed North the bullhorn, and North wasted no time in turning it on and using it. His baritone voice, amplified by the battery-powered speaker, rung down the hallway.

"This is Lt. Commander North of the *Waypoint Magellan* Marines," he said firmly. "Stand down. If you continue on your present course, we will be forced to shoot. Even now, we have a corvette's chain guns trained on your approach. If you step in range, we will shoot." When he had finished speaking, North indicated for his troops to hold their fire.

North strained his hearing in the hopes that these people would come to their senses and declare that they were surrendering. The silence went on for several uncomfortable moments, and then North heard a swishing sound followed by a metallic clink on the outside of the barrier wall.

"Grenade," North shouted, assuming the Chasm troops had used some sort of rocket propelled ordinance to move the grenade's blast radius to include the barrier.

"The barrier will hold," Leo managed to quickly shout as they all hit the ground. North winced. Three seconds came and went, and no blast.

"Is it a dud?" North shouted. His comm rang, and it was Twig, whose vantage from the elevated *Claire De Lune* cockpit gave him a line of sight over the barrier.

"Smoke bomb. It's a smoke bomb."

North looked up and began to see a think plume of gray smoke pouring over the wall. The cloud was expanding rapidly

"They are going to charge us in the cover of smoke!" Marcos shouted. The smoke had already started to cloud the interior of the hangar. Visibility had quickly reduced to 50 percent and North choked a bit on the clouds.

Twig was on the comm with North again. "Do you want me to shoot some rounds into the smoke?"

Before Twig had finished his question, North heard an audible command from Lt. Johnson, who must have only been 20 meters or less on the other side of the barrier. "All units, attack!" Johnson shouted.

A massive volley of bullets and even improvised tossed projectiles, mostly steak knives, came flying into and over the barrier. Hot metal splintered creating deadly shrapnel.

"Aughh…" Leo shouted out. He had taken a knife to the head, and blood was gushing out of a laceration a half-dozen centimeters long on the left side of his forehead.

Marco returned fire into the smoke, but could not see if was hitting anything.

"Twig," North shouted into his comm and looked up into the cockpit of the corvette positioned just ten meters away from him, "Do you have an infrared scan?"

Twig's voice was excited, "There are at least 10 people meters from your position and closing fast."

"In five seconds, let your guns free and don't stop until you hear from me or you run out of ammo. Mark."

Twig started to count out loud. "Five, and four, and three…"

Now it was North's turn to shout through the smoke. "Hit the deck, hit the deck, hit the deck!"

Marcos, Leo, Tricia, Wong and North all flattened as close to the floor as they could.

"Two and one…" The guns started consuming bullets from the chain feed, quickly ripping through the makeshift barrier as if it were aluminum foil. The air was filled with the copper-plated bullets, singing a high pitch as they traveled in less than a second to meet their targets of metal, plastic and flesh.

Some small arms fire was returned by the advancing Chasm troops directed at the well-armored bow of the *Claire De Lune*. The ballistic attack left a few dimples and dents, and even cracked the viewport, but otherwise left the corvette unharmed. The corvettes were designed to take impacts in the front from space debris and other objects that could collide with the ship as it zoomed forward through space, and the assault rifles could do little real damage with a frontal assault.

How is this happening? North's heart burned in his chest as he imagined the fate of the Chasm troops. He couldn't see anything, but he could hear the screams of profanity and raw pain, which he assumed came from Lt. Johnson's cannon fodder being torn to shreds. The hangar smelled acrid, and North inhaled the unidentifiable fumes from the smoke bomb and the sickly odor of fresh blood. North realized he felt the blood, too, as the splatter from ruptured human bodies settled on North's hair and face, arms and back.

"North!" Twig shouted from the cockpit. "*The American Spirit*! I've got hundreds of heat signatures coming in behind us. I'll see if I can spin around…"

North flipped on his belly to face behind him, toward the gangway portal which led out to the *American Spirit*. Johnson was just leading a distraction, North realized. A costly one, no doubt, but if these people coming across from the gangway were armed, North knew his half-dozen troops would not be able to hold the hangar.

"North to Moreno: Things have gone from bad to worse. We've got a hundred or so inbound bogies from the *American Spirit*. We're going to need all the backup you have and that's probably not going to be enough. We're attempting to…"

The portal door to the gangway swung open and the bullets from at least five assault rifles sprayed out into the hangar. Because North's squad was already on the ground, the initial volley missed. North could see the whole 40-meter-long gangway filled with armed people, four to five abreast, moving forward, with the front line firing liberally.

Rita Moreno's calm voice came over North's comm. "Understood. We're taking appropriate steps. We see them on our thermal scans as well. Stay alive as long as you can. Hold the approaching forces back if you can. Moreno out."

North knew that Moreno would do everything she could, but he couldn't help but feel abandoned at that moment.

North looked over at Leo while he took aim. "This could be it. God have mercy on our souls."

Leo looked white. "If you shoot a hole in that gangway, we could all suffocate."

Bullets now buzzed from behind and in front of North. *Caught in the crossfire*, North thought. *How embarrassing to let Johnson get the better of me.*

"I know, but if it looks like we are going down, I say let's take the lot of them with us," North said to Leo.

On the *Clair De Lune*, Twig had powered up the thrusters, to maneuver the guns to face the horde boarding from the *American Spirit*. The powerful thrust pushed the smoky air around the corvette toward the walls of the hangar. This drew the attention of Capt. Järvinen, who was directing the assault about five rows back from the front line. Järvinen knew if the corvette could bring its guns to bear on the gangway, he and his assault were doomed.

"Take out that corvette!" he shouted, as the first line of his troops cleared the gangway into the hangar. North expertly sniped two Chasm troops in that first line, careful to not miss and puncture the gangway.

The three men still standing seemed to North to likely be conscripted civilians, based on their poor physical appearance and general lack of confidence. They opened fire on the exposed stern of the *Clair De Lune*, which was not as well armored as the bow. Behind them a petite, exceptionally fit woman, obviously trained military, took a knee and produced at grenade launcher.

The small arms fire had already damaged the corvette's rear; burning fuselage from the engine housing starting to add to the smoky hangar air. The assault line was held up as the grenadier took aim. North took a shot at her, but missed. Instead, he hit the frame of the gangway junction, made of reinforced steel. No damage.

North shouted over his comm. "Twig! Incoming grenade!"

But there was nothing Twig could do about it. In the hangar, he had no room to maneuver. He started his 180 spin.

Too late. The RPG expertly hit its target, and the explosion sent the corvette smashing back to the deck. The stern erupted with explosive flames.

"Get out of there, Twig" North screamed, "Flames are about to hit the O-2 tank."

Twig knew he couldn't get out of the cockpit, down the short interior corridor and out the side portal in time. Or at, least, it would be close.

"I'm pulling the eject," Twig said.

"In the hangar!" North said. "Are you crazy?"

Twig reached for the red eject lever. It was completely manual, in case of electric systems failure. The lever pulled a space worthy nano-polymer dome around the pilot's seat. When ejected in space, this makeshift escape pod could provide life support for 30 minutes to an hour. Two explosive bolts blew the canopy-like viewport and the domed-chair was projected clear of the corvette. Simultaneously as the chair cleared the *Clair De Lune*, the spacecraft became completely engulfed in flames.

The pod, with Twig inside immediately smashed into the hangar's ceiling, crushing and cracking the dome, before the pod bounced down back into the flaming corvette. Fortunately for Twig, the pod had enough momentum to roll clear of the burning ship.

For a moment, everyone in the hangar was transfixed by the exploding ship. The nasty smoke coming off the burning corpse of the *Clair De Lune* nearly eliminated all visibility. North could hear Järvinen shouting orders for his troops to advance into the flaming hangar.

"Find those Marines and execute them quickly," Järvinen bellowed. North had estimated by this point, if they had followed their captain's commands, at least 30 could already be out of the gangway and safely in the hangar.

The fire suppression systems kicked on, spraying a heavy foam that quickly extinguished the hot blaze in the center of the partially molten *Clair De Lune*. The foam also cleared the air as it fell from valves above and was sprayed from jets on the floor.

"That took way too long," Leo said dryly.

North had huddled between two crates, trying to avoid being in the line of fire from either the exterior hallway or the gangway advances. He motioned for Leo to join him. Leo sprinted from his cover and slipped in the foam retardant, scrambling on his belly to the gap where North hid. Leo narrowly avoided about a half dozen shots that zipped by.

"Moreno, if you have anything, now would be a good time," North said into his comm.

Moreno's calm voice came back over North's comm. "We're working on something. Please stand by."

Lydia stood next to Moreno in the Command Center, a look of disbelief over her face. "You can't do that. That could kill North and your other Marines in there."

Moreno ignored the imposingly tall blonde. She called out to a Marine manning engineer station two on the second floor of the command center. "Corporal, are you sure you can disconnect only the *American Spirit* latch?"

"Yes, ma'am," Corporal Horner, one of the Marines assigned to the late Anderson's detail, now working for Acting Marine Commander Moreno, said sharply.

Lydia turned to Skip and Kora, who were standing off the command platform in the center of central command, trying to stay out of the way of the flurry of activity. A least two dozen Marines and civilians were attempting to get real-time information on the dozens of conflicts that had erupted as Chasm loyalists stuck on *Magellan* had been exposed and challenged by roving bands of vigilantes. The waypoint was descending into chaos.

Skip looked down. He didn't know what to do. He didn't want to see his friend, his best friend, die — even if it meant the salvation of *Magellan*. Skip knew he could never bring himself to consider trading a few lives, including one brave, good life, to save thousands more.

"Kora, you can't let her do this!" Lydia protested, looking for support from her colleague and friend's older sister. Kora said nothing, only shaking her head slightly. Her eyes were moist, and she had to focus to keep from tearing up. Kora wasn't ready to cry yet. She still had hope for North, and maybe even Amberly, too.

She would save her tears for when and if they were in glory's grasp.

"Corporal, prepare to release, on my mark," Moreno said to Horner.

"North will have about 30 seconds to make it to the manual portal controls, ma'am," Horner offered to Moreno. "Once we go, we'll not be able to stop it from here. Just contain the loss to the hangar. There is no guarantee they'll be able to get to controls before —"

"No!" interrupted Lydia. She stepped up on the command platform, face to face with the Acting Commander. She was trying to intimidate Moreno, 15 centimeters taller than the older woman, but Moreno gave no ground. "You cannot do this. North and the others will die."

"Ma'am," Moreno said, calmly but with steel in her voice, "stand down or I will have you removed. This is the only way North — and Tricia, Leo and Marcos — all of them, will have a chance of surviving. The have *no* hope if we don't we act now. Do nothing, they will most certainly be overrun. And if they are overrun, they will come here, and they will destroy this station and kill us all."

"There has to be another way," Lydia gave no ground either.

"We are out of time," Moreno said, softening her tone a bit. "Please, stand down, before I have to stun you."

Lydia hadn't noticed until now that Moreno had quietly pulled her stun gun and had it aimed squarely at Lydia's muscular abdomen.

Skip and Kora had already moved up to restrain Lydia, and she reluctantly moved with the pair off the platform.

Moreno holstered her gun and looked at the retreating Lydia. "I know this is exactly what North would want me to do."

Lydia knew Moreno was right, and out of extreme grief, turned and hugged Skip. Skip, not really a hugger, was caught a bit off guard by the outreach for emotional support, and Kora neatly helped by bringing both of them into a friendly, caring embrace.

Moreno looked at Horner and gave a thumbs up, then opened a comm channel to North. "Moreno to North, we're ready with our plan. Hold on to something. We're going to try something crazy."

North gave a puzzled look to Leo, who was crouched next to him. He and Leo had belly crawled between the corvettes *Maverick* and *Lady Katie* to avoid getting in the crossfire from Järvinen's phalanx and whoever had survived in Johnson's assault group. North had no idea what Moreno was talking about, but shouted to Tricia and Marcos, who were crouched next to a flipped desk, shooting somewhat randomly, alternating between the hall and general direction of the *American Spirit*'s gangway.

"Hold on!"

North looked toward Järvinen's troops who were cautiously making a defensive formation at the far side of the hangar. He could see clearly again and made out Järvinen and the woman grenadier. North resisted the temptation to pop out from behind the *Maverick* to shoot a volley in their direction.

Moreno's voice came over the comm. "Get ready. You are going to have to manually close the portal. Good luck."

"What do you mean, close the portal?"

"We are disconnecting the gangway. Now."

"What the —"

An automated voice spoke loudly over speakers filling the hangar.

"Warning. Gangway disconnection in 10 seconds. Portal is not secure. Are you sure you want to continue?"

Terror flashed in Järvinen's eyes. "No! Discontinue. Stop!"

But the computer ignored Järvinen's command. North knew that Moreno had already overridden local voice safety from the command center.

"Five, four, three, two, one…"

The magnetic latches holding the gangway to the *American Spirit* disconnected, and immediately, the slight tension from the *Magellan* pulled the tube clear of the ship. The suction effect was immediate, as the space-exposed end of the gangway rushed with the powerful thrust of air venting into the vacuum.

North could see the entire slaughter unfold. He dropped his assault rifle and gripped a handle on the crate nearest to him.

Those in the rear of the gangway, mostly professional soldiers loyal to Chasm, were the first to slip out into the coldness of space. Their screams were swallowed by the air that pushed them into oblivion.

Those in the middle of the gangway had a few seconds to respond. Several grabbed on to the structure beams that gave the gangway its shape, but most were buffeted by the people in the front, who succumbed to physics after a vain attempt to scramble to escape the tube into the relative safety of the hangar.

Those in the hangar were not much better off. The troops in the mouth of the gangway who had just stepped onto the hangar deck were in the vortex of the suction, with all the atmosphere being compressed through that choke point. They too were whipped quickly through the gangway and out the other side with such force that they spat out of the tube like a bullet out of the barrel of the gun and into the hull of the *American Spirit*. Some hit with such intensity that they cracked skulls and other bones, increasing the agony of their certain death.

Inside the hangar, the massive depressurization had created a tempest. The emergency curtain had fallen sealing off the hallway and the reception area of the hangar, so that North and his squad were trapped with the Chasm troops as the hangar quickly vented its precious breathable gasses into space.

Twig, still dazed from his escape from the *Clair De Lune*, had just freed himself from the ejected seat, when the gangway seal was broken. He did a quick scan of the hangar floor and, from a position obscured by several corvettes, he couldn't put eyes on any of North's squad. A gust knocked him up against the *M.S.S. Presley*, one of the older corvettes in the *Magellan* fleet. Realizing he had little time, Twig quickly found the Presley's hatch, which as Marine pilot, he was fortunately authorized to unlock with his handprint. He slipped inside, and sealed the door behind him.

Near the other side of the hangar, North figured it would take about 30 seconds to a minute before those in the hangar who didn't get sucked out into space would be exposed to a near vacuum, and even the air inside his lungs would attempt to escape through his mouth and nose, and maybe his eyeballs out of their sockets, too.

North realized what Moreno meant when she said he'd have to close the door. He looked across the atmospheric violence towards the gangway manual control panel. The access panel was at least 50 meters away from his secure position and about five meters too close for his comfort to the gangway portal that was currently sucking people out into space at a lethal rate. He'd have to get there without getting blown out the gangway, getting shot by any Chasm troops, and get the door closed before they all suffocated.

If they did suffocate, North thought, at least this Chasm force would go with them. *Blowing the gangway was a clever move by Moreno, gutsy and bold,* North thought as a smile formed on his face. *That's exactly what I would have done.*

North hand signaled to Leo to cover him, took what he thought could be his last breath, started for the manual control panel. Either he was going to get that door closed, or learn what death by venting felt like.

Leo leaned out of cover just after North started darting for the panel, with his assault rifle raised. One of the Chasm troops who had made it through the gangway and onto the hangar deck was firing wildly at North, who was sprinting in an irregular line, buffeted by the suction storm. Leo pressed himself against the hull of the *Maverick* to secure himself, aimed and put a single bullet into the skull of the shooter. The Chasm trooper fell to the ground, blood trickling from the gaping hole in the middle of his forehead. The vacuum suction drug the dead man along the floor for a meter or so, before sucking him into the open-ended gangway and out into space to join the dozens of his dead colleagues who were floating aimlessly, just out of reach of the waypoint.

The tempest had not only pulled bodies out into space, but loose articles, shrapnel and other larger metallic fragments from the explosions and ongoing battle were also being drawn out with the powerful atmosphere suction.

A sharp sheet of aluminum, probably from a desk or temporary wall, sailed toward the grenadier, who was holding with two hands onto a safety rail just a meter from the open portal. Her legs flailed out behind her, and her square face was intent and focused, as her long brown hair whipped wildly. She let go of the rail with one hand to block the flying fragment from hitting her head, and almost lost her grip as she deflected the object. It bounced off her defending arm and spun in the wind and came down on her hand that was still gripping the rail. The sharp edge acted like a knife, severing three of her fingers at the knuckles and causing her to lose her grip. She cursed God as her soon-to-be-lifeless body was sucked out into the void.

North's lungs felt like they were being sucked out of his chest as he flung himself at the manual control panel. The storm had calmed, which meant there was little to no air left in the hangar. He dare not open his mouth now to take a gasp — he would probably lose more air than he could take in. The exposed skin on his face and hands started to burn with extreme cold.

He was a meter away from the control panel now, and he stumbled as he fought to keep from blacking out. He bounced on the floor. *This is the end,* North thought, surprised at how calm he was. *I wonder what heaven will really be like? Will Amberly make it? Amberly. Amberly still needs my help. She's out there.*

North forced himself up. He slowly, painfully reached for the panel. He could see the emergency shut button. He swung his hand at it, stumbled again and missed. Now he was leaning against the wall, next to the controls, and his entire body felt like it was exploding.

Not done yet.

He slid his hand down the wall over the emergency shut button and lost consciousness, his mouth opening and the air escaping from his lungs.

"It's closed!" Horner shouted.

"Bring up the emergency curtain!" Moreno shouted with a frantic urgency that strongly contrasted her normal, cool demeanor.

Kora held Lydia's hand tightly as they watched the monitor showing a live security feed of the hangar. They saw the safety curtain slowly rise and loose items on the hangar floor were once again tossed around as the air pressure equalized.

Skip tried to reassure the women. "It will only take a few seconds for the hangar to re-pressurize. I'm sure they'll be okay."

Moreno knew she had to secure the hangar again. "Horner, Inon," she ordered the corporal and a nearby private, "Grab an assault rife and get out there. Once you secure the floor, comm me and I will send out the medics. Move."

Inon, a short 25-year-old with cropped bleached white hair and a top-heavy muscular build, already had a rifle in her hand.

"Ma'am" she shouted and sprinted down the hall to the connecting corridor that would take her to the hangar. Horner quickly followed.

Moreno joined Skip, Kora and Lydia, and they watched as the emergency wall slowly retracted into the ceiling, allowing a rush of life from the interior hall to fill the hangar with invisible gasses.

Johnson and Kyung-ah were the only two Chasm troopers assaulting from the interior who survived the *Clair De Lune*'s chain gun defense. When the safety curtain fell, they were on the interior of the station, and spared from the depressurization of the hangar. With the wall coming back up, Johnson figured they would have one opportunity to press their advantage and kill any *Magellan* Marines that survived the depressurization. If they broke through now, maybe, just maybe, the two of them could take control of the station.

The opening beneath the wall was waist high and growing, so Johnson and Kyung-ah checked the ammunition in their rifles. Johnson looked at Kyung-ah who indicated he had only four rounds left.

"That's enough," Johnson said. "Let's go."

The pair simultaneously plunged beneath the slowly rising safety wall and emerged on the other side and quickly attempted to locate any survivors. The hangar was a complete wreck. Corvettes were thrown about, flipped and rolled. The charred remains of the *Clair De Lune* were still upright, but had been dragged from where Twig had set it down about 20 meters toward the now-sealed gangway portal, black carbon burn trails marking the path where the space-vacuum had moved the vehicle.

Johnson looked past the worthless vessel and saw four figures standing at the far side of the hall. One of North's lackeys, Corporal Marcos, had a gun drawn on three men. Two of them, standing two meters in front of the third, Johnson didn't recognize. The third man, he did recognize: Capt. Järvinen, master of the *American Spirit*. Johnson then saw a fifth man, sitting propped up against the wall, with a brace in one arm and a gun in his other arm … aimed right at him and Kyung-ah.

Kyung-ah saw North at the same time as Johnson and didn't hesitate to bring his gun to bear on the injured Marine. But North didn't have to aim, he just had to pull the trigger. And as soon as he registered that Kyung-ah was moving to fire, North's hair-trigger reflexes engaged his rifle. Kyung-ah fell hard, and another corpse littered the hangar floor.

Johnson stood next to him, and his survival instincts kicked in. He knew he couldn't draw fast enough on North, so he made a split-second survival decision to drop his rifle and put his hands up. Johnson realized he wasn't ready to die for the cause.

North smiled wearily at Johnson's up stretched hands.

North's unexpected shots taking out Kyung-ah rattled Marcos, who reflexively looked over at North and his fallen target. One of the two remaining Chasm troops with Järvinen went for a gun, hoping to catch Marcos off guard, but the Järvinen loyalist was too slow. Marcos turned back, saw the gun grab, and put two bullets into his would-be assailant's leg. A scream of pain filled the restored atmosphere of the *Magellan* hangar, but the fallen man was still scrambling for the gun.

At the same time, Twig slid out of the *Presely's* hatch. He was behind Järvinen, but had lost his sidearm in the chaos, so he scanned the area and found a twisted metal bar which he grabbed and quietly began to approach Järvinen from the back.

Marcos had a clean shot on the head of the wounded Chasm troop. Järvinen and the second troop were just a quick shot away, too.

Marcos didn't want to shoot to kill. He had another idea, and shouted. "Don't do it. Put your hands up now, leave the gun alone, and surrender. I'll make sure you get Moreno's amnesty deal instead of the airlock. Do it! Now!"

The wounded troop and the other Järvinen lackey both took the offer immediately, the former clasping his hands over his head to surrender as he bled out of the two bullet holes in leg. The second troop threw his hands up and kneeled.

"How dare you surrender, you maggots!" Järvinen shouted. He produced a small hand gun from a pocket in his leather jacket, and before Marcos realized what was going on, Järvinen had shot both his own troops cleanly in the back. Marcos froze for a second as he looked at the shocked expression on the kneeling lackey as his face went blank. North was also jarred by Järvinen's cold murder of his own men, but he kept his gun trained on Johnson.

The moment the second murderous shot rang out, the door accessing the hall which led to the command center flew open and Horner and Inon popped out, guns aimed and quickly training on Järvinen.

Marcos raised his rifle at Järvinen, but before he pulled the trigger, he saw that the captain had turned his gun on himself, and used his free hand to motion to Marcos, Leo and Horner to hold their ground.

"Not another step or I'll do it," Järvinen said as he pushed the barrel of his gun into the flesh under his jaw.

"Just put the gun down," Marcos said as he slowly took two steps toward Järvinen. "It doesn't have to end this way."

Järvinen slowly moved his free hand toward his mouth, and North could see he had a comm unit sewn into the sleeve. He spoke slowly and clearly into his comm sleeve, while he still had his own gun jammed into his jaw with a finger on the trigger. "Raven One, do you copy?" he asked.

A voice crackled over Järvinen's comm.

"This is Raven One," the voice said. "Captain, have you taken the hangar yet?"

That voice... so familiar, North thought.

"I'm sorry to report that we have not. I have lost my assault force, and Johnson has been captured," Järvinen said.

"I'm never surprised by your failure, old friend," Raven One said, her casual voice was laced with a quiet, burning anger.

The gun in Järvinen's hand was trembling. He continued his conversation as Marcos and Twig slowly closed on the captain, weapons at the ready.

"I don't know why I was vain enough to believe I could be a successful part of history, of this success, of Chasm," said Järvinen, with tears now streaming down his face. "But I know you will go on to build our brave, new world. All my love, and all my hope."

"The value of your love and hope are suspect," Raven One's voice came out of the comm box sewn into Järvinen's sleeve. "Know that if Chasm fails, that it was for the failure of men."

"I'm sorry." Järvinen pulled the trigger, and his body collapsed.

Johnson saw his chance. He sprinted for some cover and slipped behind the partially raised safety curtain.

Marcos and Twig ran up to Järvinen's fallen body. Marcos felt for a pulse.

"Dead," Marcos said.

Raven One's voice once again emerged from the now lifeless Järvinen's sleeve.

"Soon you will all join him."

North shouted from where he was seated, "Who are you? What do you want?"

The comm box clicked and then only offered static.

CHAPTER EIGHTEEN

Kimberly Macready was not upset. She expected that Johnson and Järvinen would likely fail. She had another plan for getting back onto *Magellan* and in control of the command center.

Kimberly and Amberly stood on the bridge of the *Firebird*, looking through the viewport at the *American Spirit*, tethered to *Magellan* by various steel cables. Between the massive spaceship and the waypoint, the gangway slowly oscillated, like a metronome, with its base attached to *Magellan*, and the head, formerly attached to the *America Spirit*, free floating in space.

The cloud of human bodies, floating in various directions, was slowly dissipating as the Chasm troops caught on the gangway drifted off into the dark void.

Amberly felt like she had been turned to stone. The sheer magnitude of death parading in front of her was more than she would have ever imagined in her most frightening nightmare.

Dek, who was also standing, stepped behind Amberly and softly embraced her shoulders with his hands and forearms. Amberly responded warmly to the human touch, leaning back into Dek. She felt compassion and understanding in his presence, and she wanted to believe that Dek was as horrified as she was.

Unaware of the firefight in the *Magellan* hangar, Amberly wondered if this mass execution was necessary and was beginning to think that maybe the *Magellan* Marines were as evil as Chasm. Or maybe Joti was right — there is no evil, just the truth that is defined by power. Amberly's head was spinning, and she just wanted to be home, sitting in her small dining room, eating rice with her sister, giggling about boys and getting excited about discovering a new stellar anomaly. That life seemed so far away.

Thick in thought, Amberly barely noticed that her mother was chatting with Captain Järvinen over the comm unit. Something about how all men disappointed her. Then she heard the gunshot, and her head snapped up.

"Dirty hell!" Sparks said. "Did Järvinen just kill himself? Who knew the guy had a spine?"

There was a scuffling sound, then an unknown male voice came over the comm. "Dead," he said.

Kimberly leaned forward and activated her microphone. "Soon you will all join him," she said, pouring certainty and confidence into her tone.

The voice that replied made Amberly jump.

"Who are you? What do you want?" North asked.

Kimberly and Amberly both recognized the voice at once. Kimberly severed the connection.

"North!" Amberly shouted, instinctively lurching away from Dek toward Kimberly's communicator. "North! North!" She fought back the tears. She knew she had to get control of herself, if Kimberly thought that her daughter's loyalty was in question, her own life would be in peril — and she certainly would be of no help to her friends on *Magellan*.

Like a put-out teenager, Dek immediately soured at Amberly's emotional reaction to his would-be rival. Kimberly also became concerned, furrowed her brow and let out a nearly inaudible, "Hmmmm."

Sparks seemed not as interested in Amberly's reaction to hearing her friends voice as she was in North himself. "You know, it's a pity we couldn't take North with us. He makes a nice photo. When I was doing mission research, I set his mug as the background of my infopad. Mmmm. Men in uniform really fire my —"

"Sparks," Kimberly interrupted. Sparks' description of North as some sort of plaything was so anachronistic in this life-and-death scenario, Amberly looked at the other woman with disbelieving eyes.

"Sometimes I feel like we have too much brain around here and not enough brawn," Sparks lamented.

Dek cleared his throat in a way to let Sparks know he didn't appreciate her flippancy, and then turned to Kimberly. "What next?"

"Dek, Amberly," she replied, "Get your spacesuits on. Sparks, take the pilot's station. And make sure the escape pod is working, you are going to need it."

Even though she didn't know the details of the plan yet, Sparks smiled excitedly. Her faith in Raven One's ability to salvage the operation was absolute, and Sparks was ready to get off the sidelines and take matters into her own capable hands.

"Finally. Let's finish this."

Boro had explained to Moreno that the somewhat random military style assaults now being carried out by Chasm cells were probably a contingency tactic to distract *Magellan* authorities to give Chasm leadership the time to carry out the primary mission.

"The cells are just supposed to make mischief until Raven One gives the cell commanders the authorization code to move to the next phase. I'm sorry I don't know more," Boro said in his deep bass voice. "I was the lowest rank in Chasm."

North waved him off. "You chose the right time to switch sides."

The well-dressed, perspiring Jayden Adams, chief judicial officer on *Magellan*, huffed a disagreeable sound.

"They've taken hostages at Bush Elementary and the Evangelical Church, they set fires at several micro-factories in the Science Quarter," Horner reported to the assembled leadership council. Governor Thor and his shadow, Gonzalez, along with Adams and State Quarter Police Captain Remus Montenegro, a squatty olive-skinned man in his late forties, represented the civilians. Remus had been promoted to acting chief since the murderous Lt. Johnson killed Remus' former boss, Allison Kim.

Besides Moreno, the military was represented by acting Wing Commander Twig, Strike Commander North, and Corporal Horner, who was functionally serving as a sort of chief of staff for Moreno. Boro, a Marine who served under Johnson and now a confessed Chasm agent, was also in the room because Moreno needed intel on Chasm and Boro's defection made him the best information source at the moment. The only reason she trusted him was because he saved North's life.

Moreno was trying to decide what the next course of action was to bring peace back to the station and end the Chasm threat once and for all.

"North, what is our fighting strength now, police and Marines combined, those we've verified are not Chasm?"

North looked at Rita. "Including those here on base and those who are deployed across the station we have about 40, not counting officers. I was talking with Captain Montenegro, and he believes we can probably deputize another 10 to 20 civilians who have some training and could be brought on in combat support roles right away."

Montenegro nodded his support of North's assessment.

"Remus, get to it," Moreno said. "Call everyone up now."

The police officer pulled an infopad out and started typing in orders.

North spoke up. "We have our largest force guarding the Science Quarter brig right now — 10 troops. One hour left before the amnesty offer expires."

Moreno turned to Adams.

"Counselor, you've been processing the defectors. How many Chasm traitors have surrendered to us?"

North hadn't noticed it before, but Adams was trembling slightly.

"Adams?" he inquired.

"We have 25 Chasm conspirators in custody, an unfortunately small amount considering the potential size of their overall force," Adams said, trying to steady his voice. "Boro's estimates of Chasm's force on *Magellan* is off by half."

"Good thing we vented about 100 of them into space," Gonzalez joked. When an awkward silence followed, she added, "Too soon?"

North snapped his head back at Adams. "Wait. How do you know the troop strength of Chasm?"

"Isn't it obvious?" Adams stood up. "I surrender."

Something clicked, and Moreno drew her sidearm and pointed it at Adams.

"Whoa… Rita," Thor sprung to life. "Let's not be hasty. Are you saying that Adams is Chasm?"

Adams slowly put his hands up. He had stopped shaking, and his countenance changed immediately, as if a 1,000-kilo weight had been taken off of his shoulders. "I am your 26th Chasm defector, and I request amnesty from the death penalty under the executive order of acting station commander Moreno."

"I don't understand," Thor said, his shell-shocked face slowing melting into a hot rage. "Jayden, how could you be a part of this treason? This murder?"

Adams glowed. Unburdened from the secret of this Chasm membership, his face seemed to smooth. North thought he instantly looked 10 years younger.

Chief Remus pulled out a zip cuff, and Adams offered his hands. "You know your rights, Jayden."

"He has no rights!" Thor burned at Adams' betrayal. "We are under martial law. You dirt-licker, Adams! We may all die, and you were a part of this."

"Look at this place. We're an umbilical cord that is trying to continue to justify its existence. Earth doesn't want to cut the cord. But it's time to let Arara go. Humanity cannot fully realize what science, technology and social engineering have to offer as long as Arara is bound to the failings of the past." Adams shook his head. "I don't expect you to understand."

"You're insane," Twig scoffed at Jayden.

"No, I just have enough vision to understand the past and to see the future," the lawyer replied.

"Humanity will never be perfect," Moreno said, returning her weapon to its holster. "If you pulled off your Chasm and created a true gap from Earth, sooner or later your Arara utopia would be corrupted. How many people are going to have to die for your little social science experiment? You can't beat original sin."

"How quaint," Jayden's voice had taken on a thick tone of condescension. "These individual lives don't matter. Even mine doesn't matter. Once you let go of yourself for the value of the common good, for the sake of the collective, you can rid yourself of your stupid fixed-moral value ideas like murder and individual responsibility. History will remember us and honor us."

Adam's hands were now secured behind his back. Moreno stepped up so she stood face-to-face with him. Adams was about ten centimeters taller than the female Marine, but somehow, at least to North, she had the larger presence.

"Why are you surrendering now?" Moreno asked in a voice that was clearly meant to intimidate.

"Quite simply, my work is done. I am tired of living a double life. I am proud of what we have accomplished," Adams said.

"What a liar. You're a coward!" North spoke back. He pulled a chair behind Adams and then forced the solicitor to sit down, his hands still bound behind his back. North walked around the table and sat down opposite Adams. "You are playing all the angles, Jayden. If Chasm wins, you likely get a ticket to freedom on the *American Spirit*. You'll be made a hero in your so-called new world order. If Chasm loses, you avoid the airlock. That's why you are revealing yourself now. Any later and you risk someone else exposing you."

"I don't care why you decided to impugn yourself at this time," Moreno said. "I want specifics on the troop strength of Chasm. I want to know what the next mission is, and what the contingencies are. I want names. Location of weapons and resources. Strategy on other waypoints. And I want it now. What is the next move? Who is the leader, who is this Raven One?"

"Sorry, Rita," Adams said. "Just because I surrendered, doesn't mean I am going to help you. I'm not talking."

North jumped at Adams from across the table. He backhanded the lawyer with his uninjured arm.

North's voice was soaking in power and anger as he spoke to Adams. "Talk, traitor! My friends have died today, and one of my best friends is still captive on the *Firebird*. And God help me, I am not going to lose anyone else. This ends now, Adams. Tell us! All of it!"

Adams was unmoved. He closed his mouth in a tight frown and looked away from North towards the stars.

"Fine, have it your way," Rita looked at Adams, her icy stare betraying none of North's passion. "North, will you and Twig escort Adams to airlock 16b? Under the authority granted to me by the governor's declaration of martial law, I am sentencing Jayden Adams to death by airlock, the sentence to be carried in ten minutes. There will be no appeal."

Twig hoisted Adams to his feet and drew his weapon. "You heard the lady."

"What?!" Adam's face tensed again. "You can't do that. I have amnesty from being a member of Chasm. I surrendered —"

"Oh, I'm not airlocking you for being a member of Chasm," Rita said in a smooth, even tone. "I am sentencing you to death because you are withholding lifesaving information that is probably critical to the survival of this waypoint. In this crisis, I think everyone will understand why I am declaring this a capital offense."

Adams seemed to consider his options, the relief that had eased his facial features just moments earlier had evaporated. His eyes were heavy with fear, and he reached down into his soul to muster up courage.

"I will not betray the future," Adams said, his voice shaking but resolved. "The individual does not matter. To the airlock, then gentlemen."

"To hell, I think." North had no hesitation, but Twig hoped that Adams would fold.

The two walked out of the room into one of the capillary hallways. This close to the edge of the station the rooms were dense, and the passage was not wide enough to accommodate two men abreast. North led the trio, Adams in the middle, and Twig brought up the rear. He had his gun trained on the cuffed Adams. They passed the base armory, where several Marines were gearing up.

One of them popped into the hallway hearing the foot traffic, saw North and saluted.

North saluted back. "It's going to get ugly. Be sure to get your full armor gear and bring plenty of extra ammo. Not sure what the plan is yet, but I should be back shortly — I'm just taking out some trash."

The three slid by and reached the exterior wall of the Marine base. North presented his thumbprint and entered a code to release the door.

Outside, North found a group of civilians — he thought he recognized them as microfactory technicians, gathered at a hall junction. They looked up and first spotted North.

"Good, a Marine," the tallest of the group said. "I'm going to ask him."

The tall man approached North. "Hey, what's going on."

"You all need to get back to your homes and lock down. Didn't you hear the governor? There is an enemy force here, and they are not contained."

"Enemy force? Where? How did they get here? On *American Spirit*?" said another worker.

"It doesn't matter. The point is that we are all in danger, and you need to stay out of the way."

Adams saw an opportunity.

"Don't listen to these men," Adams said. "They are trying to overthrow the government. They are going to execute me!"

The third worker spoke up. "Hey, I recognize you. You're the chief justice. What's going on here? Why are you in handcuffs?" The three men moved to block the hallway.

North was annoyed. "I don't have time for this. Stand aside so we can carry out our business. You need to get back to your homes and lock yourselves in."

"Yeah, whatever," the tall man said. "Look, I don't know what's going on here, and I don't want any trouble. But you need to let the chief justice go." The tall man pulled a heavy omni-wrench from his work jacket interior pocket and waved it threateningly.

"You're right, you don't know what is going on here," Twig spoke up. "We are all in great danger. This guy is part of Chasm, the terrorist group threatening *Magellan*."

"How do we know you guys are not part of this Chasm thing?"

"That's right, they are!" said Adams excitedly.

"Shut up," Twig said.

"Why should I shut up?" Adams said. "You are going to execute me, are you not?"

"Look," North said. "Let me get the governor on my comm unit, and he can let you know the truth."

"No!" Adams said. "They kidnapped the governor and are forcing him to say lies or be killed."

The tall man looked North in the eyes. "I think you and the flyboy over there need to walk away. You can leave the chief justice with us."

"No can do."

"Well, then I am sorry about this, but…" the tall man swung his wrench at North and caught him on the bad arm. North stumbled back into Adams, then dropped into a crouching charge to tackle the tall man. The other two men prepared to join the brawl.

Twig, who was mostly still behind Adams, threw the lawyer to the floor with a powerful push from his gunless arm. He quickly aimed and discharged his stun gun three times, sending the workers painfully twitching to the floor and then into unconsciousness.

North straightened himself up, moaned over his injured arm,

which was shrieking with pain, and then used his good arm to help Twig hoist Adams off the ground.

Adams shrugged. "It was worth a shot," he said, almost embarrassed. "I am a desperate man."

"So tell us what you know about Chasm, and we can head back to base," Twig said, uneasy about his part in the coming execution.

"Sorry. I've already told you," Adams said, a wave of bittersweet melancholy washing over him, "I am ready to die with my secrets. Surely you must understand. I'm not playing chicken with you. There must be something or someone you'd be willing to die for."

North thought of Amberly.

"Yeah, the mother planet," Twig said. "Let's get moving."

Amberly could not remember ever having such intense feelings of nervousness. Her palms sweated inside her space suit, even though it was environmentally controlled to be around 20 degrees. Dek wasn't exactly comfortable with Raven One's plan either. The pair, along with the elder Macready, had just donned the space suits and were standing by the *Firebird*'s main hatch. They could now only communicate over the internal radios. The suits were plain white, except for the brightly colored *Magellan* flag patches adhered to the suit breasts.

"Sparks, are you sure you can pull this off?" Dek said over the radio to his cohort-mate.

"Are you kidding, you son-of-a-dirt-licker?" Sparks was alive. "It's just a quick bounce maneuver. And as soon as I've broken through, I'll switch the computer nav back on."

Sparks was also wearing a vacuum suit. It had no environmental control units like the ones Dek and the others were wearing, but it did supply oxygen to her sealed helmet unit. The suit was made of a dark black polymer and fit her tightly. The flight suit was made so someone could still pilot the craft even if the atmosphere had suddenly been vented. Paranoid pilots would wear the flight suit always. Then, in an emergency, putting on the suit was just a matter of twisting the helmet on. Suits were fitted, custom made for a pilot.

Sparks' lighter gloves also provided greater range of

movement than the bulky gloves on a spaceworthy suit. Sparks punched a few buttons in the magnetic screen and then pulled up the rarely-used manual yoke from a boxed unit next to the pilot's chair on the bridge. The yoke controlled the Valkyrie thrusters using hydraulics in the event of a complete computer shutdown.

In this case, the computer shutdown would be intentional, because Sparks intended to force a collision. If active, the computer's safety measures would have used the ship thrusters to prevent impact.

Her right-hand fingers slowly gripped the stick. She flexed each finger, getting a comfortable grasp.

"Let's do this," Sparks said over the radio.

"Okay, Sparks," Kimberly said. "Chasm is counting on you. With any luck, you'll be able to escape. We'll meet you at the rendezvous."

"Oh, I'll race you there," Sparks said with a jocular tone. "Tell Jayden I said hello once you take the command center."

"On my mark then," Kimberly said. "Three, two, one… mark."

"Hold on to something," Dek said. In response, Amberly grabbed a handrail next to the sealed *Firebird* hatch.

Sparks smiled and started to press into the yoke.

On the *Magellan* command center, a civilian monitoring the station's exterior sensors shouted to the center chair, where Moreno was reviewing a tactical report with Remus.

"Ma'am, ma'am! The *Firebird* is on the move."

Moreno looked up from her infopad. "Where to?"

"Looks like a collision course onto the topside dome. Impact any second!"

The governor who was reassuring members of the *Magellan* legislative council on a video call stood to attention as well. "The gardens!"

The *Firebird's* port thrusters had the ship accelerating sideways at more than 400 km/hr. The runabout smashed into the plexiglass dome, shuddered and bounced off the dome. Inside the dome, a loud cracking sound echoed, as stress at the molecular level on the transparent dome started to give way to fissures.

The *Firebird* itself struggled to steady after ricocheting off *Magellan*. Sparks pulled hard on the yoke and fired the starboard side thrusters to stabilize the ship relative to the waypoint.

The jolt threw both Amberly and Dek across the room, their grips on the handrail insufficient to keep them grounded. Kimberly, on the other hand, possessed the needed manual dexterity to not lose her grip, and her body merely jerked at the impact.

"Well?" Kimberly called through the radio. "Are we a go?"

Sparks answered back. "I see some small cracking, but no entry point yet."

"Give her another whack, and hurry," Kimberly said. "Moreno must know how we are trying to break in now."

"Check your suit integrity, Amberly," Dek said. "Make sure you didn't damage anything in that last hit. And hold on."

This time, Amberly grabbed the handrail with both arms.

"It's going to take me about two minutes to set up for the next run," Sparks said.

"Hurry," Kimberly implored again.

North, Twig and Adams had reached airlock 16b, the closest to the Marine base. It was at the end of a long, exceptionally narrow corridor.

Twig indicated with the wave of his stun gun for Adams to step into the airlock.

"I'm not going in there," Adams said. "Why should I? What, is North going to hit me again?" Adams rubbed his bruised cheek.

"Your choice, Adams," Twig said. "This is your funeral. Do you want to go out wide awake? Or we could just stun you and throw your comatose self in there. Just know as soon as I pull this trigger, you'll never wake up again."

"We're arguing over minutes," Adams said.

"But they are your last," North said.

"Please, Jayden," Twig said. "Tell us what we want to know. There doesn't have to be any more death today."

"My death is on your hands, cowards," Adams said. "And soon, you'll be with me in death."

Adams spoke boldly, but his trembling body revealed his fear. He eyed the stun gun pointed at him, and then decided to step into the airlock voluntarily. "I guess I am going to end this, eyes wide open."

North tapped a control that sealed the airlock. North spoke solemnly. He knew a part of his humanity would die if he carried out this execution, but he was a solider, trained to follow orders. North believed with all his being in the afterlife and held to the orthodox Christian view that only those who believed in Jesus Christ would go to heaven.

North quoted from Christian scripture, "'For God so loved the world, that he gave his one and only Son, that whoever believes in him, shall not perish, but have everlasting life.' Make peace with your maker now. You have 30 seconds. God have mercy on your soul."

"Spare me your religious platitudes," Adams said. "This is my end."

"It doesn't have to be," Twig asserted. "Please, tell us what we need to know."

A red light started to flash and a pleasant female artificial voice started to speak. "Warning. Airlock depressurization in 30 seconds."

North looked through the viewport into the airlock at Adams. Both men had tears forming. North, who just weeks ago enjoyed a life of peace, was now fully broken. His soul cracked over the duty that forced him to execute another living human. It wasn't just that duty was forcing him to kill the subdued Adams. He felt himself wanting to kill Adams, to take revenge for those already killed by Chasm, and for what was next to come.

Twig stood at attention. A series of snap hisses came from the magnetic locks releasing on the circular exterior airlock. When the countdown was complete, an electric motor would twist open the dog lock-style door and man and atmosphere inside the airlock will vent out into space.

The computer voice spoke again. "Twenty seconds."

"She's coming!" Jayden started to yell. "She's coming!"

"Who is coming? Who?" North said.

"Raven One," Jayden said. "You can't stop her. She's unlike anything you've ever encountered."

"Who is Raven One? Tell me now!"

"She'll have hundreds of troops. She'll overwhelm you. Her

strategies are mind-boggling. She cracked the code. She'll take the waypoint and destroy it from the inside."

"Ten seconds."

"Who is she? Last chance!" North pounded the window.

"Seven. Six. Five."

"Okay, Raven One is…"

"Three, two…"

North pounded the emergency abort button. The magnetic locks resealed.

"She is Kimberly Macready."

Jayden hung his head in shame. He had now betrayed both his waypoint and Chasm. North was right, Jayden had been playing both the angles, hoping he could survive the coming destruction. Jayden knew now that if Raven One did win, and found out he revealed her, she wouldn't hesitate to space him.

And in his heart, he knew she would win.

North was sure he heard incorrectly.

"Are you kidding me? Did you say Kimberly Macready? She was lost at space six years ago."

"No, she had cracked the *Magellan* master codes. She went into hiding until our escape ship arrived and we were ready to execute the master plan. Instead of waiting for six years on *Magellan*, she decided it would be safer to hide in the Spencer Belt. She's on the *Firebird* now. With her daughter, North. With Amberly. Now let me out of here!"

North was in semi-shock. This answer exploded a thousand new questions, but one surfaced first to his mind.

"Where is Kimberly's husband? Where is Amberly's dad? Where's Alroy?" North demanded. "Is he part of the Chasm plot as well?"

"No," Adams said softly. "He was a mark — a sap. I'm sure she spaced him the moment they were clear of *Magellan* visual range."

"No, no, no!" North pounded the interior door of the airlock.

Twig and North's comm units simultaneously beeped on the emergency channel.

Twig answered first, "Twig here, ma'am. The condemned has starting spilling infor—"

"Twig, North — I need you to head to the topside garden

access tubes right away. The *Firebird* is trying to … punch a hole in the dome. Skip thinks they may be trying to land on the gardens since they can't get into the hangar."

"What?" North said. Using a runabout to wreck the *Magellan's* farming apparatus to find a landing spot was the most crazy thing he'd heard in his life.

"I don't need to tell you how catastrophic it would be if we lost the gardens," Moreno said. "I'm sending a team of Marines and civilians to meet up with you at Rick's. From there you can assess the next course of action."

"We're on our way. Rita, is this a secure channel? No civilians listening in?" North asked.

"Yes. Why?"

"Adams started coughing up information at the last second. Please don't tell this to Kora, but he claims that not only is Kimberly Macready alive, but she is Raven One, the leader of the Chasm operation here on *Magellan*. It's so crazy: I don't know if I believe it."

"Wow," Moreno said, sincerely surprised. "Understood. I don't know if I believe it either. Get over to Rick's ASAP. Contact me when you are there. The rest of the team is leaving here now. Moreno out."

Twig tilted his head toward Jayden. "What do we do with him now?"

"We don't have time to deal with him now," North said. "Either we space him or we leave him … locked up in the airlock."

"You can't leave me in here," Jayden protested. "What if someone comes along and … lets the air out?"

"Too bad," North said. "If we survive, we'll come back for you."

With that, North and Twig started moving for the nearest tube station at a rapid clip.

"North! North!" Jayden's shouts slowly became softer as the pair of Marines double-timed down the hall.

CHAPTER NINETEEN

Sparks was having the time of her life. *Who else has gotten to ram a runabout into a waypoint?* she thought as she gave the *Firebird* a little more running space. Still manually piloting the ship, she aimed for a second collision with *Magellan*, hopefully not causing too much damage to the *Firebird's* primary thrusters. But it didn't matter. Within a half hour or less, she was going to be ditching the *Firebird* entirely anyway – or the ship would be her tomb. The life-threatening danger thrilled her like nothing before. She had never felt so alive.

"Ready on the hatch," Sparks radioed her companions waiting near the main aft cargo hatch. Amberly Macready and her mother, the infamous Raven One, stood waiting. Amberly was white-knuckle anxious and feeling nauseous. Kimberly was focused. With the two women was Dek, somewhere in-between focused and anxious, ready at the manual release for the hatch to make a jump for *Magellan*. He had the code breaking box strapped to his space suit — the same box he had used to access the gardens the day he met Amberly. Only this time, he needed it to unlock the hatch to get out of *Magellan's* green paradise. Once the hull had been compromised in the gardens, the exit hatches from the gardens would be automatically locked down.

When they touched down on the gardens, the three spacewalkers would have to remove their suits because they were too bulky to fit through the hatch into the main *Magellan* levels. Dek would use Kimberly's hacking box to open the hatch, and then they'd have to fight against the flow of venting atmosphere and seal the hatch behind them. The chances of missing whatever fissure, of getting blown out into space, of getting impaled by debris, or suffocating before they could get safely inside *Magellan* were high.

Dek knew he would have to be sharp to survive. He needed to make sure both the Macready women made it alive. Getting Kimberly to the command center was vital for the mission success. And the mission had to succeed for Dek to survive the day.

Amberly had to survive, well, because Dek loved her. He

knew that eventually the Chairman, Kimberly and the rest of Chasm's leadership wanted to completely destroy that binary emotional attachment between a man and a woman, that foundational representation of everything Earth was, the basic building block of Earth's society for thousands of years.

The love of a man and a woman had no place in the coming Arara order. In its place was the love of the greater good and a covenant commitment to the planet and the community that lived there. The pursuit of pleasure, that would remain, but a genderless pleasure, at best. But any thoughts of self-sacrifice would never be for the benefit of another individual, spouse or otherwise, but instead for the corporate best.

Dek knew all this, and in his head, he agreed with this new order. But Dek didn't want to give Amberly up. He couldn't. He didn't know how he would reconcile those feelings once Earth and its ways had been discarded and lost forever. But he would figure it out when the time came. He might not be Kimberly Macready-level genius, but he was still a clever man. Dek looked through his suit helmet at Amberly and smiled.

Amberly looked out of the tiny aft portal at *Magellan*. Were her friends even alive? Was there anything even left to go back to? She had wanted so desperately to find out what had happened to her mother that she was willing to lie and steal for Dek — and for Chasm. And she sold her soul for what? To find a loving, caring mother who was waiting to meet her and restore their relationship of love and support? No, her mother was a genius, murderous tyrant on a mad crusade to change the course of history and the nature of humanity.

For a moment, Amberly hoped that she and her mother would die in the spacewalk, that she could get off this speeding tubecar of life. Everything she loved and held dear was destroyed or about to be.

Maybe.

Her friends could still be alive. They could need her. The thought gave her a reason to live. She thought about North, about being with him. The idea seemed so beneath her back at the Shard Cave, but at this moment the patriarchal idea of being protected by his powerful arms was extremely appealing.

Dek suspected Amberly's unease, and moved to comfort her.

He took her thick-gloved hand in his. "Everything is going to be all right, Amberly. This is the rough birth of a great, new future. I'll be here for you."

Dek knew that last sentence would draw the ire of Raven One, but he chanced it. If the male protector undertones did bother Kimberly, she did nothing to let him know.

Sparks' voice came over the radio. "We're in position. Here we go!"

The *Firebird* sped stern first at great speed into the already cracking *Magellan* dome. The impact exploded pieces of ship and dome in every direction.

Shards of plexiglass were projected out into space as a jagged hole, about 10 meters wide opened in the garden dome. The immediate pressurized rush of air escaping the garden blew the *Firebird* out of the hole it had created, flipping the ship into an end-over-end spin.

Amberly tumbled rapidly in the belly of the spinning *Firebird*, colliding with the walls, Dek and her mother. Kimberly shouted into her radio, "Sparks, get us stabilized! Sparks!?!"

There was no response.

The *Firebird* was rotating nearly once a second and was drifting away from *Magellan*. Kimberly had a firm grip and a safety rail, holding herself down. Dek had floated to the center of the hold as the room span around him. But Amberly couldn't get clear of the various desks, boxes and stations that were bolted to the hull. A box full of emergency food supplies came loose and smashed into Amberly's helmet, and the woman was pushed into the spinning ceiling of the room and caught a lamp bar hard in the arm. Amberly cried out in pain, and the radio fed her outburst into Kimberly's and Dek's helmet.

Kimberly felt a trickle of worry seep into her thoughts. "Sparks? Do you copy? Get us stable!"

"Sorry," Sparks came over the comm. Underneath his helmet, Dek eyes showed visible signs of relief. "I was thrown out of my chair. I'm engaging the computer pilot now."

Once the computer had control of the ship, it quickly started calculating and executing the appropriate thrusts to bring the ship upright relative to *Magellan*.

Dek looked to Amberly. She had recovered and nodded at

him, putting a hand forward to indicate she was okay. Dek looked out the hatch portal at the gaping hole in the top of *Magellan*.

"Can you get us any closer?" Dek said. "We'll get blown into space before we get caught in the waypoint's artificial gravity jumping from this distance."

"Give me a second to see if I can get you a wee bit closer." Sparks expertly navigated and stabilized the *Firebird* just several hundred meters from the growing hole in the garden dome.

"Well?" Dek asked over his radio.

"Dek, I show we are at optimal alignment," Sparks said. "This is as close as you get. This is your best shot."

"This is our only shot," Kimberly said. "Blow the door, Dek."

Dek pulled the emergency hatch open.

Suddenly, Dek, Amberly and Kimberly were ejected out into space, sucked out of *Firebird's* cargo bay.

Everything was silent.

Then Amberly could hear her own breathing inside her helmet.

"Dek? Dek?" she said nervously into her suit's radio. She already knew Dek wouldn't be able to hear radio signals because of the jamming interference flooding space by the *American Spirit's* communication array.

She looked around but couldn't seem to orientate her body so she could see Kimberly or Dek. They were not between her and *Magellan*. Amberly assumed they must have been floating behind her, but she couldn't be sure.

She was completely free floating now, shooting head first towards *Magellan*. She was propelled solely by momentum, closing rapidly on the waypoint, but not yet in the pull of its artificial gravity well.

She could see the large, jagged hole in the garden dome and could see a plume of dusty air being projected into space. Already, she could tell she was colliding with the escaping atmosphere, and it was slowing her down. If air being expelled in the opposite direction slowed her forward progress entirely before *Magellan's* gravity caught her, the wind stream would push her back out into open space the way she came. The space suit had no means of self-propulsion.

More than 100 meters separated Amberly from the gaping

hole in the gardens, and she was rapidly decelerating. She looked to her left and saw the *American Spirit*, gleaming brightly, reflecting the blue-tinted light of HD 238921, Spencer Minorum.

She turned her head and looked forward again at *Magellan*. With her helmet blocking peripheral vision, when she looked forward it filled her entire field of view. The vast metallic disk, with its garden dome, now bleeding a mix of atmosphere, dust and various plant limbs and leaves, was both beautiful and grotesque at the same time.

Amberly had seen photographs and videos of Earth from space, and there was no denying the home world, a brilliant spherical swirl of blues, greens, browns and white, was truly beautiful. And when she compared the image of her Earth in her minds eye with *Magellan's* harshly sloping hull, jutting with tubes and metallic recesses and pocked with various-sized viewports, the waypoint was distinctly artificial. From the topside view, it was a huge, uneven grayish spinning dish with a green eye. Now that eye was cracked.

For Amberly, Earth was foreign and might as well as have been mythical. When she saw *Magellan*, now less than 50 meters away, she saw... home. Somewhere between Rick's and the Science Corp labs, the topside gardens and Chinatown, somewhere in the mess before her was her heart. In those places where she had played with Kora, danced with North, laughed with Lydia, and even beat Skip at chess, those memories and people were as much a part of *Magellan* as the bulkheads and antimatter reactor, the Tube and the hangar.

It was her home. It was worth fighting for. And now Amberly felt it was worth dying for.

The people on *Magellan*, progressives and traditionalists, atheists and believers, the native-born and the Ararans, men and women, all worth saving: They were *Magellan*, both adjective and noun. Those unique, individual lives were worth something, not just as the collective population of *Magellan*, or even as a social team that kept *Magellan* running smoothly as a key link between Earth and Arara. Individually they were worth celebrating and worth protecting.

Amberly now felt like she was barely moving at all.

The only noise she could hear was her rapid breathing as the vibrations generated by the cardio activity echoed in her helmet.

Then, she looked to her right and saw infinity: the billions of sparkling points of light, scattered throughout the universe, with no end that she could comprehend. At once she experienced basest human emotions of eternal loneliness. She felt small as she gazed out into black sea that she would never cross — at least not alive. She was a speck of nothing in the infinite universe. The blackness of space seemed to absorb her mind, pulling her focus into the places between the stars.

She imagined the sparkling stars as some sort of bitter, tragic symphony. *Tchaikovsky, maybe*, she thought, *Swan Lake perhaps*.

She looked at the stars, visually sharp, twinkling red and blue and white, separated by the eternal darkness. They were so far away. She reached out with her hand, and time seemed to stop. Something solitary in her core longed to know them. Amberly longed to know the unknowable.

She thought about her dad. Remembering his face clearly was hard, but she could still hear his voice. "That's what heaven is for," he'd say. "All the mysteries of the universe, everything we couldn't understand, we'll know." Cloaked in her mother's empirical worldview, she didn't agree with him, but even now she wondered where he had acquired his undeniable optimism. *His hope, perhaps unfounded*, Amberly thought, *would be welcome right now*.

She tried again to picture Alroy Macready in her mind's eye. A warm smile, trimmed with reddish beard and nearly perfect white teeth. His green eyes were warm and inviting, bright and full of life. He wasn't tall, but his arms were strong and reliable. Even when he was tired from piloting an excessively long trip, his spirit never seemed to lose its energy.

As Amberly thought about her dad, a particularly bright star caught her attention. *That must be dad, looking out for me*, she thought. Amberly smiled. She didn't think the spirit of her father had really become a star, and he certainly didn't believe such a thing, but the what-if of the thought comforted her now.

Amberly's forward momentum had slowed considerably when she was just a meter or less from the torn hole in the topside garden dome. Even though the escaping atmosphere was so thin now it offered no detectable resistance, for a moment Amberly thought she might be pushed back into the darkness of space.

There were probably worse ways to go than floating into infinity, Amberly frowned.

And then she felt a familiar tug: She had slipped into the reach of *Magellan's* artificial gravity field, a force she knew well. Home was pulling her in.

As Amberly slipped through the jagged portal left by the collision with *Firebird*, her suit caught on a dislodged, warped reinforcement bar. The tear immediately depressurized her suit as she started to fall rapidly and dangerously to the surface of the *Magellan* garden, now just a few meters away.

She hit the dirt hard, landing on her side. The impact knocked her air out. Although most of the atmosphere was gone, dirt and leaves and other organic material still swirled in the garden.

Amberly was breathing hard as the air in her suit became almost too thin to inhale. She couldn't seem to catch her breath. She didn't get up. *Tchaikovsky* was still playing in her head, and she began to see black spots.

"I am going to pass out," Amberly said aloud to no one. "I am going to die."

And then she looked up and saw her mother seize her by both arms and begin to drag her through the dirt storm. And she looked ahead and saw who she thought was Dek kneeling over a floor portal.

Dek had already removed his gloves and was working frantically to get Kimberly's hacking box to open the door. Kimberly set down Amberly after half-dragging, half carrying her daughter inside her space suit for several meters. Kimberly took a deep breath and removed her helmet and then quickly unfastened the rest of her space suit, stepping out and then stripping a now unconscious Amberly out of her suit as well. Dek almost had the portal open.

"I'm starting to feel light headed," Dek said as the whipping wind in the dome started to calm. The atmosphere seemed nonexistent. Dek took in a deep breath, but the air was thin and his lungs started to burn.

Kimberly was calm and focused. Dek noted the thinning air didn't even seem to bother her.

To Dek, the hacking box seemed like it was taking hours to bypass the computer lock on the portal, but in reality, just five seconds had passed.

"It won't open!" Dek wheezed to Kimberly, panic in his eyes. He wondered if he could put his space suit back on before he suffocated. "It's not working!"

"Save your breath," Kimberly said in a disappointed monotone. "It is just having to run a secondary hack because the computer knows this side of the portal is depressurized. It's a safety feature."

Kimberly's words did not comfort Dek. He felt the temperature start to drop rapidly, and the plants that did not get sucked out into space started to freeze.

Within another five seconds, the magnetic locks on the door released, and Dek pulled the round portal open. Immediately, a geyser of air from the lower decks of Magellan shot out into the under pressured topside gardens.

The force of the air blast knocked Dek off his feet, and he stuck his head into the rush and took in the thicker air.

"You go down first," Kimberly ordered. "I am going to hand Amberly down to you."

Dek was eager to comply and forced himself against the sustained upward blow down the same hatch that he and Amberly had climbed up on the night they met. Kimberly hoisted the unconscious Amberly into the hole and slowly lowered her down. Dek was on the deck below now, and he reached up and grabbed Amberly's legs, catching himself absentmindedly admiring their attractive shape. Amberly's red hair blew wildly as she passed through what effectively was a wind tunnel.

Dek immediately felt guilty admiring Amberly's beauty while she was unconscious as he took her full weight from Kimberly and set her gently down on the floor.

Kimberly slowly climbed halfway into the hole, forcing herself against the shooting air. She looked up into open space through the fissure in the top of the garden dome. *So begins the end of* Magellan, she thought, as she pulled the portal closed behind her. Kimberly dropped more than three meters to the floor, where she landed in a shock-absorbing crouch next to the prone Amberly.

The mother hovered her ear above her daughter's mouth, put two fingers on Amberly's neck and was still. Dek could see that the young Macready breathing shallowly.

"She's going to be fine," Kimberly told Dek. She ran a hand gently over Amberly's mid-torso. "She may have fractured a rib. You'll have to carry her Dek, so be careful. I know you are not strong as that North fellow; do you think you can handle it?"

Kimberly's dig at Dek's strength was a not subtle way for Raven One to remind the younger man that he was vulnerable to silly patriarchal rivalries.

Dek put an arm under Amberly's knees and an arm underneath her shoulder blades and lifted her up, careful not to show any sign of strain. Amberly wasn't heavy by anyone's definition, but she was 45 kilograms.

"Let's get down to the command center," Kimberly said to Dek, taking off at an aggressive pace toward the tube. "You know, I am glad I was able to visit this place one last time before we torch it."

CHAPTER TWENTY

North and Twig had double-timed it to Rick's. When they arrived, they found the bar empty of patrons except for the contingent of Marines Acting Commander Moreno had dispatched from the Marine HQ.

The trip from the airlock where they left Adams to Rick's was chaotic, with panicking residents scurrying about the main halls and capillaries, and various Chasm operatives attempting to cause mayhem. Twig had used his stun gun four additional times on people he believed to be Chasm troublemakers.

Examining floor schematics at the bar were three Marines, Leo, Boro and Wong, and two civilians, Kora and Lydia. Kato was the lone Rick's employee in the bar, and he was serving up drinks.

The Marines stood to attention when North and Twig entered the bar.

Kora ran up and gave North a hard squeeze. North winced as she brought too much pressure on his injured arm.

"Sorry," Kora said.

"North, Twig," Leo said to the two officers, "We have to move, now."

"What's going on?" North said anxiously, reflecting the intensity in Leo's voice.

"We just heard from Central Command," Wong said as he pulled out his infopad, "the *Firebird* successfully punched a hole in the garden dome."

"No!" Kato gasped. "Our food source for —"

Twig frowned at the barkeep. His response seemed to have a fake quality to it. *What a drama queen*, Twig thought, then said, "We'll have to deal with that later. Right now, we need to get the station locked down and make sure that the damage is contained."

"It might be more complicated than that," Wong said. "Apparently three people, well, jumped from the *Firebird* through the fissure."

"Jumped?" said North incredulously. "How?"

"Space walked right through the new hole. But listen — about four minutes ago portal 1425b from the topside garden into access hall 14Y was hacked, opened and resealed."

"We need to find those three now," Twig said. "They could be planning some sort of sabotage. Maybe they brought a bomb or some explosive material?"

"Could it be Amberly?" Kora asked, voice full of hope.

"Maybe, but with whom?" Twig said.

"Saddle up. Let's go find out," North said.

Leo pulled out an infopad from a green supply pack that slung across his back and called up a map. "If we split up and move to these three junctions and converge here, there should be no way for these guys get past us," Leo pointed to three hall crossings on the map.

"Let's move," North said. "Keep your stun guns drawn and be ready for anything. Leo, you and Twig cover this corridor. Boro and Wong, you're on hall 16Y. Kora and Lydia, you come with me. But stay back in case there is trouble."

Twig looked over at Boro and spoke to North. "Can he be trusted?"

"With my life," North smiled. "Now move. Let's catch these people."

On the bridge of the *Firebird*, Sparks had physically propped the manual yoke with an empty soup packet, and stood and quickly made her way toward an escape pod.

The computer spoke over the ship-wide speaker system, "Warning. Collision imminent in three minutes. Collision avoidance systems have been disabled. Do you want to enable them?"

Sparks ignored the computer and held down an escape pod access control for ten seconds. She counted out loud as she did. A round door, less than a meter in diameter, rolled open revealing the interior of the pod. The capsule was cylinder-shaped, designed to hold two medium-sized humans. A small viewport opened into space on the opposite side of the access door. The wall was lined with rations, air tanks and other survival gear, and two gurney-like clearings. Sparks strapped herself into one and reached over to a control panel and started to input the commands that would clear the pod from *Firebird*'s hull.

The door slid shut, and she could hear explosive bolts detonating. Suddenly the pod jerked free of the *Firebird*. Almost instantly, the pod was outside the *Firebird*'s artificial gravity field, and Sparks could feel herself become weightless.

"Time to go home," she said to no one, and then activated the pod's limited control thrusters to push the lifeboat toward the *American Spirit*. She was looking forward to getting back on the ship that had been her home for the last three years and the one that would take her back to Arara — for good.

"North do you copy?" Moreno was signaling North's radio. He was wearing a wireless earpiece, and moving down the hallway with his stun gun raised in front of him, poised to shoot. On either side of this hall were micro-factories and raw supply storage for the small production center.

Lydia also carried a stun gun North provided for her, but she held it barrel down. Kora refused a weapon, even when North insisted. "I'll just end up accidentally shooting a friend," she had argued before leaving Rick's.

"I read you, XO," North replied to Moreno via the radio. "We're moving to intercept the three potential hostiles. I hear we've lost the gardens. How do we recover from that?"

"The gardens are not important now," Moreno said in North's headset. Kora and Lydia could not hear Moreno's end of the conversation. "If your friend Skip is reading our radar correctly, they may be making a run for the anti-matter reactor. Find whoever got off that ship and question them immediately and report back."

North's face turned grim. "Understood."

About 100 meters ahead, the hall took a hard left and then converged into an area where the hallways being swept by the other two teams would intersect. North punched open the sole door on the right side of this segment of the hall and peered inside.

"Lights!" he commanded. The room responded with a flood of artificial light, and North quickly saw there was nothing in that room but tubs of polymer pellets for 3D manufacturing work. He popped back into the hallway and sealed the door behind him.

North heard what he thought were footfalls around the corner, so he held up a finger to his mouth to indicate that he wanted Lydia and Kora to be as silent as possible and then waved them to stop. North pointed to himself and then to the corner and pointed to the two women and put a palm angled down, indicating for them to stay.

North took a slow deep breath and slowly crept up to the corner. The footfalls were getting faster and closer. He closed his eyes and steadied his breathing. His index finger caressed the curve of the trigger of his assault rifle. *Steady*, he thought.

North sprung, rounding the corner with his weapon drawn. He saw someone he did not expect to see.

"Kimberly?" North said, slightly confused, as he looked at an equally shocked Raven One, who was eyeing North's assault rifle with suspicion.

Even with Jayden's recent revelation, North didn't really believe that Kimberly Macready was alive, much less leading Chasm. *How could Amberly and Kora's mother be so evil?*

North didn't want to make any hasty action. Kimberly looked lean and even hungry, but there was no mistaking her raven black hair and her round face that looked so much like Amberly's. He had remembered what Jayden had said about Kimberly's surviving six years of self-inflicted exile.

"North," Kimberly said sweetly. "So good to see you. I'm sorry but…"

North saw Kimberly reach for what appeared to be some holstered weapon, and his instincts kicked as he pushed his weapon close to Kimberly's face. "It's true then?"

The Chasm leader slowly moved her hands away from her gun, and that's when North noticed Dek, and more importantly, that he was carrying Amberly.

"Amberly!" North shouted. "Let her go, Dek!"

"What!? She's not my prisoner," Dek replied, nervous at the gun that North was brandishing. "She came of her own accord… and now she is one of us."

"No, that can't be," North said, but he didn't quite convince himself.

Kora popped around the corner with Lydia in tow, and her gaze fell on her mother.

Her face went white. "Mom! Mom? You… are… alive? I don't understand. You were dead. How…" She was dizzy and confused and thought she might faint. Kora then saw Dek with an unconscious Amberly stretched between his two arms.

Gathering her strength, Kora ran toward Amberly, and Dek slowly lowered her to the floor. "Amberly!"

North kept his weapon trained on Kimberly, and the Chasm leader sighed. Kora listened for Amberly's vitals and then stood up, and took note that North had his weapon pointed at the mother she thought had died six years ago.

"She's fine, Kora," Kimberly said, seemingly unfazed by the assault rifle pointed at her and unemotional over the fact that she was reunited with her eldest daughter after her six-year exile.

"I don't understand…?" Kora said, tears running down her face. Kora started to move forward to embrace her mother, but North forcefully said, "Stop."

"Wha... why are you pointing your gun at my mom?" Kora said.

"Kora. Your mother is Chasm," North said. "In fact, we have reason to believe she is the leader."

"North, that's my mom," Kora said, her voice trembling. "Don't you remember her? Mom, tell him… tell North."

"Ask her where she's been all these years?" North said, re-aiming his gun from Kimberly's torso to her head. "I bet hiding out on the Spencer Belt. You think it's a coincidence that she just reappears as this crazy Chasm cult is trying to destroy us all. Ask her what happened to Amberly!"

"Is that what you think?" Kimberly said calmly, without giving away any emotion in your voice. She didn't know what North knew, and she didn't want to give him any additional information.

"North, are you sure about this?" Lydia stepped up and asked. She had her stun gun in hand also, but was still aiming it down. "The Kimberly Macready I know, she was a woman of science, not murder."

"Don't science me, Lydia," North said. "Millions have been killed in the name of science."

"And religion," quipped Dek, who was half squatting over Amberly's resting body. He stood up and took a step toward North.

"You shut up and stand down!" North said. He didn't take his gun off Kimberly, but his focus was clearly burning on Dek. Dek stopped, realizing that North wouldn't hesitate to drop him with his assault rifle.

Dek wasn't ready to die yet. He had to be patient, and maybe the odds would get better. He also suspected Raven One was working on some plan as well. He decided to wait for her lead.

"You think my mom is one of the people who want to kill us all?" Kora looked like she was going to reach to grab the gun out of North's hand. Tears ran down her face. "This is my mother. I don't know how she is here, and I don't know why she is here, but … I don't understand."

"You could never put things together as well as your sister," Kimberly said.

"It's over, Kimberly," North said. "Jayden told us everything."

"You knew mom was alive?" Kora said to North, sobbing between words. "You knew she was alive you didn't tell me?"

"Kora, we only just found out," North said, "before we came over to Rick's."

"Jayden, typical male, all bravado and no backbone," Kimberly rolled her eyes. "How did he break? Did he give up everything for the promise of Moreno's amnesty, precious little that will be worth when my work is done here."

As she was finishing the thought, Twig and Leo sprinted up. Twig saw that North had his weapon drawn on the dark-haired woman, so he followed his training and pulled his stun gun and aimed it in the general direction of Kimberly and where Dek had returned to kneeling above Amberly.

Kimberly didn't like the way things were unfolding. Her mind was furiously working to find a way to escape and complete her mission. She had to get to the command center, to provide an escape for the loyal Chasm operatives, and make sure *Magellan* was not only temporarily out of commission, but utterly destroyed. The umbilical cord had to be completely severed, she knew, for Arara to rise. And with the apparent failures of the team at *Waypoint Cortez*, the Scorched Earth protocol was the only way to guarantee the gap was big enough to eliminate the influence of the mother planet on Arara.

Escaping from North and a pair of civilians, one of them her less than brilliant daughter, wouldn't be too hard, but the arrival of Twig and the Marine Leo meant she was going to have to process a new plan. She had hoped to exploit a wedge between

Kora and North while Kora was emotionally vulnerable, but North appeared to know too much about Kimberly's Raven One identity to let that happen. She had one more card to play to avoid being incarcerated and probably executed by the *Magellan* Marines. She'd just have to stall for a minute now, maybe less.

"Actually, Jayden broke in the airlock," Twig said. "Kimberly Macready, I presume. Also known as Raven One. And ugly over there must be this Dek I keep hearing North pledging to offer a free facial rearrangement."

Dek gritted his teeth, but said nothing. North took a step toward Amberly.

"I want you both to clasp your hands over your head and step away from Amberly," North said and waved his gun at Kimberly and Dek. "Slowly."

"Didn't you hear Dek? My daughter, she's with us," Kimberly said. "Didn't you know, she's with Chasm. She is now part of the triumvirate of leadership."

"Liar!" Lydia, who had been silent in the background, spoke up. "Amberly would never be a part of this madness."

"Tell me, North," Kimberly smiled, "How did Mr. Tigona here steal the runabout needed to pick me up from my secret base without an access card? Did Amberly happen to borrow a card from you?"

North cursed.

As if on cue, Amberly started to rouse. She opened her eyes and was surprised to see North's face. For a moment, she wondered if this had all been some bad dream she was just waking up from. Then she noticed the gun in North's hand, pointed at … she turned and looked, her evil mother.

Kora was really confused now. Her first reaction was to run to the side of Amberly, her beloved sister, now that she was rising, but North's command to stay back was still ringing in her ears. And Amberly had been acting strange and secretive since the *American Spirit* put into port, spending a lot of time with this strange Dek fellow, even running off with him to some sort of secret rendezvous in the topside gardens.

Amberly was still too groggy to understand what was going on, so she let her mind rest. Other people would work things out. She was just happy to have survived the space jump.

"Let me tell you what is going on here," Kimberly said, hoping to stall North and his Marines another 20 or 30 seconds from putting her and Dek in binders, and maybe Amberly, too. "You are all part of the greatest single moment in human history. Are you sure you are on the right side? What are you fighting for? Enslavement to mother earth?"

"You're crazy, Kimberly," North said. "Where's your husband? Where's Alroy?"

Raven One ignored him. "We are going to build the perfect society, where everyone is truly equal and people are free to improve humanity: where we put the good of the whole over the good of the individual. Where is the evil in that? The evil is fermenting in your hearts and the hearts of all men who resist the natural evolution of humanity. They fear change. They cling to a false sense of security through conserving the dated past. No more. Join the right side of history. Come with us on the *American Spirit* back to Arara, North. Let's not shed any more blood today. What do you say? Will you join me and fight for what is best for all, or will you stand with —"

Boooooooooooooooooooooooooooooooooooooooooom.

The lights flickered and so did the artificial gravity.

North looked worriedly at Twig, giving him a what-the-dirt-was-that look, and in that instant he took his eyes off Amberly's mother.

In a snap, she shot her arm forward, knocking the assault rifle out of North's good arm and sending it flying toward Twig. North instinctively leapt for his gun, as it fell to the floor, and Raven One gave him a much more powerful leg swipe than he would have thought her capable of. North hit the floor hard on his injured arm and yelped in pain.

Facing the opposite direction, Dek took a step toward Twig and the pilot took aim at Dek's head, and Dek stopped, slowly raising his hands and stepping back. Twig held the gun and looked over to check on his fallen comrade, when he became aware of Kimberly flying toward him, clenched fisted. Twig brought up a hand to block Kimberly's punch, but he was too slow and spun off her fist. Twig was shocked at the amount of strength Kimberly had in her punch.

Sensing Twig was off balance, Kimberly bum rushed him and

knocked him down. She pulled his stun gun from his grip in one quick motion and aimed it at Leo and discharged the weapon. Leo fell to the ground, convulsing.

Kora, still recovering from the shock of seeing her mother again, snapped into her medical training, and automatically went to Leo's side to care for him. Deciding she had to act, Lydia finally took aim at Kimberly with her stun gun, when she was sharply hit in the head by a flying infopad. Dek had flung the electronic device like a flying disc and was now charging Lydia. She dropped her gun as her hands reflexively went to the point of impact on her head.

Lydia was almost 20 centimeters taller than Dek, muscular and fit. Dek knocked her back, but she did not lose her footing. She shoved Dek off onto the floor. Kimberly shouted to Dek as Lydia stumbled, bleeding from the head.

Lydia attempted to focus on Kimberly who was charging her now. Lydia threw a punch at the smaller dark-haired woman, but Kimberly expertly stepped out of the way. Raven One crouched and expertly performed another powerful leg swipe that took Lydia off her feet and to the floor.

Kimberly had found her opportunity for escape. She ran past the fallen Twig, toward the hallway they came from, pushing Kora out of the way, and then breaking into an impressive sprint.

"Lydia!" North shouted as he tried to get to his feet, still struggling with Dek. "Shoot her!"

"No! You can't shoot my mom!" Kora pleaded.

The tall blonde picked up her gun and took four shots at Raven One, but her stun bolts did not find a target.

Twig looked at North, who waved him off to indicate he was okay. "Go get her!" North said as he struggled to get to this his feet. "If she makes it the command center, she could destroy us from the inside!"

Twig took off after Kimberly.

For an instant, the command center shook violently as a booming noise rippled through *Magellan* and oscillated every loose object in sight. Then the power flickered and the gravity jolted, giving private Inon a brief nauseating feeling in the pit of her stomach.

She blurted several profanities. "They rammed *Firebird* into the reactor!" the white-haired woman's yell was full of shock.

"These guys aren't bluffing," Skip said, holding on tightly to a rail next to the console he sat at on the first floor of the command center.

Moreno stood in the well in the middle of the command center in full crisis response mode. She turned to a civilian tech on the second balcony. "Shut down the reactor, now, please." Her voice was cool and commanding.

"Please enter your biometric authorization," the tech responded to the acting commander. Rita raised her palm in front of the magnetic screen at her station, and it accepted the input. "Okay, it's shutting down."

Corporal Horner flanked Moreno in the well. "XO, how long can we last without power?"

"Several months on back-ups with some assist from solar panels, assuming Chasm hasn't sabotaged the batteries," the tech answered without being asked.

Moreno was frustrated. She didn't think she needed to be justifying her perfectly sensible decisions to her underlings. "If we keep operating the antimatter reactor, and it is damaged; it could explode and take the whole station with it. Or it could leak lethal amounts of radiation. Either way, we have to take it off-line until we can verify that there is no potentially fatal damage."

Skip spoke up again. "It will take a least another hour for the cool down and shut down to complete, and then another hour for the anti-matter core to be securely stored."

"Inon, check the internal diagnostics. Are they giving you any readings?" Moreno asked. The private swiped at the three-dimensional rendering floating in front of her.

"I know that the shutdown command has been received and the process is starting," Inon reported. She double-checked her screen and uttered her favorite profanity again. "Looks like the service room has been depressurized. Probably exposed to space from the collision. But debris or damaged hydraulics or the sudden depressurization could have damaged the containment units, and we wouldn't know about it until after the shutdown process failed to complete."

"So we are blind without a visual inspection?" Skip asked.

Moreno turned to the young corporal standing behind her. "We need to know how bad the damage is, Horner. We need to verify the shutdown was successful."

"I'm on it, ma'am," Horner said, offering a salute.

"See if you can find the chief engineer." Moreno suggested. "But, take Inon and Skip along – if you don't mind. Between the two of them, they might have enough technical expertise to get us the information we need."

A sharp beeping sound came from the tech's panel. "Shoot. Radiation alert in the Jeffries tube 43c. That's the one connecting to the reactor tower. I don't know how high above normal."

"Sounds like we'll need to pick up some radiation suits then," Skip said nervously.

"Do you know where Engineer Zelma is?" Horner asked.

"The chief last reported in at the State power relay station, but that was before the Chasm assault began," the civilian tech muttered.

Moreno was worried that even if they could incapacitate the Chasm revolt, with a damaged reactor and destroyed garden dome, *Magellan* may already be a doomed waypoint. She forced the worry down. *Now is the time to show confidence*, she thought. *It's what Anderson would have done.*

"Better double-time it, Horner," Moreno said. "I'll radio North's team to join you once they lock down the topside garden situation."

She punched a few buttons floating in the air in front of her.

"North," Moreno said. "North, status report. North, do you copy?"

Dek and North were both struggling over North's assault rifle. Dek had his hands on the butt of the gun, while the hand of North's good arm gripped the barrel. North struggled to point the gun away from him while not releasing it to Dek.

Dek reached for the trigger, and North forced his injured arm to clasp Dek's would-be trigger hand. North pushed back on the barrel with his good arm and then twisted Dek's fingers with his bad arm. Dek howled. If North's arm wasn't injured, he probably could have broken Dek's fingers in his grip. However, the searing pain in his arm kept him from doing any real damage.

271

"Give up, Dek," North said, "and maybe Moreno will stay your execution." North gave a quick jerk on the gun, and flung it from both of their grasps. Dek and North both scrambled to their feet, with about two meters between them.

Dek charged North, and they both went flying down the hall together away from the others. The pair struggled for several more meters before the Marine found the space to land a blow.

North swung his good elbow hard into Dek's gut and almost knocked Dek's wind out. Dek grunted, took two steps back, then one step forward and following his forward momentum swung his right fist into North's jaw. The hit smarted. North was shocked. He would never have suspected that Dek could throw a serious punch.

"You think you are *good*," Dek said, with a sincere condescension, as North recovered. "You think you can save Amberly. You are wrong. Only I can save her now. She doesn't love you. She never will."

"You think I don't know that?" North parried. "I know I am not a good person. Just forgiven. Hopefully for this!"

North stepped up and punched at Dek's lungs. Dek managed to bring his arms to block, but he still was knocked back a few feet. The swift punching movement caused North's injured arm to jolt with pain, but he ignored the shrill feeling.

"I know that I am nothing to Amberly," North said as Dek struggled to catch his breath. "She made that perfectly clear to me when you showed up in her life."

It was Dek's turn to take a swing at North. The Marine dodged Dek's jab, but he was unprepared for the stealthy uppercut that followed and caught him in the chin. The impact caused the unsuspecting North to bite his lip hard, and his bite drew blood.

North jabbed back at Dek, who stepped back, fast enough to defuse most of the energy from the blow.

"I know she took advantage of my feelings for her to help you," North said. "Doesn't matter. I still care for her. I will save her home. *Magellan* is where she belongs."

Dek sidestepped to stay out of North's punching range, and then took two steps back to put more space between him and his adversary. "If you love her, you'll let her go. You'll let her come with us, with me and her mother."

As Dek circled, he could tell that North was considering the truth of his words. He also realized he must kill North. Dek figured North would not give up his cause to keep Amberly on *Magellan*, doomed or not. Dek knew Amberly's only chance of survival was to escape with him on the *American Spirit*, and North would stand in their way as long as he still drew air. Also, killing North would earn him some credit with Kimberly, possibly what he needed to get the space to have a relationship with Amberly.

Dek dodged a clumsy right hook from North's weak arm and decided to try a psychological attack to get the upper hand.

"You know she fancies me?" Dek chided. "And why not? She and I are the same: Students of the universe, masters of science. And didn't you hear Kimberly? She's one of us now. She'll be a great leader of Chasm one day, just like her mother. She'll be a founding mother to the new order, remembered for her greatness and for surviving the destruction of *Magellan*. Let *us* go, North."

North sprung across the hallway and managed to get both of his hands around Dek's throat while using his own weight to hold the smaller man to the wall. "What did you do to her?" North demanded. "How did you corrupt her?"

North pulled Dek's head forward and then slammed it forcefully against the steel wall. Dek had underestimated North's raw strength. Dek was seeing dark spots in his peripheral vision. A flash of panic made him consider that his miscalculation could be his end.

Was this worth it? Dek wondered. *For Chasm? For Arara?* North had Dek pinned, the Marine's hands crushing Dek's windpipe.

Dek's gaze fell down the hall, and he saw Amberly running toward them. Now, as he faced certain death — either by asphyxiation at the hand of this brute, or by airlock as a traitor to Earth — he knew that the new Arara order would never give him what he wanted: Amberly as his own.

Not as his possession, but he wanted Amberly to belong to him, and him to her. The want was powerful, and Dek understood why the Chasm leaders wanted to destroy this personal bond. No loyalties this strong, however personal, could be tolerated in deference to loyalty to the new order.

He couldn't be sure what it was that made him long for

Amberly. He had known plenty of smart and attractive women, but she was special. His analytical mind couldn't decipher the cause. He pictured her soft, round cheeks, blushing to match her rouge hair.

Deep down, he knew that Raven One would never permit them to have any sort of committed relationship, to perpetuate the old ways of love between a man and a woman. Dek tried to call out to Amberly, to tell her that he loved her, before he entered oblivion, but only a faint gurgling sound escaped his mouth.

"North! Stop!"

Amberly's voice was sharp and clear. "North, you're killing him! Stop! Please."

North looked at his hard hands encircling Dek's neck, where a whitish-blue ring started to form where blood was being cut off.

"Please, North, please. This isn't you."

Amberly was right. North the murderer? North felt a powerful shame that his passions had gotten the better of him. Moreover, he was ashamed because he knew his God had seen the murderous intent in his heart. North breathed heavily and fought back tears as he released his grip from Dek's marred throat, shoving the transient back into the wall. Dek gasped as air filled his lungs.

North looked over and saw the disappointment and fear in Amberly's eyes, and he felt broken again.

To see Amberly defend him so vigorously, to beg for his life, sparked a powerful new hope in Dek. Maybe there was a way he could be with Amberly, Dek believed again. He didn't have North's strength, but perhaps he was just clever enough to figure it out, how to survive and start a new life with Amberly. But there would never be a life for him and Amberly on *Magellan*. This waypoint was doomed. For them to be together, they had to survive. And for them to survive, it meant the return to Arara.

Dek took a long breath and then unexpectedly pummeled North with his free arm, landing a kidney punch that caused North to double and completely release Dek for just an instant. Dek had enough space to draw his short blade from its hidden sheath.

"Dek, no!" Amberly shouted.

Following the commotion, now Lydia and Kora had also

found their way down the hall.

North was already recovering when Dek, with all the strength he could muster, drove his knife into the heart of the existing wound on North's arm. Dek pulled the blade out and stabbed North's torso beneath the left rib cage, and in a flash pulled it out only to stab North's injured arm again, leaving the blade piercing the wound.

The large man cried out in excruciating pain and stumbled back into Kora, his arm immediately bleeding profusely. The blade remained lodged in North's muscle and bone as he collapsed to the floor.

"North!" Amberly shouted. She and Kora both moved to him as he clutched his arm.

"Lord, no," Kora said, "I think he hit an artery. Lydia grab that med-pack." Kora waved over at the nurse's bag she had tossed on the floor down the hall where they had first encountered Kimberly and Dek. Lydia retreated to recover the requested kit.

With the attention on North, Dek slowly reached over and picked up the assault rifle and aimed it squarely at North. North had to die.

"Amberly, Kora," Dek said with a quivering voice, "Please step away from him."

Lydia returned with the med-pack, handed it to Kora, and nervously noticed the gun Dek had aimed in the general direction of Amberly, Kora and North.

"Lydia, hands on your head," Dek requested firmly. The tall woman slowly complied, lacing her fingers against her soft yellow hair. "Please, step away from North now," Dek repeated with more intensity, indicating all three women.

"No!" Kora said, with tears running down her face. "He needs my help! Please."

"I don't want to, but I will kill you if you make me," Dek said, looking hard into Kora's eyes. "North will never surrender or stand down — he has to die. We've come too far, so close to perfecting humanity to let this Marine get in the way. Death comes for us all; for North it comes today."

"Go to hell," Kora growled. She knew she should pray for her enemies, but she had no place for that Christian practice now.

Dek lightly pulled the trigger and a single bullet rang out, a warning shot aimed purposefully well above North's head. Amberly yelped in surprise at the sound of the gunshot, but she stayed by North's side.

"You don't scare me," Kora said, turning her back to Dek and preparing to pull the knife from North's wound. "Shoot me. I know where I'm going when I die. Do you?"

"Apparently to hell," Dek mocked Kora.

"Save yourselves," North gasped. His breaths were rapid, but shallow. Both the Macready sisters knew North would soon die from blood loss. "Maybe Dek's right. Maybe it is my time. No reason for you to die, too. Save yourself. Be happy. Kora, you're a dish. I'll always love you, Red."

"North," Amberly said, tears running down her face. North shook his head at her in surrender.

Dek looked at his beloved. "Amberly, please step away from North," Dek begged.

North slowly forced himself to stand, blood trickling from his wounds onto the cold steel floor. He gently pushed Amberly and Kora out of the way and stood vulnerably in sights of his own assault rifle, which Dek had trained on North's torso.

North looked at Dek hard. "Kill me if you must, but promise me you'll take care of Amberly. Promise me you'll die for her." Then North closed his eyes and fell to his knees. He was bleeding out, shot up, stabbed, stunned, broken and worn out, but mostly just tired. The day had tested his mettle like none other. He leaned against the wall, and slid down into a seating position, leaving a crimson streak on the wall. Dek's blade still protruded from his arm.

He smiled, closed his eyes, and prepared to die.

Amberly knew what she had to do. It was the only way to save North. And *Magellan*.

CHAPTER TWENTY-ONE

Amberly stepped between Dek and North, confident and resolved. Her face was scratched and dirty, perspiration and dust streaked across her face.

After all this time, she finally figured out what she felt about North: She loved him. She didn't know if it was romantic or platonic or anything else, she just knew it was a *real, selfless love.* And she knew she loved him because she was ready to sacrifice herself, her hopes and dreams for the future, if needed, for his sake. She was ready to leave him, so he could live. She loved him, because he first loved her. He always had, even if he hadn't known it. And now she reflected that love back to him.

She knew that to save North, she would have to let him go – painfully.

"Dek you need to listen to me very carefully," Amberly took a step toward Dek and positioned herself between the rifle and North. "Dek, I want us. I want us to be together," Amberly said, her heart breaking as she imagined the pain these words would have on North.

Amberly continued. "But that will never happen if my mother wins. You know it. You think you can outsmart my mother? You think she'll let us be together?"

While Amberly distracted Dek, Kora removed the blade from North's arm. The pain electrified his nerves, but North didn't even have the strength left to cry out. Kora was spraying wound care on his arm while Lydia was applying pressure to his fresh torso wound.

"We'll figure something out," Dek said. "We'll run away and hide in the Arara wilderness."

"Maybe," Amberly said. "But with a mark of death always on our heads, we'd never be free. I would never be happy."

"So what do we do?"

"Surrender to the *Magellan* authorities," Amberly said. "You can still be granted amnesty. And you must know how we can stop Chasm, how we can save *Magellan*."

"They'll exile me... send me back to Earth," Dek said. "There is no escape for me. Arara is our best hope. We should take our chances with your mother and the Chairman."

"My mom will kill us just like she did Joti, in a snap, if she thinks we'll harm the cause," Amberly argued. "If *Magellan* exiles you, at least you'll still be alive. I can't see you die, not now."

"Yes, but I'll never see you again," Dek said. "That's not a round trip to Earth."

"Amberly, I can't save North here," Kora said, interrupting her gunpoint discussion with Dek. Kora was disgusted with her sister, for apparently choosing Dek, but she knew now wasn't the time. "If we don't get him to the medicenter soon, he will die."

"I'll go with you," Amberly said to Dek, ignoring her sister. "So two decades on a ship won't be so bad if we are together. Maybe we can start a family, who knows?"

How did this happen to him? How did he come to love this woman? And with love, Dek reasoned, comes trust. He had to start trusting Amberly now.

"Please Dek, surrender," Amberly said. "Let's go on a great adventure together. Do you love me?"

"I don't know what love is, Amberly," Dek said, hardly able to process the emotions exploding inside of him. Nearly his whole life he'd given his life for the cause, and the belief that the greater good, the state, Chasm and the perfect society to come, would always be more important than one person. But whatever he felt for Amberly was so powerful, he was willing to throw nearly 20 years of loyalty to Chasm away. "But how can what I feel toward you not be love?"

"Please, surrender."

"Amberly! North's unconscious," Kora gritted.

"Please, my love, surrender."

Dek lowered his weapon, and Lydia stepped forward slowly. Dek handed the butt of the gun to Lydia and put his hands on top of his head.

"Amberly Macready," Dek said, his face beaming with a strange joy, "I surrender and disavow Chasm and ask for asylum and amnesty."

As Lydia took possession of the assault rifle, Amberly stepped up to Dek and wrapped her arms around his neck.

"Welcome to the good side," she said. "Now, how do we stop my mother?"

Just then Boro and Wong rounded the corner, weapons raised.

Dek raised his hands in surrender. "Kimberly Macready will have one objective in mind, getting to the command center with as many troops as possible."

Kora, who was leaning over North's prone figure, trying to stabilize him, pointed at Dek. "Secure him. He's Dek Tigona, a Chasm leader."

Wong pulled out a zip cuff and secured Tigona's hands.

"He surrendered to us willingly," Amberly said rapidly. "He gets amnesty. Get as much information from him as you can, okay? We have to stop my mother before it's too late."

"Amberly," North spoke weakly.

Amberly knelt beside North. "North... I... I..."

North motioned for Lydia to hold his head up. "I hope you and Dek ... are happy, Red, I really do," he said, smiling faintly. Amberly could see the bittersweetness in his dark brown eyes, and she could not hold back her tears. North was crying too when his eyes rolled back into his head, and he slipped again into unconsciousness.

"We have to get him to the medicenter, now!" Kora said. "Lydia, help me carry him."

Boro reached down. "I will carry him." The large Marine gently picked up North.

Wong was communicating with his radio earpiece. "I need a dispatch of a gurney stat." Wong listened to the reply. "Okay. Tell the Science Quarter medicenter we have Lt. Commander North incoming with multiple stab and bullet wounds. Lots of blood loss. He is unconscious."

Wong looked at Kora.

"No ambulance, let's move." Wong said. "The medical response teams are in chaos right now. Either they are out responding, or they never came into work today. We'll have to get North there ourselves. Boro, you got this. I am going to get this fellow to the Brig — North said he trusts you with his life. Save him again."

"So I shall."

Boro started down the hallway, his arms outstretched, holding North. Lydia and Kora followed. About ten paces down,

Boro stopped and grunted. North was not a small man. It was at least a kilometer to the nearest medicenter. Lydia came up beside him and slipped her arms under North and locked them onto Boro's. He smiled at her and appreciated her strength. Together they carried the fallen Marine as fast as they could.

Wong pointed down the hallway that led to the tube. "Let's get you both to the command center. We can interrogate this traitor there. I am sure that XO Moreno will want to question him personally."

Amberly watched as North, Boro, Lydia and Kora disappeared behind a steel wall around a corner.

Dek looked at Amberly with soft eyes. "I'm sorry about North. I just…"

North was gone. Now Amberly could focus on the task at hand. She needed Dek's full allegiance to save North, Kora and the rest of *Magellan*, so she played the only card she had left. She threw her arms around Dek's neck and kissed him.

"Dek, of course I care about North, and I want to save him, and let's do that," Amberly said. "But this is the beginning of *us*. Now, how can we stop my mother?"

"We better hurry," Dek said. "We don't have much time.

So unfortunate, Raven One thought. *This is war, and I am doing what is necessary.*

She reached over Twig's lifeless body and took his stun gun. The pilot's arm had been snapped by the Chasm leader after she had ambushed him during his pursuit. The arm extended from his torso at an unnatural angle. *He didn't suffer long*, Kimberly mused, recalling how she broke his neck less than a minute after she confronted her pursuer.

Kimberly was in a vacant police substation and was accessing the system-wide public announcement system with her hacking box. She had to get to the command center. She couldn't remotely issue self-destruct commands — she had to be in the command center to make it happen. If only Järvinen and Johnson had been able to secure the command center — or even establish access to the *American Spirit*. But they had failed.

And they weren't the only ones who failed. The fact that they were not keeping *Magellan* as a prize of the new Araran order meant someone on one of the other waypoint cells had failed, too. *How can we build the perfect human order on people who are so susceptible to failure?* Kimberly thought.

A green indicator light strobed on her hacking box indicated that she now had control of the waypoint-wide public announcement system.

Kimberly took a deep breath. Chasm was hanging by a thread. The hopes for humanity perfected, after generations of planning, would come down to this. Could she convince the remaining Chasm loyalists to sacrifice what was needed complete the mission?

She closed her eyes, centering herself, feeling emotion and reason welling deep inside of her bosom. She spoke into the terminal microphone, slowly, pouring every ounce of confidence into her words.

"People of *Magellan*, today is a glorious day. You are all about to be a part of the most pivotal moment in human history since the birth of Christ. I am Raven One, but you might remember me as Kimberly Macready."

In the medicenter, Kora couldn't believe what she was hearing. She was inserting an intravenous needle into North as the surgeon prepared to go to work on the Marine's wounds.

"Can't we shut that off?" the surgeon asked her medical assistant. The assistant shrugged.

"I represent Chasm. For generations, we have been planning a great separation, to disconnect Arara from Earth, so we can build a truly perfect society on Arara, free from the shackles of Earth's history. Think of a society with no war, no disease, no money — where everyone believed that the community was more important than the individual, where everyone is truly equal. We are going to build that place. And some of you are going to come with us."

Dek, Amberly and Wong were sprinting toward the tube, and Kimberly's voice filled the waiting area. "We're going to be too late," Dek said, already second-guessing his choice in throwing in with the Earth loyalists.

"The gardens are gone. The reactor is breached. *Magellan* is doomed. Nothing can stop that now. Your only chance to survive is to join Chasm and escape with us on the *American Spirit*. I have complete control of the ship. Unfortunately, we don't have enough room for everyone, so only a lucky thousand or so will make it off alive."

Moreno stood in the command center well, listening to the elder Macready. "She's going to start a waypoint-wide panic. People are going to eat each other alive. We've got to get control of the PA."

A tech looked up at Moreno. "She must have cracked the command codes. As long as she is speaking, we're locked out."

"Here is what you have to do, people of *Magellan*, to survive. If you want to live and join me on the new paradise on Arara, I need you to help me get into the command center. The Chasm forces are already on their way to the hangar. Bring me the Acting Commander Rita Moreno's head on a platter, and you will get access to paradise. The Marines may try to stop you; but we are many, and they are few. Join the Chasm forces that are heading to the hangar right now. Help us take over the command center and clear a path to the *American Spirit*, and you can leave with us. Don't be indecisive, don't delay, or you will be left behind, and you will perish.

"To my Chasm siblings who are listening now, I give you this proverb from Arara's new wisdom: The whole is greater than the sum of its parts. You are worth more together than you are apart. We'd tarry three eternities before abandoning you. Raven One, out."

Kimberly sat and meditated, her eyes voluntarily rolling back into her head. She had set the appointed time for the death of *Magellan*. As she thought about what the waypoints represented, she knew their loss would be bittersweet. Without the waypoints, humanity would never have dared venture to Arara. Without Arara, there was no path to human perfection. *All things must end*, she thought. *Well, all things except the coming new order. It will last forever.*

Her meditation was interrupted by footsteps. She swung around to exit, and no fewer than twelve *Magellan* residents lingered just inside the doorway. They carried an arsenal made of various fabrication tools and culinary knives, decorative rods and bats made from chair legs. Kimberly's first reaction was a fight or flight consideration. Standing in front, a stout woman, maybe in her thirties with short blonde hair, was waving some sort of metallic bar. She spoke first.

"I am so glad we found you Raven One," the woman nodded her head in respect. "Alice Upton, Chasm code beta tango one four zeta. May we have the honor of escorting you to the command center?"

Kimberly smiled.

"Three hours," Dek said. "That's how long Raven One will wait before she leaves the stragglers behind."

"How do you know that?" Amberly asked.

"It was in the open code," Dek replied, twitching his arms against the tightly secured zip-cuffs.

"Are those cuffs uncomfortable?" Wong asked sarcastically, "Well, too bad."

Amberly ignored Wong. "What open code?"

"The proverb. There are no Araran proverbs. She was telling the Chasm operates and supporters we have three hours before the ship for Arara leaves. It's our way of encrypting communicating over public channels."

"Clever," Wong said.

"Can you communicate with the command center?" Dek asked.

"Yes, but we'll be there in less than 15 minutes," Wong said.

"We don't have that much time," Dek said. "I need to talk with Acting Commander Moreno now."

Wong looked over at Amberly to see if she was going to weigh in. "Every minute is going to count," she agreed.

The Marine pulled a small infopad out of his pocket and punched up a communication channel with the Command Center and spoke toward the devices built-in microphone.

"Command, this is Private Wong. I need a priority encrypted

connection with XO Moreno, urgent."

A civilian tech answered. "She's been waiting to hear from you; I'll let her know you are on the line, urgent."

A deep olive-skinned woman with dark eyes and dark hair appeared on the info pad's screen. "XO Moreno here. We heard from Boro that North is in surgery at the Science Quarter medicenter. Are you still *en route* with the prisoner?"

The mention of North in surgery hit Amberly in a crushing wave of guilt. North would not be flirting with death if she had not insisted he stand down during his fight with Dek, or if she hadn't taken advantage of North's feelings for her to steal his pass card. Her evil mother would still be chilling somewhere on the Spencer Belt instead of threatening the 10,000 lives aboard *Magellan*.

Still, she suspected that with or without her help, eventually Dek, Joti and Sparks would have found a way to recover her mother. And maybe they would all have ended up dead without a chance. And after the way she crushed North's heart, Amberly hoped now that Dek had something worthwhile to offer them, something that could save them. Getting his assistance had come at a horrible price.

"We are, but the prisoner claims to have vital information that could save the station in the next few minutes. He'd like to speak with you."

"Put him on, Wong."

"Ummm… commander Moreno?"

"What is it, Mr. Tigona? You are going to have to account for the lives lost today. Do you realize how many good pe—"

"Everyone on *Magellan* is going to die if you don't listen to me," Dek interrupted with a raised voice. "Raven One is coming and she is coming in force. If you think you can repel a force of 400, you might survive. I know we had several hundred operatives that made it aboard from the *American Spirit*. And there may have been that many or more among your ranks on *Magellan*. And your guess is as good as mine how many people from the mob will join her cause, desperate to live and betting she is the only way. A thousand? Two thousand?"

"I know Kimberly Macready, and I won't underestimate her," Moreno said. "I used to have a regular chess dates with her and

April Eaton before she went missing. Kimberly was quite good – one of the few people who could occasionally beat me."

"Occasionally?" Amberly butted in. "Maybe she was letting you win."

Dek couldn't believe this conversation was happening. He shouted, "We are running out of time! I have two things that will help you. The first is I can tell you how to disable her codebreaking box. She made it so Chasm could use it to hack *Magellan* during her self-imposed exile. She doesn't need it to hack anything where there is a terminal — her brain is like a computer. But it does help when she wants to hack something without a terminal, like a door. The box will wirelessly interface with most any *Magellan* coded device.

"It also helps when someone else wants to hack something when she is not around. Like me."

"You said we could disable it?" Moreno asked.

"Yes. It is only protected by a two-word code which you could use to access the box the next time she ties it into the network. If she uses the box, you could send the remote shutdown command."

"Let's cut to the chase, I suppose you want some special considerations for this infor—"

"No!" Dek said, yelling at the infopad held by Wong. "I don't think you realize how precarious the situation is. Get a tech so they can be ready to shut Kimberly down the next time she tries to login."

Moreno muted the conversation. Her hair was messy, and her eyes were tired. The command center was organized madness. Most of the people working on the three-level decks were coordinating police and military responses to the distracting acts of terror being carried out across *Magellan* by the now revealed Chasm cells.

Next to Moreno stood Governor Thor, who looked concerned but didn't carry the weight of leadership at this moment. Thor was content to let Moreno lead them through this crisis. He felt no need to accelerate his aging with this supreme stress. He nodded to Moreno to indicate that he thought cooperating with Dek was the right path.

Moreno waved a tech over to the well and gave him instructions. "Start monitoring for a hacking device and get ready to issue the following shutdown code the second it logs into our systems—" she paused and took Dek off of mute. "Go ahead with the passcode and the shutdown command."

Dek's voice seemed to project from his picture on the three-dimensional magnetic imaging screen in the command well. "Password: Bye Alroy. Shutdown command passphrase: Unity and equality forever."

The tech punched in the codes and nodded at Moreno. "If she uses her box again on any system connected to central command processes, we'll be able to shut it down. At least until she figures it out and changes the password."

"Mr. Tigona," Moreno said, her voice dripping with all manner of unspoken threats, "what happened to Alroy Macready?"

Dad, Amberly thought, *Alroy Macready, I wish you were here now. You'd make everything right.* Amberly was looking squarely at Dek. She hadn't thought to ask him if he knew the fate of her dad.

Dek dodged the question. "Now is not a good time for that, ma'am," he replied. "Can we discuss that when we arrive? I need to tell you my second idea to help."

Dek, still in zip cuffs, along with Amberly and Private Wong stepped into the President's Commons, a large, open eating area that also served as a waiting area for boarding the tubes. Hundreds of people packed the area, filling the metallic cavern with the sounds of discord and conflict and the smells of fear and desperation.

"Can't you use your rank as a Marine and get us through this and onto the tube?" Amberly asked Wong.

"It wouldn't matter," Dek said as he pointed to the tube car door. Someone from the mob had tossed several supply crates and some furniture into the tube path, and a passenger car had collided with the debris, shutting down the tube.

"Moreno, this is Wong," the Marine said into his infopad microphone, "The tube is out of commission. We're going to have to walk the extra two kilometers to get to you. And from the looks of it, there's a large crowd headed along the same path straight for you."

"Understood Wong," Moreno said. "Gather up as many loyal Marines as you can and get back here."

Dek butted in as they trio backtracked to the alternant route to the command center. "I can help you with your crowd problem, commander."

"I am not sure I trust you, Mr. Tigona," Moreno's voice projected from the infopad. "How can I be sure you are not playing us?"

"Because I only want what is best for Amberly," Dek said plainly. "And what she wants is for us to save *Magellan*. Even with my help, we may be beyond that point."

"You'll need to hold the line, XO," Wong said. "We are trying to get out of traffic here."

The main corridor leading from the President's Quarter Commons to the outer loop passage was thick with people, running in all directions. Some were trying to rendezvous with loved ones. Others were clearly trying to get to the hangar to attempt to board the *American Spirit*, and still others, anticipating danger at the hangar, were moving far away from it. Wong was trying to lead his group to use the outer loop as a bypass to get to the hangar and command center, and he was trying not to draw attention to himself as a Marine. Wong decided to try dropping to the sub level. The corridors were thin and twisty, but likely there were less people to navigate through. He found a floor portal and entered in his Marine passcode, and the portal yielded to him.

"Come on," he said.

Amberly dropped through the portal first, and Wong lifted Dek from behind and lowered him down because Dek was still zip cuffed and couldn't use his arms to help his descent.

Wong then followed and secured the portal above them. They were in a maintenance tunnel in life support — on one side of the tunnel were hundreds of oxygen scrubbers, on the other side, water purifiers. No one was to be seen. Wong got his bearings and pointed toward the command center.

"This way," he said as he took off down the hallway. "XO Moreno, are you still on the line?"

"I copy you."

"Here's Tigona again."

Dek spoke with enhanced tension. "Listen to me, right now the Chasm loyalists are in Scorched Earth mode. Their orders are to destroy and retreat. But there may be a way we could change the protocol to stand down mode, and trick the Chasm cells to stand down."

"Well, give me the code, and let's end this," Moreno said.

"It's not that simple. The code must come from a Chasm leader of rank, or it's generally thought of as invalid. And if there are conflicting codes, Chasm operatives are supposed to follow the highest-ranking issuer."

"Macready," Moreno swore.

"Exactly," Dek said. "However, if you were to, say, get three ranking Chasm agents to issue the stand down codes, that would certainly introduce some confusion in the ranks and thin out your opposing forces."

"Three?" Moreno asked, then it clicked. "You mean, you, Johnson and Jayden."

"Correct."

"This smells like a double cross to me," Wong said, as he led the trio down the thin, dark corridor. "I don't like it."

"It's not a double-cross," Amberly spoke up. "Commander Moreno, Dek is doing this for me, because he loves me and he knows that this is the only way we can be together. When Dek had the upper hand and was about to execute North, I asked him to stand down, and he did. He surrendered of his own accord as you can see. I want nothing more that to stop my mother's insane plan, and I —"

"Amberly Macready," Moreno said, with a hint of condescension, "I understand that it's because of you that we are in this mess. I am not sure what the legal ramifications are for your … actions, but we'll sort it out if we survive this. I'm not interested in your love life. God knows what North sees in you."

Amberly remained quiet. She was ashamed and embarrassed. She felt naïve and young. Surely Rita Moreno would understand the choices she made.

"Wong," Moreno said, "Get those two down here on the double. I'll have someone fetch Johnson and Jayden, and well see if we can get them to help us."

"On our way."

CHAPTER TWENTY-TWO

"I am fine," North said angrily, pushing Boro's arms away.

"You are not fine," Kora said, "You have been stunned, stabbed and shot multiple times today. You've lost blood. Have you even slept or eaten in the past 22 hours?"

"It doesn't matter," North said, pulling IV needles from his arm. He reached for his shirt and pulled it over his broad, muscular shoulders. He grabbed his blood-soaked body armor, made of advanced carbon fiber, and snapped it over his wounded torso. "Boro, where's my helmet and rifle?"

Boro sighed and begrudging left the clinic recovery room to retrieve the items.

"North, Kora is right," Lydia said. "I didn't carry you all the way here to save you so you could just go and kill yourself."

"Do you know if Amberly is safe?" North asked. "No? Didn't think so. You guys don't understand. This is it. If we lose, we die. I can rest when I'm chilling with the Almighty. Until then, I plan on running this race to win. No giving up."

Boro returned and handed the gun and helmet to his superior officer. The doctors had placed a flex brace over North's wounded arm, allowing him limited use of the injured limb. He took his assault rifle in one arm, placed his helmet on his head, and activated the built-in radio.

"North calling command. Moreno do you copy," he said.

"North, Tricia here," said Moreno's staffer, "We're taking quite a beating here. We have several hundred people trying to take the hangar and get to us here in the command center. The XO is working with Dek Tigona and Amberly on some plan that involves Johnson. We're having to put down a lot of civilians, North. This is madness."

"Moreno is trusting Dek?" North said, bitterness in his voice. "That is madness."

"Amberly vouched for him," Tricia said, "for whatever that's worth."

The words unintentionally stung North. He had trusted Amberly — he still cared for her, but he would *never* trust her again.

"North, it's really bad here. We need all the help we can get. What's your status?"

"I can walk and aim a gun," North said. "Boro and I are heading that way stat. I'll check in when I get to the quadrant border."

North looked at Lydia and Kora.

"We're going with you," Lydia said.

"Like hell you are," North countered. He picked up the stun gun Lydia had been previously carrying and handed it back to her. "You guys should head to Kora's place and lock yourselves in. I'll comm you when I get to the HQ."

"How are you even going to be able to get past the hangar and into the command center?"

"Back door. Now go. Take care of each other."

Kora jumped forward and hugged North, tears streaming down her face. "You are such a good man, North. I am so sorry about Amberly. About Dek. I don't know what happened to Amberly, but please bring her home. And make sure you come home, too. We've lost too much already."

Boro nodded his head in respect to Lydia, and she returned a smile; then he and North retreated into the access corridor.

Sparks had taken command of the *American Spirit*, which had picked up the escape pod from the doomed *Firebird*. She had efficiently ordered the 100 or so non-Chasm passengers still onboard into the cargo hold and then sealed them in, threatening to vent the chamber if they tried to escape.

She was unable to communicate with Raven One via the radio because of the massive interference being generated by the *American Spirit*'s rigged communication array, so she was forced to turn off the signal jammer.

It doesn't matter now, thought Sparks as she instructed two of the *American Spirit* engineers to disable the jamming device. *By the time anyone gets a distress message, Chasm will have done its work.*

Sparks surveyed the bridge of the *American Spirit*, luxuriously spacious for an interstellar ship, richly adorned in crimson and gold hues. She sat in the command chair, a rare faux leather seat, issuing commands to the fully-loyal Chasm crew.

"Tell me the instant the jammer is off, and I can get a clear channel with Raven One," she instructed her communication officer. She looked out the broad forward viewport toward *Magellan*. She could see the reactor fin, venting some gaseous substance, probably some sort of smoke, into space where she had rammed the *Firebird*. She wasn't sure if there was a fire inside, but thought it unlikely because of the limited amount of oxygen available.

The unmanned *Firebird* had ricocheted off the fractured reactor and spun off into unknown space.

"I have Raven One on the line," the young communication officer said as she absentmindedly smoothed her *American Spirit* bridge crew dress uniform.

"Kimberly?" Sparks offered, running her hand through her strawberry blonde hair.

"Sparks," Raven one said with joy in her voice. "I'm glad to see you did not fail, unlike the … men. We made it in, and I am in the process of taking the hangar now. In a few minutes, you should be able to reconnect the gangway."

"And Dek and Amberly?"

"I am sorry to report that Dek Tigona may have turned on us," Kimberly said.

"Dek? How? Why?" Spark said, feeling more shocked than she had ever felt before.

"My guess is Amberly got to him," Kimberly said. "I wondered if she had true feelings for Dek like she let on, but I had my suspicions she was just playing him. How typically male to fall for that little minx. This masculine weakness must be purged from the new order."

"Dek could attempt to invoke a stand down order if he had access to the waypoint wide PA," Sparks suggested. "Could you still countermand his order by accessing the PA with your hacking box if needed?"

"Yes, but be ready for anything. Get that gangway reestablished. If I can't get into the command center, I'll want to get onboard the *American Spirit* with haste. We may be forced to destroy the *Magellan* the old-fashioned way. It will be messy and take time, but this station cannot stand."

"Yes ma'am. I estimate we'll have the gangway reconnected

in about five minutes," Sparks said, "but you'll need to physically secure the *Magellan* side of the gangway so we can open up and let you in."

"That's done. We already have 20 troops guarding this end," Kimberly said. "Hopefully, I'll have taken control of the entire hangar deck before you reconnect us."

"Excellent. I'll start prepping our ship-to-ship armaments here," Sparks smiled. *The sooner we destroy* Magellan, *the sooner we get to head back to Arara.*

Raven One surveyed the hangar. About a half-dozen Marines were still holding out at the corridor entrance which led to command center. The floor of the hangar was littered with destroyed furniture, overturned ships, scattered tools and dead bodies.

About a dozen well-armed Marines were swarmed by the initial Chasm wave. The Marines hesitated to shoot the unarmed group, and that cost the Earth loyalist their lives. By the time the Marines realized they were in mortal danger, the mob had overtaken them. They couldn't clear out any maneuvering space with their stun guns. The Marines were beat to death by the crowd of Chasm agents, Chasm sympathizers, and other civilians who had joined up just because they were hoping to escape the death Kimberly had promised them if they were left behind.

The six Marines who were in the secondary position by the command center access door did not hesitate to fire when the mob had subdued the main Marine force and turned to them. They stunned or shot nearly 30 people before Kimberly ordered the remaining troops to retreat and regroup.

Now Kimberly had a new group massing, and she was about to unleash the second wave, nearly twice as large as the first, to break through the remaining dug in Marine defenders and escort her into the command center so she could finish the job.

She heard a large snap-hiss and looked to the source of the noise at the far side of the hangar: The *American Spirit* had reconnected to *Magellan.*

Kimberly's radio beeped. "Yes, *Captain* Sparks, go ahead."

"I have engineers in suits repairing the bullet holes in the gangway," the elated Sparks said. "Next time I comm you, the repairs should be done, and we'll pressurize the walkway. Do you want me to have some agents bring out extra armaments for your troops out there?"

"No, I don't think so," Raven One said. "The mob is already unstable out here. Let's not feed any more oxygen to this fire. Get ready to receive a lot of passengers. Triage them as soon as they get on board. Anyone without a Chasm serial number, put them in …"

"The cargo hold," Sparks said, and Kimberly could hear the smile in her voice. Sparks always did take joy in a job well done.

"I'm about to take the command center, stand by."

Kimberly signaled to two Chasm agents near her to begin the next wave of the assault. As she was putting her hand down, she could hear the waypoint wide PA system click on. "This is *American Spirit* Chasm leader Dek Tigona. Authorization code tango delta three beta beta four zeta alpha. Please cease Scorched Earth protocol and begin Stand Down protocol."

Moreno stood in the conference room connected to the command center, looking out the clear plexiglass at the *American Spirit* and the stars beyond.

Dek, who was still in zip cuffs, sat back in his chair, away from the microphone that had been set in front of him.

"Who is next?" Moreno demanded, looking at the Magellan's former chief judicial officer, Jayden Adams and Chasm turncoat Lt. Commander Johnson, who previously led one of Magellan's strike teams. Both men looked away from the acting commander's gaze. They were sitting on either side of Dek, also zip cuffed.

"Stick it," Johnson said. "I am not helping you. Chasm will prevail. You better airlock me, and get it over with."

"Sorry Rita," Adams said. "I am not pining for some outdated gender-based relationship like Tigona. I have no reason to help you."

Corporal Marcos DeLeon held a bullet-based pistol, aimed at the general direction of the three Chasm officers. "You want us to bring you back to the airlock, counselor?"

"The airlock, a bullet, it doesn't matter," Adams said. "We're all dead men soon. You think you can outwit Macready? Look at you. The whole waypoint is up in riots, the primary power reactor is leaking, the gardens destroyed. She's going to get in here, she'll command *Magellan* to destroy itself somehow."

"She's not getting in here," Moreno said with a confidence she didn't have. "She's not going to save you."

"Of that I have no doubt," Adam's smiled grimly. "She's going to kill me – for failing her, and Chasm."

"What about you, Johnson," Moreno said, "Is your death wish as strong as Adam's here?"

"Go airlock yourself, dirt licker," Johnson spit at his former XO. "Macready isn't going to space me. I am going back on the *American Spirit* in full glory for the new order."

"Last chance gentleman; I am out of time. Order a stand down or die."

"Ha, you're bluffing, Rita," Johnson said defiantly. "You wouldn't kill us in cold blood."

"Marcos, hand me your sidearm," the acting commander ordered, as Adams closed his eyes and started humming the 600-year-old tune to "Danny Boy."

The Marine flipped the gun around in his hand, and handed it butt-end first to his commanding officer. Moreno pointed the gun at Adam's head, but kept her eyes locked on Johnson's. "You're next."

"And if you come, when all the flowers are dying, and I am dead, as dead I well may be," Adams softly sung.

"Jayden Adams, I hereby carry out the death sentence for aiding and abetting treason and for continuing to actively support the destruction of *Waypoint Magellan*."

Johnson's eyes were wild. Adams kept his eyes closed. "You'll come and find the place where I am lying…"

"May God have mercy on your soul."

"… And kneel and say an 'Ave' there for me."

An explosive shot rang out from the sidearm. Jayden Adams, administer of justice on *Waypoint Magellan*, slumped forward, blood flowing out of the bullet hole in his forehead.

Dek uttered an expletive. "You just killed him!"

"Johnson's next," Moreno said. "I will not lose this station to you terrorists and your freak utopian cult."

She pushed the microphone towards Johnson, then pressed the barrel of the gun to Johnson's head. "Speak now."

Kimberly Macready was angry. Rita Moreno was exploiting the weak men of Chasm and making the completion of Scorched Earth all the harder. Kimberly turned to a Chasm agent she had deputized as her lieutenant, "Listen to me; Dek is compromised. I outrank him; and I tell you, the stand down order is false."

She eyed a terminal across the hangar at the gangway her troops had already secured. Sparks should have the gangway open soon. She had to get those remaining six Marines guarding the door out of the way so she could get into the command center. They had technical superiority, but she had brute numbers to take them out – if she could get her people motivated. Now there was confusion in the ranks as she was about to launch her second crushing wave.

There were more than 500 people in the corridor leading up to the main hangar entrance that Johnson had mutilated with explosives earlier. And the number was growing with desperate people wanting to get onto the *American Spirit*. But now there was a great commotion in the crowd, and instead of being unified against the six heavily-armed Marines that stood between her and glory, the people were fighting over what to do and who to believe.

She pulled over a flipped table, and stood atop it, hoisting an assault rifle and firing it into the air. Most of the commotion died. "Citizens of *Magellan*! This waypoint is doomed. Moreno and Thor want you to die with them to stop those of us working to save Arara from the oppression of Earth!"

Just then the PA system kicked on and a familiar voice spoke, trembling.

"This is *Magellan* Chasm leader Smythe Johnson. Authorization code beta zeta six alpha beta two zeta zeta. Please cease Scorched Earth protocol and begin Stand Down protocol."

"This is a lie!" Kimberly cried. "We must get to the control center now so we can obtain access to the *American Spirit* and save ourselves and our loved ones!"

A Chasm agent close to the front of the crowd shouted out, "Why should we not follow the protocol? They had authorization codes." Other murmurs from the crowd seemed to chant in agreement.

"I am in charge here, not Tigona or Johnson, who were

captured and now under duress of the oppressors. I am Raven One, appointed by the Chairman."

"Well I don't know you, but I know Johnson," the agent shouted.

Raven One pointed the assault rifle at the agent and put him down with a spray of a few bullets. There was a gasp from the crowd. "Anyone else questioning my leadership? Join me and live in paradise; oppose me and die on this space death trap."

"Raven One, look!" Kimberly's lieutenant shouted. Kimberly spun around and pointed the gun in a quick reflex. "The Marines have retreated into the tunnel."

Sure enough, looking across the hangar, the door leading toward the command center was unguarded. If she could get over there and use the hacking box to get the door open, she could charge the command center and end this resistance to the inevitable. The door was still secured by a computer lockdown, so that someone could exit the command center complex through the door, but not enter.

"What is Moreno doing?" Kimberly said aloud. She turned and looked across the hangar. "Now is the time! Get ready to charge the command center."

Kimberly and a cluster of about three dozen people made for the door, and the rest of the crowd started spilling into the hangar, the threat of the Marines weapons no longer holding them at bay. Kimberly's radio headset came on.

"Opening the gangway," Sparks informed Kimberly.

"No, wait!" Kimberly shouted, but it was too late. The mob saw the gangway door open, and the human survival reaction was instantaneous.

"We can get on the *American Spirit*!" shouted one.

"Hurry, save yourself," said another.

The crowd started a stampeded for the gangway. Hundreds of people crammed into the hangar and pushed for the gangway door leading to the *American Spirit*. Kimberly swore as she was losing her leverage over her cannon fodder.

From the command center, Amberly watched through camera views as the chaos unfolded in the hangar. Moreno and the six Marines on guard came through the door, followed by

DeLeon, gun raised, who was marching behind the bound Dek and Johnson.

"Get those two into the holding room and keep a very close eye on them," Moreno commanded.

"Where's Jayden?" Thor asked.

"Executed, by that bitch," spewed Johnson, his face full of defiance and hate.

"Why?" Gonzales asked. "How can you kill them so easily? No trial?"

"We don't have the luxury of such niceties," Rita said flatly. "Kimberly Macready and her group of crazies mean to kill us all. We are a thread snap from death. I needed Adam's cooperation, under pain of death. He chose death, which in turn, convinced Johnson to give us what we need to hopefully save thousands of lives."

"That's a sick moral tradeoff," Amberly weighed in.

"My job is to keep us alive," Moreno said, with growing sharpness in her voice, as she walked toward the command well. "I am fighting your mother the best way I know how, and I am fighting to win. There are no moral victories here. There is no high road. Just life or death. Amberly, are you with me, or should you be joining Dek and Johnson in confinement?"

Amberly felt like she was 12 again and she was just dressed down with a tongue lashing from her mother. She quietly sat down and said, "I am with you. How can I help?"

Moreno took a deep breath and looked at Amberly's pained face and took pity on the 19-year-old. Rita reminded herself that Amberly was just over half her age and still maturing into the woman she was meant to be. Rita stepped over to Amberly and took her hands.

"Your mother always loved you over Kora," Moreno said. Wong was standing in the command well and stepped out of the way as Moreno stepped in. "You may provide us with leverage at an opportune moment; or you may be able to talk your mother down like you did Dek. Stay close in case we need you."

Kimberly Macready and a dozen well-armed and deeply loyal Chasm troops stood at the access door from the hangar to the passage that led directly to the command center. Raven One produced her hacking box, and started tuning it to force open the locked door. Behind and across the hangar, hundreds of people pushed to get onto the *American Spirit*.

An elderly man fell in the rush, and Kimberly watched as the crowd quickly and unknowingly crushed him to death.

We have a lot of work to do to breed this evil out of humanity, she thought as the crowds pressed tighter and harder toward the gangway. *I'll have to airlock most of these unworthy, selfish people once we are underway. They have no place in the new order.*

"Someone is hacking the door!" the tech shouted to Moreno.

"Macready? Quick! The disable code. Send it," Moreno commanded, but it was unnecessary, because the tech had already shut down Raven One's tool.

The door did not open. Instantly, Kimberly knew what had happened. Dek knew the kill codes and the fool had given them up to Moreno. This would only slow her down a few minutes while she reset and reprogramed her box. She pulled out an infopad and started coding using a swift, one-handed data entry method she developed while on Sonnet.

The crowds had nearly filled the entire hangar now, and they were starting to push up on Raven One and her strike team.

"Keep the crowds off me," she told Upton. "Shoot to kill if you must. I need to reprogram my hacking box."

A civilian monitoring communications spoke up from her station. "I have Corporal Horner on the line for you," she said. "The commander is on; Horner go ahead."

Horner's voice came over the speakers. "Skip reported to his station at the communications hub like you requested."

"Yes, he's reported in to me already," Moreno said. "With the jamming down, hopefully we can get a warning message out before it is too late. What's more important now is the status of the reactor."

"Engineer Zelma says he has a fifty-fifty chance of stabilizing the antimatter core before it decays past the point of rebooting," Horner reported. "And about the same odds of blowing us all up in the process. The radiation is mostly contained, but we can't work on fixing the reactor until we at least get a partial seal in the service area. *Firebird* ripped a huge hole when she crashed into the reactor, but she wasn't traveling fast enough to create an immediate catastrophic failure."

"No boom then," Moreno said.

"Not an immediate one anyway. If we can get a full engineering crew up here, maybe with luck Zelma said we can be up and running at partial power in a month, best case scenario. Right now, we're just double checking to make sure were not irradiating the people inside *Magellan*."

"Get to it, then," Moreno said, and turned her attention to the private standing to her right. "Wong, what do you have?"

Wong lifted a small parcel. "Leo procured the ordinance you requested. With a timed detonator."

"Excellent. Secure the hangar and conference room access corridors, and then blow that window out," Moreno said. "Swiftly! It won't be long before she gets her magic box working again. Hopefully, if Kimberly knows it's impossible to get in here anytime soon, she'll retreat to the *American Spirit*."

"How will that help us?" Amberly asked. "You are going to let my mother get away? I'm sure she'll use the *American Spirit* to assault *Magellan*."

"And since we can't launch anything from the damaged hangar, we'll be defenseless against her," Wong added.

"I think we have a much better chance of surviving if we can get the Chasm operators off this waypoint," Moreno said. "And I am growing tired of people questioning my decisions — and you should be especially wary of that, Ms. Macready. When the dust settles, you may be defending your actions in a court of law. Truly with your best interest in heart, I think it behooves you to remain silent for the time being."

"I'll go and get this ordinance in place then," Wong said.

"Hurry," Moreno replied. "If Kimberly gets the door open before you can punch a hole into space, we could lose everything."

"On it, XO," and Wong slipped out the door into the T-shaped corridor, ordinance in hand. He passed the turn that would take him out the hall to the hangar and instead proceeded forward into the conference room. Amberly could see Wong through the hall, now a hundred meters away, fiddling with his explosives pack and arranging it next to the plexiglass viewport, next to Jayden's dead body.

Amberly turned away and looked into the security camera monitors. The hangar was utter chaos, and she saw her mom and what looked like a group of well-trained Chasm troops fiddling near the door that accessed the command center.

"Wong, what's your status," Moreno radioed to Wong, as he was just out of comfortable earshot.

"I need another two or three minutes to get the remote detonator set up," he said. "I don't want to be in here when we evacuate the air from this connecting hall."

"We don't have that long," Moreno said. For an instant, she taught about asking Wong to manually blow the ordinance, sacrificing himself, to make sure the vacuum was created that would effectively keep Kimberly out. But she couldn't do that.

Amberly watched her mother work, Kimberly's hands flying over the virtual keypad in a near blur as she recoded her hacking device. Time was almost up.

Amberly slipped out the door and sprinted down the hallway.

CHAPTER TWENTY-THREE

Raven One had assembled her strike team into a tight line about 30 feet from the command center access door.

The Chasm leader was giving instructions about how to storm the hall. "Those of you with guns, shoot to kill, do not hesitate. If you are captured, Moreno will not hesitate to airlock you if we cannot free you. Get ready, I am about to use the hacking box. The door may only be open for a few minutes before they can countermand my hack and force it closed again. Ready?"

Kimberly turned to execute her hacking commands for a second attempt to open the door, when it opened of its own accord. In a smooth motion, she saw Amberly Macready, her favored offspring, slipping out the door and quickly closing it behind her, the indicator light flashing back to a green locked indicator.

"Amberly!" Kimberly shouted.

"Mom, we have to stop this madness," she said, looking around at the half dozen weapons that were trained on her. "No more people have to die."

"You may have been able to turn Dek," Raven One said, "and I should not have expected less from my talented daughter, but you will not turn me. Surrender now, and I will spare your life."

"Is that what you told dad?" Amberly said, trying to start an argument and stall for time. "What lies did you tell him so he would go quietly into the night? Everything about you is a lie."

"If I lie, it is only because I am willing to trade *everything* for the greater good," Kimberly said waving a hand at her troops to approach her daughter. "Amberly, I could not be more proud of you. You've overcome so much and achieved success at such a young age. You have grown into such a beautiful woman. But I can't trust you. *You are the liar.* You said you believed in our noble cause when you only selfishly hoped to save yourself. You lured Dek away from us with your feminine wiles — I know you don't love him."

"Mom... how—"

"Clearly, you value your own needs and friends over the common good. Don't you see, everything is the State. I see now the fact that I foolishly let my emotions blind me to: There is no place for you in the new order."

"Mother, let's talk this over," Amberly said, trying to say anything to throw her mom off balance. "I have so many questions. Let's try to work this out. Just don't do anything else drastic."

Kimberly stepped forward, and gently kissed Amberly on the forehead.

"You are stalling for something. The time for questions is over. Time for you is over," said Raven One as she pointed to a young Chasm operative, Monique, a tall coffee-skinned woman. "You. Kill Amberly. Now. Good-bye sweetheart."

Amberly's mother had called Amberly's bluff, and Amberly was holding nothing. This was it, the end.

"Mom — I forgive you."

She steeled herself, wondering in a moment about the pain of death and thinking about Kora and North and their God. *Please accept me*, she thought, and held her breath.

Monique raised her assault rifle and took aim at the redhead.

Then a spray of bullets made her dive for the floor.

"North!" Amberly shouted. Boro was just a pace behind North, and already taking well-placed shots with his stun pistol, rendering unconscious four Chasm troops in less than a half minute.

The sound of gunfire made the already anxious queue of people waiting to board the *American Spirit* panic and push all the harder into the gangway. Kimberly Macready scrambled up from the floor where she instinctively fell to avoid gunshots. The crowds overran much of her strike team. Things were not going as planned. It was time to make a bold play.

She leapt toward Amberly. North took several leading shots at Kimberly, but he was not in top form and missed what was otherwise an easy target. Kimberly tackled her daughter, drew a small hold-out pistol from a pouch under the red utility robe she was wearing. In a swift, smooth motion, Kimberly put an arm around Amberly's neck and pressed the gun to Amberly' head, positioning her daughter between herself and North.

"Stand back, North. Train your weapons elsewhere, or I will spread Amberly's precious brains all over the deck," Kimberly said forcefully and jabbed the gun painfully under Amberly's jaw. Amberly winced. North did not take his sites off Kimberly.

Amberly knew if North surrendered, Kimberly would kill them both.

"Take a shot, North," Amberly said, "Kill us both if you have to. She's going to kill me anyway."

"I can't do that," North said, his eyes starting to water, "I can't take the chance I'd shoot you." As he was talking, North side-stepped around hoping to get a better angle on Raven One. She countered by pulling Amberly back toward the command center access door.

"Careful now, North," Kimberly said, with calm exuding in her voice. "I just want to get past that door behind me."

"Shoot us! Do it. North. If you care about me, take the shot," Amberly pleaded. "Don't you see, if my mom dies, Chasm will die with her."

"You move, I shoot," Kimberly told North, as she pulled her arm from around Amberly and fished out her hacking box, the hold-out gun still firmly planted point blank range into Amberly's head.

North's aim was too unsteady for him to get an accurate shot. Behind him, North heard Boro engaging some armed Chasm agents in a firefight. North had kept walking in a circular motion, so most of his flank was covered by a damaged, overturned corvette.

"I can't hold these guys long, North," Boro said as he laid down some random stun shots. He hit a few Chasm troops, and some civilians in the crowd as well.

"I don't have a clean shot," North cursed to Boro.

"North, don't let her through this door. End this now!" Amberly said. "My mom doesn't think I understand sacrifice — but I do. I would not give my life for her faceless new order. But North, I'll die for my friends — for Kora, for Lydia, for Skip — for you. End this, please."

"Amberly? Amberly." North's finger began to tighten on his trigger.

Leo slammed the door shut to the access corridor leading to the conference room and further out to the hangar, looking to

Moreno in the command well.

"Blow it," she said.

Leo pressed the remote detonator and instantly a thunderous smack reverberated violently from the hangar to the command center. In the conference room, the floor-to-ceiling plexiglass viewport shattered into a thousand fragments that were blown out into space along with several chairs as the atmosphere in the hall leading to both corridor exits vented into space.

Jayden Adams' body was pushed out into the void as well, and the blood that had escaped his body from the bullet wound in the head snap-froze as the coldness of space took over.

"Well, unless Kimberly Macready has learned to breathe in space, she's not coming in that way," Moreno said. "The only tactical option she has left is to retreat to the *American Spirit*."

"If we can't get our fighters launched to defend *Magellan*, she could slowly take us apart with the *American Spirit*'s armaments," Leo observed. "Are we only delaying the inevitable?"

"Timing is everything," Moreno smiled at her subordinate. "Perhaps we are not as alone out here as we thought."

Moreno turned to Thor. "Kimberly will shred the exterior of *Magellan* with the *American Spirit's* guns. We'll need to move all the civilians to the core areas and seal off everything outside the tube. Can you manage that?"

Thor nodded.

Leo looked at his infopad as a text message popped up.

"Marcos indicates his strike team has circled around and they are advancing into the hangar now."

"God forgive me," North uttered as he twitched on the trigger of his assault rifle. He was aiming for Kimberly's arm, hoping to injure her and get her to drop her weapon. To shoot for the head was too risky, because just a few inches off, and North knew he could be taking Amberly's life. He could never live with himself if he did.

North pulled the trigger the instant Leo blew the conference room window.

Kimberly was not expecting explosive sounds behind her and instinctively jerked, pushing Amberly forward slightly.

Amberly cried out in pain. North's bullet had found a target.

"No!" shouted North.

The safety light on the door went from green to red, indicating the hull breach on the other side of the door and that it was unsafe to open. Kimberly cursed. There was no way she was going to be able to get into the command center now, with several dozen meters of lethal vacuum between her and her objective. Kimberly dropped her box and again seized Amberly, now pulling her toward the gangway.

Kimberly felt warm blood oozing out of Amberly's torso.

"Don't move!" North said, re-aiming his rifle.

"Why?" Kimberly mocked him. "So you can shoot her again?"

Suddenly, a cacophony of weapons fire erupted as Marcos, Tricia, Inon and Wong joined Boro in routing out the obviously armed Chasm agents.

"Everyone down!" Marcos shouted as he put some bullets in the ceiling. The crowd obeyed and hit the deck, except for some Chasm troops returning fire. But they were outmatched.

Kimberly drug Amberly as a human shield at an amazing pace toward the gangway. Marcos was completely surprised that woman of Kimberly's size could possess such strength.

Kimberly spoke through her helmet radio. "Sparks, do you copy?"

The younger woman replied. "What's going on?"

"Prep the *American Spirit* to put some distance between us and *Magellan*," Raven One said. "I am coming on board. As soon as I am on the gangway, secure the *Magellan* side door. Also, have a medic ready. My daughter has been shot."

"What about Dek? And Johnson? Adams? We still have dozens of agents on *Magellan*," Sparks asked, afraid of the answer.

"Lucky break for them. They will be honored dead in the new Arara order."

Kimberly pointed her hold out gun in the general direction of the Marines and laid down some covering fire, unloading the four-bullet capacity weapon, as she backed into the gangway tunnel pulling the wounded Amberly with her.

One of her bullets hit Tricia in the shoulder, and the Marine collapsed to the floor.

Monique and Alice Upton were covering Kimberly's retreat.

Alice threw down cover fire while Monique ordered the crowds in the gangway out of the way, waving her assault rifle and threatening them.

"Sparks, I'm in," Raven One shouted into her radio. "Close the door now."

When the door slid shut, a sense of desperation filled the remaining hundred or so people still on the hangar, and the frenzy increased.

Marco patched into the speaker system in the hangar and with an amplified voice commanded, "Everyone remain on the ground. This is an order under martial law."

Inon let a few bullets fire harmlessly into the remains of *Claire De Lune* to help Marco get his point across, and people started lying down on the ground.

Wong was speaking into his radio. "The hangar is secure. We have lots of wounded and dead here, we need all available medical assistance now. Tell Moreno that Tricia has been shot."

North's own radio buzzed. He sat on the floor, utterly spent, and held his helmeted head in his hands. He heard Moreno's voice in his helmet. "North, report."

"I shot Amberly. Kimberly escaped. My God, what have I done?"

CHAPTER TWENTY-FOUR

After three days of continued assault from the *American Spirit*'s main plasma-based guns, the exterior of *Magellan* suffered from dozens of hull breaches. Plasma weapons were not as damaging as traditional ordinance weapons or high-energy lasers. Still, with enough time Moreno knew the *American Spirit* would be able to critically compromise *Magellan* beyond repair.

Moreno looked over to Thor, who had taken up a semi-permanent station just behind the command well.

"I'm not sure how much of *Magellan* will be left for you to govern when we suspend martial law," she said dryly.

Chief Engineer Zelma walked into the command center. His eyes were dark and his white hair was completely unkempt. "Rita, we need to think about evacuating the command center and move to the center core with everyone else."

Moreno ignored him and spoke to Tricia, who was monitoring a diagnostics station. "What is the battery reserve life?"

"It's not good," Tricia reported. "The *American Spirit* has managed to damage nearly three-quarters of the reserve batteries. I think about 10 percent of them are deep enough in the waypoint to be safe from the plasma gun's maximum penetration."

"We're making sure to use the batteries that they can reach first, while we still can," Zelma reported.

"She's going to freeze us out," North said. "Once the power is gone and we are all dead, she can come in here and destroy the place over our lifeless bodies."

"She knows, doesn't she?" Moreno said to no one in particular. "Macready knows it's coming. That's why she's focusing on the batteries and hasn't finished off the reactor yet. She wants to make sure we are dead before they get here."

"What's coming? Before who gets here?" North asked, puzzled. "We're lightyears out in space. No one is out here except us and them."

Moreno smiled, but didn't answer the question. "Any new communiqués?" Moreno looked over to Skip.

"No, the transmissions are still jammed. It was lucky we were able to get out a transmission when the jammer was briefly down," Skip said. Moreno had asked Skip, whose full-time job was monitoring transmission traffic and news aggregation, to move over from the communication center to the command center. Still, there weren't many communications to monitor. In the brief window of just a few hours that the signal jammer had been turned off on the *American Spirit,* only standard news transmissions and other historical data from Earth had been received — messages that were sent eight years ago. The *Magellan* did manage to get off a distress signal, but it would be six months before it would reach *Waypoint Gilbert, Magellan's* neighbor on the Earthside — and it probably wouldn't matter if it reached *Waypoint Cortes,* as that station was likely already under Chasm control, or destroyed under Scorched Earth protocol.

One unique message had been received, encoded from the supply ship *Magnus,* which was believed to be a half light year away. The communication was a simple text that read: "We will arrive in six." The message didn't make sense, based on the positional data they had on *Magnus.* Skip said the message must have been some sort of error, but Moreno also had another theory she did not share.

"Next time they build a waypoint, they need to build some guns into the thing," North groused.

Once Raven One had control of the *American Spirit,* she immediately targeted the *Magellan* hangar, leaving damage so severe that launching weaponized corvettes, *Magellan's* primary defenders, was impossible. Moreover, the pilot corps had been decimated too, with both the senior officers, Jindal and Twig, and more than three quarters of the pilots, losing their lives at the hands of Chasm terrorists.

"Chief," Moreno called out to Zelma, "Assuming Macready takes out the batteries next before she tries to destroy the command center, how long do we have?"

"Well, at the rate of her plasma fire, it would take her at least four or five days to puncture through, now that we've reinforced the conference side wall," the engineer said.

"We're staying put for now; if I am correct, we'll want to be ready for *Magnus.*"

"Ready how?" North asked. "Even if the *Magnus* was close,

there is no guarantee that they could do anything to stop the *American Spirit*."

"Let me tell you a story that Anderson once told me," Moreno smiled as she leaned back in her chair. "About 20 years ago, senior Marine officers on *Magellan* were briefed on a plan to build a deep space warship, the first-of-its-kind. Apparently, Waypoint Command suspected the potential of an uprising. If Chasm has been generations in its development, perhaps it's possible that 30 or 40 years ago, some intel on the operation leaked."

"Sure — it would take nine years to reach Earth," Skip thought. "They'd take a few years to work out a grand plan and then a decade or so to actually build the ship."

"And in the meantime," Moreno jumped in, "highly secret information is sent to the Marine commanders, already vetted as most trusted and Earth loyal, about the existence of this program."

"So what do you know, and how do you know it?" North asked.

"Well, when I became XO eight years ago, the standard operating procedure was for the Commander to review hundreds of top-secret, need-to-know only briefings — not even governors had access to this info — so if a Marine commander died, the next in line would know any critical secret information. We covered something called Project Prime, a new secret warship being built as an insurance policy in case any of the crazy rebellion rumors were true. I hardly remember the briefing, except for the fact that Anderson thought the intel on a potential uprising was balderdash."

"And so much time had passed since the briefing, the likelihood of the threat being real seemed remote," North said.

Skip's eyes lit up. "You think *Magnus* is that ship! You think it's been broadcasting false reports about its whereabouts and intentions, and that it's not a half lightyear away, but rather its days away — close enough for near instant radio contact?"

Skip snapped his fingers. "Of course! That explains the anomalies in the transmission reports – they were falsified. You know I've been tracking that for years."

"The only reason we haven't been able to contact them or them us is because of the *American Spirit* jamming," Moreno said. "And when the jamming was down so the Chasm agents could communicate to their teams on the waypoint, we could get our distress signal out, and the *Magnus* was close enough to receive it and reply."

Skip smiled. "But the *American Spirit* can contact them, so why aren't they running?"

"Because they believe the cover story, that *Magnus* is just another deep space supply ship. So they want to make sure there is nothing for them to save by the time they arrive, hence trying to kill our power. The quickest way to make sure that dead men tell no tales," North added. "If they run now, we could survive and *Magellan* could be saved. No, they must finish what they started. At all costs."

"My theory is that *Magnus* lied again about how far out it was," Moreno said. "They figured hostiles could be monitoring the transmission, though it was encrypted, and that those hostiles might already be suspicious that *Magnus* was more than meets the eye because it was a half lightyear from where she was supposed to be. So they lied. Maybe they were half that distance away — we could know they were coming, and they would have the element of surprise. If *American Spirit* wasn't actively scanning for them yet — and why would they if they were still days out — they could sneak up out of nowhere, save *Magellan* and stop the *American Spirit*."

"*Deus Ex Magnus*," Thor said. North and Skip both gave Thor strange looks at his use of the Latin phrase. "What? It's a literary term. I was an English major. Never mind."

Kimberly Macready sat in the captain's chair on the *American Spirit*. Sparks entered the bridge and walked up to the center seat.

"Sparks," Kimberly smiled faintly. "Status report."

"We believe we have two more days of bombardment before we completely destroy their power reserves."

"What can we do to increase the power to the bombarding cannons?" Kimberly asked, as she ran outcome models in her head.

"We have all the power except life support, artificial gravity, engine spool up and the electromagnetic jammer diverted to the weapons. The amount of power life support and gravity take up is insignificant and wouldn't change the timetable."

"What about engine spool and the jammer?" Kimberly asked.

"We could cut our timeframe for permanent decommission of *Magellan* by about 30 hours," Sparks said. "But if we powered down the standby engine spool up, it could take us weeks to bring the interstellar engines online for departure. Don't we want to be gone when the *Magnus* arrives?"

"It doesn't matter if everyone on *Magellan* is dead," Kimberly said. "*Magnus* could be an opportunity. We could commandeer the vessel if we are prepared. I'm sure the resources on that ship are substantive. We just need to be ready to disable it as soon as it is in weapons range."

"Why don't we just power down the jammer," Sparks said. "We could get the job done before *Magnus* arrives and be ready to speed out of here, so we can avoid the confrontation."

"That has to be the least intelligent idea that has ever escaped your lips," Kimberly scolded her protégé. "We can't risk *Magnus* having open communication with *Magellan*. They could already be in instant radio range. We should keep everyone in the dark. Secrecy is our security. That's our priority. Take the engine spool offline and keep jamming."

"Very good then," Sparks said.

"How's Amberly?"

"Doc Appleton said she is going to make a full recovery. Why do you care? You were going to kill her back on *Magellan*," Sparks said, with a bit of jealously creeping into her tone.

"She is my daughter," Kimberly said flatly. "And she will be a great asset to our order. Don't underestimate her intelligence and her potential. Once we get her away from the influence of idiots like Dek and that moron, North, she will be a great leader. She was born for it."

"We can't trust her," Sparks argued. "We should space her and let her be at peace with her soon-to-be dead fellows on *Magellan*."

"I'll leave that for the Chairman to decide," Kimberly said, annoyed at Sparks' impertinence. Still, Kimberly had to admit Sparks had earned a larger voice at the Chasm table considering she was one of her few colleagues to be an unqualified success in wrapping up the *Magellan* mission.

Kimberly turned to her yeoman, Groben. "Have Amberly

brought to the bridge when she is able."

The yeoman, a tall, thin man, 25 years old, with dirty blonde hair, snapped in salute and left the bridge to carry out his orders.

CHAPTER TWENTY-FIVE

Amberly Macready did not want to see her mother.

Four days had passed since Kimberly Macready took her daughter as a hostage to escape the doomed *Magellan*, when Amberly had taken the bullet that was meant for her mother.

The doctors told Amberly she was lucky the bullet missed the major organs, but Amberly thought she would have been luckier if the bullet would have killed her. She couldn't help but be half angry with North. Why couldn't he have just shot them both, mother and daughter, and ended Raven One's tyranny right then and there?

Of course, she knew the answer, and it made her even more distressed. North loved her; and even though he believed she had no intention of returning that love, he couldn't bring himself to take a chance that he might end Amberly.

Now Amberly was the one who was going to have to live, knowing that she was an accessory — albeit a naïve one — in North's death.

Amberly felt like nothing more than a prop since the day she was born in her mother's lifelong undercover operation to subdue or kill the 10,000 inhabitants of *Magellan*. That she unintentionally aided the so-called Raven One made Amberly loathe herself almost as much as she did her mother.

Still, she wanted to know the fate of her home, *Magellan*, as hard as it might be to face that truth. Amberly knew she had to see with her own eyes; she could not believe what her lying mother told her.

The yeoman escorted Amberly onto the bridge. She looked around and quickly exchanged ugly glances with Sparks.

Her mother was seated in the captain's chair, facing away from her toward the main viewport. Her raven black hair covered her round head, and Amberly looked around for some sort of weapon that she could impale that head with but saw no opportunity.

Then, Amberly looked past her mother through the viewport. The young woman gasped and choked back tears.

Nearly every square meter of *Magellan's* external hull, once gleaming in stellar light, was pocked with scorch marks and plasma holes. Smoke, water crystals and other gasses slowly poured out of some of the holes in the hull. Fragments of metal and carbon-fiber frame that had broken loose in the bombardment now created a cloud of debris which floated around the station.

"It's ironic, sweetheart, that something so horrifying will be the beginning of something so beautiful," Kimberly said, without turning to face her daughter. "Sort of like childbirth — something painful begets a beautiful future." Kimberly wore the dress uniform of the *Magellan* science corps, white and sleek, the same uniform she had worn seven years ago when Amberly was just a girl. Kimberly was not a woman of complete science however. The outfit had one military trapping: a thigh holster with her small hold out pistol.

"You're crazy," Amberly said, and then looked around at the Chasm operators standing at the various stations on the bridge. "You are *all* crazy! Humanity is not a cosmic accident waiting for you to fix. What makes us beautiful is that we are all broken. You can't purge the brokenness out of us. You can try to social engineer and rewrite everything that makes us human: our weaknesses, the love of a man and a woman, our individualism, our competitive spirit, whatever you progressives want to fix. But it won't change anything. Everything you don't like about Earth is hardcoded in your DNA and in your souls. Don't you see? You are bringing with you the very thing you are trying to escape: your humanity."

"Amberly, you're —" Kimberly tried to silence her daughter.

"You might as well airlock me now. I will not stop fighting you, and I will always help everyone remember how exceptional *individuals* can be," Amberly shouted with an explosive passion that took back the more docile Chasm bridge officers. "My friend North, who is 10 times the man of any of you emasculated Chasm dirt-lickers, believed in grace, that anyone could be redeemed. I look at you, all part of this twisted murderous insane cult, and I think my friend is wrong. If there is a hell, I hope you all burn in it."

The bridge was silent. Most of the bridge officers expected Kimberly would address that death-wish of a rant quickly, but when Kimberly said nothing, the space grew awkward.

A proximity sensor alarm sounded at the tactical station breaking the silence. A Chasm agent manning the station looked down and reported in a somewhat surprised voice, "Captain Macready, it's the *Magnus*!? She's now in sensor range."

"Bring us around," Kimberly ordered the pilot. "Let's bring our guns to bear quickly and disable the ship before it knows what is going on."

"Something's not right," the tactical officer reported. "I'm seeing five vessels now — the *Magnus* — and what looks like … four smaller, um, corvette class ships."

Realization lighted Raven One's eyes. "*Magnus* is not a supply ship," she said, alarm juicing her voice. "It's a warship. Apparently with a hangar full of fighters."

"We are so screwed," Sparks muttered.

Raven One began issuing rapid-fire commands. "Helmsman, belay that order to bring us around. Bear us back down on *Magellan*. Sparks, all power to the guns. Redirect jamming, life support, everything. We need to finish off *Magellan*. Focus on the command center. Looks like we all get to die for Arara."

"The *Magnus* is trying to call us," Sparks announced from the comm station.

"Let's hear it then," Kimberly said. "Maybe we can stall them long enough to finish off *Magellan*. Don't let up on the firing."

"*Magnus*, we copy," Sparks spoke into the receiver. "I am patching you with *American Spirit* Commanding Officer Raven One."

A clear, baritone voice came over the radio. "Captain, *American Spirit*, this is Captain Jonas Obadiah of the *U.S.S. Magnus*. Please cease hostilities and surrender immediately and unconditionally, or we will disable your ship. I have four corvettes with orders to engage, and they will not be withdrawn until you cease fire on the *Magellan* and surrender. Will you comply, *American Spirit*?"

"*Magnus*, you are too late," Kimberly said. "Our work is nearly finished. But tell me, Captain, what do you really know about us? About our attempt to save humanity."

"We can discuss that at length after you surrender. I estimate about 15 minutes before our Corvettes intercept you," Obadiah said plainly. "Please. The *Magnus* is superior to the *American Spirit* in every way. Our ship's armor plating is practically impervious to the limited fire power of your ship."

"We have no quarrel with you," Kimberly said, hoping to delay *Magnus* as much as possible. "May I suggest a 30-minute cease fire while we consider our options."

"Don't play games with me, Captain. Our spectrometer suggests that you are firing on *Magellan* as we speak. I repeat, surrender immediately, or we fire our particle beams to disable your ship."

Kimberly turned to Sparks. "Cut him off."

Sparks complied, and ended the connection with *Magnus*.

Kimberly started reciting facts to herself. "*Magellan's* batteries are gone, but it could take hours or weeks for everyone to freeze out. *Magnus* is bearing down on us and will surely destroy us before we can finish *Magellan* conventionally. There is only one way to ensure *Magellan's* destruction."

Amberly was trying to process everything that was happening. Earth wasn't caught unaware — they had been making a response to Chasm. There was a chance that North, Kora and the others could be saved, that her home could be saved.

Hope.

Amberly's hope was Kimberly's desperation, so Amberly suspected her mother would do something desperate.

"No main engines?" Kimberly asked what she already knew.

"Offline to direct power to the guns. It would take us too long to spool the engines back online," Sparks replied. "At least five hours."

"What about navigational thrusters," Kimberly said. "How much speed could we generate by employing those to propel us towards the *Magellan*?"

"Maybe, 100 kilometers an hour if we backed up a kilometer or so and got a running start."

"That's how it ends for us then, my friend. In death, we will give humanity a chance to be reborn," Kimberly said to Sparks, and turned to her daughter. "Sweet Amberly, I wanted so much to show you the north shores of the Lewis Islands where I fell in love with the ocean. Now, I am afraid you die with us."

Kimberly took a deep breath and issued the command, "All

hands, prepare for ramming. Sparks, prepare to initiate a core self-destruct."

Amberly felt the hope that sprung up inside of her when the *Magnus* arrived evaporate. An anti-matter explosion in the *American Spirit* reactor would ensure that if the collision between the *American Spirit* and the *Magellan* didn't utterly decimate the waypoint, the energy released from the explosion would incinerate it.

The plasma bombardment stopped.

"Why are they letting up?" Thor wondered. He looked particularly haggard, refusing to sleep for days and bundled in a pile of blankets.

Zelma shrugged his shoulders. "Maybe they are saving their energy now that they know we have almost no reserve energy left?"

"No. Macready knows she's close to breaching the command center," Moreno said. She was a silhouette sitting in the command well, backlit by emergency lights. All non-essential systems had already been shut down. "Something else is going on."

"*Magnus* must be here," North said, his breath visible in the near zero-degree atmosphere. "Do we have enough power to bring up the radio?"

"No," Skip replied. "And even if we did, it would probably be useless because of the jamming."

"We've done everything we can to maximize our chances of survival," Moreno said. "All we can do is sit and wait."

"And pray," North added. And he did.

The pilot double-checked his data. "We'll need to reposition several kilometers to begin the run, Raven One. But do we need to do this? There has to be another way to finish *Magellan* without us committing suicide in the process?"

Some of the other officers on the bridge murmured in agreement. Kimberly stood up and glared at each of them individually as she pulled a small handgun from her thigh holster. She aimed it at the head of the pilot.

"Don't you think if there was another way, that I would have figured it out? I am Raven One. Now is not the time to grow weak.

We are close. I cannot afford any disloyalty or questioning of my absolute orders now. Yours is not to reason why – yours is to do, and die." Kimberly pulled the trigger and the pilot slumped over, dead.

"Sparks, take his place," Kimberly said, as she returned the pistol to its holster.

Amberly had to stop this. At least she had to try.

"Sparks, this is madness," Amberly begged. "You don't have to do this."

Sparks tipped her head toward the dead pilot and then took his seat.

Amberly looked around at all the bridge crew. She could see it in their eyes. They were all terrified. She doubted if any of them wanted to die for the cause; but they would because her mother willed it, and they felt powerless to stop her.

"Listen to me, all of you!" Amberly said. "You don't have to be killers like this. You all have a choice. You are all individuals and your souls will be responsible for the actions you take, or don't take, to stop this insanity."

Kimberly looked at her Yeoman. "Summon security and have my daughter removed from the bridge immediately."

The word "immediately" had barely rolled off her lips when the bridge buckled, like a moving tube car hitting a stationary one from behind. Those standing on the bridge, including Amberly, were thrown to the floor.

"What was that?" Sparks asked.

Groben stepped into the unmanned engineering station and read the flashing lines from the screen.

"Damage report: Our rear engines are destroyed," the yeoman reported. "Fortunately, no hull breaches. Looks like it was a precision strike meant to only disable us.

"How? The corvettes are still ten minutes off," Sparks questioned.

"Laser," Amberly said flatly. "They travel at near light speed, you know."

"Impossible," Sparks said. "They couldn't have a laser that powerful —"

Sparks was interrupted by a high pitch tone being blasted over the ship wide public announcement system. Then Captain

Obadiah's familiar voice came over the speakers.

"This is the *Magnus* commanding officer. We have observed your hostile intentions towards *Magellan* and have disabled your ship …"

"How are they broadcasting this on our PA system?" Yeoman Groben asked.

"They've hacked in remotely," Kimberly was solving the riddle as she spoke. "The oppressor's technology is years more advanced. Lasers with real destructive power. Hacking computers that sliced through our 20-year-old firewall protocols."

Kimberly closed her eyes. She focused on all the variables. They were changing rapidly. What was most important now? If the *Magnus* could make it to the *Waypoint Cortez*, without resupplying on *Magellan* then the Chasm operatives needed to be ready for them. She had to send a warning now. It would only take a minute.

She opened a terminal and began keying in a message, relaying everything she knew about *Magnus* that would be helpful for Chasm. It was a miracle of intelligence and secrecy that the ship had been able to mask her true identity in its eight-year voyage from Earth, and none of the other Chasm operatives at the other waypoints were able to see through its veneer.

As she typed, Obadiah's monologue continued. "If you do not surrender now and continue your hostile actions toward *Magellan*, we will destroy your ship. We regret this course of action, but by not complying with our surrender commands, your captain, Raven One, has left us with no options. Our orders are to defend the waypoints at all costs, and that certainly would —"

"Message sent," Kimberly said rapidly. "Sparks, throw up the jammer."

The PA system went to static and the jammer flooded the electromagnetic spectrum. No more transmissions were going in and out, and Obadiah's remote control of the PA system was cut off.

Sparks spoke up, "With the jammer activated again, those corvettes won't be able to communicate or coordinate with the *Magnus*. They'll be more cautious and take more time. Time we need to complete the mission."

"Your jammer *is* a wonderful piece of technology, Sparks. An

Arara innovation is an edge against Earthen aggression," Kimberly saluted her *de facto* lieutenant. "Now get those thrusters firing, and let's finish this."

Sparks marked some commands into her control screen, and the ship started to back away from *Magellan*. With the sudden movement, everyone lurched.

"Sorry," Sparks shrugged. "Inertia dampeners must have gone offline with the mains."

Kimberly summoned Groban with a beckoning gesture. Then she turned to her daughter. "I don't expect to see you again, Amberly. I know you take no joy in our sacrifice today." She hugged Amberly.

Amberly had no more words, just tears rolling over her rosy cheeks. In their embrace, Amberly wanted to remember her mother the way she was, when Amberly respected her as a strong, loving woman who led her family to pursue greatness. But she could not. All she could think about was how that woman was a lie, and her real mother, this Raven One, was about to kill everyone onboard the *American Spirit* and *Magellan* to complete some cultic utopian fantasy.

"We almost have enough distance to achieve maximum ramming speed," Sparks announced.

Still holding Amberly tightly, Kimberly whispered in her ear. "Let me give you a gift to hold onto as you face oblivion. I know being a part of the greatest enterprise of humanity is no consolation to you, so let this piece of information comfort you: Your father's dying thoughts were of his daughters. He pleaded for me to tell you one more time that which I am sure you know, that he loved you more than life itself. I promised him I would tell you just before he died. Now I've made good on that promise."

Amberly sobbed into Kimberly's shoulder. "You killed him, didn't you?"

"Yes, it was for the greater good. Your dad would not join me," Kimberly said as she loosened her embrace. "Sacrifices had to be made."

"I hate to interrupt your family bonding time, but we've reached optimal distance," Sparks said. "Is the word given?"

Amberly quickly snapped back from her mother. Her hand was outstretched, holding her mother's gun which Amberly had slipped out of Kimberly's thigh holster during their maternal embrace.

"Not yet, Sparks," Amberly said, as she did her best to aim the gun directly at Kimberly's head. Instinctively, everyone on the bridge froze.

"Now no one make any sudden moves," Amberly said. "I've got nothing to lose. And I am ready to go down with a fight. Sparks, you move this ship one millimeter, and as soon as I put a bullet in Raven One's head I am putting one in yours."

"You're not fast enough," Sparks said, unconcerned.

"Maybe, maybe not. It's your gamble," Amberly said, "But I'm pretty sure I've got Raven One. And I might as well get it over wi—"

"Wait!" Kimberly spouted. "Why would Sparks or any of us care if you kill us? In three minutes, we'll all be dead anyway."

"Mother, you are in denial. You spent too much time alone on the Spencer Belt dreaming of this moment of glory. You think when it comes down to it, that everyone here is committed to death for your so-called 'greater good,'" Amberly said, with powerful conviction coloring her voice. "The human survival instinct — the powerful urge for us individuals to live on, is hard to erase. It's part of us. At the first chance, these people are going to make for the escape pods, and hope *Magnus* pulls them out of cold space. They can claim to be innocent bystanders easily enough. If everyone else is dead, no one will know better."

"No," Raven One said, any motherly kindness flushed from memory. "You are wrong. Humanity can evolve, improve, throw off the old ways. Chasm is that chance. These people here know that. They will die for that."

"Maybe people would die for someone they love or their children, but for your soulless, faceless future, none will die. If you don't believe me, see if your officers will eject the life pods now, empty."

The bridge officers and crew looked around uncomfortably at each other.

"Go on! Do it," Amberly shouted. "Eject the escape pods. Eliminate your only chance of survival now. Do it! Sparks, do it."

"No Amberly, I need to infiltrate *Magnus*," Sparks said in a very hasty and shaky voice, "and … look for an opportunity to destroy *Magnus* from the inside."

"That's what I thought," Amberly said, waving the gun slightly.

Raven One was furious. "I sent the message, Chasm will be ready. Launch the escape pods, Sparks! Our lives do not matter. We must be committed to the very end."

Sparks stepped away from her panel. Now that she was faced with it, the thrill was no longer worth her death. She was already calculating the distance to the door.

"So, you are all the cowards my daughter thinks you are," Kimberly shouted, her mouth spitting with rage.

Kimberly was interrupted by pounding and shouting at the door.

"Live by the mob, die by the mob," Sparks said in resignation.

"It doesn't matter," Kimberly said. "They are not getting in. And the moment any of you cowards open the bridge door, you are all going to be lynched and airlocked, anyway. No one is getting to an escape pod. So please, I beg you, let's make our deaths have meaning instead. You will never have this opportunity to save humanity again. This is it. Don't lose sight because of your selfish vanities."

Amberly looked around. The shouting at the door grew more intense. They were calling for Raven One by name, demanding her head. Looks like Obadiah's message got through. Surely someone on the other side would figure out a way to physically destroy the door.

Sparks started to move back to her seat.

"Wait, Sparks, don't do this," Amberly pleaded. In her peripheral vision, she saw the communication officer and Groban stepping toward her from two sides. Raven One had convinced her people it was better to stay loyal — or at least the mob trying to break into the bridge had convinced them there really was no hope.

Kimberly looked at her daughter, who still held the gun pointed at her head. She smiled wickedly, knowing she had deflected Amberly's attempt to foil the suicide run. Her eyes, centered on her daughter's pale face, burned into Amberly, who started to shift her weight. The comm officer and yeoman were paces away now.

"Just surrender, Amberly," Kimberly said, now reaching out to Amberly. "Let us die together, mother and daughter. It's going to be okay."

"No, it's not!" Amberly shouted.

The yeoman made a lunge for Amberly, but she stepped out of his way, simultaneously pulling the gun's trigger twice.

The sound of the ringing shots silenced the gathering locked outside.

"Amberly, my Amberly," Kimberly whispered as she collapsed to the ground. "What would your father think?"

"I'm so sorry, Mom," Amberly cried. "You gave me no choice."

The rest of the bridge crew was in shock. The demigod Raven One was mortal. Amberly couldn't tell where the bullets had hit, but her mother's robe immediately showed signs of absorbing blood.

Raven One's sacrifice conflicted Sparks and pushed her. She shook her head, sat down and started the thrusters, when Amberly stepped up behind her and put the gun point blank to the back of her head. The ships acceleration toward *Magellan* threw Amberly slightly off balance, but she kept the gun trained on Sparks. The ships motion caused the crowd outside the bridge to come back to life, and the pounding and shouting intensified.

"Stop the vessel now, and I will ask Moreno to pardon you," Amberly offered.

"No! Don't stop," Raven One said weakly as she bled out on the floor. None of the Chasm officers moved to give Kimberly aid.

"I am desperate. I will put you down, Sparks." Amberly spoke evenly. "Then I will just stop this ship over your dead body."

"Do what you must," Sparks said. "I've chosen my path now. I'm sorry I ever thought of straying."

The *American Spirit* was picking up speed. The proximity alarm blared again with an audio warning from the ship's virtual intelligence. "Warning. Collision eminent in two minutes. Warning."

"Good girl," Raven One said.

The mob outside was pounding the door with some sort of battering ram. The beats were loud and becoming more frequent.

Amberly saw two Chasm officers moving for her again.

Amberly steeled her resolve and ran her finger over the trigger, causing the officers to hesitate. Then, the whole ship rocked suddenly and forcefully.

The tactical officer examined her display port. "The corvettes are in firing range. They are firing munitions. They'll blast us apart."

"Please, Sparks," Amberly said, her voice and hand trembling. "Stop the ship. Open the bridge door."

The ship rocked even more violently. "We're not going to make it to *Magellan*. At least not in fewer than hundreds of pieces." Damage indicators lit up the bridge along with a variety of alarm sounds.

The VI spoke again: "Warning. Collision eminent in one minute. Warning."

"I'm sorry, Sparks," Amberly said as she fingered the trigger.

"Okay! Okay! I give," Sparks said as she fired the retro-thrusters, and the *American Spirit* began to slow.

The corvettes continued their bombardment.

"Slow us down! We're still going to crash!" Amberly said.

"I'm trying. Turn off the jammer," Sparks yelled. "Hail the *Magnus*."

The communication officer sat down and entered the jammer shutdown code. "Channel open with *Magnus*."

"We surrender," Sparks said hurriedly. "This is acting captain Sparks of the Chasm *American Spirit* triumvirate, and we unconditionally surrender. We are attempting to slow down our approach. Please cease fire and stand by."

The doors exploded open as at least two dozen *Magellan* refugees flooded in, armed with various pipes, knives and bat-like devices. Many of the officers instinctively stuck their hands in the air as a sign of surrender.

"This is Captain Obadiah, we accept your surrender," came the now familiar voice over the PA system. "Please continue to decelerate. The corvettes have been ordered to hold fire. We'd like to debrief Raven One immediately."

A blonde man, burly and more than 180 centimeters tall, was clearly the mob's leader. He looked at Amberly and her gun pointed at Sparks.

"Amberly Macready?" the man said gravely. "I'm Midas.

Remember me? I used to make deliveries to the science lab. Your... mother, Kimberly. Raven One? The cause of all this?"

"I shot her," Amberly said, shock setting in as she dropped the gun.

"You shot her for us?" Midas asked.

"Take Raven One!" shouted an angry mob voice.

"Please, wait!" Amberly pleaded.

"Warning. Collision eminent. Warning."

Every eye on the bridge looked at the viewport it became clear the *American Spirit* would not stop in time to avoid colliding with *Magellan*.

"Sparks? Sparks!"

"You Macreadys are so demanding," she said. "We're down to 10 kilometers per hour. I've slowed us down as much as I can, hopefully —"

A loud creaking of metal flexing followed by snap popping filled the air inside the bridge. The *American Spirit*'s nose flattened into *Magellan*, as pieces of both ship and station flew out into space. The reverse thrusters were still firing, and the American Spirit seemed to bounce backward off the waypoint's damaged exterior. Sparks skillfully deployed all four thrusters to bring the ship to a relative full stop.

"Thank you *American Spirit*," Obadiah's voice came over the PA. "The damage doesn't look so bad from out here. Please prepare to be boarded."

The forty or fifty *Magellan* refugees that had pushed onto the bridge by this point cheered. "Get Raven One!" someone shouted.

"To the airlock," screamed a woman. The mob cheered its approval of the idea.

The crowd hoisted Kimberly up and started to pass her bleeding body over the sea of people out the door.

"Mom! Mom!" Amberly screamed. Kimberly strained to turn her head toward her daughter as she was carried out.

"I'm sorry," Kimberly choked out, blood running down her arms and dripping from her fingertips.

"Mom! Mom!" Amberly tried to push her way toward Kimberly, but Midas stretched out his heavy arm and kept her from following.

"Oh, Amberly, I can hear the ocean now. It's okay. It's the

surf on the north shore of Lewis Island…"

"Mom!" Amberly saw her mother close her eyes, smile, and relax as the crowd passed her body through the busted door and out of sight.

That was the last time Amberly saw her mother.

"It's like a parade in her honor," Sparks observed with a detached voice. "Or a state funeral."

Amberly tried to follow. "Best that you don't go," Midas warned in a low rumble of a voice. "You might end up in space with her."

Amberly dropped to the floor, crying bitterly. Her spirit had been utterly crushed, and her soul was stretched to the breaking point.

Sparks sat down on the floor next to Amberly and put her arm around the legendary Raven One's daughter. "Even though I only met Kimberly in person a few weeks ago, Dek and I had corresponded with her for almost a decade. She was a mentor and a mother figure to me. You know, cohort," Sparks said pointing at herself. "No mother."

Amberly looked up from the floor at Sparks, emotionally numb, unable to process what Sparks was saying.

"That makes us sisters, you and me," Sparks said and rested her head on Amberly's shoulder. The strawberry blonde started to sob.

Several civilian men, armed with stun guns, burst onto the bridge where about 20 from the original mob remained with the subdued Chasm officers.

"Zip cuff all the Chasm officers and send them to the brig," one of them said.

Several men hoisted Sparks and Amberly off the floor and onto their feet, forcing their arms behind their backs and securing their wrists with zip cuffs. They were about to pull them off the bridge, when Midas spoke up.

"It's okay. I'll take them. You worry about the others," Midas said, and the makeshift posse moved on to the communication officer and the yeoman. Midas then whispered to Amberly, "Stay close to me until things calm down. Who knows how many poor souls will be spaced for revenge tonight?"

Sparks looked at Midas, and even though she knew that he

was really only protecting Amberly, and it was her good fortune to be with her at the moment, Sparks was grateful. "Thank you."

Sparks and Amberly stood next to Midas and watched as the bridge was cleared of Chasm officers. Sparks, hands still zipped behind her back, playfully bumped Amberly's shoulder with hers.

"You win. You saved *Magellan*."

Kimberly Macready knew she must be hallucinating. She had lost so much blood. Breathing seemed hard. She felt like she was floating. She closed her eyes and saw the Chairman. Her eyes were stern and her bleached white hair pulled back in a very tight bun. Her 160-cm tall body was a specimen of perfection. Even though she was nearly 60 years old, her muscles were taut, her skin clear and her look sharp. Her face exploded with disappointment. Her eyes were dark, lacking an iris.

"Just like your men," the Chairman said, her voice harmonious and sickly sweet. "You failed me."

"No," Kimberly said and reached out for her beloved Chairman, but the Chairman turned into a fine mist and disappeared.

In her place a man appeared. He was handsome, with a strong jaw and broad shoulders. He wore a crisp pilot's uniform and sported hair that matched Amberly's.

"Alroy," Kimberly gasped. Her husband smiled warmly at her.

She didn't feel like she was floating anymore. She felt like she was lying on a cold metal floor. She was chilled and longed for the comforting sensation of warmth one more time, but she would never feel that again. She vaguely had the sense of people angrily shouting her name – her Chasm code name, Raven One.

"Alroy, I kept my promise," she said. "Amberly knows that you will always love her."

Alroy, dressed in the uniform he was wearing the first time Kimberly saw him, said nothing, but only smiled all the more brightly.

Some electronic voice Kimberly could barely make out was counting.

"Alroy… Alroy… I'm fearful. I don't know how to die. I've never felt this before." Tears, real ones, she thought, were streaming down her face. Alroy said nothing, but his smile withdrew slightly.

"Alroy … Will you … pray. Pray for me?"

The Alroy spoke softly in his rich tenor voice. "Kimberly, my love, I never stopped praying for you, and I never will."

Kimberly coughed blood, smiled and was about to wonder if she had been wrong about everything; but before the synapses in her fabled brain could construct that thought, her body was sucked into the cold vacuum of space through one of the *American Spirit's* auxiliary airlocks.

Kimberly Macready was at peace.

EPILOGUE

Amberly rolled over in her bed and looked out the small viewport in her living quarters. In the next room, she heard Kora snoring.

Amberly's infopad spoke quietly. "Amberly? I sense you are awake. You have an urgent message from your legal council. Shall I play it for you?"

Amberly sat up, "Go ahead, Verne."

"Amberly," her lawyer's recorded voice said. "I want to go over your statement one more time before today's trial. Would you meet me at conference room h12 at nine hundred hours?"

"Tell her I'll be there," Amberly commanded her infopad.

Nearly three months had passed since the arrival of *Magnus,* and the repairs on *Magellan* were going better than expected. The garden dome was refashioned into two semi domes, with a thick metallic patch connecting them. The botanists and chemists had already begun to fashion new soil from recovered organic material that wasn't lost through the dome crack, and mixing it with inorganic material harvested from the Spencer Belt. Resources and expertise from the *Magnus* accelerated the stabilization of *Magellan.* The wonders of the repairs, however, were overshadowed by the bloody trials.

For the last six weeks, a military tribunal had been casting judgment on the Chasm agents and operatives who survived the initial rage of vigilantism. The tribunal consisted of now permanently appointed Marine Commander Rita Moreno, her newly promoted executive officer, Lt. Commander North, and Governor Thor Rillio.

Today was the last day of the tribunals, and upon completion, Moreno would end martial law and return rule of *Magellan* to its elected civilian leader, Rillio.

Amberly's lawyer was reasonably certain that the tribunal would acquit her of aiding in sedition and treason when she provided the pass card to Dek. Technically, the card enabled the attempted murder of every soul on *Magellan* and succeeded in leading to the deaths of more than one-tenth of the waypoint's permanent population. In light of this detail, the lawyer wanted to be prepared, leaving nothing to chance.

At first, that Amberly would be charged at all was uncertain. But Moreno feared if she wasn't charged, the authority of the court would be tainted because many would see only favoritism towards the longtime friend of Tribunal North.

Amberly climbed out of bed and looked out her window into the darkness of space. Even Spencer Minorem's relative brightness seemed dim and hopeless to Amberly. She let her nightgown fall off and stepped into the shower.

The noise woke her sister, and Kora went into the dining area to prepare a bitter caffeinated drink that those who lived on *Magellan* called coffee, though no one from Earth would call it such. By the time it had finished brewing, Kora poured a cup for herself and Amberly, just as Amberly was slipping into her clothes.

Amberly had neatly pressed her white science corps dress uniform, and as she buttoned the top, Kora couldn't help but observe the striking similarity between Amberly and their mother.

"Wow. You look just like mom," Kora said, then quickly adding "like in her old pictures... when she was still good."

"Mom was never good, Kora," Amberly said with the bitter taste in her mouth. "I have to go down early to prep for today's trial."

"I figured," Kora said. "Amberly, I know you told me not to, but I went over to the barracks yesterday to talk with North. I tried to convince him to call you, or at least send you a note."

"Maybe you could get him to read the ones that Amberly has sent?" Verne suggested in his electronic voice.

"Verne, shut off," Amberly said, annoyed. "Look, Kora, North hasn't spoken to me for three months, what makes you think he will start now?"

"He's hurt. He's broken. We've all been through a lot. Too much," Kora told her younger sister. "But all hurts heal over time. I know. I *am* a medical professional."

Kora grabbed a brush, sat behind her sister and ran the instrument through her red locks. "I'm worried about you, sis. You need to get out and away from the killjoys at your work. Why don't you come to church with me? You could use a good joyful sermon."

Amberly didn't feel like going to church, though she liked how going would spite the memory of her mother and honor her dad.

She didn't want to socialize with just anyone. She wanted to talk with North, but he had completely shut her out since she professed her love for Dek in her attempt to save *Magellan*. And she also wanted to talk to Dek, but he had been placed in solitary confinement until his trial. She last saw Dek when Moreno was threatening to blow his brains out to compel him to help stop Chasm.

"I'll think about it," Amberly hugged Kora. "Thanks for caring. I need to go."

"You'll be great today. I'm praying for you," Kora called after her sister.

The repaired hangar had been transformed into a makeshift courthouse to accommodate the crowds that wanted to witness the tribunals, and this day the crowds were their largest, with standing room only.

The tribunal had saved the best show for last. Those on today's docket made the trial the hottest ticket: Lt. Smythe Johnson, former commander of one of *Magellan's* Marine strike teams; Sparks, the cohort-born who ultimately surrendered the *American Spirit*; Dek Tigona, Spark's cohort brother, and who along with Sparks, was one of that ship's Chasm leadership team; and Amberly Macready, who aided Chasm by stealing a pass card, and daughter of Kimberly Macready, architect of the failed Chasm apocalypse.

The whole morning was spent hearing evidence and witnesses. A slew of people testified on Amberly's behalf, including Lydia, Kora, Dek, Boro and several others. The court convened for lunch. After lunch, they would deliver the un-appealable verdicts together. The punishment for the guilty would be carried out immediately. The political pressure to end the martial law was great, but Moreno refused to do so until the tribunals would be complete, concerned that some legal maneuvering under civilian law might allow clever Chasm agents to escape justice. Also, she didn't want the blood of these proceedings on the civilian government, which needed cleaner hands to bring about a new normal.

An airlock had been added to the portal that served the hangar gangway. Dozens of instant executions had been carried out by spacing the guilty in front of the crowd. Although some were repulsed by it, most of the lifetime *Magellan* citizens had developed a significant bloodlust toward those who conspired to kill them all.

The crowd had returned from lunch back to the hangar court room, and the three judges came in and sat at an elevated table. The military police guard then escorted the four accused to stand before the judge. When Johnson entered the make-shift courtroom, many people booed.

Moreno spoke first. "This court will now consider the fate of Lt. Commander Smythe Johnson. Each tribunal may now give their statement and vote. XO North?"

"Lt. Johnson shot and killed his fellow Marines, including Captain Anderson in cold blood in service to Chasm, at the peril of us all. I witnessed it personally. He is guilty," North said.

"Gov. Rillio, your vote?"

"I concur with North and have nothing to add," Thor said. "Guilty."

"Two is enough to convict, but the death penalty requires three votes. I sadly add my vote. Lt. Smythe Johnson, for your many murderous crimes against *Magellan*, including plotting against its destruction, I strip you of your rank, dishonorably discharge you from service, and sentence you to death by airlock, to be carried out immediately. May God have mercy on your soul."

Although the verdict was not unexpected, the crowd had a mixed reaction. Some gasped. There was not an insignificant amount of clapping and cheering.

The MPs drug Johnson into the airlock, in full view of the crowd. Johnson screamed, "There is no God, you morons. The Chairman will avenge me." He spit on the ground as the MPs pushed him in the airlock and sealed the door.

Rita signaled the MPs, and within a few seconds, the space side door had opened, and Johnson was sucked into space. There was some cheering in the crowd, and some sobbing as well. The crowd had not been entirely desensitized to the shock of seeing someone airlocked.

Of the 47 traitors on trial, only four had been acquitted. Twenty-four had been sentenced to exile, and the rest had been executed.

"Order. Order. Next, this tribunal will render our verdict on the Chasm agent known as Sparks. Governor?" Moreno polled Thor.

"I find Sparks guilty of conspiracy to destroy and have no further comment," Thor said.

Sparks sat in a plain black jumpsuit. She had trimmed her long hair into a pixie cut, and dyed it black. *Was she honoring Raven One with that color, or just trying to disguise herself?* Amberly wondered.

"While I agree that Sparks did commit conspiracy on several counts, I also believe her claim to some amnesty offered by Amberly Macready is valid, though Amberly is not an official representative of the government. Therefore, I vote Sparks not guilty by virtue of offered amnesty," North offered.

"I, on the other hand," Moreno explained, "do not find Macready's offer binding by this court, particularly when the surrender is procured at gunpoint. Guilty. That makes a 2-1 guilty vote, so unfortunately Sparks will not face the airlock. Sparks, you are sentenced to exile from *Magellan*, to serve as a manual laborer aboard the *American Spirit* on its trip to earth, upon which you will cast yourself on the mercies of the Earth's courts, lightyears from our jurisdiction."

"Oh, a 17-year labor and isolation?" Sparks said, with just a hint of sarcasm. "I thank the court for its merciful ruling."

Moreno directed the MPs to take Sparks to the brig for holding until the *American Spirit*'s departure. Dek reached over and briefly hugged Sparks, but the cohort-mates exchanged no words. Sparks was led away, not knowing if she would ever see Dek again, or if her messy brown-haired co-conspirator would be the next, or perhaps the last, Chasm turncoat to executed by the vacuum of space.

"And now let's pass judgement on Dek Tigona, admitted co-architect of Chasm's plan to destroy *Magellan*. I will vote first. The depth of Mr. Tigona's treachery and his complicit leadership in recruiting others to destroy our waypoint are unforgivable, and I declare all promises of amnesty null and void. I find Dek guilty. Governor Rillio?"

"I agree with you, Rita," the governor said solemnly. "This man is unredeemable and his crimes are too great to allow him to live. Guilty."

"Thank you for your vote," Moreno said clinically. "North?"

Dek sat nervously. His eyes darted around the room, avoiding contact with North who sat on the elevated platform with the other two magistrates, and Amberly, who stood next to him among the accused. His choice to betray Chasm had been the right bet so far, especially with the arrival of the *Magnus* and the revelation of her true purpose.

But this was the moment of truth. Would he spend the next two decades of his life with Amberly on the way back to Earth? Or was the hour much later?

Dek's heart beat rapidly as his fate was in the hands of his failed rival. Would North condemn the man who stole his love?

"This man surrendered when he had the upper hand. He could have killed me, but instead he spared me upon the offer of amnesty. I believe that his amnesty is binding, and therefore I render a vote of not guilty."

The crowd roared in anger. Clearly, they expected to see the airlock used for a second time today. Dek let out a long sigh, and was about to offer a celebratory smile, but considered the crowd and instead offered a humble bowed head.

"I thank the court for its mercy," Dek said.

"So be it, North. Mr. Tigona is hereby sentenced to an exile of hard labor and isolation on the *American Spirit*," Moreno said.

Amberly stood next to Dek. She was careful to show no emotion on the pronouncement of any of the sentences today. She would have to tell Dek the truth, that she didn't love him — she certainly had no intention of leaving *Magellan* to go follow Dek to Earth in infamy, assuming this court didn't exile her.

She used his feelings for her to save *Magellan* and to save North. She was a liar and a manipulator of men, just like her mother. Still, she admired Dek and appreciated many of his qualities, found him attractive and may have been infatuated with his intellect. But in final analysis, Dek was the author of so much pain and death, Amberly would never be able to forgive him. Nothing would ever be the same again; nothing would ever be right.

Kora had said that North was broken. But it wasn't just North. Amberly felt that everyone who survived was broken, and unlike the *Magellan* itself, the people weren't so easily repaired. This was as much Dek's fault as anyone's. Amberly did not have North's capacity to forgive, to show compassion and love for his enemies.

"The MPs will restore order," Moreno called out, and slowly the commotion from the crowd died down. "The will of this tribunal is absolute, and not even the fury of the mob will change that. Let's finish this unsavory task. Let justice be done, so we can move onto peaceful activities and pursuits."

Moreno cleared her throat. "Amberly Macready, admitted to unintentionally providing critical aid to Chasm, including helping them steal a runabout, which caused critical damage to both the topside gardens and antimatter reactor. Because of her aid in the capture of the *American Spirit*, the prosecution has sought only exile in this case. Still, I want the record to be clear that only two votes are needed for an exile conviction. Gov. Rillio, how do you vote?"

"Amberly Macready is an upstanding citizen of *Magellan* and a patriot who clearly helped save *Magellan*, though she may have misstepped along the way. My position has always been that we should be awarding Ms. Macready a medal of honor, not prosecuting her — which is something I intend to do when I am restored to office by this time tomorrow."

There was a sustained applause in the audience.

"Thank you, governor," Moreno said. "I am just as anxious as you are to see civilian rule once again on *Magellan*. It can't come too soon."

Thor smiled at Amberly. She blushed at his praise and was glad to know that the governor understood her motivations in the end, how from the moment she knew *Magellan* was threatened, all she wanted was save her home.

Moreno continued. "I am prepared to render my vote. I am not sure that I am ready to build a statue of Amberly yet, but I also vote for acquittal. We all should be proud of Amberly, not condemning her. She helped us get critical information at risk to her own life that helped us expose an existential threat to our home. Amberly, I knew your father as well as most, and I can say with certainty that Alroy would be proud of you and honored that you carry on his name."

The crowd burst into spontaneous applause again, and from the first few rows, Amberly heard Kora shouting, "That's my sister!"

When the commotion died down again, Moreno continued. "I also wanted to offer my condolences on the passing of your mother. I know the Kimberly Macready that you knew, before she left us, was someone you cherished and loved. She truly died that day when she left *Magellan* six years ago. I am also sorry that she didn't receive proper justice, for both her sake and the sake of her victims, and that vigilantism prevailed. We excuse the actions of vigilantes because of the extraordinary circumstances, but that doesn't make her execution good."

The crowd was silent. Many assembled in that hangar took part in the spacing of Raven One, and some were indignant at the scolding, while others felt guilty now that cooler heads prevailed.

Moreno decided to try to change the mood. "With two votes for acquittal, Amberly will be exonerated," she said, and the crowd responded with enthusiastic applause. "North, looks like your vote is academic."

"If it's all the same," North said. "I'd like to go on the record with my vote."

"By all means," Moreno said, smiling broadly. "Declare your vote, and then let us dissolve this tribunal."

North stood up from behind the table. "Before I do, I wanted to thank the people of *Magellan*. They have always been true, caring and good to me since I came here nearly 10 years ago. And I wanted to announce now, that I will be resigning from *Magellan*'s Marines. I've accepted a commission as the new executive officer and Marine commander aboard *Magnus*. I swear once we've buried the Araran rebels in the hot sands of New Mesopotamia, I will come back to *Magellan*, my true home."

The Marines in the audience gave a "Ooh rah" salute at the surprising news. Amberly's heart felt like it was going to explode. She was going to lose her friend, the great thing that was in front of her this whole time. She would have no time to mend her relationship with North.

"Thank you for indulging my announcement, now to the business at hand," North said, looking directly at Amberly for the first time in months. "The worst type of betrayal is that from those who you love the most. Amberly Macready is an unquestionably intelligent and gifted woman who should have known better than to make deals with the devils she didn't know."

Audible gasps rose from the crowd. Slapped with surprise, Amberly began to tear up.

"Governor, she is not a hero, she is a betrayer," North continued to look directly into Amberly's eyes. "God as my witness, I don't know why I ever let myself love her. I don't know why any of you trust her professed good intentions behind her traitorous actions now."

A single tear welled up in North's stoic gaze. "I can't believe you, Amberly. I don't know about your father, but your mother surely was proud of how you followed in her footsteps, a manipulator of people, to achieve your own goals, covert and twisted. My conscious is clear. I vote that you are guilty of treachery that led to the deaths of hundreds."

Amberly was emotionally overwhelmed, supremely shamed by North. She collapsed to her knees and buried her hands in her face, sobbing. The crowd murmur intensified. Kora and Lydia rushed up from their seats, pushing past a guard to come and kneel next to the devastated woman.

Moreno was shocked. She decided the most merciful thing to do was to end the proceedings immediately. She stood up and in a commanding voice, spoke, "The business of this tribunal is concluded, and therefore we stand dissolved. You are all dismissed."

As the tribunals stepped off the platform and moved toward the milling crowd, Dek lunged toward North, and pulled his fist back. "How could you do that to Amberly?" Dek shouted, after being physically restrained by two Marines. "I thought you loved her."

North was heading for the command center access exit, but when he heard Dek, he stopped, turned around and took two paces toward Dek. "I did the right thing today, Dek. I was right to spare you, and I was right to condemn Amberly. Sometimes doing the right thing is hard, but I wouldn't expect your crooked mind to understand that. Goodbye, Dek; I hope we never see each other again."

Dek was already calming down at this point, and North turned and followed Thor and Rita through the door into the Command Center. Dek turned back to Amberly, who was now encircled by her friends and started walking over to join them.

The MPs immediately restrained Dek. "Sorry bud, you're headed back to the brig," the more burly officer said. Dek paid no attention to the officers as they dragged him away. He couldn't stop looking for Amberly.

The next morning, the Macready sisters were up early. Amberly was wearing the same black dress she wore the night she met Dek at Rick's. Kora, on the other hand, was wearing a conservatively cut blouse and black pants. The sisters were very somber as they both had hard tasks ahead of them that day. Now that he was out of solitary confinement, Amberly would be visiting Dek.

And although North would not see Amberly, he would see Kora.

With *Magellan* patched up, the aid of *Magnus* was no longer essential. Captain Obadiah wanted to move as quickly as he could to take control of *Waypoints Cortez* and *Marquette* and confront the rebellion at Arara if possible. That was a three-year journey, with news of the existence of the warship getting to Arara with a least a year's time for their forces to get ready to confront *Magnus*, the most powerful vessel humanity had ever constructed. Obadiah had great faith in the power of his ship to steer the course of history, but he wanted the Chasm rebels to have as little time as possible to mount a resistance.

Amberly and Kora walked together, arm in arm, silently until they reached the Church Commons, where Kora boarded the tube for the Marine HQ and Amberly took the artery corridor leading toward *Magellan's* brig.

North was sitting in the guest chair in Commander Anderson's old office, remembering the murderous events that took place there more than three months ago. Moreno and Kora walked in.

Moreno turned to Kora, "Here he is. I'll give you two a moment." Moreno exited the office, leaving North and Kora alone.

"I am glad you came by to see me," North said, smiling at his friend, "but I don't want to talk about Amberly."

"That's too bad," Kora said, "because that's all I want to talk about."

"I can't afford to think about her anymore," North said. "And it would just be a futile effort anyway."

"Why are you so sure?"

"If I didn't know any better, I'd say you are the naïve sister," North laughed. "She made it clear to me how she felt in the Shard Caves. She made it clear how she felt when she professed her love for Dek. And even if she hadn't, doesn't she see how everything is changed now? The life we used to have is broken. I'm broken."

"I know," Kora empathized. "But that doesn't mean —"

"I'm not the same man I was when the *American Spirit* landed," North said. "I don't think that man is coming back, Kora. Who I am now, and Amberly becoming her mother. It wasn't meant to be."

"That's not fair," Kora shot back. "Amberly is not Kimberly. You are too hard on her. She may never be able to forgive you for what you did to her at the trial, North. Can't you at least tell her you're sorry?"

"You can tell her that I forgive her."

"Friend, you are such a stubborn ass," Kora said flatly. "I see where things stand. But take this," Kora handed him an encryption key.

"Amberly wanted to be able to send you private messages. If you get one, maybe you should read it."

"I shouldn't take this," North said. "I have to stay focused, and thinking about Amberly, corresponding with her, would compromise that focus."

"I don't understand," Kora said.

"Our waypoint is safe, but for how long? How long before the Arara rebellion burns and tries to consume *Magellan* again?"

"Stay here, patch things up with Amberly," Kora pleaded.

"I am answering the call to service," North said. "Because of my combat experience on a waypoint and my time spent growing up on Arara, Captain Obadiah believes that I would be an important asset in the coming war against Chasm. *Magellan* is my home, and if I die defending it lightyears away, all is well."

"What about Amberly?" Kora wanted to slap some sense into North.

"She has Dek. She should go with him back to Earth."

"She's not going with Dek, North. I told you that was a ruse," Kora said with a growing frustration. "She saved us. She turned Dek at the right time to save you. She turned Sparks at the right time to save us all."

"Amberly is so messed up in the head, she doesn't know what she wants," North said, trying to hold his bitterness at bay. "She doesn't know up from down. Right from wrong. Probably never has."

"You are wrong about her," Kora said, resigned that she was not going budge North. "But I understand why you believe what you do."

She changed the subject. "Hey, what's this I hear about Sparks going on the *Magnus*?"

"That was my idea," North said. "We think she could have important intelligence that could help us in our coming battle. *Magnus* is the most powerful military force mankind has ever created, a space warship — but it may still be one ship against a planet."

"Sparks has agreed to help?" Kora asked.

"No, we'll have to break her."

Kora frowned.

Moreno walked back into the room, with Skip in tow. "Better move, Jarhead," Skip said to North, trying to joke through his sadness. "Your ship is about to sail."

Kora hugged North. "You take care of yourself. I am not going to be around to patch you up, and we want you coming back in one piece."

"I am going to miss you … and Amberly. The incomparable Macready sisters," North said, thinking of peaceful days long gone. "I'll take the key, but I won't promise that I'll use it. Pray for me, Kora Macready."

"I will. Pray for us, too. Pray for Amberly."

"That's the awesome thing about prayers," North said. "They are the only things that travel faster than light."

The MP let Amberly know that she would only have five minutes. Once the *American Spirit* was away, the exiled would enjoy slightly more freedom, but until then, everything was high security with captured Chasm agents who avoided the airlock.

Amberly sat down across the table from Dek, and smiled awkwardly. She didn't know if she could do it. Dek was beaming with excitement to finally see Amberly after so many months of solitary confinement.

"I never thought I'd be so excited about getting off a spacious waypoint and onto a cramped deep space ship for 17 years," Dek said. "But spending those years with you, I'm sure will make them go by in a flash. Who knows, we may like Earth ... if they don't execute us when we get there."

"Don't joke like that," Amberly said, looking into Dek's blue-grey eyes.

"Hey, everything is going to be okay," Dek said. "We survived this far? If Raven One couldn't separate us, what can? I know we'll do fine, as long as we are together."

Amberly looked away. She was trying to find the strength to confess her lie.

Dek picked up on the cue. "Except you're not coming, are you?"

How could she tell him now that not only was she not taking the long journey with him, but that she never loved him? She played him like she played North. She was convinced that the truth was the best option, until now. Amberly saw now that the truth would destroy Dek. She knew it was wrong, but she had no strength left. She held onto the lie. *Well, it is a half-lie*, Amberly rationalized. She was attracted to Dek, and in another impossible set of circumstances, one where Chasm had never been conceived, she could see them together. But that was a fantasy world, much like the utopia Chasm was trying to build.

"Dek, I'm sorry. You mean so much to me," she said. "But I can't leave *Magellan*. This is my home. I can't leave Kora. She is my family."

Dek was dumbfounded.

"Dek, this is the hardest thing that I have ever done in my life, but since Chasm came, everything is changed now. If I went with you, even with our ... love, eventually we'd fall apart."

"I don't understand."

"You know, my mom loved my dad, despite her double identity. But I saw the bitterness grow in her," Amberly said, "How she loved my dad, but resented being away from home. She was a woman torn, and my dad saw her suffer something exponentially worse than homesickness. And he could do nothing about it. It destroyed him too."

"Amberly, I—"

"Please don't say anything. There is nothing to be said. *Magellan* is my home; I will never leave. I wish you could stay, with all my heart I wish you could," Amberly lied. "If I went with you, it would be unfair to you, and it would be unfair to me."

"Amberly. You are confused," Dek said.

"Honestly, Dek, I am thinking more clearly now than I ever have."

Amberly stood up, and stepped around the table, and kissed Dek gently on the cheek as the MP entered the room.

"Goodbye, Dek. I'll never meet anyone like you again."

Tears were rolling down Dek's face now.

"Amberly Macready, I will always love you. I will come back to you someday, I promise."

Amberly didn't protest Dek's pledge. They both knew the promise would be impossible to keep. She smiled one last time at Dek, turned and walked out the door, not wanting him to see she was tearing up as well.

Lydia, Amberly and Kora looked out of the large portal in the Science Corp lab's conference area. It was almost four months ago when she first saw Dek and Sparks standing on the observation deck of the *American Spirit* through this window.

The three women drank hot topis and now admired the *Magnus*, a gleaming light blue ship, which sat docked just outside the lab window.

"How did it go with Dek?" Kora asked.

"I lied, "Amberly said, sipping her synth-tea. "Then I kissed him goodbye."

"That bad?" Lydia commented.

"And with North?" Amberly asked.

"I called him a stubborn ass," Kora reported. "But he took the key."

Lydia stood up. "Let's go watch the ceremony."

Down in the hangar there was a big celebration, as Captain Obadiah and XO North prepared to board the ship. Many of the lab windows opened into and had a great view of the hangar. Most corvettes and runabouts had been repaired and polished for the ceremony. Someone seeing the hangar for the first time today would find almost no evidence of the battle that took place here three months ago.

Governor Rillio and Commander Moreno presented the captain with a *Magellan* flag, as was the custom for departing ships that had visited the waypoint for the first time. The Marines assembled gave a salute, and the governor and the captain shook hands. Some grand words were exchanged that the women could not hear.

North looked up at the lab, and caught Amberly's eye. The two held the gaze for a moment Amberly wished would last forever. North gave Amberly a slight smile, one that Amberly knew she may never see again.

North winked, then turned with the captain and entered the gangway connecting to *Magnus*. The crowd cheered.

Kora put her arm around her sister.

Amberly looked at her and smiled. "Let's go home."

APPENDIXES

A BRIEF HISTORY OF THE BIRTH OF THE WAYPOINTS

Moon Orbit, July 4, 2476.

From Earth, *Waypoint Columbus* was visible to the naked eye. The largest mobile object created by man, the waypoint was nearly five kilometers in diameter and orbited the moon during the final phases of its three-decade construction. Fortunately, the project engineers had learned from the process so that they would build the next one, *Waypoint De Leon*, in one-fifth the time.

Simple patterns in the grey nano-carbon superstructure conveyed a Spartan beauty, although *Waypoint Columbus* was not designed with aesthetics in mind. Viewports and other windows were almost non-existent, save for the spattering of skylights above the *Waypoint Columbus'* garden core, located near the center of the disc-shaped structure.

In the garden core, Admiral William James, the top-ranking military officer, addressed the gathered diplomats, politicians, bureaucrats and family members of the waypoint crew who would stay behind when the *Columbus* got underway.

Crew, however, wasn't the right word. They would soon be permanent residents.

To support the 5,000 inhabitants of *Waypoint Columbus*, form took a back seat to function. Future waypoints would dedicate more real estate to the psychological wellbeing of the spacefaring citizens, but *Waypoint Columbus'* primary objective was the indefinite, self-sustaining survival of man in space.

This day, *Columbus* would begin its 24-month journey out of the Sol System, to its new permanent anchorage, almost a half lightyear away. Later, *Columbus'* success proved man could live indefinitely off-planet, becoming the first step toward permanently occupying new worlds.

"That humanity would someday settle the stars was destined," Adm. James spoke smoothly, evenly. His words evoked a strong pride in those who had spent decades working toward the greatest moment in human history since man entered space a half-millennium ago.

"Science fiction has always promised that man would somehow bend the laws of physics so we could travel faster than light. Hyperspace. Warp speed. Mass effect. FTL drives," the admiral said. "In our great fiction, a spacefarer could reach the stars not in years, but in weeks or days or instantly. Reality allows us no magic trick, no *deus ex machina* that will bring us to the stars. Only the unstoppable determination that makes us human, a tremendous amount of work, and generations of patience will bring us to our destiny."

By the 25th century, humanity could not travel faster than light, but it was not for lack of trying. History's best scientists and engineers could not formulate practical light speed travel: no artificial wormholes, no tesseracts, no powerful generators that could fold time and space.

By the middle of the 24th century, the United States and her allies decided on a more practical approach to colonizing the cosmos: Project Waypoint. Using deep space probes, astronomers had already identified three Earth-like planets in other solar systems in the Milky Way galaxy. The closest planet, Arara, was eight light years away. Project Waypoint would attempt to colonize all three planets, all roughly in opposite directions from earth.

While many politicians pushed Project Waypoint to assure the survival of humanity should Earth ever be unable to sustain life after a natural or artificial disaster of global scale, ultimately it was not fear that drove men to overcome human dependence on *terra firma*. Instead, for generations a new manifest destiny had gripped the world. That humanity would expand, learn, grow was pre-ordained.

But the galaxy was a big place.

Humans could only engineer vehicles that would travel at fractions of the speed of light (c). Most interstellar ships had a cruising speed between .3c and .5c.

Even then, the amount of energy needed to accelerate — and decelerate — was amazing. But energy generation was no longer a problem. While unable to bend space and time, science did solve the antimatter riddle. Energy, the scarcity of which had once been the cause of great wars, was now plentiful and cheap. Antimatter/matter reactors — kept off-planet for safety —

generated the limitless energy needed to make Project Waypoint viable.

Over the course of the next five decades, humanity would build 72 waypoints, scattering them like interstellar rest stops between Earth and the three planets astronomers found to be fit for human life. Those taking the two-decade trip from Earth to Arara would have 18 waypoints to help them find the way. Most of them were built by the North American Space Alliance (a confederation of the United States and what was once known as Canada and Mexico). The European Space Alliance and the African Space Alliance built three each.

A LIST OF THE WAYPOINTS
BETWEEN EARTH AND ARARA

Most of the crew who left on the initial launches would never return to Earth. It was fitting then for the waypoints to be named for the great explorers who discovered the "new world" in the second millennia. The waypoints between Earth and Arara, in order from Earth, were: *Waypoint Columbus, Waypoint De Leon, Waypoint Drake, Waypoint Raleigh, Waypoint Polo, Waypoint Vespucci, Waypoint Balboa, Waypoint Coronado, Waypoint Hawkins, Waypoint De Soto, Waypoint Hudson, Waypoint Cabot, Waypoint Estevanico, Waypoint Cartier, Waypoint Gilbert, Waypoint Magellan, Waypoint Cortes,* and *Waypoint Marquette.*

"Since we started to record our own history, humanity has falsely believed that we were in control of our own fate. As long as we are dependent completely on Earth, such independence has always been an illusion," Adm. James said with confidence, hands smoothing his dress blues as he straightened, the pride of the moment seeming to give him unnatural height. "Today, however, our great fiction has become reality: We are now truly the masters of our own destiny. This waypoint will guide our path."

AN ACCOUNTING OF THE SHIPS OF MAGELLAN

Going on a recreational trip, no matter how short, on one of the spacecraft assigned to *Magellan* was quite a luxury. Besides the privately-owned space vessels registered to the mining companies and traders, *Magellan* left Earth with a complement of four Valkyrie-class space shuttles: the *Magellan Space Shuttle Enterprise*, the *M.S.S. Normandy*, the *M.S.S. Firebird*, and the *M.S.S. Nautilus*. The *M.S.S. Normandy* was the Valkyrie that carried Amberly's parents when they were lost in space in 2596, and that ship had not been replaced. *The M.S.S. Enterprise* was decommissioned three decades before that, after excessive wear and too many collisions with cosmic dust and debris made that Valkyrie un-spaceworthy. *Enterprise* was replaced with the *M.S.S. Palomino*, which came in a supply convoy from Earth in 2597, bringing the *Magellan* to three-fourths of its Valkyrie capacity. A fully equipped and stocked Valkyrie-class space shuttle could travel with a crew complement of 30 for a few billion kilometers before reaching the point of no return to *Magellan*. The Valkyries were used primarily for research trips and were also rented out to private users, notably booked by the mining companies when asteroids were in range of the *Magellan*.

Magellan also employed a complement of about a dozen corvette-class shuttles. These small two-seat shuttles were mostly military, and about half of them had been constructed on *Magellan* itself in the larger microfactories. The corvettes built on *Magellan* were not off an assembly line, but hand crafted with their own unique modifications and style. The Marines controlled eight corvettes, armed with repeating 50mm chain guns.

These small two-seat shuttles were mostly military, and about half of them had been constructed on *Magellan* itself in the larger microfactories. The corvettes built on *Magellan* were not off an assembly line, but hand crafted with their own unique modifications and style.

Follow the continuing stories of the brave men and women of humanity's waypoints in Flight of the Magnus, *the next exciting novel in the Project Waypoint Series from Shadowlands Press. Sign up for e-mail news and announcements online at ShadowlandsPress.com*

To report errata and other mistakes found in this edition, please e-mail us at editor@ShadowlandsPress.com.

www.ingramcontent.com/pod-product-compliance
Lightning Source LLC
Chambersburg PA
CBHW070639180626
46817CB00006B/2168